Branded Sanctuary

JOEY W. HILL

ELLORA'S CAVE
ROMANTICA PUBLISHING

An Ellora's Cave Romantica Publication

www.ellorascave.com

Branded Sanctuary

ISBN 9781419961441
ALL RIGHTS RESERVED.
Branded Sanctuary Copyright © 2010 Joey W. Hill
Edited by Briana St. James.
Cover art by Syneca.

This book printed in the U.S.A. by Jasmine-Jade Enterprises, LLC.

Electronic book publication February 2010
Trade paperback publication August 2010

The terms Romantica® and Quickies® are registered trademarks
of Ellora's Cave Publishing.

BRANDED SANCTUARY

ॐ

Trademarks Acknowledgement

⅀

The author acknowledges the trademarked status and trademark owners of the following wordmarks mentioned in this work of fiction:

Barbie: Mattel, Inc.

Cirque du Soleil: The Dream Merchant Company

Cool Whip: Kraft General Foods, Inc.

Disneyland: Disney Enterprises, Inc.

Dom Perignon: Schieffelin & Co

Dove Promises: Mars, Incorporated

Fisher Price: Mattel, Inc.

Jeep: DaimlerChrysler Corporation

National Geographic: National Geographic Society

Nike: Nike, Inc.

Tinkerbell: Disney Enterprises, Inc

Twilight Zone: CBS Broadcasting Inc

Viagra: Pfizer Inc.

X-Men: Marvel Characters, Inc.

Y or YMCA: National Council of Young Men's Christian Associations of the United States of America

Chapter One

ജ

With a wrenching scream, Chloe bolted out of her second bad dream of the night. She stopped, swaying in the middle of the room, fists clenched in defense, body cringing in anticipation of pain. Blinking, she stared around her and slowly remembered that she'd left candles burning on the dresser so she wouldn't wake into the clutches of darkness. The small floating votives, shaped like lotuses, were still burning in their rose glass bowl, which told her she'd had the nightmare soon after her head hit the pillow.

Settling on the edge of the bed, her legs shaking, she scraped her hands through her hair and rocked herself for self-comfort. She needed to go to the bathroom, but the narrow doorway was a tunnel of darkness, and the mirror in there reflected the shadows from the flickering candle flame. Goddess, her heart wouldn't stop its racing, sending alarming sharp pains through her chest.

Twenty-four was a little young for a heart attack, considering she was in pretty good shape and had no history of heart disease. A panic attack was far more likely, since she was plagued by nightmares of a man trying to beat her to death while enjoying the hell out of it. Kicking her body, punching her face, overwhelming her and teaching her what being helpless really meant.

A lesson she'd give anything to forget.

Up until it had happened, she'd been a firm believer that all things happened for a reason. To teach lessons, increase wisdom, allow a karma exchange for all parties involved. But when something truly horrible happened, all that wonderful spiritualism sounded like New Age bullshit peddled by celebrities. She vacillated between anger, fear and something in between that kept her from doing anything to change it. That was the worst thing of all.

"Help me. Help me, please." She didn't even realize she was saying it until the whisper grated on her ears. For the first time she wished she lived in town, not in the rural area outside Tampa, in a rundown rented two-bedroom farmhouse nestled in a tangle of trees, shrubs and flowering vines. At this second, she'd give up her tiny garden and natural sanctuary for the comforting sounds of apartment neighbors watching late-night television or walking down the hallway from a nightshift job.

She was so tired. Marguerite, her boss, would see the shadows. It was one of the reasons Chloe called her "M" for short, because she was like the savvy head of MI-6. Once dawn came—and please, let it come soon—maybe she should pull a flighty Chloe routine, call in and say she was staying home to hug trees all day to balance her chakras. Marguerite was way too smart for that as well. Chloe didn't ditch work. She loved being at Tea Leaves as much as she loved being at her own home. Or used to.

That was the crux of it, wasn't it? She was afraid of everything, enjoying nothing. But she was being stupid. She could get through this.

Thump. Thump.

She scrambled over the bed with a startled cry, knocking over the side table, the lamp and the cell phone on it. When she landed in the debris, the night table jabbed into her hip as she rolled over it. Snatching up the lamp in nerveless fingers, she scooted back into the corner, her intestines coiled in painful knots. *No, no, no.*

When the thump came again, her scattered mind struggled to place it. Gradually, over the momentous pounding of her heart, she realized it was the maple she hadn't cut back. It held one of her bird feeders. The wind was up and the feeder, as well as the branch holding it, were striking the backyard shed. A noise she'd heard a hundred times.

She couldn't take it anymore. Her chest constricted as if it was being crushed, her breath strangling in her throat. This *was* a panic attack. Full blown, and while one part of her mind rationalized it, the rest of her was freaking out. As she let the lamp fall to her side and pushed the side table off her legs, her hand brushed a slip of paper that had fluttered to the floor when she knocked over the table. Glancing down, she saw the folded note that she'd slid under the lamp base almost a year ago.

No, she couldn't. She really couldn't. She didn't even know him, for heaven's sake. They'd met at Marguerite's wedding. Yeah, they'd hit it off, and she'd meant to call him. She'd kept the dang note by her bed, after all. Of course, she and Gen had really had their hands full, running Tea Leaves while Marguerite had been on her honeymoon. But when that had passed and he'd tried to reach her a couple times, through Marguerite, she'd given this and that bogus excuse not to get in touch. Every time she thought about calling, she felt hesitant. For the first time in her life.

At one time, she'd been tremendously confident, buoyant with energy. She'd reach out to anyone, sure that she'd find something worthwhile in the contact. A gorgeous guy who'd seemed interested in her? Hell, she would have been on the phone to him the next day, practically before he had his morning coffee.

Her mental argument against calling now didn't seem to matter. Her errant fingers had already flipped open her phone and were dialing. On the fourth ring, her good sense caught up. Oh Goddess. She was calling him at three in the morning.

He answered before she could jerk the phone from her ear and snap it closed.

"Hello?"

She cleared her throat. He'd been asleep. Obviously. She should just hang up. "Brendan?"

"Yeah?" Then a pause. "Chloe? Is this Chloe?"

"You recognize my voice?"

"Of course," he said, as if it was the most normal thing in the world to wake out of a dead sleep and recognize the voice of someone he'd only met once before. "I was hoping you'd call. In fact" — a throaty chuckle, sensuous and warm — "I think I was dreaming about you."

"I—I'm sorry about the time. I didn't realize it was so late." God, didn't that sound lame? Calling at ten o'clock at night—that was a mistake. Calling at the freaking dawn-of-the-dead hour, she had to be a vampire not to know what time it was. Or a mental case. She'd really liked this guy, and he was going to consider her completely nuts. But oh, his voice sounded good, all sleepy and sexy.

"You okay?"

"Yeah. I'm fine. I'm just—" A sob caught in her throat. "I can't...I can't breathe, Brendan. I had a nightmare, and I'm so sorry, I couldn't call Marguerite or Gen, I didn't want them to worry." Her words tumbled over one another, making her incoherent even to herself. Maybe that was good. "Your number's been on my side table, and I just found it and..."

What did that say about her desperation, keeping his number by her bed? Of course, she didn't typically play coy with guys. So why was she worried about it now? It wasn't like he was ever going to want to hear from Marguerite's crazy employee again. "I'm sorry for waking you. I needed to hear another voice, and I've done that, so—"

"Chloe."

She stopped at the one word statement. A gentle poke into the flashing spokes of the running wheel of her mouth. "Y-yeah?"

"Okay. What would you like to talk about?"

She blinked at the dark opening to the bathroom that seemed to be watching her. "Can you...can you just talk?"

"Sure. I'll be happy to do that." Just like that, he started talking. "You know, I was still hoping you'd call, even though I'd decided you weren't as interested in me as I was in you."

She stood up, made it two steps toward the bathroom. As she drew in some deep, calming breaths, she remembered the way he'd looked at the wedding. Beautiful in his tuxedo, his dark hair brushed back but too silky and fine to prevent several tempting strands from tumbling over his forehead. A childhood friend of Marguerite's, he'd walked Chloe's boss down the aisle to Tyler, then had taken a seat in the front pew next to Komal and Mr. Reynolds, more of Marguerite's eclectic assortment of chosen family. The front row of chairs had been close enough to the altar that the tips of Brendan's polished shoes had nearly been under the hem of Chloe's dress as she stood up to do her part as bridesmaid.

She'd noticed he had a lean swimmer's body. Marguerite said he swam every day and that he taught drama at the community college. She remembered the shades of gray, green and gold of his hazel eyes. She visualized them now as she took another step. She *really* needed to go to the bathroom.

"No. I was interested. Am. Can you…keep going?"

"But then," he continued, "I thought, well, she and Gen are taking care of the tea room while Marguerite's on her honeymoon, so maybe it's that. Maybe she'll still call. So here you are." She could hear the smile in his voice as he tactfully avoided all the months where Marguerite's honeymoon wouldn't have been an excuse. "I'm so glad you did. I've been thinking a lot about you. You made a big impression."

She stopped again. One small step from the bathroom, she stared at it. Maybe she could hold it until daylight. Too many shadows. "A bigger impression than I'm making now?"

"If I could have picked one person in the whole world to call me at three in the morning, it would have been you."

"Why?" She imagined him lying on his back in his bed. He slept shirtless, she was sure, and maybe he'd have one

11

muscular arm propped behind his head, the other holding the phone. How delighted those sheets must be, sliding along that lean, bare body. Maybe he slept naked.

Okay, that was more like herself. She was at the threshold. Quickly, she groped around the corner and snapped on the light. She let out a short scream.

"Chloe?" The instant, urgent concern in his voice jerked her back.

"It's okay," she gasped. "Just clothes…hanging in the shower. Looked scary."

"Oh." She heard him draw a steadying breath as well. "Well, cotton blends can be menacing. I'm convinced my shoes come out of the closet at night and form a ring around my mattress, stare at me through their eyelets, like spiders waiting to pounce."

It startled a giggle out of her. "You do not think that. You're trying to make me feel better about being a big chicken."

"On the contrary. You're a petite, cute chicken."

"Ugh." She wrinkled her nose. "People always call me cute."

"Try being a guy born with the innocent expression of Beaver Cleaver. I thought the longer hair and a bit of stubble would help, but all the hair does is make women want to pet me like a golden retriever. The stubble itched."

"I didn't think that at all. When I saw you, I thought you were a handsome guy."

"Yeah, but if a bunch of terrorists had crashed the party, you all would have flocked behind Tyler and that other guy, Mac."

"That's because Tyler is ex-CIA or some other freaky secret agency thing, and Mac is a homicide cop."

"And because they look manly and heroic."

She smiled. "You're being very manly and heroic right now. But I know what you mean. Just for once, I'd like a guy's first impression to be how sexy I am."

"I thought that. I would have jumped you at the wedding if you hadn't been on crutches. It didn't seem very sporting."

She laughed outright. "I'm going to put you on hold a second, okay?"

"Are you all right?"

"Yeah...I just... I need to go to the bathroom. Can you wait a second?"

"As long as you need. But come back soon."

It was amazing, but the soothing timbre of his voice stroked her as if he were standing in the room with her. She wished he were. While usually she could flirt and tease with the best of them, and virginity was a distant memory, she really didn't go to bed with a guy on the first date. However, in this vulnerable moment, she'd have taken him to her bed in a heartbeat. She wondered if Brendan would be the rare type of guy willing to just curl around her, hold her without doing anything else, if that was what she wanted.

After taking care of her bathroom needs, she found her nerves had steadied even further. She was certain it was as much because of his presence as her now more comfortable physical state. She pressed the button. "Are you still there?"

"As promised. What can I do for you now?"

She sat back down on her bed. "Well." She made a game attempt to be the person he'd met at the wedding, when everything had been magic and light, no room for fear or shadows. "You could tell me what you're wearing. Sorry, I'm tired and I can only manage clichés."

"Do you want me to go—"

"No," she said, probably way too quickly, but he sounded pleased.

13

"Okay, then. When it comes to nakedness, guys really don't consider anything a cliché."

"You're naked?" She squeaked it, then cleared her voice. "You're bullshitting, to distract me. You probably wear footie pajamas, Beaver."

"You found me out. No, seriously." His voice lowered, murmured in her ear in a husky tone. "I am completely, entirely, head-to-toe, naked. Under a light sheet."

"How far up is the sheet?" She held her breath, waiting for the answer.

"I can see my right hipbone. The other side is up a little higher, on my stomach."

With a hipbone bare, if he was on his back and she stood at the right side of the bed, she would see his bare ass against the mattress. She pressed her lips together.

"What about you, *le poulet petit?* Are you naked?" The French rolled off his tongue and turned the remains of cold fear in her belly to heat.

"Would you like that?"

"I would," he said. "But I'd like a nightgown as well. Sometimes what women wear is as provocative as the flesh beneath. You have a way of making the two work so well together."

"What would you do first, if we were together?"

"Hmm… Well, considering we're both naked…" He waited a pregnant pause and she stifled a giggle, refusing to answer. "I'd pull you in my arms and hold you. Just hold you, until all those shakes went away. Rub your back, stroke your hair. Wipe the tears from your face. Promise you no one is ever going to hurt you again, because I won't let them. I'd make the nightmares go away."

Chloe swallowed over a jagged ache developing in her throat. "Oh, Brendan. You're really being far too nice. I'm never going to hear from you again, am I? You're going to help this pitiful wretch through her nightmare and then decide you want to go date a nice normal girl who doesn't call you at 3 a.m. I'd tell you I'm not usually like this, and I'm not, but I don't know...lately I haven't been myself."

He was silent a long moment. "Chloe, you took on a crazy psychotic, a convicted felon who'd served hard time. You fought him tooth and nail to protect a child. Jesus, he had to beat you nearly to death to get her away from you. You were brave as hell."

"No," she quavered, brushing away the few tears that rolled out of her eyes against her will. These days, she always seemed ready to cry, but she'd become tyrannical about it, refusing to allow more than a few to squeeze out at a time. A contrast to the easily emotional person she'd been, who'd accepted tears as easily as laughter, feeling both were cathartic. That was before.

"It wasn't that. All I could think about was what he'd do to Natalie if he took her from me, and I knew he was going to. I knew I'd rather have him kill me than survive to find out what he'd done, all because I wasn't strong enough to stop him. When Marguerite found me, I wanted to be dead. If she hadn't gotten to her in time..."

"No, don't think that." He responded immediately. "No matter what happens in life, Chloe, no matter how bad it gets, you can get through it. There's always someone out there whose hand you can hold, so the abyss doesn't pull you in."

"Like yours." She wiped at her eyes again. "Thanks."

"Like mine. From now on, I want to be the first person you call when you feel this way, okay? Then you'll feel so guilty, you'll have to go out with me."

"You'd *guilt* me into dating you?"

"Oh yeah, pretty much. With this pretty-boy innocent face, I don't get many of the hot women."

"Yeah, right. Now you are bullshitting me. I've seen you. Women would catfight to go out with you."

15

"Anytime you feel like staging one, I'm there. Clothing optional. Heated body oil would make my year."

Again the laughter rolled over her. Chloe curled back in the bed, pulling the covers up and watching the candles burn inside the glass bowl. "Thanks. Thanks for making me feel not so pathetic."

"That's the very last thing I consider you. Now we were on the whole naked thing…"

She chuckled. "One-track mind." On a whim, she wriggled out of the sleep shirt and panties. "Okay, I'm naked now."

Another pause. "Really?"

"Really. I was wearing a Save the Whales sleepshirt and pink underwear."

"Lace, cotton, thong?"

"Lace, cotton, no thong." She smiled. "Not really comfortable for sleeping, but if you want to imagine…"

"Men prefer to think women sleep in teddies or thongs and demi-bra sets. And slip into stiletto heels when they get out of bed."

"So their butts will do that provocative swing as they walk to the shower?"

"Absolutely. Are you really naked?"

"*Brendan.*" She laughed at him. "Tell me more about *you* being naked."

"Is that a command?"

There was a curious space of time after the question that tingled with something unusual. Intrigued by it, she bit her lip. "Yes."

"All right, then. I'm lying on my back. I'm using an earpiece, so I have both hands laced behind my head. I've propped up a knee, so the sheet has slipped."

"What can I see now?"

"You'd pretty much see all of me, except for part of one leg, about to mid-thigh. I'm being a slut for you, but only to help you through your nightmare."

"Oh." Even as she smiled, her breath sighed out of her. "Will you…touch yourself?"

"I don't know. May I?" That pause again that made her chest tighten, like the panic attack but far more pleasurable. "You have the control, Chloe. I'm all yours."

She had to find her tongue, but when she did, the answer came without hesitation. "Yes."

"All right, then. I'm sliding my palm down the center of my chest, over my stomach…slow…"

Chloe closed her eyes, imagined that tanned hand moving over muscular pecs, a taut brown nipple, down to the ridged abdomen she was sure he'd have. Down, down.

"Do you want me to go lower, Chloe? Touch myself there?"

"Yes," she breathed.

"Your wish is my command. Do you prefer a certain word for…"

"What do you call it?"

"Depends on the day. Cock, dick. Bane of my existence, reason for living…"

"Cock." She stumbled over it a little, grinning, but nervous too. "I don't like penis. It makes me think of my six-year-old nephew playing naked in the sprinkler. He kept shouting out the word penis to shock everyone."

"Well, I definitely don't want you thinking about that." That sensual amusement was in his voice again. "So I'm gripping the base of my cock, stroking upward. I'm hard for you, Chloe. If that doesn't offend you."

"It doesn't," she said with a dry throat. Her nightmare seemed very far away.

"I wish I could see you. You had beautiful breasts. Perfect. I wanted to touch them at the wedding."

"That might have been awkward."

"Fortunately, I restrained myself. Will you touch them for me now? Imagine it's my hands on them?"

She remembered his hands. She'd watched them avidly, whether they were clasping a utensil or wine stem, or holding out a chair for someone. When he'd asked her to dance, his hand had folded over hers, the other low on her back, warm and strong as they turned together. Why the hell hadn't she called him earlier? He likely would have been in her bed tonight, and this never would have happened.

He was taller than she was, and her head had fit perfectly into the hollow of his throat. He'd laid his jaw on the crown of her head, and she'd almost fallen asleep as they swayed, because her injuries had still been healing. Despite his joke about crutches, she'd actually been using a cane that day. Though her leg had ached horribly, she'd wanted one dance. By the time she finished that one song, he'd been bearing almost all her weight. He'd have carried her back to her chair if she'd let him.

Sliding her hands up, she cupped her breasts, feeling self-conscious, though of course she'd aggressively cupped them before in this room, when she'd pleasured herself. Imagining countless alpha heroes, she'd even fantasized about Tyler more than once. Not that she'd ever tell Marguerite that, but Goddess, no woman with a pulse could help but fantasize about that man. After the wedding, she'd fantasized about Brendan quite a bit, but with the nightmares, she hadn't had the energy to see any of it through in some time. It had probably been six months since she'd managed an orgasm alone, let alone with anyone else. Of course, she would have to go out with someone to become more than a party of one, and that hadn't happened either.

Regardless, her libido was stirring in quite an alert fashion now, as if recalled from sabbatical on a NASA rocket

18

red-eye flight. She was pleased by his comment, because she had generous C-sized breasts on her short, curvy frame. It contributed to the hourglass look that Gen had said most women would cheerfully commit all manner of sins to have.

"Are you touching yourself?" he asked.

"Yes."

"Are you imagining my hands? I'm imagining yours. I'm imagining you stroking me, setting the pace, wanting to torment me as long as possible while I strain in your pretty small fingers." When he spoke again, his voice was rough with a passion that told her his desire. "Do you want me to take this all the way, Chloe? Do you want me to come for you?"

"Yes." *God, yes.*

Chapter Two

ɞ

She heard the rasp of his breath elevate, knew his pace would be quickening. The curl of that capable hand would be stroking closer to the head, working the skin up against it, thumb probably pressing on the sensitive vein beneath. His balls would be drawing up, getting ready, his body turning into a hard statue of muscle and focused male need, buttocks getting tight as a drum head against the mattress, pushing his cock into his grip.

"Talk to me," she whispered. Her fingers crept up her right breast, making a tentative pass over the nipple. The sheer jolt of response arched her up, startling her such that she captured it between the knuckles of her middle and forefingers, increasing the clamp as she imagined his teeth closing on the hardening tip.

"I want to be inside you. I'm imagining...that. Your cunt, slick...wet, closing over my cock, stroking it like my hand now, only so fucking much better. Straddling me, sitting up...coming down hard on me...your gorgeous nipples in my mouth...hard...biting them... God, I want to fuck you."

"More. Tell me more." She was usually more generous, but her body was too needy, in the midst of a punishing storm after a long drought. Her other hand slid down her abdomen, called by the fresh, eager need between her legs. When she reached her clit, she let out a soft moan as it gave her a welcome pulse, responding to her touch. The way her heart lurched in response, she realized her absent desire had affected her mind as much as her body. *I'm aroused. I'm alive.*

"You're touching your pussy now. I can tell from that sound you just made. I want to lick your fingers, so when you

20

slide them inside yourself, it will be my mouth that helped make you ready."

His mouth was doing that already, on so many levels. She eased two fingers into miraculous wetness, just up to the first knuckle, playing in that sensitive opening. Her thumb and ring finger compressed her clit, following instinct to find the most effective pattern of strokes and pressure that could change every time, thanks to a woman's ever-shifting demands when it came to what turned her body on.

"I'd get you so wet, Chloe. With my hands, my mouth. Whatever you demand, I'm giving to you."

Her rhythmic rubbing on either side of that quivering nerve center, the feel of her own slick flesh against her knuckles, was probably less rapid than his pace, but still the tempo was catching up, like the swelling overture of a composition of strings and keys at once, strumming and pounding together.

She pinched her nipple harder, gasped as she felt his fingers, the way his large palm would cover her breast, squeeze it so the nipple, when taken into his mouth, would be even more sensitive. "Don't stop..."

"Can't think of anything...but wanting to come for you. Seeing you...in my mind. Naked...glorious...so fucking sexy."

"Come for me, then. I want to hear you."

"Want to wait..."

"No. Come now." She didn't dare let her mind think anything was expected of her, anything that could dissipate the wave of pleasure that listening to him reach crescendo was building.

There was a scraping sound, a short bump, as if he'd hit his elbow and jarred the earpiece, but then she heard his expulsion of breath, the guttural sounds that built into a succession of helpless groans.

"Yes," she whispered. "Like that. Come hard for me, Brendan."

She wanted him to have to wash his sheets tomorrow. She imagined his seed spurting thick and messy over his clenched grip, coating his fingers in a way that would make her want to lick every one of them, suck them into her mouth and then clean his cock the same way, swirl her tongue over his balls, taste and tease them with her teeth. She'd work her way up his delectable, muscular body one perfect inch at a time. She wanted to be there with him, trailing her fingers through the thick cream where it hit his belly, painting it over those impressive abs.

"Ah…" She caught her own moan in the back of her throat. Even as his climax was winding down, he heard it.

"Please come for me, baby. I want to hear you too. Stroke your pussy. Imagine it's my mouth, sucking on you, tasting that wetness. Your legs are wrapped around my shoulders, grinding yourself on my face, marking me as yours, taking your pleasure."

"Oh Goddess…" The flush raced up her body, a wave of heat as her clit spasmed under her fingers, her inner labia clamping around the digits inside, a poor substitute for what she wanted filling her there.

Despite that, it took five desperate more minutes, her body locked up, straining, afraid she wasn't going to make it, but his whisper was a hand pulling her up over that cliff, not letting her doubt herself and give up.

"Don't get in your way, Chloe. You can do it, baby. My mouth is on your pussy, fucking you with my tongue, my cock so hard, wanting you. When you're all done, I'm going to lie between your legs and suckle your tits for hours, so easy and gentle, until you're wet and wanting again. Until you give me permission to fuck you into the stars. Give this to yourself…"

It was a hard, hard climax, pulled from inside a room that had been locked for too long. Long enough that one, two, three convulsions, a short scream, and the door slammed. She vibrated with the aftermath, making a long, low cry of need, her body clutched in a trembling weakness. Curling around her hand, still clenched against her pussy, she brought her knees up to rock herself, keep that sensation going as long as she could.

It didn't matter. She'd done it, damn it. A baby orgasm was still an orgasm. It was like the first time she'd had one, when she was twelve. Something unexpected, that she immediately knew she'd want to do again. It had been an innocent accident, instigated by her bemusement at how good it felt to hold her giant teddy bear between her legs and rock against it. Just like then, she was in the secret sanctuary of her bedroom, but she'd since learned there were better things than teddy bears to fill that need, no offense to Balthazar Bear.

She wanted the real thing, Brendan's cock inside her, his body lying upon her, giving her that sense of safety and intimacy, an only-the-two-of-us-in-the-world feeling.

Unlike when she was an adolescent, though, she was breathing too hard, and her chest hurt again. Her other hand was still cupped over her breast, cradling it, and she tried to calm herself, imagining his hand there, his body spooning in behind her.

"You all right?"

His warm murmur over the phone made her eyes close tight as she held onto the resonance. "I wanted...more." Needed more.

Then she realized how that sounded. "I didn't mean—"

"I wanted more too. But this is a good start, don't you think?"

It was okay. Though he hadn't completely understood the nuances of her statement, she hadn't offended him. Listening to the easy honesty in his words, she realized that it could be that simple, for both of them. She'd adopt his truth for her own.

"Yes," she said. "I hope so. What now? Is there a phone sex version of cuddling?"

"Leave it to a girl to think of that."

"Well, if we didn't, you guys would start using phone sex exclusively, thinking you could get out of it."

"As good as phone sex is, I'm pretty sure we wouldn't give up actually being inside a woman, for any reason. I know I wouldn't."

That little trill of sensation skittered down her breastbone again, like a cool drop of water on a hot day. "Anyhow," he added, "I'm not ashamed to admit I like cuddling. As long as you don't report my violation of the universal male code to the proper authorities. Then I'll deny we even had the conversation."

She smiled. "I liked hearing you. When you came...it was like heat spread all over me, as if you were here."

"I was imagining being there. Or you being with me. Are you warm enough? If you get cold, you should get under the covers."

"I notice you didn't say I should put my sleep shirt back on."

"Well, no need for drastic measures if you have a blanket. Are you tired?"

She'd yawned. She was glad to hear the reluctant tone in his voice, though, as if he wasn't ready to let her go.

"Not really. It's just the time of night. Remember, it's you guys who get sleepy after sex, not us. So if you start snoring in my ear, I'll get my foghorn and blast you."

"You have a foghorn?"

"Yep. I dated a ferry boat captain for awhile, and he gave me one from a boat being refitted. It makes that deep two-toned sound, like you hear in the movies. It can blast your eardrums if you're too close to it."

Loosening her hand from around her breast, she drew her handmade quilt over her. A soft, familiar *mrrr* noise gave her fair warning right before St. Frances leaped onto the end of the bed. The dark tabby usually went out prowling while she slept, using his cat door to come back in during the later hours of the night. Stomping over with a look that suggested she was messing with his schedule by being awake, he situated his long, lean bulk into the curve of her body and began to ferociously wash, rocking against her.

"Why are you giggling?"

"St. Frances is tickling my chin. My tabby cat," she added. "Named after St. Frances de Sales, not Assisi. He was a medieval bishop, the one who said *Nothing is so strong as gentleness, nothing so gentle as real strength.*"

"And what saint-like, gentle qualities does your St. Frances have?"

"He doesn't hurt anything, not even bugs, unless it's an accidental squishing when he lies down. He catches creatures all the time, but he holds them so gently in his mouth they're still alive when he brings them to me. One morning I woke up to find an ibis strutting about the kitchen. When he catches chipmunks, he lays them on the linoleum and then looks puzzled as to why they're cowering there."

"Like cat, like Mistress. Marguerite told me you're the official bug catch-and-release officer at work."

"You asked about me?"

"She mentioned that at the wedding reception, when one of your customers brought up stories about things that happen at Tea Leaves." He paused at her silence. "It's not that I didn't want to learn all about you, Chloe. I wanted to learn it from you. And Marguerite...she pointed out if you weren't interested, I'd only be tormenting myself if I asked her all these questions about you."

There was more to it than that, she could sense it in his voice, but before she could pursue it, he switched topics. Since she was drifting in a dreamworld, not wanting any unpleasant reality to intrude, she let it go.

"A ferry boat captain?" he pressed. "Gen said you'd also dated a biker. No wonder you haven't called me. A drama teacher's pretty boring compared to all that."

"Yeah, didn't you hear me yawn earlier? Rescuing me from my nightmares with out-of-this-world phone sex and talking to me in French. Geez, it doesn't get duller than that. Idiot." She cradled the phone under her head, her eyes drooping despite herself. "Tell me more about being a drama professor. If I was going to walk into your class, what's the first thing we'd do?"

"If *you* walked into my class?"

"Brendan." She snorted. "If I was a brand new student."

"Well..." She heard some rustling, and imagined him turning on his side, still naked, his damp cock against his thigh, his dark hair brushing his shoulders. The moonlight would be filtering through his windows, kissing every curve and plane of his lean body. "We warm up with facial exercises. I have them grin, really wide. Scream. Screw up their faces tight and release them after thirty seconds. There are so many muscles in the face that give away expression. You have to exaggerate them for the stage, but it helps to know how to do it minutely as well, if you plan to act for film."

Chloe scrunched up her face, held it, and released. "Wow. It's like doing yoga or isometrics for your face."

"Try a big, exaggerated clown smile, take it down to a quick smile, then a faint one, as if you're not really happy, but you're going through the motions. Then back to the big one again."

"Okay..." She laughed. "It's hard. You have to concentrate. Like trying to pat your head and rub your stomach."

"You're training your muscles to respond on command, versus instinct. Once you get that down, you go back to instinct, only instead of responding to emotional stimulus, you're cued by lines, the tone of the scene."

"I bet your female students imagine you naked when you talk like this. I get the perk of *knowing* you are."

"You're not focusing," he said in mock offense.

"Ooh, a stern tone. And I am too. This is really interesting."

"As interesting as getting to blow a ferry captain's foghorn?"

She laughed outright but snuggled into the blankets, folding her arms across herself like a bat, scooching St. Frances down lower into the cradle of her lap. "For your information, I didn't blow *his* foghorn. Or anything else. It was one of those casual dates that turned into friendship."

"He must have been blind, or stupid. Not saying that being your friend wouldn't be great, but if a man could have more, he'd be crazy not to go for it."

"Maybe he discovered *I* was too crazy." She sobered. "You know what you said, the faint smile, going through the motions? I've been doing that for awhile. Sometimes I've wondered, if I do the fake smiles long enough, will it become like you said, an instinctive learned response, but nothing I really feel?"

"You've been real with me tonight. You haven't forgotten how to feel."

"How do you know?"

"Because some people are great actors. You're not, Chloe. You're as genuine and without artifice as they come. What you feel, it's in your voice. And you can feel and be whatever you want to be with me," he added.

"Charmer. You're just hoping to get lucky."

"I got lucky the moment you dialed my number. Want to do another exercise? This one I call WPS. It helps the beginners get over self-consciousness."

"I'm afraid to ask what WPS means."

"Worst Possible Song. Basically, I come up with a song for you to sing to me, the one you'd least likely pick for yourself, because it wouldn't fit your voice or comfort zone. Of course, I usually have a karaoke machine to help them with the words. For our purposes, I'll pick something familiar. You can sing what you remember and improvise the rest. Learning to think on your feet, in front of an audience, is also important."

"I honestly can't believe you're on the other side of this phone, sounding so teacherly. Not wearing a stitch. It's really turning me on."

His laugh made her grin, an expression so out of practice, instinctive or deliberate, it was a real surprise to feel it stretching her face. "Focus," he repeated, even more sternly. "You're already a problem student."

"That's what my teachers said. I just learned faster than everyone else and got bored."

"Sounds like a challenge to me. *Lucille*, by Kenny Rogers."

"Oh my God, I love that song. I dated a guy who was a roadie for him on his nostalgia tour a few years back. There was this seventy-year-old woman up front and, no kidding, she threw her panties at him."

"Your roadie or Kenny Rogers?"

"Kenny Rogers, jerk. But Stan had to retrieve the panties so nobody slipped on them. He was a sweetheart. He made a point to get them back to her after the concert. Told her that, while Kenny appreciated the gesture, he thought some lucky guy probably couldn't wait to see her in those crotchless purple mesh panties."

"You made that up."

"Truth is always stranger than fiction. Are you really going to make me sing *Lucille*?"

"I'd never make you do anything."

"But you'll think I'm a chicken."

"*Le petit poulet*. Already do, remember?"

"Will you say something else in French? Or Italian? Can you do an Aussie accent?"

"You give me a song, love, I'll do anything you want."

A shiver ran up her spine at the broad tone that brought to mind Heath Ledger. "All right, here goes. But you really do have a masochistic bent."

"That's sadistic, love. A masochist craves pain. A sadist gives it. Though that's a brush with too broad a stroke, to my way of thinking. Start singing, pretty sheila."

"I have an Australian friend who says that word's old-fashioned now." Chloe rolled over on her back, guiding her fingers through her headboard and holding there as she stared at her ceiling. "I wish it wasn't. Don't talk that way anymore, though. I like your voice, just as it is."

"Anything you want," he said softly. "Will you sing for me, Chloe?"

Closing her eyes, she hummed a few bars, taking a moment to collect her thoughts before starting the first stanza. A man seeing a woman in a smoky bar, thinking he was going to get lucky, never realizing he'd stepped into a tragedy of love lost.

When she was done, Brendan was quiet. "I like *your* voice," he said. "Nice and off tune, pretty and feminine. I can't believe you knew every word. You sang it like you felt it, no self-consciousness at all. You'd be great in my class."

The sincere compliment was a small thing, but it was an accomplishment. Giving her a feeling she hadn't had in awhile—that she had something worthwhile to offer. She wanted to push away the morbid thought, and the emotions that crowded in behind it, but the refrain of the song haunted her mind. *Why did you leave me?*

"Brendan, would you do something for me?"

"Anything."

"Are you really still naked?"

"Mm-hmm."

"Good. Can you put your hand on your heart?"

A space of time, then: "It's there now."

29

"Can you count out the beats? There's this theory, that when two people focus on the rhythm of their hearts, it synchronizes them. Brings the beats together."

"One beat. Two beats. Three beats… Is your hand on your heart too?"

"Yes," she answered, closing her eyes. She whispered the cadence, and though hers leaped when she realized it was working, it settled back down, slowly aligning with his verbal count. She began to speak aloud with him, in unison. "One beat, two beats…

He was with her. It felt like that thump against her hand was the true beat of his heart. Relaxing her head against the pillow again, she let her other hand drift down between her legs, finding the matching pulse there, holding her hand cupped over her still moist sex. The need to sleep that had been waiting behind the door of her nightmares was rising, a warm, relentless force, pulling her into its embrace.

"I'm getting sleepy, Brendan. But I don't want to go."

"Sleep, Chloe. I'm here. We can play later."

"Good," she murmured. "I can think of some really terrible girly songs for you to sing. *Like a Virgin, Girls Just Wanna Have Fun…*"

"Now who's the sadist? Sleep, sweet girl. Just sleep."

"*Hero,* by Enrique Iglesias. Sing that to me. Do you know the song, the words?"

"I know it. Close your eyes. I'm curled up behind you, holding you. Nothing will bother you any more tonight. I'm here."

"Don't forget the sappy whispered part at the beginning."

He hummed a few bars first, just as she'd done. When he made the soft plea to be her hero in that sexy whisper, he did it perfectly, not silly or awkward at all. She bet he was the best drama teacher ever. He began the ballad, taking her toward dreams, a slow spiral, no darkness. As candlelight guided her way, the shadows were a comforting cloak from reality, rather than its deceptive camouflage.

Believing he would keep her safe, she slept.

Chapter Three

ဆာ

Chloe rubbed at her eyes blearily and checked again to be sure she had her embroidered Tinkerbell knapsack, the bag she carried as a purse. Yep, still on her shoulder. Same place as when she'd checked two minutes ago. She hoped her license was in there. She'd mislaid her keys twice in her stumbling morning departure ritual.

She was already running late for Tampa traffic. Technically Marguerite and Gen had opening responsibility today, but the pre-work crowd could be demanding. She liked to be there to help. Plus, once she'd awakened again at 6 a.m., a scant ninety minutes after she'd hung up with Brendan, she hadn't been able to get back to sleep.

Stepping out the door, she pulled it closed and gave St. Frances a fingers-to-the-glass kiss. The cat, sitting in his side window shelf seat, gave her an indifferent look, which normally would have made her smile. Suppressing a sigh, she turned, and found herself confronted by something far more reassuring and unsettling at once.

Brendan, in her driveway, leaning against the door of a silver Jeep. Mortification warred with the indefinable, though she wanted it to be pleasure.

He looked...well, there was nothing a girl could do but stop and take a long, thorough look. Which required the indulgence of other senses because of course they were like jealous siblings. If the eyes got a look, the lips wanted a taste, and then the nose wanted a deep, long drag of that nice male musk. At the wedding, it'd been threaded with the fragrance of the lavender sprig in his tux lapel. She'd been bathing in lavender lately, and the idea of it, a bath with lavender and

Brendan spicing the waters... How could anything be better than that?

Those direct hazel eyes met hers, a gray-green-brown color she imagined would grace Fae wings to help the creatures blend into the forest. Silken black brows and straight-out-of-a-teen-heartthrob-magazine hair. It had the casually styled multi-layered look, and his jaw was clean-shaven. At the wedding, Gen had remarked, albeit in a low tone, that his hygiene and fashion confidence were stereotyped gay male, icing on a solid, dense cake of hetero sexual preference. The best of both worlds.

Maybe he was Italian. A pretty Italian momma's boy without the momma's boy part.

She was babbling in her own head. Not a good sign. As he straightened from the Jeep, walked toward her with a loose-limbed stride, the relaxed athlete, she had to remind herself to breathe. He stopped at the bottom of the stairs, looking up at her.

Months ago, she would have blithely skipped down the steps, wrapped her arms and legs around him and given him an enthusiastic kiss. She was painfully aware of that. She also would have had a hundred things to say by now, but the images of last night crowded in, the uncertainty of where that left them today, and she couldn't think.

He braced a booted foot on the bottom step. She liked the combination, scuffed black cowboy boots underneath his stressed jeans. When he'd been at the Jeep, she'd tried not to obviously linger on the nice presentation of his groin as he'd leaned against the door, ankles crossed, one hand hooked in the jeans' pocket. The casual blazer and button-down shirt complimented the outfit, screaming sexy college professor. All his female students probably had wet dreams about him. Hell, she was feeling that response now.

"How did you know where I lived?"

"I have friends in law enforcement who owe me favors. You were worth calling one in."

Before she could untangle her tongue at that, he withdrew his left arm from behind his back. In his hand was a stuffed puppy, a Rottweiler with a floppy red felt tongue and a blue bow tied around his neck. The laugh snorted out of her like a Jack-in-the-box surprise that made her jump a little, startled at her own noise.

"Thought you could use a guard dog."

"The bow kind of ruins the ferocious reputation, don't you think?"

"He says he's as capable of being cuddly as he is of ripping someone's throat out." Something a little dangerous went through his gaze, making that aroused response intensify. The tingle reminded her of a satellite photo she'd seen of a star cluster, one solid ball of heat in her stomach, light flashes radiating out from it into the other parts of her body.

His gaze remained on her face, making her suspect he was studying the shadows under her makeup free eyes, the lines around her mouth. "I don't know what to say," she ventured.

"Then don't say anything." Sliding an arm around her waist, leaving the puppy between them, he drew her down to him. Her arms automatically threaded over his shoulders, and when he brought her close, she pressed her face into his neck and all that silky hair.

Oh he was a dream come true, for sure. She should know better. But a part of her still wanted to be the Chloe she was months ago, who wouldn't question good fortune, who would embrace it wholeheartedly. She hadn't marked time. Instead, when something ran its course, she anticipated the next stroke of luck, beauty or happiness, rather than grieving on what had changed or passed.

But this Chloe saw all the shadows, the dark corridors and remembered her fear of a thumping branch in the middle of the night. The sly, malicious voice in her head told her this wasn't real, that she was merely using this temporary shelter to hide from those things.

Then Brendan turned his head toward hers, brushed his mouth over her lips. Not a sweet brush, but a sensual, lingering drag that came back to center and steadied as the comforting arms tightened, one hand palming the back of her head. Instead of pity, he gave her heat, a simmering, slow curl-the-toes-up-in-the-shoes heat, teasing her mouth open, tangling with her tongue so everything from chin to knees went tight, tingling, fluttery or wobbly.

The bag slipped off her shoulder as she slid her own hands up under his arms, inside the jacket, and dug her fingers into his back through the thin stuff of his shirt. She was acutely aware of the body under the clothes. How could she not be? He'd lain naked in his bed last night, gripped his cock and followed her direction to climax, leaving her vibrating, taking her to wonderful dreams.

Okay, instead of being flighty Chloe, staying home to hug trees and balance her chakra flow, she could be raging hormone Chloe, staying home to fuck the daylights out of the most irresistible thing that had ever shown up on her doorstep.

No, she couldn't. Because here it came, the pleasure turning to desperation, a simultaneous need to pull him closer and shove him away. She'd never been a needy, clingy kind of girl. She wouldn't become that. She wouldn't do that to herself or Brendan.

As if he knew, though, he'd already eased up, lifted his head to give her a sexy half-smile. "I hadn't planned that, but after last night, I couldn't get this close and not taste you. Feel you."

"Okay," she said.

His smile became a grin. "Can I give you a ride to work? And a ride home tonight?" He drew her down the steps and to the Jeep, where he leaned back against it, bringing her close again.

"I'm a little out of your way."

She wasn't sure where he lived, but she was pretty sure that he lived in town. He'd told her that during their conversations at the wedding, which had been light and easy as two butterflies playing and chasing one another over a moonlit meadow, occasionally stopping to sip nectar from flowers. Or, in their case, champagne.

"You're as out of my way as a fork in the road, and just as intriguing." He was still holding her close, but Chloe realized she was pressed against him as though she was using his ability to stand in lieu of her own. Every curve fitted into the shapes and planes of his body, so his chest was against her breasts, his groin against her belly, for he'd shifted his legs apart to cradle her in between. Long thighs stretched out on either side of her, his hands gripped low on her hips.

His aftershave was mixed with faint chlorine pool smell. When she slid her fingers through his hair, he tilted obligingly, eyes locked on her face. It was like passing her fingers through flowing water. She dropped her touch to his side, then his thigh, following it to his fingers at her hip. They flexed beneath her touch. His cock had gotten hard from her proximity, the increased pressure of it against her belly, but he didn't seem concerned about acting on that. He simply let her keep moving her hands over him. That increased pressure brought a sharp need of her own, though, one that had sharp teeth and the threat of darkness.

"I want you to take me back inside and have sex with me," she said abruptly. "Right now."

Holy God, where had that come from? She didn't know, but it was a plan of action, something to do other than this stillness, this standing by his car, in his arms, the world slowing down so that all the things racing by would stop as

36

well. They would see her, and worse, they would make her see *them*.

"Chloe." A muscle flexed in his jaw as he released her waist, brought his other hand to cradle her face, drawing her eyes to his, but that wasn't what she wanted. Everything in her pooled between her legs, driving all of the focus there. She'd earned him, earned the mindlessness. She didn't want a Tantric stillness or lazy, building pace that had to involve the mind, the spirit, the inner chi or whatever the fuck she'd normally bring into it to make her think it was something extraordinary. She was against a visceral wall of muscle and testosterone, and her blood was pumping hot with the need to embrace it. A hard fuck, no gentle kisses, no hands on her. She'd tie his hands to the rail of the bed, tie them tight so it would hurt a little. She'd bite and tear, consume, devour and take, until there was nothing left.

Stretching on her toes, she found his mouth, growling with pleasure as it opened for her. A clever tongue tangled with hers again and sent sensation rippling through her nerves, sweeping away the debris inside her like a hot, scorching wind.

"Chloe." He repeated it then, and though he held her face in a gentle grip, it was unshakable. She closed her eyes. "Tell me again what you want. I need to hear it. What do you want?"

What was it in his voice that pulled her out of that whirlwind, even as she tried to claw back to it, wanting to spit at him? But he said her name again, in a whisper this time. Just her name.

"Chloe."

It became an echo through all those empty spaces, the places she hadn't known were empty, or maybe they hadn't been. Whatever had populated those rooms was gone, and she wasn't sure how to bring back the comfortable, quirky furnishings that had been there before.

"I want to be me again. I want to feel safe."

A sigh left him, a warm breath that caressed her face as he curved his hand around the back of her neck then, bringing her face into his chest. She'd been close to him a moment before, pressed tight, but this was somehow closer, maybe because some of that tension left her and she melted into him in truth. Her arms slid up under his again so she could flatten her palms over his shoulder blades, her nose burying in his chest, seeking the comfort of shirt and skin and their nice smells. His other arm wrapped around her waist, holding her between his braced legs so close. He was still aroused, but it was a natural, easy pleasure now, a reminder of all the wonderful things it meant, that were possible.

She prided herself on being independent, but she welcomed the subtle message he'd been sending to her with that blue bow on the Rottweiler. Male, protective.

How long they stood like that, she wasn't sure, but he held her while the sun warmed the Jeep and emanated against her. Myriad bugs, frogs and other creatures that lived in the thicket of tangled foliage she'd encouraged around her cottage sang, chirped and made their discordant morning noises. Clicks, sawing violins, pops. Sounds hard to describe, but everyone understood the feeling, the familiar reassurance of them, that came on a sunny early morning. Much like this feeling.

He brushed his lips across her forehead. "Why don't I take you to work now?" His mouth pulled in a smile against her temple. "But if you want to revisit that other idea later, I won't object."

* * * * *

In fact, Brendan knew if she'd made the demand once more, he would have swung her up in his arms and taken the stairs two at a time, even knowing it was the wrong thing. Well, wrong was the incorrect word. It would have been sweaty, slick and satisfying to the parts of their bodies that were impatient with emotions, though. But he knew how it would have played out. Shame would have drowned her because "I want to have a rough fuck with somebody I barely know" didn't mesh with the Chloe he'd met at the wedding, or talked to in such an extraordinary way on the phone a mere few hours ago. He didn't want to lose that Chloe. He was more than a little concerned she was in danger of losing it herself.

The person he'd met at the wedding had let her emotions lead her, despite her injuries and close brush with death. He knew magical nights like that made nightmares temporarily go away, but even so, he'd sensed he'd been talking to the real Chloe. Unabashed, unrepressed. That Chloe might have made the impetuous decision to make love to him so quickly, but if she did, it would be because she felt a connection that told her coming together physically would be a joyous, fulfilling experience. Where, if there wasn't love, there would be learning, friendship, laughter, things worth taking the emotional risk.

Her desire to be taken now, such an abrupt, harsh and cruelly worded decision, was just the opposite of that. She was completely shielded, the quick desire a way to avoid or outrun her feelings, not open them.

He understood all that. But he had his own needs and vulnerabilities as well, and her demand was like a witch's spell. If it had been uttered twice, or more catastrophically, the irreversible three times, it would have taken him over. He would have obeyed her without thought.

Or maybe not. Surrender and submission were inseparable from love, care, protection. Without those things, the soul was lost, along with the treasure. A Mistress had taught him that. His Mistress, or rather, *the* Mistress, the one who'd allowed him to be hers, even if she belonged to another.

Not for the first time in the past few hours, he realized that history might be problematic. *Yeah, that's an understatement.* He was in uncharted territory, pursuing someone who wasn't part of a life that was a large part of his. Maybe that was the real reason he hadn't called her for months, even knowing he could have gotten the number from Marguerite. But he hadn't forgotten her, had wanted her, and when he'd heard her voice on the phone, he knew he didn't want to deny himself the pleasure of getting to know her. He'd accepted it as fate, but he was well aware he could be rationalizing a path to catastrophe, for both of them.

As he helped her into the Jeep and made sure her seatbelt was securely fastened, he noted her downcast eyes, bruised with lack of sleep. Brushing her cheek with his knuckles, he won an attempt at a real smile.

It was never easy or simple. Something worth having never was.

* * * * *

When Brendan dropped her off, he told her that he'd come back for her at the end of the day. Walked her to the side porch of the tea room. Held her hand. A part of her wanted him to kiss her, but she had no idea what she herself wanted. She'd never realized her own thoughts could turn her into a lunatic.

She must have conveyed that indecision, because after a steady, searching look, he squeezed her hands and took a step back, nodding to her before heading back down the narrow path to the roadside parking. She thought she detected an expression of regret, like he'd hoped for more of a signal from her for the kiss. Or she might be reading way too much into it. He could be thinking, "Okay, be a good kid, play well with others, and don't give away the carrots I put in your Barbie lunchbox."

He hadn't fucked her, though she'd all but begged him. Maybe she understood why he'd turned her down, but his decision not to kiss her now took some of that understanding away. A *nice* guy? Was that what she really wanted? Any other day there would have been callous, insensitive, only-thinking-with-their-dicks Neanderthals lined up ten deep everywhere she looked, ready to take advantage of her desire for rough, violent sex.

He'd stopped at the Jeep, his hand on the latch, and now he looked back, met her gaze. What was it that showed in her face? She didn't know, but he let go of the handle and considered her from head to toe, standing on the steps.

She hadn't worn anything particularly alluring today. She was dressed up enough to be presentable for work, no more, no less. Usually she went for some kind of amulet, a few strings of colorful beads, unique costume jewelry that fit her flowing clothes or faded jeans and quirky T-shirts. She loved wild, floppy hats with feathers, decorated the brims with vintage brooches she found. She might wear a ribboned cameo at her throat, or poison vial amulets. Some days she went for the natural look, her jewelry just a seashell or rock she'd found, strung on a silk cord.

Rather than being the armor they were for many other people, her clothes and accessories were part of her honest language, the way she laughed and talked to the world, which sang back in multiple colors and textures.

If anyone could live on the curve of a rainbow, it would be you. Gen had said that to her. Over a year ago.

Today, her throat was painfully bare, her outfit bland. Jewelry and color were the last things she'd been thinking about this morning. But as his gaze coursed over her throat, instead of feeling like she'd failed herself, she imagined his hands or mouth as the embellishment there, a sensation as vibrant as whatever sparkling color she would have chosen. She almost forgot how tired and pale she must look.

His focus moved back to her face. All he'd done was look at her, and she couldn't move, could only tremble. Could he devour her body with a look, the way she wanted him to do? No, of course not. No more than he could take her up on her needy demand earlier, or give her one damn kiss now.

On the other hand, if he'd given her a brush of lips the way he would a pathetic invalid, a psycho charity case, she might have had to pluck the Welcome to Tea Leaves wall plate off the porch pillar and slap it against his head hard enough to spin him.

"Chloe." His voice was a caress, feathering the twenty feet of air between them. "What do you want right now? Tell me."

"I want you to kiss me, like you would have last night. I don't want you to give a damn about how I feel or what I want. I don't want you to be sensitive or caring. It's choking me, damn it."

He cocked a brow. Pivoted and opened the Jeep door. For a second, she thought she might crumble right there. Or scream like a madwoman, ripping all the innocent flowers from their pots to throw clods of dirt at him. Then he shrugged out of the coat, broad shoulders delineated by the pull of the white shirt beneath, and tossed it over the passenger seat. Turning around, he strode back up the walk to her.

His eyes were back on hers, but his expression was very different now. He showed her fire, purpose, a sensuous set of his mouth that had her own lips tightening in anticipation. He moved swiftly and gracefully, such that she had approximately one indrawn breath to think "I have no idea what the hell I'm doing". There was panic, that odd conflict again, wanting him and yet fighting not to bolt and hide. Before she could decide, he'd slid one arm around her waist and put one foot on the step next to hers. When the weight of his body shoved her against the railing, her hands flew to his shoulders to grab.

In a blink, her feet were barely touching the porch boards, then not touching at all as he took another step up. The height difference, along with the strength of his one arm, brought her up against his chest, put her thighs flush against his. Before her feet could scrabble for purchase, he'd shifted his hands, gripped her thighs and yanked them up so they slid around his hips, pressing his body into that carnal cradle, denim to soft fabric.

She'd worn drawstring cotton pants with her T-shirt, hand painted with a jasmine tea leaf. One of her faded and frayed ballet style slippers toppled off her toe so that her bare foot curved around the back of his thigh. Even though the outfit was thin, it felt like too many clothes as the sensual overload of the previous night rushed back in, the remembrance of his cock spurting at her command, that steel organ now pressed against her center.

Then his mouth claimed hers and all of her brain cells spun out of control. He did exactly as she'd craved, making the kiss hot, demanding, basically pure sex administered in oral form. Tongue invading, teasing, plumbing, his other hand wrapping around her head, fingers buried in her hair. The arm around her waist was low enough his hand splayed out over her buttock, gripped her hard so she moaned into his mouth and moved in hard, restless anger against him. He made a masculine noise in her mouth, urgent, sexual. Tearing his mouth away from hers, he tasted her throat the way she'd imagined, only sucking on her flesh, scoring it with his teeth. He sucked hard enough to leave a mark upon her, something she could finger through the day and remember. Gen might see it and tease her, which was good, because that would convince them she was doing okay, make them worry less.

As he kissed her, her nerve endings reacted like reeds bending before the touch of a warm wind. At the same time, that coil in her lower belly drew into a needy fist she felt in all the right places, above and below. Her mouth, face and throat had never been so sensitive to a man's touch. She wanted him everywhere, his mouth, the beat of his breath, the tips of his fingertips, so she could shiver and moan, lose herself in sensation, thoughts disappearing.

When he lifted his head, she was clinging to him, her breath panting, heart trip-hammering.

"I could never kiss you like I don't give a damn about what you want, Chloe," he murmured, intense gaze upon her face. "But I can kiss you like it's the most important thing in the whole fucking world. I could stand here and kiss you like this forever."

Staring into his face, she forced her fingers to let go of him, one at a time. "You don't do anything in half measure, do you?"

He eased her down, ran a thumb over her moist lips. "I'll see you at six."

Turning, he went back to his Jeep, and left her there.

Chapter Four

≈

"Chloe?"

The door had opened behind her and she hadn't even realized it. Thank Goddess it was Gen and not their boss, because she wasn't sure how she could have held it together in front of Marguerite at this raw moment. There was just something about her and Tyler, both of them seeing past all layers to who a person was. It was a loveable quality only when you weren't desperately using those layers as camouflage.

Gen was a different kind of friend. The comfortable kind. Though there was concern in her eyes, she put a hand on her hip and gave her a tart look. "Are you done necking with your boy-toy and ready to go to work?"

"Apparently more than you, if you had time to press your nose to the window." Chloe attempted a smile as she managed to shuffle to the door. Gen slid an arm around her waist and squeezed, unspoken affection and care.

"If it's a pretty day, I look out the window. I just didn't realize how pretty the view was going to be. Wasn't that Brendan, the one who gave Marguerite away at her wedding? About time you called him. I should have slipped him your number to get things going sooner."

Yeah, because I want to rush my inevitable trashing of the relationship so he can treat me like a leper sooner. But she had really liked that kiss. In fact, if she set aside her insecurities, she knew she'd never enjoyed a kiss more in her whole life. Her body knew that was the kiss of all kisses, specially tailored for everything she wanted and needed.

Awkwardness, excitement and laughter were all part of first kisses, as much as passion and potential. But there was something about Brendan that took her right past awkwardness. She should have been pretty embarrassed when she first saw him this morning, but that mortification had been immediately brushed aside by desire. Everything felt the way it should. As if nothing he said or did, or even she said or did, could be wrong. As natural as breathing, as perfect as lovemaking in the tranquil hush of a church. The quiet beauty of the sacred meeting the child's need for joy.

Her mind had gone straight to the land of poetic fruit loops.

Grimacing, she put down her tote bag and came into the main kitchen. The day's tea offerings had been written on a piece of floral stationery and left on the counter for her to transcribe to the board. As she was looking it over, a cup of tea, steam rising off the liquid, was placed at her elbow. "I think a chamomile this morning, mixed with lavender and our freshest green blend for energy." A square of chocolate was placed next to the cup by long, elegant fingers, graced by a silver wedding band etched with Japanese characters. "And this, for pure indulgence."

Chloe looked up into the face of the tea room's owner, Marguerite Winterman. Tall, beautiful and as remote as the ice queen of fairy tale legend was the way most would describe her precise features, moonlit hair and pale blue eyes. Chloe and Gen both knew her well enough to call her friend. She was more than that too. Chloe couldn't exactly put a finger on it, but though there was not a great distance in their ages, Marguerite possessed qualities she might have assigned to a favorite but strict teacher, a tribal chieftain or temple priestess, with Gen and Chloe as her acolytes.

Chloe didn't resist authority or rebel against it; she just flowed around it like a cheerful brook, integrating it in her bubbling froth. But there was no going around Marguerite, which was why Chloe knew she'd needed more sleep before coming in. Even now, Marguerite's fingers drifted to Chloe's face, tipped up her chin.

"Why are you here today?" she asked quietly.

Because I don't know where else to go, Chloe almost said. The person she used to be had plenty of casual friends. On any given week she might head off to a hike in the mountains, or dress up in Goth gear for a heavy metal concert. Spend a weekend working a table for a charity event in one of Tampa's many parks. But she'd cut herself off from those friends over the past months. Put them off by saying they'd do something soon. It had been a gradual thing. She'd tried participating in her usual activities, but felt more and more like a remote wooden doll. She did and said the right things, but came home exhausted from the pretense, the emotional drain of being totally detached and pretending not to be.

As a result, during the past few months she'd done little to nothing, other than putter around her house, sit on the back porch and stare into space or nap, with St. Frances curled in her lap, an undemanding weight.

Sometimes she wished the work day would never end, that she could stay in a continual loop like one of those Twilight Zones where she could always be here, where she understood what she needed to do and who she needed to be. Much like she'd felt when kissing Brendan, not wanting to go back or forward.

She'd been nervous the first day she'd come back to work after her attack, since this was where it had happened. But Marguerite's renovation of the tea room must have included a cleansing ritual, because the second Chloe stepped back across the threshold, she'd felt relief, a sense of home. Which she hadn't felt anywhere else until this morning, when she stepped into Brendan's arms.

"I..."

"She was dropped off." Gen came to her rescue. "Brendan brought her to work."

Marguerite's gaze didn't waver from Chloe's face, but a speculative look entered her gaze. You couldn't distance

Marguerite or evade her when she wanted a straight answer, but offering a new variable that changed the nature of the question had an effect. "Did he stay the night with you?"

Yep, that was Marguerite. Direct. "Not exactly. We stayed up late on the phone and he came by this morning, offering to drive me."

"So he'll be driving you home tonight."

Chloe nodded.

"Good." Marguerite released her from that penetrating look, but slid the tea and chocolate closer.

"It was a really hot, tonsil-sucking kiss," Gen offered.

"It was not."

"It had those take-me-now electrons bouncing all the way across the porch. You were wrapped around him like a monkey on a branch."

"Like some kind of slut?" Chloe snapped. "Some dirty whore?"

Marguerite's head whipped around as Gen froze. Chloe put down the tea list with exaggerated care, the roaring in her ears a tsunami. "Sorry," she said faintly. "I...that's not what I meant."

"Not what I meant either, honey," Gen said softly. "You're usually so uninhibited with your feelings, and I could tell you really like him. It was good to see."

"Yeah, I like him." Chloe cleared her throat, managed a ghost of a smile. "We had this totally over the top time on the phone last night. We talked and talked, and did lots of stuff..."

Marguerite she drew closer again. "Chloe—"

"I'll make cupcakes today," Chloe said desperately. *Please don't ask, please don't ask.* She felt like a bomb ticking down to detonation. "You know you're working on taxes and you always feel better afterward if you have some of my cupcakes."

Marguerite studied her another long moment. "Chloe, you *will* start taking care of yourself, or I will make you move in with Tyler and me and do it for you. Are we clear? I love you, and I won't tolerate this much longer." She nodded at the girl, gave her another even look and disappeared into her office, though she left the door open.

"I don't know how," Chloe whispered. That was the crux of it all, wasn't it? She had no answers, and she'd always been so very sure of herself. She needed something different, something to give her that confidence. She just couldn't figure out what the hell it was. Clinging to the cliff edge by her fingernails was hard enough; she couldn't begin to think of how to pull herself back up. A plethora of hands might be waiting, but something inside her head crawled into a ball and wouldn't reach out.

Like Brendan. She loved the kiss, but if she thought beyond that, the anxiety rose. Damn it, damn it, damn it. A gorgeous, wonderful guy was interested in her. What was the matter? Why couldn't she fix what was broken?

Gen had moved to take over the brewing that Marguerite had started, but she gave Chloe's lower back a gentle caress as she passed, thankfully saying nothing further. Chloe shifted her attention back to the counter and stared at the list of specials. Something pleasurable, safe, part of the routine. She loved seeing what Marguerite had put together to offer their customers each day. Loved how she always wrote it down in careful calligraphy, on different types of stationery. This one was a gray mist, with the hint of shadowed fairies and silky daisies behind the writing. Even though the list's only purpose was for Chloe to copy it to the white board, it was a ritual. Marguerite understood the power of ritual, as intuitively as she anticipated what teas would be needed each day to best meet the needs of her clientele.

That intuition was probably why Chloe wanted to be so far away right now...and yet she needed to be here too, more than she needed to be anywhere else. Except, perhaps, in Brendan's far-too-open arms.

* * * * *

He arrived right at closing time. Chloe's heart leaped foolishly in her chest, even as her hands shook a little, pouring out the tea for the Dupont party. They didn't notice though, because the all-female table was watching Brendan come up the front walkway. He was bearing gifts.

As he stepped in, she saw it was a theater mask. It had the face of a cat, with long winsomely curled whiskers and tufted ears. When he found her, obviously looking for her, he gave her a smile and came right over, reaching for her hand to give it a quick, caressing squeeze. A female wave of amiable yet gratifying envy pulsed at her back. "Hey there. Thought about you today."

"Oh sure. Until the next psychotic woman calls you in the middle of the night. Then I'll be old news."

"True. But I'm a live-in-the-moment kind of guy." He gave her another squeeze as Marguerite came from the back. Chloe noted he straightened, dipped his head respectfully to her. There was always an odd formality between them, but yet she knew they were very close. The mystery thankfully distracted her from her momentary discomfiture.

Marguerite offered a tray. "How about a cupcake? Chloe made them at lunch."

Brendan considered. "Has Mas...Tyler had his share yet?"

"Yes, the alpha wolf has had first pick, and is probably nursing a sugar crash for his incurable sweet tooth." She pushed the tray at him. "Take this in the kitchen and see if you can help Gen loosen the lid on the Darjeeling. What's the mask for?"

"A surprise for Chloe." He winked and disappeared through the swinging door, the only thing that was capable of getting every woman's mind off his tight ass and back to whatever it was they'd forgotten they were talking about.

"Oh dear." Mrs. Dupont leaned over. "Chloe, I think I've dumped some tea on the floor, and my napkin doesn't seem to be picking it up."

Choe squatted, her always available washcloth pulled from her apron pocket. She stopped in mid-motion, however, her gaze riveting not on the small, brandy-colored puddle, but a dried, older stain.

It was a small smear, one that would be missed except at this time of day, when the sun was coming in at just the right angle. It might not even be a stain. It could be a discoloration of the wood that the sunlight turned into the memory of blood. Her blood. Biting down on her lip hard enough to create more of it, she wiped up the tea.

* * * * *

When they reached the Jeep, Brendan stopped before the passenger door. Rather than opening it, he turned her toward him with a touch on her shoulder. With a quick meeting of eyes to confirm she had no immediate objections, he slid the mask over her head. She peered at him through the eye holes, not sure how to react. He didn't seem like he needed a response from her, however. He was occupied with settling the mask on her nose in a comfortable, surprisingly snug fit. When he at last stepped back, he gestured to the side mirror. As she checked herself out, she saw the mask made her eyes look feline, the painted lashes adding an exotic, mysterious flavor to them. Her curly, short hair fluffed around it, giving the cat's face a whimsical, very feminine flavor.

She looked toward him, and knew her lips had curved in a pleased smile when his eyes warmed. "Beautiful," he said, with satisfaction, and she couldn't help but agree. The half mask left her cheeks, lips and chin bare, making them much more sensitive to touch when he brushed his fingertips across her lips. As he traced the skin below the mask edge, over her cheekbones, her lips parted. Easing his fingers into her mouth, he touched her tongue, the secret moistness within her bottom lip.

"Now you can be whoever you want to be." He spoke in that voice that seemed designed to elicit total trust and enable seduction at once. "While you wear that, you're a mysterious, gorgeous creature who can do anything she wants to do and it's okay, because tonight she's a mystery to herself as well. She's going to be the side of herself she doesn't know, not the side she does."

With any other guy, she'd have thought it was a way to get her to be what *he* wanted, relieve him of the burden of another night of dealing with her personal demons. It would have hurt, but she wouldn't have blamed him in the slightest. But when she looked up at him from behind that form fitting mask that already felt like part of who she was in this exact minute, she knew he didn't have that kind of duplicity. There was something about him so centered on what she was feeling and wanting, it was a part of him too. What she couldn't give herself but wanted to, he did. Totally crazy but totally fine.

She'd never been with a male with this kind of sexual and romantic confidence. He was unreal, but also so real he made her ache in every place a woman ached when she saw the epitome of what she wanted, needed, desired, even before she knew how to name it.

She lifted her hand, closed it on his wrist, stilling him. They stayed that way for another long minute, her staring at him, him holding her gaze with all the reverence of a worshipper come to the shrine of a goddess. Of a sudden, she felt clean and...not powerful, that wasn't exactly the right word. Grounded. She felt grounded, for this brief, all important moment.

She guided his finger into her mouth, tasted him. Bit down a little. Then harder. His hazel eyes heated, the sensual mouth curved, and she felt his response, his need reach toward her in that heat. A man's power and strength, rendered motionless, reined in by her touch. She wondered if she bit hard enough to break skin, if he would let her, take her need to inflict pain and let the desire to accept it from her become overwhelming.

"I want to touch you. Kiss you."

She wasn't ready for that, so she shook her head. "I want to touch *you*," she said instead. "While you drive."

He opened the car door for her, and she got in. After he made sure her seatbelt was fastened, he strode around the front of the car. Though he kept his gaze on her face, she let hers course over him, blatantly appreciating the way he moved. As a stage player, he could probably stride with warrior purpose, lazily saunter, or manage a seductive swagger with lots of hip. He was mesmerizing to watch, but she had another way she wanted to appreciate him.

As he got in on his side and lifted the key, she closed her hand over his, not hampering him but holding on as he put it in the ignition and turned it over. He'd shed his jacket from the morning and had rolled up his sleeves at some point. She let her hand glide down his wrist, his forearm. The mask made her feel brave. Dangerous. "Will you keep two hands on the wheel?"

"I'll do anything you tell me to do." As if he read her intent and was already feeling the arousal from it, he said it with a soft fierceness, nothing meek about his compliance. Not when his body was like a taut wire that, if snapped, might wrap around her and bring her the sharp edge of his loss of control. Giving her a look that made the mask feel even more erotic in its close hold on her face, he put the Jeep in drive, put his hands on the wheel and headed out for the main highway that would take them to her home.

She knew she should care about whether she was being a hazard as he navigated the busy traffic, but it wasn't a reckless self destruction. She knew he'd keep her safe, just as she knew he wouldn't take his hands off the wheel until she said he could, because it was the requirement itself in addition to the explosive energy between them that brought it to a combustible level.

She slid her fingertips under the sleeve to find the crease of elbow, the tender skin there at odds with his firm, tanned forearm and callused hand. While she did that, she put the other hand on his knee, and began to move upward along faded denim.

He shifted, though she sensed his self-imposed restraint. It made her want to test that leash. She slid higher. Stressed denim loved Brendan's body, outlining the lean thighs and cradling his groin. As her touch progressed, he adjusted his legs apart for her, anticipating her desire before she had it. The inseam curved over his testicles, tempting her to cup him there. She wanted to stroke the base of his cock with her thumb, a straining thick crescent beneath the zipper, not enough room to expand to its tumescent length. But she didn't touch him yet, leaving her hand high on his thigh.

His throat worked as he swallowed, his fingers tight on the wheel. Long, strong fingers. She thought of him last night, and imagined how he gripped and stroked his organ, starting slow and teasing, getting faster and faster, rougher, his body jerking as his climax finally spurted, wetting his abdomen and thighs as she listened, breathless, on the other end of the line.

Her hand was so close she could feel the pulse of blood in his groin, the heat emanating from it. He'd merged onto a familiar stretch of two-lane highway edged with mature oaks dripping Spanish moss. Not the interstate, that would have been too impersonal. Too separate from the smell of marshy land dotted with small lakes. She was conscious of the dwellings they passed, trailers and fishing getaway cottages nestled on overgrown lots. Other, more opulent homes were set back on manicured lawns, interspersed with cottage clusters, the occasional citrus groves or fields with cows and horses. The eclectic zoning of the Florida coastal areas. It kept the scenery surprising, unexpected, hard to classify.

She felt the same about the choices she had inside the Jeep. She wanted to touch his cock, but she wanted to wait as well. Either option would allow her to tease him while he tried to drive, unable to do anything but endure what she wanted. So she deliberately skirted his groin, gliding over his hip bone to the belted waist of the jeans, then across his tense abdomen, to the buttons of his shirt. One, two, three...she unbuttoned it in reverse order, working her way up to his throat. She wanted to turn sideways in her seat to lean in further, but when she reached down to unbuckle the seatbelt, he broke his promise for the first time. His hand left the wheel, closed over hers.

"You can adjust it a bit to make it slack, but leave it on."

"To keep me from crawling on top of you while you're driving?" She wanted to inject humor in her voice, but there was too much of a bite.

He glanced at her, the setting sun glinting off his riveted gaze, a touch of amber fire in the hazel. "To keep you safe."

As he suggested, she loosened the belt and turned on her hip. When she did, she enjoyed the view of his naked chest framed by his open shirt. His cock strained against his jeans, obviously aroused, the display constantly shifting as he let off the gas and applied the brake as needed. She returned her hand to his bare chest, touching his flesh there for the first time, pushing her knuckles beneath the cloth of the open shirt to cross the terrain of a pectoral, drop down to fondle a nipple. The abdomen against which she had her elbow contracted as he drew in a breath. Leaning forward, she pushed aside the shirt and closed her mouth over the nipple, the whiskers attached to the mask tickling his skin.

"Ah, God. Chloe..."

She slid her other hand between the seat and his back, stealing down to the waist of his dress jeans. They were loose enough back there, even with the belt, to permit her fingertips to caress the upper curve of his buttocks. She didn't find any underwear. Of a sudden, she was very, very hungry. She

55

wanted to eat him alive, leave nothing but bones when she was done.

When at last he turned into her driveway, he brought the vehicle to a jolting stop, car parked in a skewed manner behind hers. Releasing her seatbelt then, she left his in place but climbed on top of him, barely giving him time to reach down and slide the seat back. That space gave her hips room to clear the steering wheel as she sat down on his lap and rubbed herself on him, making a desperate mewl at the resulting friction. She was needy, savage, not herself. Yes, he'd told her to be whatever she wanted to be, and this was it, but it was wrong too.

She wanted to savor, but she was incapable. Savoring meant going slow, letting the emotion saturate the moment, and she couldn't bear that.

He reached up toward her face, those graceful male hands intending to cup her jaw she was sure, overwhelming her with the tender, romantic pleasure of his fingers passing over her lips. Clamping her hands around his wrists, she shoved them up to an awkward angle above his shoulders. She couldn't hold him there of course, but as he held her gaze, he slowly slid them back behind his head and curved his fingers on the head rest bars, restraining himself for her.

It was a cue, and her body responded with the mindless violence of a gladiator. Trained to leap the moment the grate opened and the vulnerable opponent entered the ring.

If the shirt had still been buttoned, she would have torn it open, buttons clattering across the console. Instead, there was no barrier to the next step. She put her mouth on him, tasting, using her teeth, her nails to rake across hard male flesh and leave welts. He shuddered beneath her and yet she put a hand up to his eyes, demanding that they close, unable to bear his scrutiny even though she was hiding behind a mask. He obeyed, his biceps hard curves, thighs taut beneath her legs.

She moved down his abdomen, the seat pushed back enough she could slide down between his splayed knees, unbuckle the belt and open the jeans to find just him beneath. His ass had been rubbed by denim all day long, one thin cotton layer between him and whatever female lusted after him. It made her angry in some way, possessive and greedy at once, goading the aching, gnawing lust she couldn't seem to assuage, that didn't seem to belong to her. More like a symptom of an illness she couldn't shake.

Shoving that aside, she focused on what lay before her. Released from its confines, his cock straightened and rose, stiff with blood. Smooth and hard, perfect. He had no hair at the base, she noticed. In fact, he was smooth all over. Swimmer. Did he remove it for that? Still, he'd kept that gorgeous black silky hair on his head, the sweep of eyebrows that saved him from being too pretty. They gave him a determined and dangerous look, particularly when he was protective, as she'd seen him be, several times now.

A faint exotic scent told her he put cologne on those smooth balls, and it worked like an aphrodisiac charm with the natural male musk. She put her mouth over him. No teasing seduction, no taunting lick. She didn't care about his response, except for what she demanded for herself. She was using his body, pure and simple, and with his hands clasping the headrest, keeping himself open to her, she took it as a sign that it was her right to take what he was offering. She sank down on his cock, sucked hard, licked. She was pretty good at giving head, had always enjoyed the act, the way it could drive a guy wild, her mouth giving him a gift he couldn't give himself.

But this was a gift only for herself. Putting her hand up once, she squeezed his clenched knuckles as mute reinforcement of her desire. She didn't want him to touch or speak to her, or look at her. His cock was a delectable piece of meat she would exploit until it gave her what she wanted. The arch, jerk and thrust of his muscled body, the ripple over his abdomen, the rhythmic clench of his buttocks against the seat as he thrust into her mouth, she would wrest it all from him.

Clamping her teeth on his thick organ, she held him still in mid-thrust, flicking her tongue along his shaft behind the hold of her teeth. A languid serpent, playing with prey. The throbbing pulse beneath her tongue leaped and she tightened her jaw further. With one hard bite, she could make him scream, cry for mercy. Bleed. Or she could do as she did now, one slow, slick glide of her mouth down, replacing her savagery with deep throated acceptance, then back up, calling forth what he was helpless to deny her. That vein pulsed, and his cock jumped in warning.

"Shit...Chloe..." He coiled up. "May I... I can't... Please..."

No guy had ever asked before, certainly not on a knife edge like this. It gave her a flood of searing power to hear the plea in his voice. "Come for me," she whispered against his flesh, and held him tight, her fingers curling around his balls. They contracted, drew up as he thrust into her mouth. His whole body arced to her, booted feet pushing into the car floor as he spewed.

She took most of him in the back of her throat, but some of it she let run back down over her fist, making his cock that much more slick. As he cried out, that harsh animal sound, she milked him to the last drop, fanned her sticky hand over his stomach, spreading his seed there. As he finished, his cock making tiny jerks against her tongue, she slowly slid off him. Pressing her open mouth to his abdomen, she licked each individual crease and ridge, cleaning the stickiness away as he shuddered and trembled beneath her.

Her body was as aroused as she'd ever experienced, but she still didn't want him to touch her. She couldn't go forward or back. This agonized yearning was all she dared to feel. She wanted so much more, but why ruin it by asking for more than she could get?

Moving back into the passenger seat, she felt dizzy and almost weak, her skin so hot and cold at once. Pulling off the mask, she left it, opened the door and stumbled out into darkness, twilight gone to night.

She stopped, swaying, not sure which direction held the front door, but before she could decide, he was there in front of her. Shirt hanging open, jeans zipped, though he'd left the top button open and the belt loosely buckled. It made her aching body shudder worse. But still she backed away. "No." She shook her head. "Don't touch me right now."

"Chloe." He spoke softly, but there was strength and purpose in his voice, determination in that look. "You need me to touch you."

"I can't... I don't know how I need you to touch me."

"Will you trust me to know?"

She put her hands over her face, uncertain. He took a step forward, then another. She swayed as he came close. "I might break if you touch me. A million pieces."

"I won't let that happen."

He slid an arm around her back, bringing himself so close there were mere inches between them. Just as she was steeling herself for him pressing against her, possibly pushing her up against the Jeep, he leaned down and swept her legs so he was cradling her in his arms, a movement so smooth it was as if he'd levitated her into the position, her body naturally flowing with the movement of his.

Wondering, she slid her arm around his neck, her fingers tangling in his hair. "Wow," she managed.

He smiled, but his features were somber. "I'm staying tonight. I'll stay on the couch or I'll sleep in the Jeep, but I'm staying."

She didn't reply, only laid her head on his shoulder and let him take her inside the house. He shifted her easily as he handled the opening and closing of the door. She liked being carried by him. She was usually more active in her physical interaction. Typically, a guy ended up carrying her because she'd done a little hop and wrapped her legs around his waist, so he could waltz her to the bed, or maneuver her for a kiss in chest-high ocean waters, or wherever they happened to be for the pleasurable, ultimate moment.

But despite what she and Brendan had just done—or rather, she'd done to him—she wasn't ready for sex. This, being carried by him, was a welcome kind of intimacy, however. As if by lifting her off her feet he was simultaneously lifting any burdens, letting her drop them as she'd dropped the mask. She wanted to lose herself in simple delight.

He took her to her bedroom, moving slowly in semi-darkness. He didn't turn on any lights, which she also liked, using just the early evening light to guide his way. It kept the mood soft, easy…dreamlike. No truths highlighted by harsh light.

"I want to undress you for bed. May I have that honor?"

"Yes," she whispered.

Setting her down on the mattress, he guided her T-shirt over her head. His gaze flickered over the lace bra she wore and then he stepped in closer, reaching behind her so she was in the loose circle of his arms as he unhooked the bra.

"You've done that to lots of girls, hmm?"

He shook his head, but slid it off her arms and set it to the side before he knelt, giving her breasts a lingering, appreciative look that warmed her. Taking off her sneakers, he caressed her sensitive arches. Moving his hand to her waist, he tugged the drawstring loose. Easing onto her elbows then her back, she stared at the ceiling. A crystal mobile hung there, smoky and rose quartz, selenite, black tourmaline. They picked up the dim window light, throwing off dull gleams of color. Curling his fingers into the waistband, he worked the pants off her hips. The rustle indicated they were being folded and put to the side.

She didn't realize she was holding her breath until the pad of one finger traced the low waistband of her silky swatch of panties. Followed the crease of her thigh, then crossed over her pubic bone, a gentle warning of his intent. His thumbs hooked the sides and he slid them off, moving in sync with her helpful wriggle to get them free from under her bottom.

Now she lay naked, and she knew the nerves were going to start again. But he didn't lean over her, didn't suffocate her. Instead, he stayed kneeling as he had throughout and closed his hand over her foot, bringing it up so he could tease her sole with his mouth.

It caught in her weirdly twisting mind, a really bad Haiku poem in the making. *He enclosed her sole / A substitute for her soul / Since her soul fears him.* He had to settle for her foot, for a homonym. A facsimile, something that wasn't what he really wanted. Word games. All of it games.

A moment before she'd been apprehensive of his more intimate touch, but now the sensual caress on her foot, her ankle, made her upper body cold and yearning for the same attention. "Brendan," she murmured. "Come lay on me."

He rose. There was a clink as he unbuckled his belt again, the sound of it sliding free then dropping to the floor. At her curious glance, he brushed a light finger over her bare stomach. "So I don't hurt this soft skin."

Putting a knee on the bed, he braced himself over her, a handsome silhouette with certain features highlighted. The gleam of a shoulder and eye, the plane of his jaw, the angle of his hip. Reaching up, she spread his shirt open wide, fanning her fingers over the firm musculature beneath. "You're not one of those workout freaks, are you?"

"If I am?"

Curling her hands in the loose fabric, she wrapped her knuckles in it so they disappeared in the cotton brushing his sides. "We won't suit. I'm allergic to exercise unless it masquerades as something fun and unrelated to fitness nazi-ism."

His lips curved. "I like hiking and swimming, because I don't like sitting still too long. Doing laps helps me get into that mindless zone, gives my worries a break."

"The Zen of YMCA Laps." She found a smile inside herself and shyly shared it with him. "I can go with that. The Y's a place of great spiritual peace. And karaoke nights." She tugged at his snort. "Why haven't you laid on me like I asked?"

"I'm getting aroused again, Chloe."

His impressive recovery time goaded the devil in her once more. She arched a brow. "Can you lay on me without doing anything about that, if I tell you that you can't?"

"Yes. It won't stop me from getting harder. In fact," his voice dropped, so it shivered along her nerves as his gaze slid down her face, touched her breasts and the slope of her bare belly, "It's likely to make things worse."

"Good," she whispered. "Can you hold back, no matter how hard you get?"

Was she *trying* to torture the poor guy? But she didn't take it back as his gaze returned to hers and held.

"If you command me to. And if that's what you want."

In answer, she pulled at him again. This time he started to lower his body onto hers, but in an unexpected and pleasurable move, he slid an arm beneath her, palmed one buttock and shifted their bodies up the mattress so her head could be on the pillow, comfortable. Then he brought his body all the way down, readjusting his arms so his elbows were propped on either side of her head.

Bliss. When his weight settled on her, it was perfect. Holding her down, pressed into the mattress, sheltered and anchored at once. Freeing her hands, she slid her palms with savoring delight down his bare back, following the line of his spine to the beginning rise of buttocks. As a result of his removal of the belt, the waistband rode lower on an ass she knew was delightfully bare. But when her palms brushed the small of his back, she found something the tail of his shirt had concealed in the Jeep.

She moved her fingers over it more carefully. "Is this a scar?"

"Yes."

Something in his voice drew her gaze to his face. "It has a shape. I can't tell..."

"It's a brand. A *fleur de lis* design."

Scarification. Marguerite had hired her from a body piercing jewelry kiosk in the mall, so body modification didn't bother her, but somehow she hadn't expected it for Brendan. He seemed so...straight laced, white knightish in a way. She hadn't yet seen evidence of tattoos, no piercings and he dressed with conservative fashion sense, his jeans and shirts good quality, enduring styles, not trend-trash types of stuff.

"It must have a special significance."

"Yes. It does."

When he met her gaze, she felt it, a wall. Suddenly, she felt a little trapped beneath his body, where a moment before it had felt so good. Secrets and shadows made the fit less comfortable. "You don't want to talk about it."

"Chloe." He framed her face. "I won't refuse to answer any question you ask, but I'm requesting that you hold off on that one."

Her brow wrinkled. "Why? For me, or you?"

Brendan shifted. "Both. You, because we're at the point it might scare you off, and me, because I don't want to scare you off. I like being with you too much."

She swallowed. The perfect moment was a balance between words spoken and things left unsaid. Change and dread often walked hand in hand. She could feel the bite of loneliness threatening, and she didn't want to feel that way with him.

"Okay," she said. "But you have to sing to me. Whatever song I choose."

He raised a brow, his expression easing. "Is this payback for last night?"

"You bet your ass. And I'm not reciprocating and singing something else. One moment of abject humiliation is more than enough."

"One way only," he promised. "My punishment for breaking the mood."

"No." She shook her head. "You didn't do that. That was me."

His fingers tightened on the sides of her face, stroking and awaking nerves that shimmered over her whole body, particularly the places that pressed against him.

"The brand is on my skin," he reminded her. "Anything I do that makes you sad, frightened or lonely, should have consequences. I'm willing to do anything to fix it."

Chloe traced his brow, feathering her fingertips through the fall of hair over it. "*I Don't Want to Close My Eyes*, the Aerosmith version."

He smiled, brushed a kiss across her lips. Chloe tightened her hand on his neck to increase the pressure and he obliged, pushing her into the bed, his cock pressed in sensual promise against her mons as he devoured her mouth. He could make a kiss into a slow rhythmic dance with circles of tongue, pressure of lips, his hand holding her face on the other side and fingers stroking. In minutes she was rubbing against him in instinctive need. Her legs rose, clasping high on his hips. The barrier of denim between them helped dissolve some of her unease, reminding her that he was her toy to play with as she wished. Toys were safe, right?

It was a mean thought, an ugly side of her taking advantage of what he'd just offered, more than anyone should offer another human being, really. The guilt increased as he raised his head and she saw how much he could offer her. It proved how shallow a vessel she truly was right now, because she knew she'd waste most of what he gave her, unable to contain it. Her walls were too brittle to hold a gift of such weight.

"Sshh," he murmured. His fingers were at the corners of her eyes, collecting the tiny pair of tears she didn't know had escaped. "I'm whatever you need me to be, Chloe, as long as you need me. I won't ask for more than you can give."

Even if she wanted and needed him to demand more? She didn't know how to say that, though. She wasn't even really sure what it meant.

"Sing to me," she said, a soft plea. She needed him to sing, and to sing that song specifically. She wanted to hear that poignant wish that the moment between them never had to end. That she'd never have to close her eyes and give herself to the cold, deadly dreams of the reality she couldn't face.

In the long, searching pause that followed, her heart dipped into apprehension. Whether or not he asked for more than she could give, she feared he already saw more than she could bear him to know.

Then he began the first yearning bars. Closing her eyes, she held on, his untrained voice soothing her nerves like a lullaby.

Chapter Five

❧

They lay in the bed and talked for four hours, as if they hadn't talked most of the previous night. She learned more about his drama classes and swimming, and gave him anecdotes about Tea Leaves and her comfortable, large family who lived up in New England. She talked about the wide variety of characters she'd met through her job at the piercing kiosk, as well as a hundred other small adventures.

He listened, let her go on like an idiot, but it was as if a dam had broken. For the first time in a long while, she could talk about anything and nothing. She felt no pressure to act like nothing was wrong, covering the obvious fact it was with inane, babbling chatter. Nor did she feel like he was ignoring it for his own comfort. Rather, she felt his understanding and acceptance of where she was right now, giving her complete ownership of the choice of when to talk about it. It made her feel almost…free.

Of course she realized the miracle of it was possible for a couple reasons. They were here, quiet and sequestered from the rest of the world, no outside triggers to those dangerous poison clouds of memory drifting inside her. The other reason was the man himself.

Amid the conversation, they'd pulled together a meal. She still had a loaf of the French bread she'd made a couple days before. With that and some honey butter, a few sliced fresh tomatoes he'd gone out and pulled from her garden, he'd seemed perfectly happy with the light fare. They'd eaten it in her bed, keeping the lights off.

There'd been more kissing. During the meal and after. Lots of kissing, until she thought she could have come from that alone. But stretching out and facing one another, her still naked and him with his jeans on, her toes playing on the denim over his calves, they made a new game of it. Who could do the hottest kiss without moving the lower body or using the hands below the throat. Goddess, he'd brushed her collarbone once and she reacted as violently as if he'd touched her clit, making him groan fiercely in response, though he'd kept his hands there, not taking advantage of the moment.

When they finally agreed to call it a draw, they lay side by side, hands tangled in a loose knot on the mattress, their unreleased bodies damp with perspiration, touched by the breeze through the open window. Shudders twitching the muscles so they'd grinned at one another like spasmodic children. As she closed her eyes, Brendan's fingertips whispered over her mouth, and she knew the look lingering on his face was far from that of an adolescent's. A man's desire, a man's emotions.

He had an unprecedented ability to stay on the innocent side of lust she craved, indulging that side without pressure. Everything she wanted and did to him, he responded just the right amount, so artfully she only felt a twinge of guilt here and there, knowing she was keeping him in a state of arousal and liking it far too much.

Even in his aroused state, though, he had a subtle skill for gauging the level of her own desires so he never pushed on them too hard, never allowing his own to overrule hers. She was fairly well versed in sexual matters, but she'd never experienced anything like this. It was fucking sexy as hell and crazy unreal. Some part of her wondered how long he could manage such a miracle, but somewhere along the journey, she stopped worrying about it and just enjoyed.

He put his arms around her, and she easily adjusted her body into the curves of his, the joy of spooning. It was only a little after nine, but so many sleepless nights had taken their toll. As she drifted down from arousal into somnolence, she fell into blissfully dreamless sleep, wrapped in his scent and arms.

Still, she was amazed to wake up just before dawn, rather than the middle of the night. She had remained in the loose curl of his arms, but had to slide out from that welcome shelter to attend to nature's call. After leaving the bathroom, she shrugged into a Japanese style robe, a gift from Marguerite, and slipped into the kitchen. She warmed up some Earl Grey from the previous day, and cradled the hot mug in her hands, looking out the kitchen window.

In an hour or so, it would be daylight. A faint violet and azure combination in the sky told her the weather would be clear. Bless God and Goddess for sunny days, where shadows were banished and the twisted meeting of desire and destructive emotions parted company, leaving just playful lust and a cautious excitement about what the day could bring.

She wandered back to the bedroom. He'd shifted in his sleep so he lay on his stomach, his arms stretched over his head and curled around the pillow, his jaw shadowed by a day's worth of stubble. She liked the loose, low riding fit of his jeans, but was startled at the hard pulse of response between her legs, so fierce she felt moisture dampen her thigh.

Maybe it was just the cumulative effect of what they'd been doing before they went to sleep. Despite his perfect balance of desire and restraint, part of the delicious nature of it was her lack of such inhibitions, making it even harder for him.

Her lips twitched. An accurate if unwise choice of words, if she wanted to calm herself down. Every sexually experienced woman knew that a man woke up hard. Brendan was likely lying on a very nice erection right now.

Her gaze landed on that mark low on his back. Goddess, a brand hurt, and this was fairly precise on the edges. As she drew closer, she realized there were three, the *fleur de lis* and a decorative element on either side of it. If she dripped the hot tea on them, would it invade his memories in a pleasant or disturbing way? A lot of people who did the body modification were turned-on when they were touched there, heightening erotic response. Could she make that erection harder, thicker?

Setting the tea aside, she leaned over. Blew softly on it, and heard him murmur, but not stir. When she placed her mouth on it, her hand molding the curve of his buttock, a wave of proprietary feeling swept over. Despite whoever had asked him to do this, it was as if she was taking possession of the significance. A transfer of ownership. An odd thought, for certain.

She tasted it and him, her tongue following the design. Her other hand was bracing herself on the mattress, and his fingers slid over hers in the folds of the sheets, their hands curling and tangling like mating birds compelled to brush together in flight and then intertwine, moving in the same rhythm, guided by the same natural compulsion.

When she raised her head, he was looking at her, sleepy desire in his eyes. "I want you, Chloe," he said, his voice rough with desire. "Right now."

It trembled through her. Raw honesty, which made it a demand that her own body was fully willing to embrace.

"Sshh. Don't think." He turned on his side, still holding her hand, and drew her down next to him, so dawn light limned the pleasing shape of his broad shoulder. An inexorable pressure, the gentle touch of his palm pushing her to her back beneath that shelter, and then his hand slid down, down, down. He hovered, so close but not kissing her yet. He didn't press her down with his body, as if knowing if he did too much, too soon, she might release the breath she was holding and break the spell.

Those long, clever fingers opened her robe and stroked over the scar tissue left by her navel piercing, then drifted lower. Like flowing water, nothing fast or sudden.

If he asked permission now, she'd have panicked, because her mind was in an odd paralysis, but he wasn't talking, either. He was surrounding her with his intent and desire, weaving her into it in the very air, so that even as her body stirred, she felt like her heart beat was slowing. She was so in tune with him, so much a part of this moment with him, permission wasn't relevant.

That was why, when he shifted his hand down, her reaction startled her. She grabbed his wrist, as if her fear was something separate, a monster she couldn't predict. He merely kept going, her grip sliding uncertainly to his forearm as he made his way down.

"I'm not going to hurt you," he crooned in that sexy, soft voice. "But I'm not going to stop, Chloe."

Thank Goddess. It was a reassurance and she took it as such.

He slid his fingers over her clit and then down to her labia, covering her. Her grip moved to his biceps as he began to stroke her, the way he might a kitten. An apt comparison, she thought with wry desperation. He moved his fingers in small, massaging circles, learning her, not just following a prescription for response, making her feel...well, like the center of his universe.

"You're beautiful," he murmured. "So pretty and soft." He moved so slowly, but it wasn't an easy touch. There was an intensity to it that had every part of her quivering.

His gaze moved to her breasts, their faint tremble with her elevated breath, and lingered on her nipples.

"Fragile pink there too," he observed. "You're a flower, Chloe. A perfect, pale pink rose." He let his knuckles drift up her breastbone, fingertips grazing the rise of her right breast until he reached her collarbone, turned his hand over and caressed the base of her aching throat. His fingers spread out and curved there, covering that sensitive column as he bent and touched his lips to her breast. He didn't start with the nipple, but worked his way around it, nuzzling, teasing, then giving her bites, some harder than others, the suggestion of pain.

Her legs grew looser, opened further to his touch, wanting to pull him in. But he was the ocean, following his own natural pattern and pace, so she rode the direction he set, breathing his name in the semi-darkness until he lifted his head, his lips moist from the intricate track his tongue had left on her flesh.

"Do you want me inside you, Chloe?"

She wanted that and more. She'd gladly throw out entire roomfuls of things she didn't want to feel or see inside herself to make room for everything he was, everything she wanted to know about him. But she didn't even want it to be that conscious. She simply wanted to absorb him in the quiet dawn, become as peaceful and passionately alive as the day itself, and as instinctive.

"Yes," she said.

His hazel eyes were so close, the mouth a sweet curve. Women were so pleasing aesthetically, but there was something so uniquely beautiful about a well-formed male, a strength-coated vulnerability, such a yin and yang. Ironic, since women were often the mirror, vulnerability over steel.

Reaching down to the waistband of the jeans, she pressed her knuckles into firm flesh as she unhooked the button and parted the teeth of the zipper, loosening the waist further.

"Off," she breathed.

He complied and then did something else remarkable. He took a cross-legged position on the bed and slid his arms beneath her, helping her rise to straddle him. Guiding her legs around his waist, he brought her moist lips in contact with the heat and stiffness of his desire.

"I don't want you to use a condom," she said, a whisper. "I'm protected from pregnancy. I trust you if you say it's okay."

"You can trust me, Chloe," he confirmed it, his eyes darkening with pleasure. "Nothing would please me more than to be inside you, nothing between us."

Feeling his release inside her. She nodded.

"Hold onto my neck," he murmured, as if knowing her emotions were rising to overwhelm her again.

She crossed her arms over his shoulders, buried her face in his hair, pressing her temple to his skull, fingers tangling in dark strands. He used the adjustment of her body to lodge the broad head of his cock in her opening, so that her breath caught in her throat. When he moved, she did, in natural accord, and then she was sinking down on him, wresting a male purr of approval from his throat, a breathless moan from hers.

It had been over a year. She hadn't used anything in her frustrated self-pleasuring other than her fingers or something to vibrate against the outside. His cock stretched tissues anew that hadn't been used in a while, and it felt good, because he took his time with it, as if he knew. It was like that first stretch of the morning, the muscles going beyond learned response to reach even further, send a spiral of pleasure through the whole body.

His arm tightened on her waist, bringing her home, all the way to the hilt, then snugging her up close, long fingers splaying over her backside.

"God, Chloe," he muttered. "You feel fucking incredible."

"That's you," she whispered into his hair.

"Has it been awhile?"

"Yeah."

"Good. For me too." He pressed a hard kiss to her temple, holding there. And not just his mouth. His body remained still, heat energy vibrating from it, as he gave them both time to absorb the way it felt. Her thighs were quivering, and she couldn't keep herself from tightening on him, moving incrementally, testing. Oh Goddess.

A pleasurable starburst of almost forgotten sensation went from the point of friction where her inner muscles gripped his head, worked against the ridge, all the way to the womb.

He speared the fingers of his other hand through her hair, gripping, and then, blissfully, he began to move. One strong, rolling movement that took him out, slow, and then back in at the same pace, lifting and bringing her back down in a nerve reaction so delicious her face tightened because of it, her fingers clutching, eyes closing and head dropping back. She did little more than hang on as he did it again, then again, so slow each time that she whimpered at the pleasure cautiously uncoiling from her belly. He kept her wrapped so securely in his arms, both of them bathed by tranquil dawn light, his heated breath brushing her ear like a tropical breeze teasing the lobe. Her breasts pressed into his chest, her arms holding him as close as she could manage.

She loved him.

People thought the word was misused, often confused with lust. But she knew she could in fact love him, no matter how little she knew about him. In this incredible, astounding moment, she thought she loved him more and differently than she'd ever loved anyone in her life or ever would.

"Brendan." Her voice was a broken whisper.

"I'm here, baby," he whispered back, never faltering. His pace was increasing because hers was, and she realized he was following her pacing, anticipating it, to ensure the maximum pleasure for her. It couldn't have been easy, because her movements were becoming more fractious and insistent, the slick slide and retreat starting to smolder to flame, bodies urging toward even faster movement, piston velocity, straining into one another. The grip of his hands on her buttocks became bruising, kneading, awakening sensitive nerve endings. When she came down harder this time, smacking on his pubic bone with a reaction that rocketed through her clit, his cock lodged deeper, pushed her closer.

"I want to feel you come," he managed, his eyes fastened on her face. "See you lose control. Hear you sing. Feel your pussy ripple on me, because of what my cock is doing for it."

She spasmed against him and his voice got rougher. "That's it. Will you come for me, Chloe?"

"Go...with...me." She demanded it, clutching his hair and tugging, bringing a spark to his eyes, a feral curve to his sensual mouth. Her breasts wobbled before his greedy eyes at each jarring contact. She was goaded closer to that precipice by the way his eyes devoured their movement, the distended tips of her nipples.

"Suckle me," she demanded. "Hard."

His mouth fastened on her nipple, back curving, one hand continuing to hold her, another coming around to grip the breast, squeeze it into his mouth, so that the touch of his tongue ignited erogenous zones all over her body.

"Goddess, yes. That's it. Brendan..."

It came up on her so fast and unexpected, because it had been so long since it had happened so easily. This was like a dam breaking over jagged rock, so she felt the rush and the broken pieces at once.

Now," she demanded, part plea, part command, as she toppled over that edge. The climax arched her into his body, his mouth. Her hips pushed down, working hard and fast against him, muscles squeezing him relentlessly inside, feeling every inch of that hard organ. Her nails dug into his shoulders, hanging on for dear life as those wonderful, rolling, punishing waves took her over and rational thought was lost.

Cries wrenched from her throat, ratcheted up to a wail of victorious pleasure as he obeyed, letting go mere seconds after her. Those delightful arm and shoulder muscles stood out with the strain, rippling with the motion, his cock's friction rubbing within her, the rim of the broad head, the thick heat of him keeping her climax roaring through her, an engine fueled by the driving piston motion.

Her arms banded tight around his shoulders as the sensation overwhelmed her. As she held him close to her breast, her hips ground down on him. She snarled, throwing her head back, nails driving in further as she took every drop of his release. Closing her eyes, she embraced the ride, far beyond any worries of what the day would bring.

It was the best her body had felt in a long, long time.

Chapter Six

ဢ

She should have known it wouldn't last. After a brief post-coital nap, he'd kissed her good morning warmly enough, run through the shower when she'd wanted a few extra minutes of snoozing, then made them both one of her organic, free-range eggs while she got under the hot water. He handed her forkfuls through the curtain since they were running a little late. So accommodating. He hadn't coaxed her to bathe with him, hadn't even taken more than a friendly glance at her naked body in the shower.

She had a tiny shower, so there was no way they could have shared it, but she'd expected him to try. Yeah, it was a work day for both of them, but that wasn't it. If she were more sure of herself, she would have dragged him in with her, soaked his jeans and gotten both of them laughing and easy with one another again. She'd always been attuned to any sign of instability around her and gone out of her way to balance it, had enjoyed the power to do so. But she couldn't get past her own reaction. She couldn't bear knowing the first perfect thing she'd experienced in months had rotted in the course of an hour. The intuition that had guided her to so many adventures and new things had become an enemy, shedding a bright light on the things she didn't want to see.

He was distant, damn it. She could sense it, see it in his eyes. It couldn't have been something she'd done, since they'd basically fallen asleep in each other's arms after what was undeniably a wonderful experience for both of them.

"What is this?"

His casually interested voice disrupted her internal argument. Peering cautiously around the bathroom door, she kept her brush in hand to give her something to do that didn't require direct eye contact. Brendan was leafing through a notebook holding magazine cut outs and newspaper clippings, pen scribblings. He glanced up. "I assumed it was okay to look, since it was sitting here with your books."

"Yeah, it's fine." She cleared her throat. "I call that my happiness book."

He was sitting on the quilt chest at the end of her bed. Like her, he was dressed now, having used her iron to make his shirt presentable for a consecutive day. He'd even shrugged back into his jacket, though she would have thought it was too warm in the house for it. *Additional armor.*

"Happiness book?" he prompted.

She had to quell an unexpected desire to ask him to set it aside, say it was time to go. She didn't want to share any more of herself with him when he obviously was having second thoughts about all of it. Damn it, *damn it.* What had gone wrong?

"I used to... I like a lot of things I see in stores and catalogs. I can get carried away with shopping." When he smiled at that, she managed a wooden one in return and turned away, going back to the mirror, speaking with the thin wall between them. "So I started cutting out pictures of things I liked but couldn't afford. Then I found I liked them better that way. As if it was even better to look at it than to have it myself. Sometimes, acquiring it lessens the appreciation."

So it would seem.

When she came out of the bathroom, those words echoing in the quiet room, he briefly met her gaze, reached out and took her hand, but it wasn't a gesture to encourage a breakdown of the wall. His unreadable expression didn't match the gesture, or the invisible tether of restraint that seemed to be holding him back.

They'd moved too fast. Hell, she had no idea what his personal baggage was, and maybe this morning he'd woken up immersed in it.

She retrieved her hand. "Well, I guess I better get going."

"I can drive you—"

"No, that's fine. That was nice of you to do yesterday, but it will be fine."

Goddess, now she was doing it. Instead of saying what she was thinking straight out, she was playing the same hateful game as him, putting distance and intimacy together in a confusing way to make it seem like everything was okay, but really using it to construct a barrier that didn't encourage conversation about what really mattered.

He nodded, moved into her bathroom to do a quick swipe at his hair now that it was dry. She turned, caught his reflection in the mirror in an unguarded moment and saw the regret and frustration there, confirming what she was already thinking.

Picking up her tote, she left the house, went and sat out on her front steps. Last night, she'd never wanted him to go. Now she was counting the seconds. She felt like a puppet on a stage, fake and stiff jointed, in a spotlight she was unable to leave.

During one of their long kissing sessions, he'd shared some music from his player with her, a Celtic woodwind selection she loved. He knew so much about her, but he'd kept himself a closed book. She'd let him make it all about her. Stupid men.

When he came out on the porch behind her, his boots scuffing the boards, she locked her fingers together, hard. "If you say last night was a mistake, I swear I'll never forgive you."

She rose then, turning to meet his expression. Her directness may have surprised him, but the words obviously didn't, driving the knife in deeper. After a contemplative silence where she felt like he was twisting the blade, he shook his head. Coming down to the bottom of the steps, he faced her. She was a step above him, bringing her to eye level. This time when he tried to take her hands, she pulled away.

"No. Something's wrong. Last night was perfect, as perfect as things can be, because I trusted you. You're not supposed to play games with me. I can't take that, and if you're going to do that, then you should just…fuck off and leave me alone. I won't take that kind of bullshit, you hear me?"

When he said nothing, his gaze turned inward as if seeking words he couldn't find, no instant denial coming to his lips, it welled up in her, huge and unwieldy, making her almost lightheaded. She felt betrayed. That was the only reason she could fathom for what she did next, something she'd never done in her whole life.

She slapped him.

It wasn't as easy as they showed on soap opera dramas. Aim and force weren't easy to coordinate, though she had plenty of rage behind it. She hit his neck more than his jaw, but it unleashed something else. She followed it with an even wilder slap that went high, hit his temple and eye, but she didn't care. If she blinded him, he couldn't look at her like this.

She flailed at him like a child on a playground, a flurry of slaps that canted her weight forward and made her fall into him. She was still pummeling at him when he turned her, waist secure in his grip as he got her feet safely on the ground. Later she would find it remarkable that he did so little to protect his face, a natural instinct for most people.

Right now, though, she was occupied. One part of her stood to the side, horrified and fascinated by the shrieking, irrational, rage-filled Chloe, spewing foul curses in language she didn't use, but then a couple things penetrated. He was holding her, bringing her in to his chest so her punches had shorter and shorter range, until she was gripping his shirt and shaking him. He was sitting down on the upper step, putting her between his knees. And he was trying to tell her something.

She blinked at him, her body vibrating. "What? What did you say?"

He framed her face in one hand, holding her body so close with the other she could feel his heart beat beneath her shoulder. "I said, last night was different for me too, different from anything I've ever felt, Chloe. I'm sorry. It spooked me, and I wasn't ready for it. You're right. I shouldn't have acted this way this morning. It was unforgivable. I didn't handle it well, okay?"

The anguish of that was in his eyes. He wasn't just soothing her, she could tell. That frustration she'd glimpsed in the mirror was with himself, struggling with his own feelings. She bit her lips, anger deflating. It left weariness, and the beginnings of mortification.

"No, you didn't," she agreed. Closing her eyes, she buried her face in her hands, rounding her body inside the shelter of his, conscious that her soft-soled canvas sneakers were curved over the toe of his left boot, pressing down on the foot beneath. But he didn't complain.

"Oh Chloe." He passed his hand over the defensive hunch she'd made of her spine. "I am sorry."

"Don't be. It wasn't my best moment, either." She blew out a sigh, feeling sick at heart. "I completely fall apart over a second date, which happened to involve sex, so who am I to cast stones?" Shaking her head, she pushed herself to her feet, making herself let go of him on a couple different levels. "I'm not ready for this, Brendan. I should never have called you that night, never should have taken it any further. It's not fair to you. Apparently, I'm not even emotionally prepared for sex right now, let alone a relationship. We should cut our losses now."

"Chloe Davis." He captured both of her hands, bringing her gaze back to his resolute expression. "You're brave, and lovely, and I've never wanted a woman more in my life. Never." He repeated it as if she should understand how significant that was, and it made her wonder what women he'd had in his life that would make this moment so obviously...more. The emphasis was so sincere it made her tremble. "If I fuck up or if you don't want me, you end it, but you don't cut me loose because you think it's too much trouble for me to hold your lifeline. Okay? No more talk like that."

"You're already having reservations yourself. Why push something that's putting off wrong vibes on the second date?"

"You need me."

Could he have chosen a worse thing to say? Bitter anger clogged her throat, back as if it had never left. She took a step back, pulling her hands away. "So rescuing girls is your particular sick little fetish? That's what turns you on?"

When she saw shock flash across his face, followed by hurt and anger, incomprehensible, detestable triumph flooded her. Who was this harpy, this thing that had possessed her tongue, turned it into a slicing weapon?

Then he gave a nod, his mouth hard. "If you want to call it that. I think it's every man's responsibility to protect a woman, to rescue her if she needs rescuing, whether or not he has the white horse and armor. But you're more than that to me, Chloe."

"Am I? Because something real is holding you back, and the most logical thing is that it's me. What, you didn't think I was all that fucked up the first night, but now you've reconsidered? Was I not a good enough lay? Too assertive? You didn't like me calling the shots?"

He rose, giving her a look that she expected hawks gave mice before they plummeted. But then he snagged her right hand, the one she'd used to slap him first. It was still stinging. As if he knew that, he put his lips to her palm, closing his eyes and holding his mouth there as her fingers curled, uncertain, over his brow.

He held her there a long moment. That contact made her lightheaded, his hair under her fingertips, the stillness between them, weighted with ugly words and confused feelings. It made her want to sway forward, perversely ask him to comfort her for the pain she'd caused him. His hand went to her waist, steadying her, but as soon as it was clear she had her balance, at least physically, he let her go. "I'll talk to you soon, Chloe."

He cut around her to walk to his Jeep. Chloe closed her hands into useless fists. She wanted to scream at him some more, but she knew it wasn't he who enraged her. She needed help, but she didn't want to be rescued by the guy pulling her heartstrings into knots. That wasn't who she wanted to be. When he put the Jeep in drive, she turned. He met her eyes. Though she wanted to be comforted by that lingering kiss she held in her tight hand, she saw the shadows. She wasn't wrong, what she had said. But that didn't mean she was right, either.

* * * * *

When she got to work, she spent as much time in the restroom as she could, under the excuse that she needed to put on makeup because she'd slept in. Fortunately, once she came out, Gen was working on the brewing for the first half hour and conversation was limited. But when Marguerite came in and they began to set the tables, she braced herself. It was the unofficial time for not-so-idle chatting, at least for her and Gen. Marguerite would throw in dry observations on occasion. Chloe knew the question was coming, but that didn't mean she had an answer ready.

"So how did it go with Brendan yesterday?"

Any normal human being could say "fine", give a smug little smile and that would be the end of it. Normal workplaces didn't pry in-depth into sex lives, but Chloe had set the tone, always asking for every romantic, sexy detail she could wrangle out of Marguerite and Gen on anything. *Karma was a bitch,* she thought.

Hell, she'd give it a try. "Fine," she said, faking a smile.

Gen raised a brow.

"That bad? He seemed really nice."

"He was. He was fine."

Marguerite, preparing the napkins with a complicated origami fold, raised a slim brow. "It sounds as if you expected more of the evening."

Chloe shrugged, stared at the teacups she was methodically drying before placing them on the settings. "No...he..." She set the teacup down with a thud, in hindsight glad that it was one of the heavier styles. "All right, fine. It was incredible, wonderful, transcending and then the show was cancelled. Apparently for reasons the network doesn't care to share, because he's too busy guarding my feelings from whatever the hell has a stick up his ass. But last night...he gave me kisses that went on forever, that rolled over me like surf. There's this part of me that wants to tie him up and eat him alive, but this morning it's like I'm the one tied. He's holding himself back. I can't tell which hang ups are mine or his. Damn it."

When she flicked her gaze up, she saw her reflection in the glasswork of Marguerite's display cabinets. Her eyes looked like the bloodshot melon ball scoops of a Pekinese. "But it's fine. That's the way guys are, we all know it. I'm going out to the storehouse to get that extra teakettle. You know the a.m. shift will be busy."

Her voice started sounding strange and too high as she got to the end of her diatribe, but she escaped before either woman could point out they didn't really need the extra kettle. They didn't say anything to stop her, though. Maybe they were as sick of dealing with her shit as Brendan was.

Breathing fast, she slid out the back and cut through Marguerite's private garden, practically running to the small shed and slipping inside. One breath, two breaths, three… The quiet storeroom, smelling of old wood and dried herbs hanging from the ceiling, had become the place Chloe ran when she couldn't hold it together. She was never bothered there. Which meant they knew why she came here.

She squatted on her heels in a shaft of early morning sunlight and closed her eyes. Maybe she was just as sick of her own shit. She refused to have a panic attack this morning. The last time she'd had one at Tea Leaves, it had occurred when she was writing the specials list. For awhile after that, Gen had quietly taken it over until Chloe could handle it again.

Writing the specials list had been a daily ritual she'd loved, peaceful and normal. She'd used the different colored whiteboard pens to create pictures of tea cups and herbs, things to jazz it up. Added wise and thoughtful sayings for the day, sometimes from famous people, sometimes ones she'd made up.

Natalie had come up with the one for that horrible day. It had been as perfect and simple as a child's mind. "Smile. It makes everyone feel good." A few minutes later, he'd come up behind them…

No. This shed was a true sacred place, baptized daily by Marguerite's lovely rituals of preparing tea leaves, working on different mixtures, the herbal magics she created with her elegant, beautiful hands. Chloe wouldn't allow that memory here. Squeezing her eyes tightly shut, she imagined a white, protective light over the place, keeping such a stain out. But what if *she* was the stain?

Stop it, Chloe. Go into work mode. You can do that. Leave all this outside the door, and if you can look nice and normal enough, maybe Marguerite won't look at you in that way that strips you bare naked, and Gen won't touch you a hundred times a day as if she's stroking a wounded animal. But if they don't do those things, I might fly apart as well.

Of course she was in danger of that either way.

I have so had enough of this. She banged out of the shed, intending to march back to the tea room, but came up short.

When she'd flown down the garden path to the drying shed and storeroom, she'd completely missed that the garden had an occupant. If Marguerite stayed overnight at her rooms in Tea Leaves, she wasn't alone. After her morning yoga, she usually left Tyler finishing his coffee and reading the paper at the bistro set, placed near one of Marguerite's many fountains. The peaceful area was surrounded by green ferns and jasmine bushes.

Wearing tailored slacks, he had his coffee cup in hand, one ankle resting comfortable on the opposite knee. Thanks to all the gods, he hadn't yet buttoned his dress shirt, because his broad chest, the soft mat of hair over it that arrowed down to a hard abdomen, was a welcome distraction. But he was looking at her as she came out of the shed. She found herself drawn by those serious amber eyes, pulled in his direction by a need that—when she voiced it—shocked herself.

"Will you teach me how to use a gun?"

Tyler considered her. He didn't seem surprised by the request, but then Tyler always seemed prepared for anything. There was a self-possession to him so absolute, Chloe was sure most would have guessed he was a former government operative, even after learning about his current profession of erotic cinema screenplay writer and sometime producer. But even that wasn't his main profession. He had his fingers in lots of pies, probably because he had the money to own a whole pie-making factory.

"Chloe." His voice had a rich timbre, flavored with a cultured Georgia drawl. "You take flies out of Tea Leaves in a cup. You apologize when you kill mosquitoes sucking blood out of your skin."

"I know. But I thought..." She sighed, miserable. "I know, Tyler. I'm just so afraid...of being afraid, and I don't know how to stop. And I don't know what to do about it. I'm not going to some idiot shrink because all they do these days is put you on drugs. But hey, what else is there? He can't convince me that there's nothing to fear in the world, right?"

Rat toes, she was blinking back more of the hated tears. But at least she was back to her normal creative expletives, instead of the more common, crass ones.

"Come here."

She stepped forward obediently without thought, always amazed at his ability to do that, but even more amazed when he took her hand and drew her into his lap without any awkwardness or hesitation. Closing his arms around her, he brought her in to his chest for an all encompassing masculine hug. "Oh God," she mumbled, her voice muffled in his shirt. She wanted to curl up in his lap like a kitten and thought since his other arm was behind her knees, she might already be. "No wonder Marguerite married you. I'd marry you for the hugs alone."

He rubbed her back, probably because he felt her trembling, but he spoke with a trace of humor. "She tells everyone she married me for my great wealth."

"Well, there is that. And the incredible ass, if you don't mind me saying."

"Just as long as you don't feel compelled to grope it."

"Well, I am feeling vulnerable, and it's the least you could let me do..." But instead she gave a little sob, and he tightened his arms around her.

"Chloe, it will get better. You've known such joy in your life, and the idea of someone like Marguerite's father is so alien to you. Why don't you come stay with us for awhile? There's no shame in it. We'd love to have you there."

"She doesn't..." Chloe closed her eyes tightly. "Does Marguerite feel guilty about any of this? Because it was her father? I couldn't bear it if she did."

"Marguerite understands the nature of evil. She was sorry you were drawn into her particular brand of it."

"I would have done anything to protect her place or her, Tyler. I don't regret that, not ever."

"I know that." He shifted his hands to her shoulders, drawing her gaze up to his face, the steady expression. "You did. You're so very dear to us, Chloe. Give yourself time. If you still want to learn how to use a gun in a month or two, I'll teach you. But like most things, it's a decision best made when you're in the right frame of mind for it. Until then, I'll shoot anybody that needs shooting for you."

"Just the kind of friend I need." She stared up into his handsome face, the expression that looked as if it could weather any storm. "Can I use you for the other thing that friends are known for?"

"Sure, little flower," he said gently, his pet name for her. He curved his hand around her neck, caressing her cheek as she laid her head back on his chest and let herself be held some more. Curling her body up against his, she used it as a bulwark against the tears she refused to spill.

* * * * *

Brendan had wanted to turn around and look at her again, but he'd made himself walk to the Jeep. Drive into Tampa, handle his morning classes. Keep a vigorously maintained wall between who he was to his students and what he'd been to Chloe last night. How he might have failed her this morning. But after lunch, the wall fell. He had a work period before the advanced drama class would arrive to start the Camelot rehearsal. He stood on the auditorium stage, staring out into the darkened seating, only stage lights casting a dim, antique yellow glow on the assortment of props around him. Things to create realities not necessarily his own.

Damn it. With a curse, he brought his fist down on the table they were using as a centerpiece for this scene. It had a tapestry draped over it, so he'd forgotten it was a solid oak piece they'd picked up from a rummage sale, rather than a far more advisable and expendable card table. He cursed again, with a violence and frustration that startled him as it echoed back from the vaulted ceiling. But it was the dry female voice from the darkness that made him jump.

"I don't think they used that particular turn of phrase in Arthurian times."

The thin brown institutional carpeting on the aisles was worn to holes in some places, and the downward slope was broken up by the occasional single shallow step, but Marguerite navigated the unfamiliar terrain as if she were the Lady of the Lake herself. The Lady of the Lake in stylish, earth-colored, ankle strap heels, high enough to be sexy but not impractical for Tea Leaves.

She came to a halt within twenty feet of the stage, and he marveled as always at her Mistress's intuition. It put her just above his eye level. If she'd come all the way to the stage she would have had to tilt her head back to look at him, something that would have been vastly unacceptable, to him at least.

"We need to talk," she said.

"I have a class." Not for another hour, but he just couldn't face this conversation now. There was no rancor in his tone, but since he made a point to deny her nothing, those four words were as insolent as he'd ever been to her. It underscored that he was fucking up on all levels today.

"Then you'll be late," she said coolly. "Come down here. Now."

He sighed. Inwardly. *Fine.* The day could only get worse. Might as well accept it.

As he moved to the stage edge, she took one of the front-row seats, crossing those killer legs, her long slim hand lying on the armrest. Though she was a Mistress, a formidable one, she submitted to one Master's touch, and that was Tyler. As such she often wore his collar as she did now, a beautiful choker of wire and pearls, as much evidence of their bond as the wedding ring on her finger.

When he approached, she leaned forward, extending one long-nailed hand toward the hand he'd used to pummel the hapless table. With reluctance, he placed it in hers. Examining his swelling knuckles, she tsked under her breath.

She didn't invite him to sit next to her. It was automatic and steadying to drop to one knee in front of her. Bracing his free hand on his thigh, he stared at those feminine shoes, the slim ankles. Chloe had worn pumps for the wedding, but this morning she'd preferred a pair of sneakers that were a fading rainbow of hand-painted colors that had seen better days. Her closet was filled with a dazzling array of shoes tumbled together like shiny gumballs, but she'd chosen ones that had gone dull with the effects of time and wear.

"What's going wrong, Brendan?"

"I'm not sure what you mean, Mistress."

He'd been the one to slow things down. One intense phone call, a drive to work and an amazing night of lovemaking happening within a two-day period seemed, on its face, a reason to slow things down. But he knew as well as Marguerite did that something *was* wrong. As the silence lengthened, his Mistress waiting him out, he wryly reflected that no one could lie to that intent blue gaze, even though he wasn't really lying. He *didn't* know exactly why he was slowing down. "She's been through a lot. I don't want to force anything until she's stronger. I don't want to make her deal with anything else."

What he'd wanted to do this morning was frame her elfin face in his hands, taste the sweet pink bow of her mouth until it heated beneath his, until all of her heated, proving he could drive the cold out of her hands, her mind, the pit of her stomach and behind her eyes. The day after their phone call, he'd thought of nothing but her all day, to the point his students had teased him for his absentmindedness.

"Did you know Chloe had an operation when she was five years old?"

Brendan's gaze shot up, but Marguerite shook her head. "Nothing serious. One of those things better handled while she was still small. When they rolled her out of the hospital room and toward the operating room, she asked the nurse where they were going. The nurse made up some silliness about an enchanted fairyland. Chloe was an intelligent little girl, and the fact this well-meaning woman wouldn't tell her where she was truly going terrified her. She started screaming and thrashing.

"When she tells the story, she jokes about them plopping a Fisher Price musical toy next to her as they strapped her to the operating table and administered the anesthetic. But you can see the memory of the fear she felt. If the woman had simply told her they were going to the operating room, she would have been fine. Nervous, but informed."

Brendan shifted as Marguerite continued. "Men often make the mistake of thinking a wounded woman needs a lie to protect her, when just the opposite is true. Most of us have a radar for bullshit. Feeling uncertain only enhances that instability. She's too fragile for anything less than total honesty."

Marguerite locked eyes with him before he could obey etiquette and sweep his gaze down. "With you, Chloe is a different, deeper, more troubled part of herself, something she can't allow herself to be with us. The joyful Chloe still exists, but she's facing that dark side now. No one I know is more prepared than you to guide someone out of darkness, Brendan, because your own demons have never overwhelmed your light. An Arthurian knight in truth." A faint smile touched her lips as she glanced toward the stage. Then she sobered. "You might best serve Chloe's needs right now by taking the reins. Show her how to drive the horse before handing them over. You understand?"

He nodded. "I do. I'd already started...before I realized I was going to do it. Which is why I pulled back."

At her raised brow, he stared down at his hand, still held inside the brace of her slim fingers. Tyler's silver wedding band shone softly in the dim lighting. "She's not natural to it, Mistress. She's messed up right now. She should only deal with one problem at a time."

"Why are you assuming it's a problem? Perhaps it's part of the answer."

"She's not part of our world. Even if I introduced her to it, it wouldn't be...innate to her. I won't make her feel like she's failed at something that's not a test." He shook his head. "I'm a transition for her, and we both know it. I lost sight of that last night, and I didn't handle it well this morning. I'll call her later, apologize and smooth things over."

"You want her to open up, make it easier for you to fly to her rescue, but you aren't willing to open up your world to her."

"The soft stuff, the hints of it, give her some relief, but I'm a painkiller, not the cure. I'm a way station."

"You're being a coward."

His head snapped up. Now he felt the unthinkable toward Marguerite. Anger.

"Damn it, I'm trying to protect her. I thought that would mean something to you."

Her pale blue gaze frosted. "The truth means something to me. The entire truth. Have you forgotten that, Brendan? Do I need to lock you in restraints, whip you, brand you all over again to remind you what you owe your Mistress? Don't you ever try to shield yourself by using my feelings for Chloe."

Miserable need spiraled up from his gut, his fingers spasming on his knee. He'd spent time with this and that Mistress at The Zone since Marguerite's marriage, but with all their considerable skills, none of them could pull from him what she could with just the sensual threat.

"Kneel before me, Brendan," she ordered with quiet firmness. "All the way. I locked the door."

She didn't have to add that. He did it without thought, going to both knees and locking his hands behind his neck, his eyes down. It was a position he'd assumed enough that, once there, a quiet sense of rightness usually settled over him, being there, obeying a Mistress's will. But not today.

She was poking sticks into places that were ready to snarl and snap to keep things out of those burrows.

"Tell me what *you* want, when it comes to Chloe."

"I want to make her happy. I don't want her to be unhappy or frightened. I want to be there for her, as long as she needs...and wants me."

Rising, she set her hands on his shoulders, nails piercing enough to register pain. "Brendan, what do *you* want?"

The emotions that rose up hard and fast within him were too difficult, too painful. He dug his hands into his neck, couldn't look at her, even when her hand touched his jaw, a usual command for him to look up. He just couldn't.

"I can't. Forgive me, Mistress."

She withdrew, a punishment as harsh as a single tail, but her voice was neutral. "You'd be risking a great deal to let Chloe all the way in, wouldn't you? You don't want to be shut out right as you've gotten your foot in the door. I assume a foot has gotten into a door, euphemistically speaking?"

The dry tone might have made him smile, and the memory of it might have steadied him, if his gut wasn't roiling. "Yes."

"You're not only taking the chance it could make things worse for her, but also that she may turn away from what you have to offer. You trusted yourself to Tim, and he betrayed that trust. You lost your parents young, and it creates a paradox. A need to find that sense of home in another's heart, while fighting the fear that it's a magic trick. An empty lie once you step into the magician's box."

He clenched his jaw. "I'm protecting myself. You're right. I'm a coward." That wasn't who he was, and he shouldn't be letting his fears or insecurities interfere with caring for her. "If I give her what she needs, and she walks away afterward, when she has her feet under her, serving her well should be enough." *It should be enough, damn it.* "I have no right to demand more."

"Brendan." Now she tipped his head up, forced him to look at her with a hand gripping his hair. She gave him that look that saw so much, could strip him bare, but she took several moments before she spoke, things in her expression he couldn't read. Perhaps didn't want to read. "Submissives of your generosity are very rare. In a vanilla relationship, you'll give someone like Chloe everything she thinks she could ever need. Every romantic gesture, every mindblowing sexual experience. And without that remarkable intuition of hers, she'd never realize, not for an instant, that she hasn't even scratched off the top layer of who you are."

Those animals snarled and burrowed, but she saw them, saw what he wouldn't face, even now. He wanted to pull away, but he didn't. "But she does have that intuition," she continued quietly. "It may be damaged, but it's still working. She already knows you're holding back on her. You really want to help her? You're going to have to let her in."

He tightened his jaw, but couldn't deny it. Anymore than he could deny that Chloe was probably right, that it was a bad idea, one they shouldn't take further. Marguerite might think he was using her feelings again, but he had to say it. "She doesn't know how you and I…"

"What you mean to me."

It startled him, spoken so intimately. Marguerite's gaze was gentle now, and she grazed her knuckles over his cheek. "You're afraid of how she'll react."

"Yes. But…" He closed his hand on her wrist, a gentle circle, always amazed by how fragile that arm was. She ate more now with Tyler bullying her, but she'd always been slim, ascetic. When he met her pale blue gaze, he let her see it, rather than saying it, wanting her to know that this part at least was the truth.

"You're afraid of hurting me." Marguerite's fingers curled, her lips pressing together.

"What happens to your friendship when she finds out? You don't love easily, Mistress. I won't deprive you of even one friend."

"Even for your own heart?"

"It's not a matter of loyalty. If it causes harm to you, then that's a message I won't question. It's not meant to be, and I'll let it end here. I can keep being there for her, but not take it to the more intense levels. That's what frustrated me too. I wasn't thinking ahead until this morning. And now…"

"You're already in so deep there's no way to pull out without someone getting hurt. Including you. Oh Brendan. Do you really think that you can keep it from getting inside you?"

He sighed, closing his eyes. "You know, sometimes being around you is like being in front of God, confessing sins."

Withdrawing, she sat back down, but opened both her hands, extending them toward him. Bemused, he laid his into them, closing his hands gently over the slender palms, respecting the great gift of her touch, of holding her. "Whether you realize it or not, I'm no longer your confessor, Brendan. I think even I didn't realize that until these past few minutes. You've changed. What you need now is more than a Mistress."

At his look of surprise, she inclined her head. "You've let go, surrendered to me, but our shared history kept me from going over ground that wasn't mine to plow. You're going to have to tear yourself open to let a *lover* see what's there. Where there are no rules or etiquettes. Where you have to risk everything you are in a way you can't even see right now. Will that person be Chloe? Or will you hold yourself from her? Only let her see a part of who you are?"

"I can't lie to her," he admitted after a long moment. "If I thought I could be everything she needed without it, maybe I could keep it secret, but it feels wrong. What she needs is a hundred and twenty percent of myself, not bits and pieces like a puzzle with parts missing."

"And by doing that, she'll have the chance to handle each piece, feel the edges and curves, and decide if she fits in the same picture. Give her that chance, Brendan. Don't treat her like glass."

Swallowing, he let his gaze course over the stage. The grail prop sat on a dais. During the performance, it would be brilliantly lit among all that darkness. He'd always liked the idea of being one of the knights seeking that grail. Damn it, if he didn't know anything else, he knew Chloe needed him right now. And if what she needed was for him to be braver than he'd been before, then so be it. He'd go on the quest, even knowing the grail would always elude him, because that wasn't the point.

He lifted his burning gaze to Marguerite, his chest so constricted he could barely get the words out. "I thought about asking you to invite her to your annual carnival." There. He'd said the ridiculous. He lifted a shoulder. "I know she knows something of your world outside the tea room. Will you invite her?"

While he couldn't tell for sure from her expression, he was pretty sure she had some reservations about the idea. But he was too wound up to retract it or suggest anything different. He expected her to deny him, tell him why she would refuse, but at length, she spoke. "Come back to Tea Leaves this evening and issue her the invitation, on my behalf."

He let out a breath that still managed to claw at his insides. He'd committed himself. The chaotic storm that had been brewing in his mind and gut most the day died back at last, though it felt as if he'd gone through a fully draining, three hour dungeon session, where he wasn't sure what he'd done or who he was now.

As Marguerite rose, obviously preparing to leave, he knew he needed to say one more thing. Something less difficult to say, but not less difficult to accept. "Mistress, there's more that happened that day. At the tea room. With your…when she was attacked. She won't say what, but it's there."

Her lips tightened. "I know. Her emotions have dammed up. We can't seem to break things loose in her. She's protecting us so hard, she's formed a barricade. But you…she's willing to strike out, reach out." Her gaze lingered on his face and he realized one of Chloe's flailing hands must have caught him well enough to leave a bruise. "If she has a different bridge to cross, such as learning more about you and what you can offer her, it may break things up further. She won't be so focused on keeping everything in."

An ironic smile touched her lips, this lovely, difficult woman who was the closest thing to a family he had. The tenderness behind that smile, the trace of sadness in her gaze as she looked down at him, as if seeing a path she wished she could keep him from taking, only underscored that she loved him as he loved her. Fiercely and unconditionally. It steadied him, despite the fact her parting words created more than a little trepidation.

"I know you don't want to hurt her, Brendan, but I want you to remember something. Sometimes loving someone means not letting them hide from themselves. It means they need to experience pain to heal. Don't underestimate your own knowledge of that," she said softly. "Because the only one who understands that better than a Mistress is her slave."

Chapter Seven

ഔ

"Gen, I'm about to head out," Chloe called out as she collected her tote bag from the back. She'd stuffed a variety of things in there yesterday, when distracted by Brendan's behavior. Now she noted a black tuft of hair, a slip of silk bow, and remembered she'd included Brendan's stuffed dog. Pulling it halfway out, her fingers passed over the playful face. Was it something pitiful, or clean desire, that made this coil of longing tighten in her belly, made her wish she hadn't been so hateful? She'd thought about calling his cell and leaving him a message, but what would she have said? Was she falling in love or in need?

No, she'd been right. She didn't need to be involved with anyone right now. But when would it get better? The first couple months after her body had fully healed, she'd told herself anyone would need time to recover emotionally from something like that, but since then, it had only gotten worse. The more she tried to push it away, the larger it got, like the monster in her closet was one of those add-water sponge things that only grew bigger with every tear.

Gen poked her head into their coat room. "You may want to hold off a minute. You have a visitor. He just pulled up."

Wow. The tide of despair was simply swept away by a sudden, dizzying euphoria. She wondered if she was becoming manic, or bi-polar, or whatever the mental-illness-of-the-month was. All day long, she'd vacillated like this, between regret and longing, brief spurts of wretched rationality and unreasoning need. With those few words, all of it was gone. Brendan was waiting for her out front.

At Gen's easy smile, Chloe couldn't help but answer with a curve of her lips. "Guess I didn't completely scare him off."

"You assume it's all about you." Gen sniffed. "Maybe I flashed my tits at him through the front window this morning before he drove off. Or Mrs. McGovern did. She was here the earliest. You know she got new breasts for her sixtieth birthday and she's showing them to everyone. Even Marguerite. You should have seen her face."

"Marguerite's or Mrs. McGovern's?"

"Marguerite's, of course. Not even a facial muscle twitched. She just nodded, polite as you please, said they were lovely and asked if she wanted milk in her tea."

"Well, I'd believe Mrs. McGovern flashing him long before I'd believe it of you. Stodgy old thing." She sobered a bit. "I was pretty hideous this morning."

"Well, go say you're sorry. The only thing a man finds more irresistible than a woman who's mean to him is one willing to make it up to him. If he's back, I'd say he's in a forgiving mood. He obviously realizes how wonderful you are." Gen gave the tote bag a hitch onto Chloe's shoulder, another quick smile crossing her face at the sight of the puppy. "Go enjoy every inch of that beautiful man. You owe it to the rest of us who're going home to frozen food and old movies."

"You wouldn't have to do that if you'd go out with the guys I've told you would be perfect for you." But Chloe let herself be ushered out the side door even as she said it, overcome with an eagerness that superseded even her ongoing desire to see the twice-divorced Gen find her soulmate.

"I prefer my own brand of self-destruction," Gen snorted, but she gave Chloe a steady look. "I'll be here for about another half hour, okay?"

Chloe nodded, then the door closed behind her. She had one last glimpse of Gen's face, caught between hope and worry. It made her stop on the bottom step despite her eagerness, testing that positive feeling rolling through her. It felt strong and real. It was a feeling she'd lacked for too long, and seemed in this moment to be solely concentrated on Brendan.

She really hadn't realized how it had weighed her down throughout the day, such that his reappearance seemed to have temporarily not only lifted that oppressive feeling, but some of her other ones as well. The reservations of a blink ago were gone. She could harbor worries, like those she saw in Gen's face, or grab this feeling in both hands like a rope, swing high over that troubled valley. Run with it. Literally.

He was almost at the garden gate that would take him up the front walkway, but when her sneakers crunched along the gravel of the side alley drive, he stopped to look and saw her.

Chloe trotted to him, cutting the corner, skirting Marguerite's tulips. Dropping her tote, she did as she'd wanted to do that very first day. She leaped upon him, trusting his arms to come around her quickly enough to prevent disaster, wrapped her arms around his neck and her legs around his waist and put her mouth on his. Instantly, a surge of fiery, sweet sensation went through every extremity, from the tips of her breasts to her lower belly, strumming through her thighs, a reaction impossible to avoid given that she had them locked intimately over his hips.

He gloriously, wetly, kissed her back, cupping the back of her head and bracing them against the gate, lurching only a little at her first hop. But he knew how to improvise, and he had a quick recovery time, because he took control of the kiss, telling her without question he'd missed her as well, and regretted their morning parting. His fingers tightened on her hips and at her nape, conveying his urgency. She wanted it to go on forever, but she made herself tear her mouth away for a vital moment.

"I'm so sorry. I was terrible. I don't want you to forgive me because you feel sorry for me. I'd hate that. You can say mean things to me, or tell me I have to make it up to you in some awful, vaguely demeaning way. I can wash your car, or do your laundry."

Though desire remained high in his eyes, humor flickered in them. "I wouldn't subject my worst enemy to my laundry, Chloe. I shouldn't have reacted—"

"Yes, yes, you should have." She interrupted him with heat. "I don't want to be treated like some fragile thing." *Just because I might be. That's not the point.* Realizing she'd tightened her fingers in his hair to distract herself, she saw it had an added benefit. It had given his eyes that decidedly dangerous look. "I know how to do other things to say I'm sorry."

"Well, that's all you had to say then. Males are pretty straightforward. We'll forgive a woman anything for sex." Definitely laughter in his eyes this time, that sexy smile lodging just under her heart.

With obvious reluctance, he let her slide to her feet, but she was gratified at how he held onto her, bare inches between them. His hands remained at her waist, fingers sliding beneath her skirt, his thumb turning inside the waistband, stroking the elastic edge of her panties. Very subtle, nothing vulgar, a hot, secret caress, so confident and easy her blood remained at high simmer.

"Going to follow me home tonight?"

"It depends on your answer to a question." Taking her by surprise, he lifted her onto the still warm hood of the Jeep, bracing his body against her knee, letting her hold his shoulder to keep her there. "Do you know about Tyler and Marguerite's annual carnival next weekend?"

"Yes." Chloe was intrigued enough by the change of topic to answer automatically.

"So you know it's a little different from most carnivals?"

"Yeah. I know." She colored a little. "I guess I'm a little surprised you know about it, even with you being Marguerite's friend. I mean, there's 'family' close—which means you're close, but you aren't told things you wouldn't tell your mom — and then 'knowing about the carnival' kind of close."

Chloe had thought Gen and she fell more into the "family" definition, but things had changed since a year ago. Not just with her, but with Marguerite. The woman who'd given them so little of her personal life before Tyler now cautiously gave them more glimpses of who and what she was, and they accepted it like the gift it was, protecting her privacy, which was why her initial answer to Brendan was guarded, his friendship with Marguerite notwithstanding.

"Marguerite was so involved in the planning this year, we both agreed to help her on this end of things. You know, fielding calls from caterers, dunking booth operators and other unlikely things." She cleared her throat. "She handles most of the unlikely things, though."

He pressed his lips together, perhaps against another smile, but she couldn't tell, because his expression had gotten more serious. She shifted on the hood, which was a little too warm for comfort through thin cotton. He noticed immediately. Opening the door, he gave her a hand down and guided her to take a seat in the passenger side of the Jeep. He flanked her in the open door, his hand braced on the window frame.

"How'd you feel about it, finding out that Marguerite and Tyler — "

"Shocked right down to my freaking painted toenails," she admitted. "But then, on second thought, probably not. I don't know that much about people who practice it as bone deep as they do, you know. Marguerite hasn't really given us a seminar on her and Tyler's particular brand of it, but once you have your foot in the door, you kind of start noticing things. I mean, I've had friends who like to be spanked or tied up, in a fun way, or girlfriends who get off on a guy sweeping them off their feet and ravishing them, like a pirate in a romance novel. In fact, Lorraine, one of my college girlfriends, her boyfriend actually did that, turned our room into a ship's cabin and tied her up with red sashes, and I walked in on it—"

Chloe was stopped abruptly by Brendan's mouth on hers, his lips curved even as he kissed her to a slower pace, her nervous hands now clutching his chest as his arm slid around her waist. Eventually, decades later, he lifted his head. "Sorry, can't resist when you start doing that."

"So I'll shut up?"

He chuckled, the flash of his smile and the warmth in his eyes mixing with the easy desire. *This is the way it was meant to be,* she thought, *what I thought I lost.* And here it was, a gift he was easily giving her.

"No. You just make me feel lots of things, Chloe. I want to kiss you when I feel them."

"Okay," she said. "What question was I answering? Oh God. If this is where you tell me you were talking about something entirely different, that you didn't know that about M, I'll have to disappear into the pavement. And move away, because she'll kill me."

"No. I was actually hoping you'd say something that blatant so I'd know we *were* talking about the same thing." He tucked a lock of her hair behind her ear, used the excuse to play with an earring. She'd put some on today, before things had gotten strained between them. She'd been feeling better at that point. In fact, she was feeling better now.

"I guess I don't understand all of it. I've looked online, seen some scary things, things that don't seem like Marguerite and Tyler to me at all, and yet, I understand in some way it's that intense for them. Maybe it's the kind of thing that feels different on the inside than it looks from the outside. You feel it between them, from them, you know. M said it's something that's done at all levels. For some it's a way to liven things up, but for others it's like being gay or straight. An undeniable orientation, down to the blood. I think it's that way for them."

She fluttered her hands in front of her, then let one land on his knee, propped in the door. His glance went to it, then to her face, and the warmth there matched what she felt beneath her palm. She had to clear her throat again. She knew she wasn't on her A-game, but honestly, she'd never dated a man this beautiful and sexually...aware. It gave a girl a permanent case of frog-in-the-throat.

"Sometimes I've wanted to quiz M on it, take advantage of those moments when she and Gen were really coddling me to find out more. But I love her too much to exploit something like that. M's still a really private person, and I want her to know I'm her friend and respect her."

She furrowed her brow at his fascinated expression. "You look like you just discovered a talking monkey at the zoo."

It startled him enough that he barked out a handsome laugh, making her grin. Really grin, and it was amazing how such a gesture could chase shadows away. But she managed to get herself back on target. "Why are you asking about the carnival? The admission price is like ten thousand dollars a person, so if you tell me you're going, I'm going to want to know what you do other than teach drama at a community college."

"The friendship with Marguerite helps," he explained vaguely. "But yeah, I'll be there. I've been authorized, for lack of a better word, to ask you to be there as well. As Marguerite's invited guest."

"Oh." Her voice drifted off, as he continued to regard her steadily. "*Oh.*"

She knew Brendan and Marguerite had known one another as children, but she didn't know any further details than that. Whatever it was, that history had been strong enough that he'd been the one who walked her down the aisle to Tyler. This moment didn't shed any further light on that; if anything, it made it more confusing. But one thing was fairly clear. "Marguerite didn't invite you only because you're an old family friend, did she? Like when you invite your relative to go to a party with you because he's in town, but you really don't—"

"Chloe." His hands closed over hers. "Will you come to the carnival?"

"Does that have a double meaning? A significance I'm missing?" Suddenly she was feeling more uncertain again, because she sensed a lot of things shifting in the air around them.

He shook his head. "I would never try to trick you. You'd be coming as Marguerite's guest, not mine. I just...I'd like the chance to see you there, be with you when it's appropriate. As a guest you can do, or not do, whatever you wish."

Chloe considered that, looked at their linked hands. "I was dying to go," she confessed with a small smile. "Definitely not as a participant. I don't think I'm that brave—but something safe, like waitstaff or a potted plant. I've never been to anything like that, and it was all I could do not to ask M a million questions."

"Well, now you'll get to see it firsthand. Since it's for the whole weekend, Marguerite said you could stay in one of her guestrooms."

"Oh? Will you be staying in a guestroom?" She dared an impish look at him, and was gratified that it felt genuine to her, no shadows chasing the feeling. "My guestroom?"

"If you want me in your bed, you only have to tell me so, but..." Brendan blew out a breath, squeezed her hands. "Chloe, I'm going to say this straight out, okay? I'm a sexual submissive. I'll be there in that capacity. Do you understand what that means?"

She stared at him several moments. "I'm not sure." Though her mind was going a hundred miles a minute, revisiting those websites in her mind, the hints of things. No, she didn't really understand, couldn't reconcile those graphic images with the man in front of her, the one who'd taken such gentle command of their lovemaking when she was too frightened to hold the reins. "But I guess you're trying to say I'll understand better if I go this weekend. That's really why you want me there, isn't it? You asked Marguerite to invite me. Because it's easier to show than explain, right?"

"Marguerite is glad to have you there. But yeah, something like that." His jaw had tightened, though, as if he knew all the conflicting thoughts tumbling through her mind.

"This is a big enough part of you that you feel like I need to know it now, before we even have our first official date with dinner, flowers, et cetera," she continued slowly. "That's why you acted so weird this morning, wasn't it?"

He looked surprised that she'd drawn the right conclusion, but inclined his head.

"Do you put all your potential dates through this?"

When he flinched, she blanched. "Brendan, no. Oh God, I didn't mean it that way."

"No, no apologies." His poignant smile melted her insides, though the shadows in his eyes still made her wish she hadn't said it. "I don't date, Chloe. Not in the traditional sense. All my more recent, committed relationships, and there aren't many, have grown out of who I meet at my preferred club. The Zone, same as the one that Marguerite and Tyler attend. You're the first I've ever reached out to like this, and I know it's too soon. This doesn't obligate you to anything. Honestly." He closed his hand on the Jeep window frame. "It's the reason I'm asking, really. I want you to know before you get too deep in, so you can decide how you want me. I'm a good friend," he added. "I can be. I'll be anything you need me to be, Chloe."

She considered that, then looked full in his face, her own thoughts pushed aside as what wasn't said penetrated, disturbed her. "But what about you, Brendan? What do you want for yourself?"

"You come first." He shook his head, lifting her hand to his mouth, but she drew it away, giving him a sharper look.

"What do you want?"

That demand seemed to shock him, like a curious moment of *déjà vu,* but when he locked with her gaze, the singular intensity pulled at her and unsettled her at once. "I want you to come to the carnival."

Squaring his shoulders, he added, "I'd like you to see this side of me, Chloe, but I'm also kind of afraid. Afraid you'll be repulsed, or worse, that you'll put some polite smile on and say, 'that's nice', and I'll never hear from you again. But I guess that's a risk I have to take. After all, you can't very well prove you're falling in love with someone if you don't offer up your whole self to them, right?"

She stared at him, and it was his turn to look startled with his own words. "I'm sorry, that was entirely unfair. I'm not saying that to make you feel—"

"Stop," she said softly. He stilled as she stood. Gazing up into his face, she reached up to touch his hair, fluttering across his brow. When he lifted his hand, she shook her head. "Please...don't touch me right now."

His hand dropped, and he swallowed. She caught the essence of something, a glimmer of understanding, intertwining with her own confused reaction to the moment. "Brendan, I wish I didn't know how damn honest you are. Then I could pretend that you said that because you're afraid I won't hang out with you anymore, ride the amusement park ride until it's done. But I know you are that honest. Just as I know, crazy as it sounds, that I want to hear those words, even if they make me a lot more afraid than they would have before you asked me to the carnival."

At his puzzled look, she bit her lip. "I'm scared I'll react exactly as you said. Find out more and realize I can't accept a vital part of who you are. That I'll paste on a forced smile, because I won't want to hurt you, while my heart will be breaking because I really wanted to give us a go. I've dated a lot, had a lot of fun, even had my heart broken once or twice, but in hindsight, they were markers in life, you know? Those things you expect to experience, to learn about who you are and what you want. This is more, what's between us, and that means it's going to hurt a lot more if that happens."

He nodded, a quick jerk. "I know. I'm sorry, Chloe. If you don't want to go, though, you don't have to. You don't have to be in that part of my life to have me in yours. I promise."

Of course I do, silly man. Her knuckles stroked down his sculpted jaw, her thumb passing over his lips. The quivering restraint in them, his desire to tease her flesh, made her tremble as well. "So I guess I'll be packing up some clothes in a few days and going to Marguerite's for the weekend."

She was glad to see a wary pleasure enter his gaze, though a regret as well. "Then I have to leave you here," he said. "One of Marguerite's conditions for you attending is that I can't see you until this weekend. She thought it best if you had some time to think about it, be sure. She said if you were worried about staying at your place in the interim, you could stay here, in her upstairs bedroom, or at their Tampa house."

Chloe wondered what all had been in that conversation, because she saw some tension remained in his shoulders. It suggested all the things this meant, things she knew she didn't truly understand. It brought some of her own worries to the surface. "Brendan, you said I'd really be M's guest, not yours. And that you'll be there as...what you said." For some reason, it felt odd to say it, though she could tell her inability to do so closed him off a little to her. Not in an obvious way, for he still stood near her, head attentively cocked, but something shut within him so she wouldn't have to look in there, be forced to walk into that room, as he'd said.

If she did that often enough, she'd have to be the one to turn the latch, open the room again. No matter what her own conceptions were of what he'd just called himself, she realized there were more layers and complexity to it than the stereotypes or websites could address. Strangely, that reassured her. It meant that there were no hard definitions. Like love.

"Does that mean other women can...will..."

Though he'd respected her desire not to be touched right now, the way they stood so close put their hands so near touching that when he shifted, their fingers brushed. Curling her pinky over two of his large fingers made a tight smile cross his handsome face. His eyes roved over her features, following the curling strands of hair moved by the breeze across her cheek, to her lips.

"That will be up to you, Chloe."

Chapter Eight

ဆ

"This is just amazing." Chloe sat back in the lawn chair, her tired muscles protesting. "It's like watching an adult Disneyland being built in a week." She tried to curl her legs up underneath her, her favorite sitting pose, and managed it with a little groan. "Okay, I'm no longer worried you were coddling me when you made me come here early to help with this instead of Tea Leaves. Are you sure you weren't a slave overseer in a former life? Or worse, a personal trainer? I think that's what slave overseers become in this life. Physical trainers, math teachers... Of course, I guess from what I've been learning over the past few days, you're kind of one in this life. Though I get that submission isn't forced, that it isn't slavery, even though some like to be called slaves. I—Argh." Chloe gave Marguerite a narrow look. "You're doing that thing you do, where you don't say anything and I babble along like a brook on whitewater steroids."

"It's because I like hearing you talk. You don't filter, Chloe. It comes straight from your mind and heart to your mouth. If we're sticking to water analogies, straight from a spring's source, before anything can contaminate it along the way."

"Like bear or moose droppings," Chloe said brightly.

"Then again, some filtering can be wise." Amusement wreathed Marguerite's typically somber features.

Manual labor aside, Chloe was sure Marguerite had also invited her to keep her from going bonkers this week. No visits from Brendan, right after they'd discovered that new flush of desire, lust, laughter. To reinforce Chloe's barely there resolve, Marguerite had taken away her cell in one of those only-M-could-get-away-with-it moves. Told her it would build the anticipation for when she'd see him again. Chloe had wondered why they both accepted Marguerite's edict about no contact without question, but she knew in a way Marguerite was right. She needed to think about this.

Maybe Brendan did too. That is, whether he really wanted to show her this side of himself. Some moments she felt overcome with what it might all mean, images crowding in her head. Her body ached with those images, unsure how to react. Other times, she couldn't bear to think about it, how it might end something between them before it even began.

One thing was for certain, though. Whether it was the enforced absence from one another right after she'd rediscovered her libido, or the fact they'd spent the last three days doing all sorts of set up work on a carnival that was going to be all about sensual pleasures, she was nearly feverish with unmitigated desire. Remarkably, she hadn't pleasured herself in Marguerite's guestroom *because* she wanted Brendan so badly. She wondered if he was the same, or—an even more tormenting image—was he in his bed at night, in that state of glorious nakedness, working himself furiously into his hand. Thinking of spilling himself in her cunt, her mouth...

"M, does Brendan like me? I mean, do you think he's seen enough of me, to know that's who he likes?" *Or is he one of those who gets off on the damsel in distress?* She couldn't bring herself to ask that, was somewhat embarrassed she'd asked what she had, so abruptly.

Marguerite crossed her ankles, her legs bare to mid thigh from a pair of belted tailored shorts. She wore a neat cotton blouse tucked into it, showing a tempting and classy line of cleavage. Her long hair was in a tail, tumbling over her right breast. She smelled good. Maybe because of her heightened sense of the erotic, Chloe could well imagine how a man might beg to have some part of that. She felt an odd desire to touch and stroke Marguerite herself. "Yes. Whoever you need to be, at any point, that's who Brendan will want. It's the type of person he is."

"Hmm." Chloe drew a steadying breath, looked away. "You have a Ferris wheel on your lawn. A freaking Ferris wheel. I can't believe it."

"We mix the traditional trappings with the untraditional. We want to keep the sense of play, childish adventure, mixed with the more adult versions of it."

"A carnival's perfect for that." Chloe watched workmen hang a sign over one tent. The Marvelous Freak Show. Unlike a fair or festival, a carnival was a blend of light and dark. The macabre with the fantasy. "I remember going to one by myself when I was younger, about sixteen. There was so much light, but it was like the bug light that draws you in before you see the shadows. There were rides and games, but the carnies, they had these intent eyes, and this right-out-front sexuality, like you'd imagine gypsies would have. A fringe society living by a different set of rules."

She tuned in to find Marguerite regarding her intently. "Yes. It's a good description."

"Brendan is part of this world. He's one of the gypsies. You haven't answered many of my questions, you know," Chloe added. "At least not with a lot of detail."

"You've already done a lot of looking yourself, on the internet." Marguerite also wore a pair of dark glasses that, with her folded hands and straight carriage, gave the sense that she was a statue. The only thing that disrupted the illusion was the wind, rippling the Gulf waters behind her and playing in the pale strands of her hair.

"But you haven't really encouraged me to do that, either. In fact, last night, you made yourself scarce while I was web surfing."

"This is a very hard world to truly understand, Chloe, unless you already feel it in some part of you. Even those who do often have trouble explaining why it draws them."

Chloe curled her hand over her bare toes. Her sneakers overlapped on the grass below her chair. "That kind of feels like an ultimatum, M. Like if I'm not...one of you, then he and I have no chance."

Why that should ruffle her feathers, when she'd nursed the same fear at Brendan's invitation, she didn't know, but it got her back up. It was uncomfortable to feel defensive, almost...competitive...with Marguerite, so she was relieved when M didn't seem to take offense. Instead, she pushed a plate of sugar cookies, sitting on the table between them, closer to Chloe's side.

"Every submissive is different, Chloe. Most of what comes up on the internet about BDSM looks the same. Violent, kinky, garish. But in actuality, every submissive is different. Imagining that every male submissive is a bedwetter who wants to crawl around and suck on mommy's toes is erroneous, not to mention judgmental. Just as boiling down what each of them needs to a tall woman in leather beating their asses with a paddle is too simplistic."

Chloe couldn't imagine Brendan in either of those scenarios, but she kept thinking about that first night, the things he'd said. *Is that a command?* The way he'd framed what he wanted in terms of her needs, not his own.

She frowned, picked up a cookie and turned it over in her hand, smelling the tempting aroma of the baked sweet as Marguerite continued. "I haven't said too much, Chloe, because it's up to you to find out what Brendan is. You've always been a creature of exceptional intuition, and it's my belief that when we let our fears drop away, truths are much clearer. In time, I will answer any question you ask, but I think the best way to understand is to simply experience these three days, not based on what you've seen on a website, but on what those finely tuned senses of yours feel." Reaching over, Marguerite touched the cookie, then ran a fingertip down the side of Chloe's hand, spreading grains of sugar there. It gave Chloe a not-unpleasant shiver.

"We place a great deal of emphasis on knowledge, understanding, comprehension," Marguerite continued. "But in a truly tolerant world, things don't always need to make sense to us to be accepted, or to become a vital part of our lives."

"Like the biblical fruit, the knowledge of good and evil. Kind of screwed ourselves there."

"Yes. Because understanding good and evil is intuitive, not scientific. We both know that." Marguerite's look arrowed directly into Chloe's soul. Toward a room she was determined to keep locked. Even if she ultimately couldn't, the last person she'd burden with what was in that room would be Marguerite.

Chloe cleared her throat. "I guess my break is over. I need to go get—"

"Stop." The firm command stopped her in mid-sentence as those blue eyes became cooler, more intent. Irrefutable. "Chloe, I will never, ever make you tell me something you don't want to say. So the discomfort you are feeling comes from the fear of what you know you need to say, and the fact you're not sure you're ready for the consequences of it. But know this."

Marguerite rose, came to her and settled on her heels next to the low chair, surprising Chloe as her long, cool fingers settled on Chloe's folded knees. "Those shadows at the carnival. If you get lost in them, or feel you need to walk away from the light into them, you will not be alone there. Whenever, whatever you eventually must face, we will be there. And I suspect Brendan will as well, no matter where or how fast you take your relationship with him."

Chloe shook her head. "I don't want to make you part of that. Or him."

Marguerite reached up and cupped the side of her face, her thumb moving over Chloe's lips in a way that felt...Well, Chloe couldn't exactly describe it. Since Marguerite had invited her into this world, she'd seen glimpses of the Mistress she now understood Marguerite was. It wasn't like Marguerite was putting the moves on her or anything, but there was a definite sexual, authoritative undercurrent in Marguerite's touch and in the way she held Chloe with her gaze. Chloe felt most comfortable capitulating, staying still and quiet under that touch, not thinking, merely accepting that it felt good to be touched, that she felt sensual awareness of the pad of Marguerite's thumb tracing her lips in that stroke. It was okay.

"Chloe, by inviting you here, he's inviting you into a part of himself that you will only find if you reach deep into *his* soul. Nothing at that level is rushed or forced. It simply is. And you know that I am here for anything you need."

Before her emotions could embarrass her, Chloe watched Marguerite sit back on her heels, change the subject. "You know, after today you're off work detail. You get to be a hundred percent guest."

"Oh, but I can help—"

"No." Marguerite shook her head, but her expression had eased, releasing Chloe as if she'd loosened a tether. "Despite my willingness to exploit your labor to the nth degree, once the clock tolls midnight, you are a guest, entitled to immerse yourself in the experience. Tyler has hired more than enough people to handle things. Even he and I will only be overseeing the occasional detail once things start. This is the seventh one of these he's hosted, so the people who run it know what they're doing. We can all enjoy the experience." Marguerite cocked her head, gave her a piercing look. "Do you miss Brendan?"

"Terribly," Chloe said, without hesitation. He was uppermost in her thoughts. Particularly that one night he'd stayed with her, so close, his body warm and strong, folded around her. The way he smelled, the softness of his hair brushing her cheek when she'd pressed her lips to his throat.

The first night she'd been here, Marguerite had worked her so hard, she'd fallen asleep sitting up on the couch after dinner. She'd woken in a pair of strong arms, carrying her to her guestroom. Her mind had leaped to the conclusion she desired most.

"Brendan," she mumbled.

"Tyler, sweetheart. But he'll be here soon." She'd been tucked into the bed, M's cool, gentle hands removing her skirt and shoes, covers drawn up. As they were leaving, she'd felt the only stirring of fear she'd had all day.

"Light. Please leave light on…in bathroom."

That same female hand came back, smoothing her hair. Then Tyler's firm touch on her leg, his lips passing over her brow as well. "No harm will come to you here, little flower. But we'll leave it on for you."

Tuning back in to the present, she wondered if Brendan had thought of her half as much as she had him. When she got her cell phone back, would she have a dozen missed calls from him? Or had he possessed the discipline she lacked?

Just hormones. Right. The *"God, I-want-to-fall-in-love-so-hard-with-him-I'll-give-myself-a-permanent-concussion-and-never-wake-up-from-it"* kind of hormones.

As Marguerite said, she'd always relied on Chloe's intuition. Intuition hadn't protected her from evil, but maybe she never should have expected it to do so. That wasn't the purpose of her particular super power.

Despite the wry smile the thought gave her, she couldn't dissipate the ache that never left her, which had nothing to do with Brendan. While Chloe refused to burden Marguerite, she did desperately want the answer to the question the woman was tragically capable of answering.

"M, how did you keep it from eating you alive? The fear, the… Is it a smokescreen? When something really awful happens, and we build walls to hold it together, hold it back, but something knocks them down, shows you how pointless those walls are, what do you do?"

Marguerite had taken a reclined seat on the adjacent wide Adirondack lounger. Her hand still rested on Chloe's arm, and now her fingers curled around it. "Come here."

Nonplused, but compelled by that velvet voice, Chloe unfolded from her chair and shifted, letting Marguerite guide her down, so she was curled up against her. Marguerite wrapped her arm around her back, pressing Chloe's head on her shoulder, tucked beneath M's chin and fall of moonlit hair. The lean strength of Marguerite's body had an unexpected softness to it, the pillow of her breast, the skin of her thigh underneath Chloe's as she crooked her legs over it. Marguerite stroked her hair.

"You learn to do without the walls, Chloe. The point isn't building them, but building a life that is so much of who you are, nothing can destroy it. If you're lucky, when you figure that out, you find—or discover you've already found—a person who will help you keep the darkness at bay. Someone who gives you the strength to live as who you are, not a prisoner of your own mind."

She'd always wanted to touch Marguerite's hair the way she was doing now, her fingers running through the thick tail, letting the strands drift back down onto the incline of her right breast. Go from there to trace her fragile neck. Marguerite allowed it, because it was so obviously okay to do that here in this quiet place, the crickets humming, and M so lazy and relaxed. It wasn't as if she wanted to have sex with Marguerite, but just indulging the desire to touch someone she loved but didn't necessarily desire, with impunity, was bliss. Marguerite's hand continued to stroke her back slowly, down to her hip and then back up, to her nape, teasing the curls, then going back down again.

"This feels weird," Chloe said quietly. "But a good weird. I like touching. More than most people do."

"Well, you'll be in heaven for the next several days, because at this carnival, you're free to touch quite a few people."

116

"Even that one?" Chloe grinned as her gaze was drawn to the stage going up further down the side lawn. The four men working on the placement of the support structure included Tyler. He'd arrived to answer questions and ended up lending a hand. He'd stripped off his T-shirt, like most of them in the Florida heat, and was helping raise a beam in nothing but a pair of jeans and a lot of gleaming muscle.

"Within reason," Marguerite said dryly, but there was a tone in her voice that suggested she wasn't entirely uninterested in the sight.

"He's your knight, isn't he? The one who keeps the darkness at bay."

It didn't require the nod against her hair, but she liked feeling it.

The beam placed, Tyler's attention shifted, as Chloe knew it would. If Marguerite was ever in his proximity, he was always quick to find her. It made Chloe wonder if maybe Marguerite helped keep Tyler's nightmares at bay as well. Because she knew one thing for sure—everyone had them.

He strode across the lawn, relaxed and easy, a feast for feminine eyes with damp muscled flesh and well-fitted jeans. Yet he still managed to project the Southern gentleman even in the casual dress, amber eyes focused on them as he approached.

"You two make a provocative and lovely picture. Giving those boys all sorts of ideas."

Chloe grinned. "Well, tell them to meet us all down at the hot tub, then."

Tyler smiled, slow and sexy, and her heart did a somersault, despite herself. Of course, she also noted that Marguerite's heart rate increased as well. Understandable, considering Tyler's gaze was fastened on his wife like he was going to take healthy bites out of every inch of her bare skin.

Since she had at least an ounce of brain left, Chloe noticed the way Tyler looked at M was not only possessive, but something else. Marguerite had explained they were both sexual Dominants, but Chloe hadn't really gotten far enough to think how that might work. But in this moment—intuition versus knowledge—she got the gist of it. With each other, one was more dominant than the other. She knew exactly who that was when Tyler's gaze shifted to hers. Chloe read the intent—and the command—loud and clear.

It wasn't the first time she'd cleared out for them. For the past few days, probably because of what kind of carnival this was, the sexual undercurrent between them had been about as "under" as an undertow, capable of dragging a whale from the shallows out to sea.

"I'll go help Marcia set up the game booths," she said, every nerve ending coming alive under that gaze, making her want Brendan even more. Maybe she could bribe Marcia into letting her borrow her cell phone. "She said after lunch there'd be a million stuffed bears to set out."

"No," Marguerite said, her arm tightening around Chloe's back. She held Tyler's gaze a moment, an unspoken communication. When he gave a slight nod, her lashes swept down, acknowledging his...permission. That was clear enough and amazing as well, but then Chloe's brain checked out as Tyler settled on M's side of the wide lounger. He removed Marguerite's sunglasses, tossing them beside her lemonade glass. As her blue eyes sparked, he braced his arm on the far side of Chloe's hip, caging both women inside it as he leaned in and captured Marguerite's mouth in a kiss.

It wasn't a brush of lips. It was a hard, press-her-back-against-the-lounger, take-her-mouth-and-dive-in, unrestrained plundering. Chloe's breath shortened, her body yearned. She closed her hands into fists to restrain herself, because she hadn't been invited to participate and wouldn't even know where to start. She was here, though, her body pressed against Marguerite's, Tyler's braced forearm pressed intimately against her hip and buttock. Then he did something that astounded Chloe more. His hand curved under her hip, his fingers firm but gentle, and he pressed her in tighter against Marguerite's body. Marguerite's leg shifted, and whether intentional or good fortune, it pressed solidly between Chloe's thighs.

Chloe gasped, her hand automatically clutching onto the closest thing, which was Tyler's biceps. He continued kissing Marguerite, moving across her cheek, down to her throat, where he bit. She arched up at the strength of the bite, where Chloe could see teeth marking skin. Tyler squeezed Chloe with his other hand, moving her against Marguerite's leg. Oh Goddess, it felt good, and he began a massaging motion that kept her in a slow, subtle rhythm.

With the two of them drawing her in like this, she couldn't help but obey the motion. She was vibrating all over, just watching, working herself in involuntary, semi-restrained jerks against Marguerite's leg as Tyler multi-tasked with riveting efficiency, making sure Chloe kept building that fire in herself even as he moved to Marguerite's shoulder, teased at her bra strap beneath the blouse with his teeth. Then he lifted his head, his gaze fixed on Marguerite's face with fierce brilliance.

"Move it out of my way."

Chloe's sex spasmed at the authority in his tone, irresistible. In response to his demand, Marguerite slid open a couple of buttons on her shirt and drew the fabric aside then released her front-closing bra. It slid back, giving Chloe a glimpse of the nearly exposed curve. Then Marguerite lifted her hand above her head, clasping the top slat of the lounge chair so there was no impediment to his access to her body, her face.

As he bent, Chloe watched his mouth seal over the already aroused nipple at close range. Taking it in, he began to suckle in a way that made her own breasts ache in envy. Tyler's hand descended further, took a firm hold of Chloe's right buttock at the most sensitive part of the curve and squeezed. With the right pressure and manipulation of fingers, he had Chloe shamelessly working her clit against Marguerite's body. Marguerite's hand slid up the back of her shirt, playing with her bra strap, and Chloe didn't know how they could even think, let alone coordinate all this. Her mind was just completely immersed in the close-up sensory input. After working out in the sun, Tyler's biceps were hard and slick under her hand.

The men working on the stage were just across the lawn, their view impeded only by some light vegetative screening around the patio. They could get a hint of what was going on, but not the full view. While he didn't mind sharing with Chloe, she doubted Tyler was amenable to exposing his wife's body and arousal to other men. Still, the possible voyeuristic glimpse, with Tyler protective and in control, was enough to stir Chloe further.

Amid her haze of desire, she also realized she didn't fear him. There wasn't that hesitation, that self-sabotage that had occurred with Brendan, perhaps because she wasn't the focus, the bull's eye center of the target. She was only a passerby, a witness so close she was drawn in, in an entirely non-threatening way.

Tyler's other hand had coiled on Marguerite's clipped-back tail of hair, wrapping it to hold her head at the angle he desired, keeping it back as he sucked her. Chloe's hand slid down his arm and back up, digging into his shoulder. The slow rock of her body against Marguerite's leg kept her arousal in a lazy, sweet spiral that mercifully kept her thoughts at bay. Tyler's pace on Marguerite's breast had likewise slowed, and Chloe found it explosive to watch the way he licked and nibbled, sweet and easy, nuzzling her at his own pace. Obviously showing it was his pleasure he was indulging, to tease and taste his wife's nipple as long as he wished, no matter how much she might shudder or plead beneath him.

But Marguerite was still, as if she understood what he required. However, her stillness wasn't dispassionate. Chloe felt the heat coming off her skin now, the little involuntary jerks the intense arousal made it impossible to suppress, reflecting the tremendous effort it took to remain motionless under stimulation. If Marguerite's desire was as great as Chloe's, it had to be building to a combustible level.

She was amazed she was doing this, but she supposed she shouldn't be. Being around Brendan had left her hormones in chaos, and setting up for a fetish carnival was all about sensual delight. It was more than enough to keep her in a stir. Sexual arousal had the same effect as alcohol, lowering inhibition, making unwise decisions seem completely okay. This wasn't unwise; she trusted Marguerite and Tyler more than she probably trusted anyone, but it was certainly unsettling to find herself swept up in their erotic wake.

Tyler's head lifted. His gaze devoured Marguerite's bared upper body. With careful movements, his expression registering every tremor of reaction under his touch, he slid the bra back in place, smoothing it over the aroused nipple. He bit the curve of her breast, eyes going molten as he earned one more suppressed gasp from her before he slipped the buttons closed. He also brought Chloe's movements to an effective, shuddering halt by sliding his grip back to her hip, squeezing her there.

"Be still now. Ride the feeling, keep it going, but don't let it go. Not yet." He flashed teeth at her, more tiger than man, showing how he fought his own desire. His voice was a low rumble. "We've found that starting the carnival with unreleased desire is one of the best ways to enjoy it. To ensure the body and heart override the mind."

Chloe became aware that Marguerite's stroke on her back had become more calming and on the outside of her T-shirt, though she vividly remembered the touch of her fingers under her bra strap. Tyler's arm was still braced behind her, his body and male heat so close. "Oh I think I'm there," she said. "If I saw a puppy about to be run over, or Brendan naked, that puppy would be a greasy spot." She gave a nervous little laugh. "I don't know whether to be embarrassed now, or awkward, or..."

"What would you like to be?" Marguerite dropped her other hand from the top of the chair to rest on Tyler's forearm. With Chloe's hand still on his biceps, they formed a reassuring, connected circle.

"I'd like to not have to say anything. To think about it, or not think about it, and just be kind of worried it happened. And flustered, in a good way. Why did you guys do that?"

"To help you understand, give you a taste of what it will be like," Marguerite said. "So you don't have to worry over it so much. Instead, you can think more about the possibilities."

"That's her explanation." Tyler shrugged. "I saw two beautiful women twined together and went from there."

Despite herself, Chloe laughed. He gave her a lazy grin. But when he straightened, reaching for the carafe of sweet tea that Sarah, their housekeeper, had left on the side table with the lemonade, Chloe slid off the lounger. "I think I will go help with those stuffed bears." Because if she didn't go do *something,* she was going to melt into a puddle of sexual frustration. Particularly if she hung around the two of them, with those pheromones still zinging like electrons around their nuclei. Her clit was astonishingly swollen, giving her a sense of the discomfort a man felt walking with an erection.

She wanted Brendan so badly right now she could almost smell his scent on her skin from a few days ago. Whatever other thoughts she might have about the carnival, she knew that she wanted to see him. It could have been a root canal marathon for charity. She would have happily attended if he was going to be here.

She turned and backpedaled. "So the carnival starts at midnight tonight, right? Is there an opening ceremony before we get to play and visit?"

"Yes." Tyler's gaze held amusement, and a male awareness of her state that had her nipples tightening up almost as much as his wife's had been under his clever, hot mouth. "There's a welcome speech, very brief, and then the unattached submissives, or those willing to be shared by their Masters or Mistresses, are auctioned as the first fundraising event. We even have a couple Doms who will offer their services up for bids, since all the money goes to the battered women's shelter."

"Do you know when Brendan will get here?"

Tyler paused, glanced at Marguerite, then came back to Chloe, meeting her eyes with a steady look. "You'll first see him on stage. He's one of the slaves being auctioned."

Chapter Nine

ஐ

To someone *else?* Yeah, he said he'd be here in the capacity of…a sexual submissive. But he'd wanted her to be here. He'd asked M to put her on the guest roll. To watch him have another woman do… What the hell *would* they do to him?

Marguerite was not a chatty person, so Chloe knew everything she'd said earlier had meaning, significance. As she got ready that night, she thought over those words, her emphasis on simply "experiencing".

She'd have to accept this, see where it was going to go. There was no way she could outbid anyone for him, even if she thought she had the nerve to do that. As she'd told Brendan, just to be here was ten thousand dollars per person, unless you were a special invited guest, like Chloe. Or him. Of course, now she knew what he was doing to pay his way, right?

Stop it. She closed her eyes. She'd learned that some Zone club regulars, like Brendan, volunteered to be floating "slaves" for those who attended unattached. Was it like going to a boyfriend's job and hoping for the chance to make out with him on breaks? She felt ungrateful and catty for even having the thought, but damn it, the excitement she'd felt at seeing him tonight had a big black cloud hanging over it. She wasn't sure if she'd rather just go home. Why hadn't Marguerite told her earlier?

Resigned, she gave herself a look in the guestroom mirror. She'd been told that dress code ranged from anything to…nothing. Literally. So she'd been encouraged to wear something festive, but whatever made her feel most comfortable. Tonight's opening sounded a little dressy, though. Five hundred exclusive guests with ten thousand dollars to blow, plus auction money and whatever else they anticipated spending on the events? The couple of nearby hotels were booked solid, plus temporary private quarters had been set up across the back lawn. Lovely colorful pavilion tents like for a knights' tournament, in case guests didn't want to leave over the two nights the carnival would be held.

She'd worn one of her favorite dresses, made of a soft wine-colored viscose fabric, a Renaissance style creation with a diamond neckline and vine embroidery that flowed down to the first of two satin inlays. There were touches of lace here and there, but the arms were left bare, and then there was a flowing crepe hem. She wore silver upper arm bands with Celtic scrollwork that matched a similar choker style necklace, and she'd piled her short set of curls on her head, enhanced her eyes with dark kohl. True to herself, she'd left her feet bare except for Indian silver anklets on each foot. They jingled with soft music beneath the flowing hem. She'd also added toe rings with yin and yang symbols on them. If nothing else, her feet would be spiritually balanced.

The dress was definitely feminine and yet sexy at once, the thin fabric giving glimpses of the outline of her body, the diamond neckline generous with the curves of her breasts and cleavage for anyone who cared to look. Though it was one person in particular she cared about, if he wasn't too busy "serving" some other woman.

Curling her lip, she gave her chosen outfit another tug. On the bright side, she certainly hadn't had any time to have nightmares these past few days. Though she still felt like bolting, it was for entirely different reasons now.

* * * * *

The view of the side and back lawns was breathtaking. She'd been part of the set up, but the final result was like an array of fairies had come and sprinkled the whole Carnival with glittering magic dust to give it that finishing touch, an enchanted look. Everything had lights. The Ferris wheel, the tents, and even the lawn had strands of tiny lights crisscrossed and stretched between poles. A breeze was coming off the water. The stage area was down by the oaks, framed by their long, gnarled branches, the wispy strands of Spanish moss.

It was impossible not to be affected by the fantasy of her surroundings, allow it to transport her mind to a place where many things were still possible. As she came down the hill, a tendril of the *joie de vivre* that she'd once spun into her own unique form of magic flickered to tentative life.

Chloe had never worried about class status before, and she was determined not to start tonight when she had enough worries on her plate. Besides which, the few faces that turned toward her as she approached the back tables were curious, but not unfriendly. Of course, she couldn't imagine Tyler and Marguerite tolerating a guest who was anything less than classy.

Her stomach tightened as she saw the opening remarks were just concluding, Tyler turning over the microphone to another man. She was sorry she'd missed that, fussing with her appearance, but she knew her increased tension was because the auction was the first event scheduled for the evening. She'd arrived just in time to see what role Brendan would be playing tonight.

She'd have expected the auctioneer to be Tyler, since the main purpose was to raise money for the battered women's shelter. Chloe could well imagine the bids Tyler's combination of Southern charm and commanding presence would elicit from his audience. But he and Marguerite were seated at one of the candlelit tables near the front, Tyler's chair pushed back so he could comfortably speak to friends at an adjacent table. Marguerite's fingertips barely touched his where both their hands rested on the cream tablecloth, though Chloe could almost see the arc of kinetic energy that flowed through the small space.

She slid into an empty chair, choosing to stay in the back. She gave a courteous nod to the two closest tables when the occupants glanced her way. One table held three people. A woman with hair like the spun gold that Chloe thought only existed in books wore a white full length beaded sheath and silver heels. The man next to her was in a tuxedo. In contrast, the third man wore jeans and a dress shirt with cowboy boots. He looked as if he played professional football. Since his face seemed familiar, she thought it was possible.

The table to her right was occupied by two men, obviously lovers. One man's hand rested on the other's thigh, tracing a path up and down it. While they weren't in black tux, their clothes were dress shirts and slacks, expensive-looking shoes. Looking back at the three at the other table, she thought they were more sexual playmates, rather than ongoing lovers. There was an easy banter between them, and a lot of smoldering glances, but not the casual intimacy of the two men.

As her gaze swept the crowd, she saw different versions of the same, as well as her first examples of blatant submission. People kneeling at the feet of their Masters or Mistresses, or standing behind them, positioned so they wouldn't block the view of others. One pair in particular intrigued her, because the woman wore a short cocktail dress, stockings and ice pick heels, yet she knelt on the grass next to her male companion, or Master, Chloe corrected herself, though she assumed both terms were true.

He wore a more casual outfit of jeans and T-shirt. As he fondled her auburn curls, he ran his fingers along the edge of a thick diamond choker to which a tether was attached. What caught Chloe's attention, though, was that the girl wasn't kneeling on the grass, but his jacket, which he'd spread beneath her.

It was a harsh contrast to what she saw to the left of them, a man completely naked and kneeling at his Master's feet. He wore a harness that caged his genitals. When he shifted, she

127

noted the plug in the rear ring of the harness, explaining the gingerly way he knelt. He also wore nipple clamps with a chain running from them to a metal band around the head of his cock. It was obvious that the heavier and more erect his cock became, the more excruciating the pull on the clamps might be. Since his cock was hard and thick, begging for attention, apparently the pain was a stimulant. His Master seemed oblivious, chatting with friends. However, watching their body language, Chloe could tell the clad man was anything but indifferent to the pleasurable torment he was causing.

She looked away from that, a little overwhelmed. Varying versions of the same were displayed across the over one hundred small round tables. Though she found it hard to look at the more extreme examples, she picked up on a couple consistent themes. There was a strong sense of...connection between the groupings. Pleasurable cruelty existed here, and pain, but also care, trust. Love. Her gaze passed back over the woman kneeling on the suit jacket, then drifted from there to Marguerite and Tyler. She suspected that had to do with them, the tone they set. Charity or no charity, it was obvious the exclusive guest list had considerations beyond money.

The murmur of the crowd fell to a hush, the waitstaff moving with smooth precision to stay out of the direct line of the lit stage as the auctioneer stepped up to the podium.

As irresistible as Tyler was, Chloe couldn't fault his choice of emcee. He was a Viking, tall and broad, with blond hair loose around a face strong enough to give Fabio in his prime a run for his money. His blue-gray eyes were warm but assessing, giving a dual impression of kindness and command of any situation. The latter made her wonder if he might be a friend of Tyler's from his time with whatever government agency he'd served. Of course, the Viking's looks suggested a film industry contact. His voice rolled over the crowd like a radio professional, but she thought he might be more at home inside a Roman arena, announcing gladiator games. Or participating in them.

"Welcome, Masters and Mistresses. We are glad to have your presence—and your wallets—for the most important event tonight." He paused for the murmur of appreciative laughter, eyes glinting at a smattering of suggestive comments, some of which made Chloe's eyes widen. "I have to tell you, it's a drug, inhaling the sweet nervousness of the slaves behind this curtain. They're anxious and aroused, wondering who will take them in hand for the next three days. Who will give them the discipline they crave, the punishments they need. Which of you will earn their surrender, and all the pleasure that comes with that."

Like Brendan, he had the voice training of a stage performer, his change in tone from amusement to seductive promise igniting the atmosphere with anticipation. Chloe tried to focus on that, rather than the sinking feeling in her stomach. As her gaze passed again over the tables, she noted many occupants had picked up thick, glossy program booklets, and were turning to already marked pages.

"Our gracious hosts, Master Tyler and Mistress Marguerite, mailed you your auction programs last month, so you should have had ample time to peruse the choices and make your selections. As you can imagine, having any one of these beautiful slaves as your own for two whole nights is a gift without price. Almost." He quirked a brow to another wave of chuckles. "Master Tyler advises you to show your appreciation generously. Looking out at this assembly, most of you would have to pay dearly to get the chance at slaves as pretty as these are. I'm of course referring to you Masters, not our assembly of lovely Mistresses."

"Nice way to save your ass, Kale," a call came from the crowd. The emcee grinned to the ripple of laughter.

"We'll start with Slave Number One. I'll run down the highlights to jog your memory. Slave Number One is a pain and punishment junkie, a real handful who requires the most

129

extreme Master or Mistress. As you can see, we already had to take him well in hand."

Chloe froze in her chair as two men, almost larger than Kale, brought a struggling male slave out from behind the large curtained area adjacent to the stage. His cock was in a similar harness to ones she'd seen in the crowd, only this one appeared to have prongs that jabbed his sizeable erection. She could see the pressure of the points digging into the tender base and scrotum. He also had some sort of bridle on his head, and a blindfold.

"Slave Number One is wearing a scold harness. For those of you not familiar with this lovely item, there's a flat metal piece holding down his tongue until a Master or Mistress is ready to put his mouth to more creative use." At a nod, they turned him. When he resisted, Chloe gasped as one of the handlers zapped him with an electric charge from a prod. The sparks were blue. The slave bellowed but turned, displaying a muscular backside and broad shoulders, already reddened with stripes.

"He needed a good caning to settle him down, at least enough to get him up here. Ladies and gentleman, he needs a great deal of your attention. Who wants the challenge of taming the beast? Who can make him serve as a proper slave should?"

"Three thousand," came from the table next to her, the threesome. The woman in the white sheath made the bid as the other two males nodded. The football player leaned forward, his expression wreathed in determined anticipation.

Chloe's pulse fluttered, and she realized she had her fingers clutched in her lap. She wasn't sure what to think. Was it the elegant-coated brutality, or something she didn't consciously understand, that made her shamefully fascinated? The slave roared in protest around the metal piece in his mouth. The two men used strength and the prod to drive him to his knees. They shoved him to his elbows, making him face the back of the stage so they could knock the knees out wider and show the assembled the large testicle sac, cinched by the sharp prongs. With his ass high in the air, the anal region was clearly displayed. A plug was in it, held with another form of clamp that had more prongs, digging into the buttocks like fingers.

The bid was up to five thousand, but Kale wasn't done tempting the audience. "Ladies, I know you're dying to put the largest phallus you can find up that stubborn ass. He takes fisting with barely a blink."

"It couldn't compare to my monster cock, Kale. He'd be begging for mercy."

"Big words, Master Luke." Kale shot a humorous glance in the direction of a slim male toward the front who looked like a barely legal Leonardo DiCaprio. Chloe thought he'd be broken like a twig by the struggling behemoth. "Do you have the money to back it up?"

"Does Luke have the *cock* to back it up? Let's see *that*." This came from a voluptuous black Amazon several tables back. She had auburn curls pulled back on her bare shoulders, a teasing smile on her wet lips. With admiration, Chloe saw she gracefully wore thigh high red boots with stilettos that should have mired her in the grass of Tyler's lawn like a croquet hoop. Her latex dress fitted her like a serpent's sleek skin.

Master Luke sent her a feral grin, pure sex and danger. Seeing that, and the intensity in his gray-blue eyes, made Chloe rethink her opinion that he could be so easily overpowered. Rather than accommodating the taunting Mistress, though, he lifted eight fingers toward Kale.

"Outstanding. A bid of eight thousand. Anymore? No? You all want to see the match between these two, don't you? Going, going, gone." Kale brought down a gavel. "Well, you'll get your wish. Master Luke already agreed that whatever slave he takes in hand tonight will be broken in public. Perhaps Mistress Regina will get the chance to see Master Luke's reputed endowments after all." Over the approbation and more bawdy comments, Kale raised his voice. "Slave Number One will be shackled in the main tent for public viewing until Master Luke gets started. And remember, baiting and feeding *this* particular wild animal will be allowed, under supervision. Thank you, Master Luke."

The slave was led off stage. Chloe jumped as a waiter poured a glass of water at her elbow. He was dressed in slacks and suspenders, no shirt, because of course it would have been sacrilege to cover up the smooth bronzed muscles she was seeing at point-blank range. She might have taken him for a Chippendale except, instead of a bowtie, he wore a slave's collar with an elegant silver tag on it that read *Marius*. His eyes warmed and sensual lips curved as Chloe glanced up at him.

"That's Caleb," he murmured, nodding toward the recalcitrant slave. "He's done this five years in a row, Miss Chloe. Everything Kale said is true. He needs the fight, the pain, to truly let go of control and immerse himself in pleasure, surrender his emotions. No one I know can do that as well as Luke Gant."

"His mother must be a Thomas Wolfe fan." Feeling like Alice in Wonderland, she looked toward the slim man again. "Are you serious?"

"It's not about physical strength, love." When the waiter winked at her flirtatiously, she realized Caleb wasn't the only one who liked to test the boundaries. Particularly as Marius gave her a lingering appraisal. But his tone was serious. "It's about the will, and what the slave truly needs. The best Master or Mistress knows that. Case in point? There's only one other Dominant here who has taken Caleb all the way to subspace, and held him there until he was ready to worship her for the rest of his life."

The waiter nodded toward the front table where Marguerite and Tyler were engaged in conversation with a couple who'd joined them. "Mistress Marguerite. Master Luke has some lovely shoes to fill."

Thinking of the things she often felt from Marguerite, that inner strength and sense of command that belied her slim, feminine body, Chloe felt a little more credulity when she looked toward Luke Gant. Marius's hand whispered across her knee, drawing her attention back up to him as he squatted next to her.

"Course, she didn't tell me to tell you all that. She just said to come assure you, remind you, that everything you're seeing is consensual. But I can tell you these are some of the best Masters and Mistresses around, the ones who can keep sense in their world, when their slave can't. Hell, Caleb can get so lost in it he'd let someone cripple him if they didn't know the right way to make him reach bottom." The waiter gave her a casual shrug, ran a quick, ticklish finger over her knee under the silky viscose. "Safe words aren't any use with him. Most of us don't know jack shit about what we need. We only know what we *think* we need."

She gasped as he brushed the carafe of ice water against her leg, leaving a trail of condensation. Affecting an apologetic look, he efficiently slid the hand towel off his shoulder and caressed her bare calf beneath the hem to dryness. It couldn't help but make her lips quiver against a laugh, even as she pushed his hand away when it tried to drift upward again. "You are not a very well behaved waiter."

"I'll take that as a compliment. You let me know if you need anything, Miss Chloe." Giving her a wink, he rose and moved on, making it impossible not to take a surreptitious look at his ass, nicely outlined in those slacks, the play of muscle over his back. And of course he threw a look over his shoulder, catching her at it, before moving on to the next table.

Chloe shook her head, but whether or not Marguerite had sent Marius on purpose, knowing his playful effect, she did feel a little easier than she had a moment ago. The auctioneer was now offering a woman who, she was relieved to see, was far less volatile than Caleb. While the two men escorted her as well, it wasn't a prison detail. They each supported one of her hands as she ascended the steps to the stage. When she drew near Kale, she shrugged with perfect grace out of the diaphanous silk blue robe she wore. The indrawn breaths were proper appreciation for a body that was pale cream, her well-proportioned and quite natural breasts tipped with pink nipples. She had no pubic hair, so her flushed and aroused clitoris was readily visible. She had a fall of ebony hair almost to her waist.

"She's the most delicate of hot fudge sundaes, Masters and Mistresses. Meant to be savored one creamy bite at a time. How would you like to be the one to redden these pretty buttocks with a spanking? Feel the wobble of that generous flesh beneath your hand. She's a level three pain threshold, but to use a whip on this one, rather than savoring the flesh-on-flesh contact, would be plain wrong. I know every man here is thinking what it would be like to slide into this already wet, needy pussy. Give Master Joseph in the front row a taste, Slave Number Two. He's already devoured you enough with his eyes to be three courses through dinner."

The resulting chuckles didn't dissipate the edgy sexual tension in the air. The young woman smoothed one delicate hand down her body, her palm sliding with a courtesan's seductive skill over her breast, then her abdomen. As she reached her goal, she adjusted her knees open wide. Chloe saw quite a few members of the audience lean forward as she dipped two fingers inside herself. Moving slow, deep, she worked them several times so her knuckles glistened. In the hushed silence, they could actually hear the sucking sound of a well-aroused woman, if the parting of her lips and her tiny gasp didn't give her away. But after those several strokes, she withdrew her hand. Moving to the edge of the stage on her hands and knees, she kept those two fingers lifted so they didn't come in contact with the stage floor. Any other time, Chloe would consider moving on one's hands and knees crawling, but this woman moved with the sinuous grace of a feminine cheetah, her hips swaying back and forth in a way that had even Kale and the two attendants distracted.

As she reached the edge of the stage, Master Joseph rose from a chair. Like Tyler, he was in a traditional tuxedo, looking urbane and self-possessed. With brown hair clipped short, he was a ruggedly handsome Latino forty-something. When he closed his hand on her wrist, she visibly trembled. Chloe heard the audience give a soft sigh, an ocean of passionate response, as he took her fingers in his mouth and sucked them gently.

"Beautiful," he murmured in a voice weighted with his Hispanic accent. He touched her hair. "I'll start at a thousand."

Chloe realized it was no insult. Apparently Caleb, as one of the more seasoned subs, and because of his almost limitless tolerance for any type of play, commanded a larger price. However, this woman's presentation had engaged the interest of more than Master Joseph, so he had to bid forty five hundred at the end to win her for his own.

Several more were auctioned after that. As each moved off the stage, he or she went to their knees, and their winning bidder came to them. The Master or Mistress was offered a selection of collars and leashes from a display board. The pain junkie had been the exception. Caleb had been hobbled above the knees, so he had to follow his handlers in a shuffle, his tether attached to the bridge of the nose plate of the scold harness. She assumed he was taken to the tent that had been discussed.

Slave Number Two, in contrast, was collared by Master Joseph with a braided silver ribbon choker, a thin sparkling chain attached. As he'd put it on her, his hands had caressed her throat, making Chloe swallow. The woman lifted her chin, keeping her eyes swept down. His palms had passed over the tips of her bare breasts, just a teasing contact. As the aroused woman swayed toward him, an involuntary movement, Chloe had felt her own nipples respond to the visual.

Chloe noted the age and sex of each subsequent slave varied, every one of them beautiful in some unique way. She was becoming intensely curious, despite herself, at those programs that were being liberally referenced by the potential bidders. From glimpses at those of her table mates, she saw Tyler and Marguerite had not spared expense. They'd been bound with a silk clad hardcover, and appeared to have an elastic silver book strap to mark pages and hold a silver pen for making notes.

"Miss Chloe, we thought you might enjoy your own program." Another waiter, as handsome as Marius, slid one onto her table, along with a chocolate truffle drizzled with raspberry sauce, presented on a crystal plate.

Chloe had only seen Marguerite glance toward her once, at the beginning of the event, to ensure she was happy with her seating and didn't want to join them up front, but she was beginning to think her boss was psychic. "Oh I can't bid."

"It's a keepsake," he assured her in a smooth voice. He gave her a smile that, despite being more reserved than Marius's, still suggested sweaty sheets and tropical breezes on bare skin.

She looked down at the stamped silver lettering on the cover, noting the name and date of the seventh annual carnival event. While she knew Brendan's picture and information would be in that book, she wasn't sure if she could handle seeing it yet, so she flipped through the book only up to the page of the slave about to be auctioned.

Marguerite and Tyler took the protection of their guests seriously, including those who agreed to be auctioned. While the photos provided were professional quality and erotic as hell, all slaves were shown with masked or averted faces.

Slave Number Twelve's mask was form fitting and black, allowing the potential bidder to see firm lips, a well-cut jaw. The rest of the man was completely nude, artistically posed so muscles gleamed and shadows only enhanced the rugged physique. His cock was erect, showing his potential to give pleasure. The text provided further coding on the types of bondage he embraced, pain levels, play preferences. Chloe skimmed the terms, some familiar some not, her fingers holding the edge delicately, as if he might reach across the page and brush her fingers, startling a jump out of her. A keepsake indeed.

According to the front program, eighteen were being auctioned tonight, twelve more tomorrow. Before she could decide whether she dared to turn the page, there was an expectant shifting as the latest slave was led off. It told her whoever was coming up next was as well-anticipated as Caleb had been.

As a result, she didn't know how to feel when she realized she didn't have to look in the book to seek Brendan. He was coming up on stage.

* * * * *

"This is the third year this slave has been on our docket, and there are three of you in the audience tonight who know he is worth every dollar that's offered for him."

"More."

That succinct, throaty one-word opinion came from the Amazon in red. Unlike the audience, Chloe didn't feel like laughing at all.

"Truly versatile," Kale continued, with a nod in Regina's direction. "Slave Number Thirteen can be as hardcore as you wish, with a top level ten pain threshold. But he is equally ready to be your gentle poet, your romantic fantasy. He is whatever you want him to be, ladies and gentlemen. His heart's desire is to please the Master or Mistress who demands his submission. Please note, this year his services are offered for only this night, a limited engagement. Bid accordingly for this rare experience."

Chloe did turn the page, her fingers resting on the main photograph, but she hadn't looked at it yet. Couldn't tear her eyes away from the stage, for a couple reasons.

The first was his sheer magnificence, for lack of a better word. He was handsome, she already knew that, knew she

137

was probably half in love with him, or at least in love with the things he'd done and been for her these past few days. She knew enough about love to know a person fell in love based on deeds first, with the soul deep connection, the one capable of saving or destroying her, coming later. However, with the strength of her reaction to him, she wondered if it was possible to have it all happen at once, a trembling skein of interwoven strands of color.

She understood immediately what it was about him that had made him so popular for the past three years. He had an aura that would have drawn the attention of any sultana or princess in a bazaar centuries ago. Or a prince, because she was all too aware he was getting as much male attention, particularly from the two men at her right. Such a prince or princess would have offered a small fortune to purchase him, because that aura said clearly, *I am yours, if you'll have me. I'll serve you with everything I am.*

When he came onto the stage, she was dimly conscious that he offered brief bow to Marguerite's table. But Chloe's attention was riveted on him. Every muscle gleamed, not the overly oiled look that suggested greasy fingers. It was the shine of perfect lighting along a statue's muscles, the fine arch of a foot, length of calf, etched shoulder and pectoral, the corded throat.

He was not entirely naked, though provocatively close. A kilt of chain mail fell to mid thigh. The mail gleamed with dull gray and sparkling silver metal links. A belt held it low on his hips, so low the diagonal line of muscle that led to the groin was visible, making a woman think of placing her hand on that muscle, following it with teasing fingertips…

The weight of the chain mail would conceal his erection, she realized, and the knowledge of that was as tempting as seeing it revealed. She lingered on the belt, noting how blatantly sexual a man's belt could be. Designed to draw the eye just above where the cock and balls were, there was a less-than-subtle implication of sex. The tongue was run through a buckle, tied over and pulled through to drape alongside the groin area.

With hungry eyes, she climbed his flat abdomen to the expanse of shoulders and strong arms, the column of throat. His hair was loose, nearly brushing his shoulders. The attitude and posture of his body conveyed absolute focus in this moment, but when she reached his eyes, she realized that focus had one single target.

It was the second reason she couldn't tear her gaze away to look at the program. Those beautiful eyes, so intent beneath the silken brows, were alive and full of desire, need, and pure male intent. The most determined force on earth, one that had carried man through fire, flood, ice age, Biblical retribution and into the modern age. And that intent was zeroed solidly, solely, on her.

As if he knew the moment she recognized it, he took another step forward on the stage.

She was vaguely aware they'd started the bidding, but she heard Kale's sensual chuckle, a pause in the action. "It appears our slave has made his choice. You might have to work extra hard to hold his attention, ladies and gentlemen..."

Brendan didn't acknowledge the comment, merely kept looking at her. She couldn't really describe what was in his expression, any more than she could describe what welled forth in her now and made her stand up. Or raise her program and call out, though her voice cracked with nerves.

"One thousand, two hundred and eighty-nine dollars. And eighty three cents."

Though the crowd had been attentive and quiet during the bidding, there was now an abrupt stillness. Every head turned toward her, making her feel like a child caught licking the butter knife at an adult banquet. Brendan's gaze, however, didn't waver. Something coursed through it, an expression she still would be hard pressed to describe, but one which spread warmth through her like the certainty of Heaven and proof of true love, all rolled into one. Even if she had just made an ass of herself, she refused to regret it.

At least that's what she told herself, as the auctioneer's commanding voice drew her attention away from her folly and presumption. She didn't dare look at Marguerite and Tyler.

"Slave Number Thirteen's ability to mesmerize an audience never fails to amaze. Miss, you may not have heard the previous bids, but the current bid on the floor is at fourteen thousand. That's five digits. One comma, no periods." There were some chuckles, and Chloe's cheeks burned. "Did you wish to raise your bid to match that, perhaps?" Despite his humor, Kale's tone was cordial, not unkind. There was that same knowing Master's look in his direct gaze that she'd seen in Tyler's, such that she couldn't seem to stop her next words.

"No...I... That's all I have in savings. I—" She couldn't bring herself to withdraw the bid, so she sat back down, shaking her head.

"Very well, then," the auctioneer said after a moment. "Then we shall continue. Master Tyler, you wish to bid?"

"No." Tyler's voice held amusement, perhaps at the unlikelihood of him bidding on a male slave, or perhaps at Chloe's pathetic bid. She couldn't look at his face to see which, but at least he didn't sound mad. "Before the bidding continues, I invite you all to raise a glass to a bidder who offered all the money she has to secure a slave. While we may all understand the feeling, rarely do we act on such overwhelming desire. Here, here, to the lovely lady in the back."

Chloe lifted her head at the chime of glasses being raised and struck with utensils. She found she barely had the courage to meet Tyler's vibrant amber gaze over the lawn, but she managed it. As well as a nod. She wasn't sure if she was supposed to stand to acknowledge the compliment, but figured remaining motionless was her best option. Her only option, because the next bid was called out.

"Minus two thousand."

Kale peered over the crowd, focusing on the table next to Chloe with the two men. "Pardon me, Master Neil?"

Master Neil rose, all sensual male and perfect fashion sense. Chloe thought he could have graced the cover of a Regency romance. "I said negative two thousand. Those of you who have attended proper schools might surmise that adding fourteen thousand to negative two thousand brings the bid to twelve thousand. However, please note, with respect to tonight's cause, I will honor my original bid to the shelter. On the positive side of the balance sheet."

Tyler raised his glass to Neil, gave him a nod. The Amazon lifted her program then. "Indeed, Neil. I raise your bid, under the same terms. Negative twenty five hundred."

The auctioneer's brow lifted and he glanced at Tyler, who simply offered a slow smile and sat back down.

Chloe realized both bidders must have put in bids on Brendan in the amounts they'd just offered, only on the plus side of the balance sheet. Now it was picked up across the room by the others. Her hands closed into balls as she heard the callouts. "Minus three thousand. Minus fifteen hundred."

Another wave of the utensil-to-glass applause. When she lifted her gaze again, she sucked in a breath. Brendan's eyes were still on her, only now there was such an intensity to his face that it made him seem like a warrior in truth. Or a poet, as Kale had suggested, a Druid priest, a young, beautiful god, hungering to be at her side. These people were crazy. She'd be bidding upward, completely ignoring her shoddy little offering. He was worth so much more...

"Mistress Lyda?"

The auctioneer's attention had turned. Chloe realized he was looking toward the final bidder, the one who'd pushed it to fourteen thousand with a hefty five thousand raise. She didn't look the type to be moved by sentiment or Chloe's gesture. She looked like the type of woman who would use

Brendan hard and leave him with a smile on his lips. Long red hair with dyed silver streaks, milk white skin, lots of it available for view with her lush breasts nearly spilling out of a white corset. Matching creamy latex pants topped by laced thigh high boots. Diamonds sparkled at her throat like ice, and she had silver eyes, obviously contacts to match her platinum hair. It was an ensemble that made even Chloe's loins stir to look at her.

She wouldn't give him up. Chloe wouldn't blame her at all. If Brendan was what he said he was, how could she possibly compete with what this woman could offer him, anyway? The Mistress had picked up her wine glass, taken a delicate swallow then put her finger in to slowly swirl it before tasting it on her fingertip. She had everyone's attention, but it was Brendan who drew Chloe's eyes from her.

He had turned toward the Mistress, at last breaking his focus on Chloe. He met the woman's eyes briefly, then he dropped to one knee, bowing his head. The movement hiked the kilt up on his thigh, revealing the line to his buttocks, shadows gathering and suggesting the heavy curve of smooth testicles. His biceps tightened as he placed a hand on his thigh, held the position.

It was clearly a petition for her mercy.

"Minus thirty-seven hundred," she said clearly, in a voice that was a cross between smoke and a kitten's purr. "I believe that brings my bid to thirteen hundred. But I think I could be persuaded to enter another minus twenty. If this particular slave put his lips to my boot heel, showing his gratitude for my generous spirit."

Chloe didn't really want that paragon of Domme perfection anywhere near Brendan's mouth, boot heel or anything else. She dug into her small purse, fumbled it so she dropped the change with a resounding clatter on the glass table, but she was already shooting to her feet, doing a quick calculation. "I have thirty-three more dollars."

The woman shifted her glance to Chloe. Chloe met her look head on, the money clutched in her fist.

Slowly, the woman's lips curved. She looked toward Kale, gave a slight head shake.

"The slave is sold to the bidder in the back for one thousand three hundred and twenty-two dollars. And eighty-three cents."

The musical discord of glasses and utensils started up again as Chloe let out her breath, feeling her cheeks flush at the nods of those closest to her.

"Congratulations," the Regency romance hero said, giving her a smile tinged with regret. "Go collect your prize."

Chapter Ten

Chloe was conscious of eyes on her as she skirted the tables to go to the side of the stage, but thankfully, they started bidding on the next offering, a pair of male slaves, twin brothers, who came out with awesome endowments that might have made her jaw drop if she hadn't been absorbed by her own purchase.

There was an attendant waiting, a slim female Domme who'd volunteered to handle this part of the auction coordination. She wore a dark vest, tailored slacks and sensible heels, her long and dark hair pulled into a neat braid. Brendan had come down to the side of the stage where she'd apparently had him take a knee, for he waited, his head bowed, the silken hair shading his face, emphasizing the jaw line. She liked seeing his face, his eyes, the reassurance they offered her, but she assumed this must be some kind of etiquette.

The woman nodded to her. "Master Tyler has indicated he will secure your payment, since you are staying as his personal guest. Would you like to pick out the collar for your slave? You may also choose a leash if you wish. They are available for loan or purchase."

She gestured to a board behind her, outlined in tiny blue lights, the selection against a backboard of green velvet draping. Chloe saw everything from a standard thick leather studded dog collar — wryly, she wondered if it was considered a "classic" by the BDSM crowd — to what she was alarmingly sure was a choker of real diamonds, since there was a certificate of authenticity from the diamond company attached to it. There were collars obviously meant for other parts of the anatomy, even though some were cruelly spiked or — she swallowed—set with electrodes. When she saw several plain neck collars, she imagined buckling them around Brendan's neck, making her claim of ownership in a way that, up until now, had been a foreign concept to her.

She'd let intuition guide her to make the bid, not thought. Since she was already treading, it was a little too late to think about how deep the water was, or how far she might be from shore already. She took the satin blue ribbon she'd tied around her head to keep her front curls back from her face. "I'd like to use this instead," she said. "If that's okay."

"Your Mistress gifts you with a symbol of ownership from her own wardrobe. You are most fortunate." The woman nodded and withdrew, her attention on the two men now coming down the steps, their large cocks moving in a most distracting way. Chloe cleared her throat, cheeks flaming again when she could tell from the flicker of Brendan's lashes he'd noticed her looking.

"Not thinking of trading up already, are you?" he murmured.

At the sound of his voice, the familiar dry humor, some of the anxiety loosened in her belly. "I guess I'll settle for you. I'm tapped out of funds, you know." But despite their banter, when she threaded the ribbon around his right biceps, tying it there like a knight's favor, she noted the quiver in the firm muscle. She remembered how the audience had responded when Slave Number Two had trembled under a Master's touch. While she hadn't entirely understood why they'd considered that shudder a gift to them all, a part of her had. Her own hand wasn't steady. She knew why she was rattled. What bemused her was him. He'd obviously done this before, with women far more demanding than her, she was sure. So why would he tremble, if not at her touch?

"Look at me," she whispered.

He obeyed instantly, so instantly it reminded her he was hers to command for the next twelve or so hours. Literally. This wasn't some play auction like "Win a Date for Charity", where'd they go to dinner, make small talk. Within the bounds of that brochure, he would be and do whatever she wanted. *Holy God*. And she didn't have to feel guilty, because it was what he wanted and craved. The unknown variable wasn't him. It was her.

Her fingers were twined in the ribbon, pressed against hard flesh. "I want to go somewhere to be alone with you. How about the gardens?"

No. She corrected herself. "I want to go to the gardens." She'd been adventurous once, sexually and in myriad other ways. She was safe here, so she'd try it out, see the way it felt to be in control. Though as he rose, his greater height taking him above her, the way his eyes held her, she thought it might not be as simple as all that. His desire was an overwhelming force of its own. In fact, there was a plausible argument that, with that intense stare over the audience, he'd chosen *her*.

"Yes, Mistress," he said. She knew she could tell him to call her Chloe, but it was a peculiar feeling, the way he was waiting on her to make that determination.

"I like you looking at my face," she said as she drew them away from the group. "I'd prefer that, instead of you looking down like some of the other...others." She still had her fingers coiled in the ribbon, worrying the silk as well as rubbing him with her knuckles. She hadn't seen him in three days, but it felt so much longer. If she thought about it too much, she might let it overwhelm her.

"I like looking at your face too." His voice was low, as if he felt the weight of the physical and emotional need bottled between them. He covered her hand on his biceps with his other one, steadying her as they walked over uneven ground. "You look incredible," he said. "The sexiest woman here."

"Yeah, right." But when she met his gaze briefly, she almost believed he meant it. "You look pretty mouthwatering yourself."

He measured his pace to hers and she leaned into him, her hip brushing his, cotton against mail, feeling the shape and sense of his leg sliding against her thigh.

Tyler had a small forest of fruit and crepe myrtle trees. The fruit trees had a few unexpected fall blooms amid the green leaves. Their branches and those of the mature crepe myrtles framed winding brick paths that meandered through statuary, fountains and quiet pools, private nooks for reading or napping, or stolen moments, like this. If she had a choice of what Heaven could look like, she wanted it to look like Tyler's gardens. He'd expanded it since he and Marguerite had married. There were times she believed Tyler pulled off his green thumb miracles in the salt-laden Florida climate all to create a Paradise on earth for his wife. Probably to make up for the dark shadows of hell that her early life had been, a life Chloe had seen first hand.

She pushed that away. *Not going there tonight.* Not here, not now. They'd made it ten steps into the tree area when she turned into Brendan. Before he could touch her, she'd caught both of his hands. Holding his gaze, she backed him up, one step, two steps, moving under a citrus tree. The green leaves closed in a curtain behind them, several of those late blossoms caught in his hair.

When she had him against the trunk, she guided his hands upward. Though she couldn't reach to the full length of his arms, her intentions were clear. Watching her the whole time, he curled his hands around the branch above him, leaving his body stretched and open to whatever she wanted to do to it. Her imagination caught fire and the desire rippled through her, almost paralyzing her at all she wanted to do.

He was taller, much stronger, and yet she held him with a word, a gesture. Because she'd given him permission to look her in the eye, all that combustible desire was like a dangerous current rising between them, making her wonder how hard she could push before it would arc and snap, and he'd take them both over. How far did his control go? Would he beg? Did she want him to?

She put her hands on his chest. When she'd finally dared a glance at his program page, it said he'd take pain, pleasure, it didn't matter. His drug of choice was a Mistress's desire. She dug her nails in and his gaze darkened.

"Chloe—Mistress," he corrected himself.

She kept digging, but moved her touch down, scoring red lines in his skin. Over the washboard abdomen, down to the belted mail tunic. She dropped one hand lower, came up under it, finding bare thigh. She hesitated, then a boldness gripped her, validated by the atmosphere, by the driving need inside her that had been growing for three days. She moved her stroking touch to the cock and balls he'd displayed so temptingly when he'd knelt toward that other Mistress. Heat and steel, the kiss of moisture at the tip. He groaned as she found he was quite aroused, just as she'd expected. He'd teased them with the weight of that mail, kept it hidden from view.

"Turn around," she whispered. When he did, she indulged in cupping her hands over his ass under the tunic, watching the movement of the mail over the shape of her hands. She wondered abruptly what it was like to create welts on a man's broad back, his flexing buttocks, make him arch from the pain like they had Caleb.

Was the power she was feeling akin to violence? It wasn't a violence she'd ever experienced before. This was hot and molten. She wanted to touch, bite, mark. She was dangerously out of control and she didn't care. He was hers. All hers. She'd given everything for him. She recalled the brochure. *Will do anything to serve…*

"Will you…" She stopped. "Get on your knees."

As he went down, his gaze was down, probably watching where he was placing his knees. She saw the passion in his eyes, though, the building lust and something else, an emotional storm building with every order she issued. Was he responding to her specifically, or any Mistress who could press the right keys? She didn't care to tarry in those waters right now. It didn't matter. With that penetrating look from the stage, he'd chosen her tonight. Impatience with her own insecurities flooded her, and a little bit of anger. Tonight, she wasn't tolerating anything but what she wanted, making apologies for none of it. Damn all of them, though she wasn't sure who "them" was.

She had no plan, no idea what she was doing, or even why she was doing it. Maybe it was like deciding to jump out of an airplane or parasail while on vacation in the Caribbean. Visiting a new place, where the chance existed to be a stranger to oneself, made it possible to explore and discover something entirely new.

When the vacationer finally came back, the adventure would be an amputated part put in a photo album, the memory like the occasional ache of the missing limb. Because that amputation was inevitable, a certain wild abandon to the adventure was acceptable. The thought gave her courage. That, and hazel eyes fixed on her face, watching her every move, demanding touch. Or permission to touch.

She cleared her throat. Tried a crazy, wild demand. "Kiss my feet."

He bent with such lithe male grace, bracing his knuckles on the outside of her bare feet. His hair fell forward, head turning as his lips brushed her instep, taking a teasing taste of the arch. Her body's response shot straight to the wetness between her legs. And he took his blessed time on that one foot, nipping, suckling. She'd never realized her foot was such an incredibly erotic zone. She wanted him to stay there for hours. Sinking down on the decorative bench Tyler had wisely placed beneath the tree's shelter, she put her palm flat between his shoulder blades. It allowed her to touch him, to feel his heat and heartbeat, and also told him he was exactly where she wanted him to stay. Sliding her other foot up, she put her sole on his lower back, her toe tracing the belt, then the curve of his spine, sliding the drape of her skirt over his back.

Oh God. He hadn't moved above her ankle, but he didn't need to do so to get her writhing. He moved from the fragile bones of the ankle, teasing the anklet, down toward the toes again. Licking each one, he traced the lines between them, tickling the skin beneath the toe rings, then moved to the ball of the foot, caressing her with a brief touch of fingers before he continued.

Chloe let her other hand drift up his back, to his nape, then over his hair as she leaned back against the bench. Sliding her fingers down her body, she navigated under the skirt and found her pussy. Already stimulated by the evening's entertainment, she found her folds wet and needy. At the very first touch, she sucked in a breath, worrying her bottom lip as her fingers teased her own clit, the sensation now going between his mouth and her hand.

He brushed her ankle, his gaze flickering up so she saw burning hazel beneath the thick lashes. "Let me do that, Mistress. Let me put my head beneath your skirt and eat your pussy as long as you wish. Give me the gift of your sweet honey on my tongue, grinding yourself against my face."

She spasmed, imagining him there. She was taken back to that first night, the phone call, his subtle ways of directing her into commanding him, taking control and giving her back power amid her fear of the dark. But something different was stirring in her now. She was used to being a generous lover. Though she knew how good he would feel, his mouth there, she wasn't ready for that now, didn't want that now. Cruel pleasure was what laced the air, and she was infected with it. "No. I want to make myself come while you stay at my feet."

He grazed his temple against her ankle, an acknowledgment, and then he proceeded to prove what she was denying herself. Every sensitive curve and crevice of her feet was nibbled and teased. He stroked her with a tongue that, by the time she was rocking on the bench, her other hand braced on the concrete surface, was as responsible for her near climactic state as her own fingers. Her wrist trembled, starting to ache.

Though he continued to obey her, his mouth on her feet, suddenly his strong hand was there, closing over her wrist. Not to take control or guide her, but wrapping around the slim bone to steady it. His thumb teased her pulse. How had he known?

"Oh God." That was it, all it took. Her fingers jerked over her clit as his thumb stroked that innocuous place. He bit down on her instep at the exact right moment. She used his hold on her wrist as a counterpoint to her fast pumping against her hand. The convulsive jerking was as hard and intense as any orgasm she'd experienced, and yet she ached to be filled. Her hand wasn't him, his hard cock sliding inside her, but she couldn't bring herself to demand it when the world was fragmenting into twenty galaxies, and she was worried her cries were reaching the other guests. But it didn't matter, because she knew this weekend Tyler's garden would become an outdoor place of pleasure, filled with moans, breathless sighs, sounds of need and hunger like a forest of nocturnal animals on a mating hunt.

As she slowed down at last, his fingers loosened, even as her own fingertips found his head, stroked his hair, trembling, wanting to grip. He raised his head then, eyes full of such irresistible desire for something she felt she alone could give him.

"May I clean you with my mouth, Mistress? I'll be very gentle."

"Oh God, Brendan." She breathed it, but then reached for him with both hands, using his body to help shift her own as she lay down on the bench to gaze up at a million stars in the night sky. "Yes," she whispered.

Her hands slid reluctantly off his shoulders to fall above her head, a fairy princess lying among the summer tree spirits. She realized she was right, that the gardens were punctuated by sounds of other guests taking pleasure with one another. Like her, they must have felt the need for a short tryst to release some pressure on their explosive desires before proceeding to the other carnival activities. It was a night literally filled with the sounds of passion, reminiscent of her own such that when he folded her skirt over his shoulders, and his breath touched her, she gave a new, soft cry, her own contribution.

Slowly, so slowly, his mouth descended, touching her labia in an almost reverent, chaste kiss. It made tears come to her eyes, her fingers curl into balls of need. One slow, dragging lick, then another, taking away her fluids, leaving only the dampness of his tongue, his sweet lips. She knew she would shudder from the memory of his mouth ever after, and if she found herself in her bed alone her fingers would become that mouth once more. She wanted to be sated, to go over again with hard, wild abandon. But she wanted to be in charge. Needed to be, even though the thought gave the desire still simmering in her lower belly a hard twist.

It made her put a hand on his head, stilling him. When she folded her legs and turned to sit up, he helped her, moving his body back from where it had been between her knees. She felt that loss, but concentrated on something else. She remembered one of the booths she'd helped set up, remembered what she'd seen there. The auction was over, the carnival goers spreading out to those areas as well as in these gardens. Did she dare do what she wanted? If she couldn't here, where the hell could she? But it was one thing to do it in the quiet of this garden, a whole other to be public with her inexperienced game of control.

Rising, she trailed a hand along his shoulder, keeping him on his knees. She was barely five feet, and he was tall, so his head reached her throat, his eyes close as he tilted his head attentively to her. His mouth was moist from his cleaning, and she caught the scent of her climax. It made her heart trip. "Do all the things you wrote in your program apply to me?"

His hair curtained one side of his face except for the flashing gold-green eye. The thick heat of his voice reminded her she'd never pushed a guy up to this level, where his cock was probably so hard he could barely walk. She'd always felt his release was her obligation. But this environment said it was okay, right? She could keep pushing. She'd read all about safe words and such. Brendan could tell her no if she pushed too hard.

"It does. And then some." Leaning forward, he pressed a kiss to her thigh through the thin fabric of her skirt. "Whatever you want. It's yours."

She took a step back from that touch which cracked open the Pandora's box of emotions swirling through her. "All right then. Follow me."

She hadn't realized how she'd internalized so much of what she'd seen so far, such that for one moment she toyed with having him leave the kilt, stride naked like some she'd already seen here. It tightened in her gut, even as she wasn't sure she wanted so many ogling the gifts Brendan had to offer. In the end, she let it remain in her mind only, a particularly twisted fantasy. Turning on her heel, she moved away, not offering to walk with him this time.

Remarkably, he fell in several steps behind her, as if she had him on a tether in truth. As they emerged from the gardens, headed for the tents and rides of the carnival area, she began to see the guests in their varied groupings. Slaves manacled at the ankles or wrists, tethered at the throat, a heady environment of those willingly being subjugated to whatever dark pleasures the Masters or Mistresses here desired.

She realized she could stroll through the sights without hurry, or concern that he was behind her, though she did glance back several times to confirm it, and for her own pleasure. He didn't look at all the distractions around him. His entire focus was on her, his eyes watching her feet, occasionally sweeping over the rest of her, attuned to where she was going, prepared for whatever she might say or need. He was her devoted slave in truth, and the power of it thrilled, frightened and dug into her with angry, needy claws.

Seeking a way of centering herself, she turned to her surroundings as she wandered through the offerings. There was a shooting gallery, where the ducks were submissives who'd been lined up with protective blindfolds, their hands chained over their heads. The guns were loaded with pellet rounds that stung, but did no real injury. Another submissive knelt below the firing line in front of each "target", suckling at cocks or tonguing the wet pussies, so that the bound submissive was hard put to stay still while the Masters or Mistresses were firing. Prizes, amusingly, were the same types she'd see at any fair. Kaleidoscopes, cheap necklaces, and colorful stuffed animals of all sizes, like the teddy bears she'd helped Marcia set out.

Cirque du Soleil styled players wandered the grounds in provocative costumes, performing tumbling feats, juggling, eating fire and blowing it out in dramatic plumes. Athletic dancers, with long ribbons twining around their otherwise naked bodies, entertained small groups of passersby. Chloe reflected a person could sit down somewhere and be dazzled for hours by everything they were seeing.

Another booth had eating contests, where food was of course being devoured off the bodies of submissives stretched out and chained on the boards. An apparently famous erotic food expert, Chef Rayne Davidson, used volunteers to decorate submissives in artistic food renderings for display at Master and Mistress social gatherings. Next to that area were advanced demonstrations of whip use. Chloe flinched at the pop of the single tail along a woman's nipple. Her dress was pulled down to her waist, and she realized it was the woman in the white sheath. The male in the tux was doing the whipping while the football player was watching, already quite visibly aroused. It made Chloe realize they were both Doms, and the woman was their shared submissive. The strike made her cry out, though her chest was already flushed with post-climactic bliss, and her eyes lingered hungrily on her two Masters.

Her breath even shorter, steps a little more unsteady, such that she felt Brendan's heat pressing closer behind her, she turned her attention elsewhere. Vendors sold food and drink, the offerings expected at a carnival. Pink and purple cotton candy, popcorn, funnel cakes, the smell of them filling the air. Masters and Mistresses offered such treats from their hands, not allowing their slaves to feed themselves. She saw a Master who had scattered popcorn across the ground. Using a quirt, he was guiding his male slave to eat each piece he indicated.

The slave seemed subdued, though there was some of Caleb to him, in the way he watched his Master like a dangerous dog would, waiting for his chance. At least that was what Chloe thought, but then he lifted his head, holding several pieces between his lips. The Master gestured to a female slave, apparently another he'd bought or brought with him. She moved forward, unashamedly naked, and knelt before the male. Going to her hands and knees, her back arched so her buttocks were high and breasts thrust in a tempting display, she stretched out toward the male submissive, like a poodle before a hulking mastiff. Chloe held her breath as she delicately took the popcorn from his lips. The Master's hand fell on his slave's nape, caressing the thick collar he wore.

"I don't really get the ones who want that," she said.

Brendan was close enough his thigh brushed the back of hers. When she curled her fingers, she touched the hem of the chain mail.

"The hardcore pain and humiliation?"

"And being treated…I want to say like an animal, but you shouldn't treat an animal like that, either."

"Like a slave." His breath teased her ear, made her shiver.

She lifted a shoulder, didn't look at him yet, though she wasn't sure why. "I guess so. A lot of them here are called slaves, but they're treated differently. There was one guy who was letting his 'slave' sit on his coat on the grass, even though it was probably a pretty expensive coat."

He nodded. "Masters and Mistresses can be vastly different, just as submissives are. They're all unique."

"You understand it," she realized, looking up at his face. "You understand why Caleb, or this guy, gets off on the extreme stuff."

Before Brendan could reply, a sharp crack rent the air. Snapping her attention back, she found that the male sub had incurred a punishment. His Master had his booted foot on the slave's neck, forcing his face to the ground, his ass high in the air. The crack came again, from a paddle hitting the man's buttocks hard enough it drove him forward. The first strike was already welling up like the brand of an iron.

Brendan's hand had closed on her arm, making her realize she'd started to move forward. "Does he... Are you sure?"

"I'm sure. Don't worry. I'll try to explain it, though sometimes explanations don't help."

She wasn't sure she could handle watching more of the violence in that demonstration area, so she turned her back to it to face him. She much preferred Brendan's handsome face. "What do you mean?"

Intuitively, he drew her away from the area. It loosened her shoulders a bit, but his words didn't give her much ease.

"If it's entirely foreign to someone, no frame of reference, inside or out, then he or she can hear the explanation, but it doesn't change their thinking on it."

A hard world to understand to those not in it... She uncomfortably recalled Marguerite's words. "It still gives them a different perspective."

"To be given something, you have to take it, or accept it. If you reject it, then it served no purpose."

"Do you think I'm that closed-minded?"

"No." Chagrin crossed his expression at the coldness she couldn't keep out of her tone. "I didn't mean it that way. It's not a matter of being closed-minded or intolerant. There are plenty of people who live and let live, as long as what their neighbor is doing is consensual and no one's being hurt, technically. But they still have no clue why their neighbor does the things he does."

The look in his eyes made her uneasy. Fortunately, she'd reached her intended destination, a welcome distraction.

The innocuous building materials, ones she'd seen brought in straight from the area hardware store, had been arranged for an erotic purpose she couldn't have imagined. Three male slaves had already been bound, their arms restrained to the horizontal bar, their feet spread and manacled to the platform, which was set with spaced cuffs for that purpose. As she and Brendan approached, she saw Master Luke and Caleb were there.

Master Luke had an enormous dildo in hand, one that had been liberally lubricated by a guest attendant. The slave was still wearing a cock harness, and the straps had been tightened such that those hooks in the rear area bit with cruel barbs, spreading his buttocks wide, revealing the glistening anus that had obviously also been well lubed. Caleb snarled against the scold harness, his impressive muscles bunched, but as intimidating as he was physically, there was something even more terrifying in the calm of Master Luke. An aura of pure psychological dominance emanated from him. He set the head of that monstrous phallus to the slave's anus with strong and capable fingers, and began to ease it inward. Putting his hand on the man's shoulder, he gripped the juncture at the neck.

"Better stop your growling, Caleb, and breathe. Push out, or this will hurt more than you'd like. I won't be taking it out until you come, you know. And that's going to be a very, very long time."

Amazingly, she saw the man respond, not to the meaning of the words, but the tone, the touch, both containing a hint of...gentleness. Caleb obeyed it. "They fit," she wondered. "It doesn't make sense."

"It's like that, a lot of times," Brendan agreed. Her shoulder blade brushed his bare chest when she took a steadying breath, reached back and let herself cup his jaw, finger his hair. "Some submissives need a particular type of act or device, or regimen, if you will. A few just need to find the right Dom, and then nothing else is that important, because they're wired into one another. What one wants, the other can give, and it's a two-way street, no real planning or thought to it."

Chloe was conscious of being watched. Other Mistresses and Masters, watching the dynamic between her and Brendan. Was it her imagination or did she see a trace of pity in the eyes of the Amazon, as if she already knew that whatever she thought she could give Brendan, it wouldn't be enough?

"Does that happen often?" she asked, struggling to push it away, telling herself her insecurities were playing with her imagination.

"It's rare," Brendan said. An upward glance showed his focus was on Master Luke, watching how he held Caleb still with a mere word, calming him with a touch. "You can find that, or something close to it, when you work with a Master or Mistress regularly, but what you're seeing is a Master/sub's version of falling in love at first sight. Doesn't mean the working-at-it kind of love isn't as deep and special in time. Sometimes you have to get some other baggage out of the way, or the timing isn't right."

"Sounds like most relationships."

"Yeah. Doesn't matter the way it looks, it's always pretty much the same struggle. Or pleasure." He slanted a smile down at her.

His fingertips grazed her waist. She could feel how much he wanted to simply take her somewhere else, maybe back to the garden. Sink down on the grass and slide into her, hold her, cherish her, give her the climax she wanted in the way she desperately wanted it. He was so good at that, at knowing exactly what she really desired. Wanting to give her that, above and beyond everything else. *Give Mistress what she desires…*

Yet his gaze kept straying back to that tableau in front of them.

She saw the others here. Their subs stayed a respectful distance, didn't touch without permission, while he was pressed up close to her now. The way the Doms looked toward her, she was sure it was clear she didn't belong here. Or belong with him. She wasn't a Mistress, but he knew this world, was taking advantage of her inexperience to try to manipulate her back to a sheltered, isolated place away from them. Where she wouldn't be an embarrassment.

She knew that was her baggage rearing its ugly head, not a true reflection of his motives. But she still had something to prove to herself, and to him. It all seemed clear here, like the act of a brightly lit play, so bright that no other scenario seemed possible.

"Mistress, my name is Niall. Would you like us to bind your slave?" A helpful male attendant was standing before her. She met his eyes briefly before he lowered his with a courteous nod. There was a faint Scottish burr in his voice, and his impressive upper body had a variety of vibrant, mesmerizing tattoos of fighting dragons. While a submissive, she sensed he might have some switch capacity when needed. From his firm, reassuring manner she expected he would also provide non-patronizing guidance if asked.

"Yes," she said, though her throat was dry. Should she ask Brendan? But in the garden, he'd said anything. In the program, he'd stated he was willing to give any Mistress that much of himself. Why not her? She tightened her jaw, and her resolve.

"Do you want the full punishment set? That would include full headmask, ball gag, cock harness and hooks."

"N-no." Though a vicious part of her was appallingly tempted, that part of her was starting to scare her a bit, because she was acutely aware of the fact she wasn't looking at Brendan. Part of it was she didn't want to lose her nerve, but on another level it was like Brendan was becoming an object to her. "Um... Other options?"

Niall cocked his head, and she noted he didn't have any problems looking behind her at the object of her intense avoidance. With lingering appraisal. She shifted in front of Brendan. While both men were taller, the intent was unmistakable. *Mine.*

Niall's brow lifted, his lips quirking slightly, though Chloe couldn't tell if it was approval or simple amusement at her naivety. "If my lady is seeking some relief, and with this slave, that's perfectly understandable, then we can bind his hands and feet on the scaffold. We will provide you a strap-on with a dual head or just a clitoral stimulator. You can penetrate him to your heart's content, have your own climax and allow him nowhere near the treasure between your legs. He'll have to smell your arousal and hunger for it until you grant him release. A cock harness can be provided if you want to make sure he doesn't lose control."

When he nodded toward the platform, she saw there was a Mistress already there, doing just that. It was an older woman with striking long silver locks tied back in a barrette. She had a strap-on affixed over the tight bodysuit she'd donned and wore very well. As she thrust inside the man in front of her, also silver haired and handsome, he was flushed with the effort of holding back his own climax, his cock sheathed in a condom and locked in a harness. His fingers clenched in his bindings.

While that woman had chosen the clitoral stimulator alone for her own pleasure, Chloe hungered so much for something to fill her inside, for Brendan to fill her, she liked the sound of the dual headed dildo better. Not giving herself time to think, she gave a nod. Another male attendant stepped forward and gestured to Brendan to follow him. Chloe couldn't help but notice the tension in Brendan's shoulders, and the sidelong glance he gave her out of those hazel eyes as he was led away.

She was darkly thrilled by it.

Chapter Eleven

ഇ

There was a place for her to change out of her dress and into a body suit. The one she was provided had an overlapping panel in the crotch to allow her to insert the phallus of the dual headed dildo. The dildo also came with a clit stimulator that fit snugly beneath a rubber guard that contoured over her crotch area, maintaining her modesty. As she eased in the naturally sized, lubricated dildo, she gasped at the sensation. Her fingers were fumbling so badly, she couldn't quite figure out how to tighten the straps. Eventually she did, though she almost called for the help of the female attendant.

When she took her first steps to move out of the changing area, a wave of amazing sensations swamped her. They weren't all physical, though having the slight movements of that dildo inside her was enough to make her steady herself on the support frame of the changing stall, take a calming breath. The tiny rubber feet of the clitoral stimulator made her want to put her hand down there, press, but she managed to quell the urge. She expected the power of her own arousal would be necessary to numb her self-consciousness, help her mount that platform in front of the casual audience that kept moving past it.

It wasn't as though she'd never engaged in low-level exhibitionism. She'd never considered herself traditional vanilla. However, after the things she'd seen tonight, she realized she'd stayed closer to that safe pasture than she'd realized. She'd always considered herself open sexually, not really limited by labels and preferences. Until recently, she'd embraced life the same way, indulging in all forms of happiness and pleasure like a wood sprite. Tonight, though, she was exploring some rooms she hadn't known she had. Maybe she did understand this better than she realized, because those needs and cravings were coiling through her now, exploring the terrain of her psyche unfettered.

She stepped around the corner, and those needs ramped up about a hundred degrees. Brendan had been stripped out of the kilt so he was naked, body gleaming in the light of tiki torches and carnival lights. For a moment, she regretted intensely not hanging around to watch him be stripped and bound, because the submissive wasn't allowed to do that for himself. Niall and his attendant would have done it, hands lingering over the aroused body, getting him even more worked up for his Mistress's touch. He was oiled up, his buttocks glistening with the liberal application of the lubricant. She was starting to understand how this worked. The more tormented the sub was, the better the Master and Mistress, and the sub himself, seemed to like it.

His arms were pulled overhead, so the muscles in his back, thighs and buttocks were displayed like artwork. Feet spread, manacled down, so she saw the testicle sac, the erect cock curving out and up in front of his body in a way that was inviting comments from a far more sizeable audience than she'd expected. Well, voyeurism was a major part of this event, and, having nabbed one of the choicest pieces of meat, she and what she was doing to him were now at center stage.

Still, it gave her pause. Niall had told her a thin curtain could be drawn around every pairing if privacy was preferred. The audience would still get a show, artful lighting providing a detailed silhouette. She thought about it, realizing she should be appalled to be thinking of Brendan as a piece of meat. But the desire to take him like this, in front of them, staking her claim in front of those smug faces, secretly thrilled as well. It was so primal, barbaric and savage. It felt right, like what life was really like at its base. The rest was false, make believe.

As she came out, Niall was there. "May I prepare you for your slave, Mistress?"

At her curious nod, he inclined his head, and went to one knee. It was downright arousing to see him lubricating the rubber cock as if it were part of her, the tiny movements massaging the stimulator against her. She lifted her head and found Brendan had turned his attention to her. While his gaze was on Niall's hands, massaging the dildo, making those slight movements against her she wasn't entirely sure weren't intended, every rigid line of him suggested Brendan might not be pleased that someone else was doing that. It was jealousy, but a different form of it. When he lifted his gaze to hers, it was clear Niall was doing what he felt was his job to do, and his alone. It prickled along her nerves.

"Done, Mistress." Niall finished, and as he did, his hand slid down her thigh, a whispering caress along the inner seam. Chloe gasped as a Dom she hadn't noticed earlier twisted around. The short whip he held landed with accuracy on Niall's bare back, hard enough that Niall caught his lip in his teeth to bite back the oath.

"The Mistress didn't give you permission to touch her anywhere else. Nor did I."

"No, Master." Niall bowed his head, but she thought she detected a slight smile on his face that suggested he enjoyed the consequences of the infraction.

"I'll punish you more thoroughly later. When I next check on you, don't let me catch you doing shit like that again." The Master, a man with close-cropped dark hair and emerald eyes, lifted his gaze to Chloe. That gaze gave her pause. It was…overwhelming. Powerfully sexual, compelling, and for a moment it was as if her feet weren't on solid ground, as if she'd backed up into a swamp in front of a hungry predator. However, the Dom merely gave Chloe a courteous nod and moved off, sending Niall one more quelling look.

"Wow. Are you…okay?" She'd seen Doms flogging their submissives several times now, and even at the whip demonstration they'd made it clear some restraint was needed to keep from breaking skin. Niall's Master had put all his effort into it, it seemed to her. In fact, she could see the strike welling blood, even now. "Oh my God, Niall..."

Shaking his head, he rose to his feet before she could reach out and touch the wound. "It will be fine in no time, Mistress. My Master and I...are a bit unique here. Just as you are, aye?" He gave her an easy smile. "Don't trouble yourself. Tell me instead what I can do to make this a more pleasurable experience for you."

He didn't seem concerned or disturbed by his Master's behavior. If there was any tension in his face, she registered it came from arousal. She didn't dare look down, because she was pretty sure she'd see hard evidence of it, literally. Yeah, maybe she might have dark rooms she was exploring for the first time, but her rooms were a shack next to the sprawling castle full of them here.

It brought her feet back to earth, a little bit. She didn't want to hurt Brendan. That wasn't who she was, and she knew ignorance did far more cruelty in the world than malicious intent. Warring with shameful pride and ego, the desire to protect won out, particularly in the face of Niall's concerned expression.

"I've never done this before." She let it drift off, hoping she wouldn't have to explain further.

He nodded, shepherding her toward the platform with a bracing hand on her lower back. With the strap-on positioned so intimately on her, the touch of a male hand on her flesh made her shiver, heating her blood further. He brought her close enough to stand a couple feet behind Brendan, though not up on the platform with him yet. It was a very distracting view, looking up the length of those lean thighs, to the mouthwatering display of tight ass and stretched back muscles, the wide shoulders pulled high by the chains holding him to the horizontal bar.

"You don't want to keep his arms hiked up like that too long," Niall murmured. "I'll let you know when we need to take them down. As for the rest, you just ease in, let his muscles give before you move forward. You never push when it comes to the anal region. Don't worry." Despite his earlier punishment, he brushed his knuckles along her spine. "Your slave's experienced and knows what he's doing. He'll pull you in, and when you're balls deep, so to speak"—he flashed a smile—"you can fuck the hell out of his ass, hard as you want. That dildo is average cock size. Would you like the curtain around the two of you?"

Chloe nodded. Now faced with the reality of doing this in front of way too many curious eyes, it was a no-brainer. She just wished she could understand why else her gut was turning cold. She was pretty damn aroused, and she'd done some kinky stuff before, though granted not this extreme. However, the environment, everything, said Brendan was into this, so why was it feeling wrong? Everything should be all right. He was gorgeous, every inch of him waiting for her.

He couldn't see her now, but his head was still tilted so she could see the shape of his forehead and bridge of his nose before it was hidden by the length of his bound arm. Completely naked, nothing on his body except that brand on his lower back that teased her fingers to touch, and then run lower, through the oil she could see slicking the taut muscles. There was a faint quiver when he shifted as much as his bonds allowed, and it made her mouth go dry, her loins tighten over the shaft inside her. Which in turn moved the clit stimulator enough to make the decision. Her gut be damned, she was going to do this.

She accepted Niall's hand to ascend the stage to Brendan's left. There was a separate set of risers to each position, so no one had to come up on stage and wiggle past someone else. She could easily see an awkward moment or two coming from that scenario. The clit stimulator stroked her as she lifted her feet to manage the steps and her pussy contracted, hard, on the dildo inside her. It was an unsteadying sensation, and so she stopped, swaying off balance, but Niall easily moved up next to her, letting her lean for a second. He smelled like pumpkin spice, and she remembered they were selling spice cakes at one of the booths. Niall had a sweet tooth. It was a reassuring thought.

"I make a really good spice cake," she mentioned, apropos of nothing. Niall gave her a sexy smile.

"I just bet you do, Mistress. You're driving him crazy, you know. He's wanting you something fierce about now."

"Isn't that what Mistresses do?" She looked at the fighting dragon tattoos, one of which was eye level with her gaze. The two in the center of his chest appeared to have locked claws as they tumbled through the air. Maybe they weren't fighting at all, but something as physical.

"Some of them. But this is about you and him. Not anyone else. So up or down?"

Brendan strained his neck to give her a brief look over his shoulder, and she saw the serious mouth, the hazel-green eyes, also somber. But desire was there too, in the set of his lips, the tense line of jaw. She got a glimpse of his cock, which told her it was having no trepidation at all. She hadn't specified wanting him in a harness, but apparently a condom was required, in case he lost control. Wouldn't want him baptizing the crowd. A strangled hiccup hurt her chest.

"Up."

She wasn't really sure if she was supposed to look toward or wave at the crowd, and suppressed another mildly hysterical chuckle at the thought. She kept her gaze on Brendan instead as Niall made sure she arrived behind him.

She moved directly behind Brendan so he couldn't look at her again. She stared at the slope of his back, focused on that brand as Niall drew the ivory curtain around them. The faint heat of the lights at her back reminded her that the crowd would be able to see what they were doing in silhouette, but they wouldn't get to see their faces.

Pressing her lips together, she reached out with her fingers and brushed flesh. Glancing down, she saw Niall had placed another single riser behind Brendan's heels, properly gauging their height differences for what she intended to do.

The Mistress several feet away, now hidden by that screen, wasn't having any second thoughts. She was enthusiastically ramming a slave Chloe knew wasn't even her own, one who was there as "punishment", shared by his Mistress. Chloe knew it was consensual, but she and Brendan weren't strangers, were they? This wasn't a punishment. Hell, she wasn't a Dominant, so why was she getting into acting like one?

She thought back to earlier in the day, Tyler and Marguerite, that overwhelming power Tyler had used so effortlessly to take over the situation, sweep them away. What had been underneath it had been a sense of caring and protection so utterly unquestionable, it was reflected in the trust Marguerite had projected. They'd cloaked Chloe with it, taking her along for the ride. Thinking of that, it took no brain cells to realize what was missing here. That feeling was something she wanted with Brendan, and while she knew it took time, what she was about to do might take it even further from her grasp. She'd had hints of it with him a couple times now, when her fucked-up mind didn't interfere.

He had his head lowered between his arms, body still beneath her touch, waiting on her will. She felt that quiver under her fingertips, sensed the crowd waiting behind the curtain. She didn't like knowing so many people were looking at him like this. This was what he did, though. Right? Probably stripped down every weekend at The Zone, gave himself to any Mistress with a big enough dildo to handle him. Took the pleasure. This wasn't about giving anything to her, but about taking. It was always about taking.

Stop it. Her fingers had curled against his lower back, dug into the thickened skin of the brand. Her thumb was pushing against the indentation at the top of his buttocks, feeling that oil, his readiness for her. *This is about you and him, just as Niall said.*

She didn't know how to project the right emotions, how to tell him how much she cared. Because at the moment all she wanted was to hurt him, the way she'd been hurt.

Oh God. Had she really just thought that? *Don't do this, Chloe. Don't do it.*

And yet, her hand drifted up to his nape as she stepped up on the riser, leaned into him. The lubricated dildo painted a line in the curve of his spine as her breasts pressed high on his shoulders. Lifting her hands to cup his elbows, she molded her palms over his biceps as she slid down the path to his armpits, the stretch of muscle and skin over his ribs.

"Chloe."

"Don't talk."

She could feel the resistance in him, as if he knew something was wrong. But he couldn't know her eyes were squeezed tight, her heart hammering in her throat. All she had to do was position that phallus between his buttocks, slide all the way in. Her pussy was already soaking wet, penetrated by the hard rubber, and she could well imagine what it would feel like, the thrust of her body into Brendan, him pushing back against the stimulator and dildo so they would be essentially fucking one another. He'd strain against those restraints, and she'd feel the power of it curl with her rising desire, headed toward that pinnacle where she'd be tangled against his body and in his mind. Deep enough to be trapped, where the impending orgasm would instead become a drowning. A drowning with no intimacy, lonely and cold.

The Mistress beside them was finishing, because she heard the woman's whisper, "Come for me now, slave." The male released with a harsh groan that prickled over Chloe's skin, the woman's own gasps of release sending that quiver through her ham strings again. Her hands had fanned out on the upper rise of Brendan's buttocks and were kneading, her thumbs sweeping over the muscle and teasing the crevice, her body taking over where her mind was hesitating. She could ram into him, fuck him hard and rough, like Niall said. Make

169

him groan like that Mistress had done to her borrowed fuck toy. Tear his flesh with her nails and teeth, demand he scream with pain as he released, letting him know that pleasure came at a cost. A cost that might be too dear to pay.

No. She fumbled at the clasp of the strap-on and yanked it loose before her body could lodge its vehement protest, though her cunt sucked hard on the dildo as she pulled it loose, forcing her to take a deep breath and lean her shoulder against Brendan's back so she didn't topple.

Letting the device fall to the ground, she turned her face into his back, against the bare flesh, pressing her mouth against him. Her body vibrated with emotional and physical need so fierce she knew nothing could ever assuage it, because she couldn't get there anymore. She didn't know how.

"I'm sorry," she whispered.

"Chloe." Brendan tried to twist his head around again, see her, his fingers clenching in the restraints. "Wait."

But she was already stepping down from the riser, finding her way out of the curtain with unsteady hands. She scrambled down the steps, not looking out toward the side of the stage, where there were people hoping to get a different profile of what they were doing. Fortunately, they had several other demonstrations happening up there, keeping their attention, but when she glanced around for Niall, wanting to reclaim her clothes, it was her luck that the person whose eyes she met was the woman in silver and white, the one who'd made her empty her purse to purchase Brendan.

Brendan had apparently been the only offering she'd desired for this evening, because she appeared to be without a submissive, enjoying the company of several other Doms strolling through the carnival. But she came to a halt when Chloe's gaze met hers. Unfortunately, they were close enough that some type of acknowledgment was needed, and Chloe hadn't looked away fast enough.

The woman must have been watching her through the screen, or Chloe's expression wasn't that hard to read. Maybe both. Though the woman's perfect face didn't reflect cruelty or cattiness, her words cut all the same. "You don't have what he needs, you know," she said quietly. "You can't be what you're not."

Chloe tightened her jaw, even as Niall came up beside her. "Maybe he needs something different," she said.

"He's a good enough submissive that he can convince you of that. That's the tragedy of it. And you don't understand enough about what he is to keep him honest."

"Mistress Lyda, with every respect, you're out of line, and you know it."

Niall spoke in a neutral tone, even gave the woman a slight bow as he said it. Lyda didn't appear to take offense. "I may be out of line, Niall, but she needs to hear it from someone, especially if she loves him. Good evening to you. And good luck. I mean that sincerely." The woman moved away, rejoining her companions, the two men who'd sat near Chloe at the auction. They gave her an assessing look, a nod, and offered Lyda their arms to continue through the carnival offerings.

"Mistress." Niall touched Chloe's arm. "He's calling for you, and he's getting agitated."

She could hear it. Brendan had spoken her name several times and he was getting louder. She flinched as she heard the chains clank, as if he'd pulled against them, followed by a muttered oath. He could hear her voice, she was sure, but she doubted he'd heard the exchange. She hoped he hadn't. A girl's pride could only handle so much.

"It's Chloe. That's my name. I'm not a Mistress." She swallowed the ache of bitter tears and shook Niall off. "Let him down, or call her back here. She'll take care of him. She's right. He's better off, and I don't belong here."

Collecting her clothes, she fled like the coward she knew she was.

* * * * *

She kept her head down and her pace sedate until she got to the outskirts of the carnival grounds. Then she took the quickest route outside the lights. She needed darkness, anonymity, even from herself. Once there, she shed the body suit and put her dress back on. Then she ran. She had to outdistance the feeling in her chest that threatened to choke her, and needed to feel the earth, the cool grass, under her feet.

Once she ran out of breath, she'd find the path to the chapel Tyler had on his estate. These past couple days, she'd occasionally gone there to sit in the front pew and watch the inlet water flow outside the large picture window. She'd stay there until things quieted down, at dawn. Like vampires, the carnival goers slept at daylight, coming back in the late afternoon for festivities to start again. Guess they understood as well as anybody that the darkest pleasures weren't as pleasurable under the harsh light of reality and daylight. Maybe she'd sleep in the chapel until then, watch the sunrise pour through the stained glass windows.

She pushed herself harder, harder, not caring which direction she headed now, just so it was away from the lights, from the feelings she couldn't face, from the overwhelming sense of failure. She'd wanted him, but she'd wanted to hurt him more, and there was no way she could tell him that. God, she was too fucked up for anyone anymore.

She yelped, startled, as she was caught around the waist and swung around, so abruptly her head snapped back and vertigo sent her mind spinning. She crumpled against Brendan and went down in a tangled heap with him. She'd known it was him the second he touched her. She shoved against him, though, because she wanted him to hold her so much she couldn't afford to let him do it. Instead, he simply shifted so he was sitting with her cradled securely between his thighs and inside the span of his arms.

"No," he said. "I won't let you go. I won't."

His voice was strained and determined, his body solid and strong, and she couldn't fight him. She held stiff against him for all of two heartbeats, then she melted. His breath went out in a sigh, and she thought she heard a soft "good girl" before he pressed a kiss against her hair.

He must have sprinted like an Olympian to catch up with her after they let him down. He'd tugged on a pair of jeans from somewhere, though his upper body was still blissfully bare.

"So have you thought of a career as a track star?" she asked, at a loss.

"I was afraid you'd fall." When he gently touched her chin, he directed her attention to what was ahead. As she blinked in the dim light thrown by a mere slice of moon, she realized what she'd thought was a continuation of the natural area was in reality the bulkhead to the water. If she'd run across it, she would have tumbled six feet down, into the inlet's high tide current.

"Ouch." She drew a shaky breath. "I guess I wasn't really looking."

"No. I thought you weren't." His arms tightened around her. "Chloe, you didn't do anything wrong. You know that, right? Whatever you want to do, or don't want to do, is acceptable here. You didn't need to run. You could have just said it wasn't your thing and let me down."

The problem was she *had* wanted to do it, but in a way that had frightened her. She couldn't say that, though, because he'd need her to explain it, and she couldn't explain it to herself. It was like she was carrying a demon inside her and only her continued silence would keep it contained. Rather than answering, she slid her arms under his, banding them over his back, and held on, pressing her face into his chest.

"It's all right," he murmured, stroking her hair. "Just relax for me, all right? We'll just sit here. That's all that's needed."

She nodded, and let him comfort her, savored how his hands felt, sliding up and down her back, the way he caressed her nape as he fondled her short curls, the rough lullaby of words rumbling unintelligibly through his chest. In time, her heart rate settled, and she could hear the water, the breeze through the trees, and the sounds from the carnival behind them. Laughter, the occasional rift of music and perhaps a cry of pleasure. Her body tightened anew as she caught a mental scent of it, reminding her how revved up she'd been before her emotions had derailed her.

Her fingers had gone from a functional kneading of his back to a questing slide over the muscles, down toward the loose waistband, where she found he wasn't wearing anything but the jeans. His five o'clock shadow rasped against her cheek as he nudged her head back against his shoulder and settled his mouth over hers. He didn't have to coax her lips apart, her mouth opening to his heat, the glide of his tongue over hers, the way he seduced her body to arched response with nothing more than that movement. His arms tightened around her so her breasts pressed harder against his chest and he cupped her skull, holding her in the kiss until she was moaning softly in his mouth, her fingers back to kneading, only now it was a spasmodic reflection of the yearning emptiness between her legs.

"Easy," he said softly, drawing his mouth away to her cheek, over to her ear, nuzzling it and teasing the shell with the tip of his tongue, before pressing his mouth to the sensitive part of her throat below. "It's all easy."

Like the flow of the inlet behind them, inevitable but nothing forced. One part of her was soothed and rocked like a baby to a still peace, while her body hummed with a woman's fully awake libido.

"I have an idea," he said against her brow.

"So do I. Several."

He chuckled, passed a hand down her hip to her thigh, tracing her flesh through the skirt to her knee, creating a ticklish circle that made her squirm and realize he wasn't at all uninvolved when he stifled an amused curse. Looking up at him, she slid her hand between them and put the heel of it on his erect cock beneath the jeans, rubbing deliberately as she held his gaze. "I want this. I really do."

"It makes me even harder to hear you say it. Do you feel it?"

She gave him a nod, but she moved her hands to his chest, resting them there with a faint quiver in her fingers. This was good, this feeling, and she didn't want to lose it. She also didn't want to worry about where to go from here. She wanted him to do that. "What's your idea?"

He pressed his lips together, a gratifying expression of near pain at the removal of her touch, but managed to give her another smile. "I'd like to enjoy the carnival with you. The traditional parts of it. Just as we would if we were in town."

"So you wouldn't be mine anymore?" She thought of Mistress Lyda of the perfect silver eyes and any-man-is-my-slave boots.

"Chloe, I was already yours."

She didn't know what to say to such a heartfelt declaration. She wanted to say she was sorry about what had happened at the platform. She wanted to ask him what he was thinking. She wanted to be able to tell him what was going on with her. For a second, when he'd been rubbing her back, rocking her, she'd almost opened her mouth to do it. But she just couldn't.

Instead, she simply said, "You could have told me that before I blew my savings."

Another half-chuckle, though his eyes remained serious. "Want to ride the Ferris wheel? And we can both try the hammer at the Strong Man booth and see who wins."

"I like cotton candy. They have that, right? I thought I saw some."

"Purple. Huge swaths of it so you'll be bouncing with the sugar rush." Leaning back down, he took her lips in a sweet, tender kiss that deepened into heat, encouraging her to sigh in his mouth as she slid her arms under his again and pressed her palms into his back. She let herself be cradled once more in a way that felt safe and pleasurable at once. As they kissed, he moved, scooping her up to bring them both to their feet. When he guided her soles to the ground, he slid his hand up the back of her leg, pausing on her thigh so it stayed momentarily hooked over his hip, keeping her on her toes enough that groin brushed groin, making her want to rub.

He let her ease all the way down only when he lifted his head. Chloe kept holding his biceps, staring up into his face. "I feel embarrassed to go back," she admitted.

He shook his head, coiled one of her curls around her ear. He still wore her ribbon, and she didn't care if the hair blinded her, she wasn't asking for it back. "A hundred dramas happen at these things, big and small. It's games and play, but there's always a lot more than that happening. It all fits in. Don't worry, no one will give you any grief about it."

"Did I ruin it?"

"No." His brow creased as he dropped his hand to her shoulder, squeezed to emphasize the point and then drew them into a walk back toward the lights. "Chloe, I wanted you to see this part of who I am. There's no right or wrong response to that. You understand?"

She did, but she also wondered if what they'd really accomplished was seeing a part of her that it would have been better for no one to see, let alone herself. Catching both her hands, he turned in circles with her as they moved in a forward direction, coaxing a silly smile to her lips.

"Do you like being with me?"

"Yes, but what if I can't be—"

"Then nothing else is necessary. I want to make you happy. That's all. The end of it. All right?"

She nodded, though his response moved uneasily in her stomach, remembering what Mistress Lyda had said. Plus, if she couldn't find happiness for herself, how successful would he be at it? She thought of his chain mail, of knights on hopeless quests.

"Let's make a deal, you and me. You're happy to be here with me, right?"

"Yes." She was sure of that, and his expression lightened, making her glad she hadn't held back.

"Well then, for the next little bit, we're not going to worry about anything else, all right? Hey, look over there. Marguerite and Tyler had the same idea."

Chloe followed his gaze as he pulled her back into the lighted area. True to his word, he'd brought her to the more traditional part of the carnival, where things were what she expected them to be. Well, somewhat. At this shooting gallery, instead of ducks, the moving targets were empty Dom Perignon bottles.

She was further bolstered to see Tyler and Marguerite had changed into more casual attire after the auction. Tyler wore slacks and golf shirt, while Marguerite was in a flowing sundress, covered by a cashmere sweater against the night chill.

Chloe was charmed to see the two holding hands like she and Brendan. Their stop in front of the shooting gallery was apparently Marguerite's idea, because Tyler was trying to move her onward and she was digging in her heels with a rare playfulness.

"Hey guys," Chloe said.

Marguerite turned her serious near-smile on them. Chloe was glad when Brendan's arm slid around her shoulders, because she could tell in an instant that M knew what had happened earlier. That wouldn't have been unbearable, but she registered something in Marguerite's eyes that suggested…disapproval. Of her?

Tyler spoke. "Good, Brendan. You're here. Do you shoot?"

"Not really. Fencing and wrestling are my manly combat sports."

Tyler snorted. "Doesn't matter. Marguerite wants to see someone do this."

"I suspect she wants to see you do it. She likes it when you show off. Sir." A twinkle went through Brendan's gaze. At Tyler's mock scowl, he held up both hands. "I'd like to learn, but I won't stand in the way of what Mistress Marguerite wants. I think you should satisfy her desires first."

Tyler muttered a mild oath. "Fine. Put them on maximum speed," he told the operator. He cocked a brow at Marguerite. "So this gets you hot, hmm?"

"Volcanic," she returned, a sparkle glimmering in her gaze. "If you don't miss."

With Chloe still tucked close under his arm, Brendan quirked the corner of his mouth down at her. Still worried, she tried to respond with an appropriate smile.

The booth operator was a young man whose crew cut and well-fitted T-shirt suggested active Marine rather than a carnie. He stepped aside, a grin on his face. "Maybe I should stand outside the booth, old man. Don't want to get hit."

"Be just as easy to shoot you out there, especially if I'm aiming for your ass, Jack." Tyler closed his hand on the pellet rifle. In a blink, he'd swung the gun up to his shoulder. Chloe didn't know how he even had time to take aim, but he shattered five bottles without hesitation, his amber gaze never wavering, his upper body barely moving as he found his targets. The glass rained down into the catch area behind the conveyor belt like the sound of pirate's treasure.

"Repeater is a little sluggish," he noted, placing it down.

"I'll tell my gun distributor we need the M-4 line of pellet rifles next time," the Marine said dryly. "Going to pick out something for the lady you're too damn mean to deserve?"

"Keep talking, jarhead." Tyler looked up at the stuffed animals and other toys just above his head and arched a brow at Marguerite. "What do you want?"

"Nothing hanging on those hooks," she responded, making Jack laugh. Giving her a sexy smile, Tyler pulled down a toy anyway. He presented her with a black stuffed gorilla bearing an armful of silk red roses and a heart that said *I'm yours.*

"That will just have to hold you for now, because I have to show Brendan how to do this, so he can impress Chloe just as much."

"I'll be lucky to hit one," Brendan snorted.

Tyler handed him the pellet gun. "No worries. Three's all you need to give Chloe any trinket her heart desires. Take it to your shoulder…"

As the men conferred, Chloe drew closer to Marguerite, despite her wariness of that earlier look. But Marguerite merely lifted her arm, drew her to her side, much as Brendan had. Letting out a small relieved sigh, Chloe leaned up against her as they watched their guys. "Are you all right?" Marguerite asked.

"Yeah. I am." She was better now, more steady. She could say it without feeling like it was a lie. "It's a great carnival. I guess I got a little overwhelmed. I didn't expect to get so carried away or freaked out at once, you know. Brendan's been great. Fantastically great."

Marguerite made a noncommittal noise. For some reason, it made Chloe want to squirm, but since she was looking toward the shooting booth, Chloe let herself do the same. With pure female pleasure, she watched Tyler help Brendan shoulder and angle the gun, a brief press of hip to hip to show him the proper stance, adjust it. All very appropriate, and yet there was a component between the two men impossible for her to miss. She creased her brow, trying to identify it. It wasn't that Tyler wanted to have sex with Brendan, or vice versa. No, that wasn't it at all. Tyler was a Dom dealing with a male sub, who was equally aware that the one touching him was Dominant. So the sexual thrum was there, even if it wasn't directed.

She could recognize that thrum, but it didn't make her part of their world, knowing how to react or handle it. Or what it truly meant.

"M." She spoke without looking toward Marguerite. "What kind of friends are you and Brendan?"

"Do you feel you've earned that information, Chloe?"

Chloe stiffened. "What do you mean?"

Marguerite shifted her stance so she was facing Chloe, kept her voice low. "Have you decided what Brendan is going to be to you? Is he a toy you're playing with on the store shelf, trying to decide if you're going to take him home? If you do, will you cherish him while it lasts, or treat him as a toy still, simply because he won't demand any more from you than a toy does?"

"You're angry with me."

"No, I'm not." Marguerite studied her with her pale blue eyes. "But I do expect more from you. Honesty, and a love given freely and unstintingly to those around you. The lack of one is hampering the other. Cruelty doesn't suit you."

"I stopped. I didn't—" Goddess, how could Marguerite be in her head, know what she'd almost done to him? But she did, Chloe could see it in her gaze, and didn't know whether to be mortified or insulted.

"No, you didn't." Marguerite's long fingernails brushed Chloe's forearm, a balm to the stinging words.

"I got carried away, like I said. What I've seen here...I was just fitting in." Chloe realized she sounded defensive, almost belligerent, but Marguerite nodded.

"It's easy to become a chameleon in this environment, if you're not sure who or what you are anymore. But though a chameleon can look like her environment, she isn't really a part of it. She doesn't gain an understanding just by blending."

Chloe stared at her. "You invited me here."

When Marguerite's expression flickered, Chloe's mind stuttered to a halt. Rewound to when Brendan had told her about the invitation. "No," she realized. "Brendan asked you to invite me. You didn't want me here. You—"

"I'm always happy to have you as a guest in my home," Marguerite interjected. "But I didn't think the carnival was the best way to introduce you to this part of his life." There was no accusation in M's voice, merely reserved observation. That was worse, because it left Chloe no real target. And Marguerite was continuing, flaying her with the even tone, the far-too-truthful words.

"You're right, what you said to Niall. You're not a natural Domme. What you are is an extraordinary young woman, one in emotional pain, trying to regain control of yourself. Either fortune or disaster has brought you together with an extraordinary submissive, one who might let you do anything to deal with that pain. As long as I've known you, you've been about healing and laughter, love. Always love. It's the one thing you've believed in, allowed to lead you, no matter what happened."

Chloe knew that Brendan was shooting, that she should be watching, but those words were as sharp and staccato as the pellet gun, kicking bitterness into her voice. "What if I don't believe in that anymore?"

"You don't." Marguerite said it gently, but Chloe still flinched. "Which is why you're trying to get it back by using someone who still does."

Anger welled up. "How can I believe in love? Love isn't strong. It doesn't help keep fear away, it doesn't make you feel safe. Power and control, that's what makes you feel safe. I thought that was what all this is about." She gestured around her. "Oh right, I forgot—I can't understand this. I don't know the secret handshake."

In all her time working for Marguerite, she'd never argued with her, never lifted her voice. However, the frustrated fury was an all-too-familiar companion of late. She had enough sanity left among her turbulent emotions to scramble to hold it back, but her voice had climbed several octaves. Fortunately, this corner of the carnival was relatively unpopulated at the moment. Still, she could feel the speculative glances of those nearby at other booths. Great, first she embarrassed herself at the auction and with Niall, now this. The seventh annual carnival would be remembered as the year that Marguerite brought her mentally unstable employee.

When Marguerite stepped closer to her, closed her hand fully on Chloe's arm, she realized she was shaking with the effort of holding her ground, not flying into pieces. "Deep breath, sweet," her boss murmured. "Take a deep breath."

"I'm sorry," Chloe managed, though she wasn't sure she was. She still wanted to scream and rant. She wanted to throw off Marguerite's touch, but she didn't.

With a light touch to her chin, Marguerite drew her gaze back up to her face. "Trust and surrender is what all this is about, Chloe. But you don't have to understand Dominance and submission, and people who practice it as we do, to understand that those two elements are at the center of *every* relationship, the core of what every person who falls in love is seeking with another. My concern isn't so much with you using him to heal, but to fight demons. Careful of the latter, or it may take you down a path you don't want to go, a place that, once you're there, will be hard to find your way back."

Those words made her want to break, spill out everything, and she couldn't. She was pretty sure once that glue came loose, she'd never put it back together again. Hell, why was it she could tell herself she wasn't ready for any of this, and yet she still kept trying?

"I should leave. You probably want me to go, anyway."

"Chloe, I would tell you if I want you to go. I'm not in the habit of concealing what I want and do not want from the people around me." Marguerite's hand tightened on her chin, a seamless transition from concerned employer to that 'other' quality. Chloe's body stilled, held by the tone and the look in those direct eyes. "What I want is for you to heal. Which means whatever infection you've been trying to bury since you were injured needs to be drained." Her touch became a caress on Chloe's jaw as she closed her eyes, unable to face Marguerite's. "You just have to find that trust within yourself, and surrender to it. It's time, whether you tell me, Gen, Brendan or even that confused cat of yours."

It startled a half-chuckle out of Chloe, though her eyes were burning and her throat ached. "St. Frances isn't confused. He just refuses to be defined by his predatory nature."

"Hmm." Marguerite cocked her head. "Chloe—"

"I have to go to the restroom," Chloe said desperately. Pivoting on her heel, she made her getaway between the tents.

* * * * *

Brendan had hit four out of ten, but when he looked over his shoulder to see if Chloe was indeed impressed, he'd seen her and Marguerite engaged in what was obviously not a good conversation.

Tyler had held him back, telling him with the pressure of a hand and a look that it was best to let the two women finish their conversation. But when Chloe dashed off, her cheeks too pale and eyes too bright, it was all Brendan could do not to follow. However, Tyler kept him at his side as they returned the gun to Jack and came back to Marguerite. The husband and wife exchanged a glance that was a communication all its own, the language that people in love, in perfect sync, shared. People with no secrets.

Brendan knew if Chloe had followed through on the platform, the orgasm they would have shared would have been intense, overwhelming. Physical. The moment she'd brought him to the platform, he'd known it wasn't a good plan. She'd taken away the gift of intimacy, withheld it, a punishment. She wasn't experienced enough to recognize it that way, and her decisions had been about what was going on inside her, not a loving or healthy expression of the lust between them. Even knowing that, he'd have let her do it. Even knowing it was wrong, because his job was to give pleasure, make her happy, keep her in a safe place to help her experience that. He hadn't done what he should have to help her get there.

As he bowed his head, thinking about that, Marguerite touched his hair, a soothing caress. She didn't offer such things often, which made it that much more potent when she did.

"I'm not going to allow this to continue. I knew this wasn't a good idea, and I should have handled it that way from the beginning."

Before he had a conscious thought as to the wisdom of doing so, Brendan had closed his hand on her wrist. "Mistress, let me solve this one on my own. I don't need you to fight my battles."

Her blue eyes went to frost and fire. But she inclined her head and extricated herself with a sharp movement and an even sharper glance. "Then start fighting them."

When she moved away, she'd added to that weight of immeasurable failure in his chest. Tyler put a brief hand on his shoulder. "She's angry with me," Brendan observed tightly.

"No." Tyler shook his head. "You've been around Marguerite enough to know she's unique in how she loves others. It isn't always an easy love. I'll take care of your Mistress's heart. You take care of Chloe's."

He nodded, letting him know that Chloe was coming back.

Brendan turned. The young woman's face was as fragile as glass, and she looked like she was ready to go home—alone. Yet he also had the memory of her heat pressed against his back on the platform, and before that her broken rasping breath after the climax they'd shared in her bed, her fingers clutching his skin. She was seeking that connection subconsciously, even as so many of the other things she did were attempts to push it away.

"When's the last time you rode a Ferris wheel?" he asked as she got within hearing distance. He nodded toward it, the multi-colored lights bathing her unsure face.

"Brendan..."

He took her hand. "C'mon. Don't think. Let's just go do it."

Chapter Twelve

ಐ

As the wheel hitched upward one click at a time while people were loaded into the cars, Chloe watched the world below become a tapestry of colorful tent tops. The moving people looked like they belonged in a macabre version of the glittering carnival world, with all the sensual trappings, manacles and leather straps. She saw the silver sparkle of Mistress Lyda's embellished corset.

Brendan's arm slid around her shoulders. "You won't fall out if you stay really close," he said somberly, the twinkle in the hazel eyes giving him away.

In answer, she laid a hand on his bare chest, pressing her ear to his heartbeat. He did pull her closer, so her hand fell on his thigh. "This is weird," she said with a strained smile. "You're half naked, you know."

"Well, if you want to join me so you won't feel self-conscious..."

Instead, she traced the attractive thigh muscle under denim. "You're a very strange man, Brendan. You let me do...what I almost did to you. You're part of this world, but you ask me to ride the Ferris wheel like we're fourteen. You like to hold hands and bring me stuffed puppies. And have phone sex with me at three a.m."

"You wear pink Save the Whale sleep shirts, make great cupcakes and debate whether or not you'd like to push a six-inch dildo up my ass." His eyes laughed down at her, though his mouth remained in a serious line. "We're all a mix. We see things through the eyes of the child we once were and the adults we become. This place, this way of thinking, brings that out."

He covered her hand with his own, lacing with her fingers. "For instance, if I could have what I want most right now, I might pull you onto my lap, sink my cock deep inside you, and then hold you as you lay back against my hands and let the wind blow through your hair." He leaned down, but instead of going for her mouth, his lips found her neck below her ear again, that erogenous zone which made her teeth sink down on her bottom lip. "Your body would be arched back by the gravity of the ride," he continued in a sensual murmur. "I'd listen to your breathless laugh, see the sparkle in your eyes from the wonder of it, making love on a Ferris wheel, keeping the best of child- and adulthood together."

He straightened then, after a quick nuzzle of her hair. "But I also like being here with you like this, pressed hip to hip, holding hands. Getting the chance to put my nose into your hair, smell you, feel you. It's as good, in a different way. I want both."

As he met her gaze, he let her see that he meant what he said, that he was holding onto nothing bad about the evening, choosing to immerse himself in the simple pleasure of being here. With her. It lessened the humiliation of the platform, the pain of Mistress Lyda's words, the discomfort of Marguerite's. Her anger had dissipated, and some of the awkwardness she'd been feeling as a result began to do the same, because of him.

Plus, for right now, he was all hers. Up here, floating up into the sky, where the only stimulus was each other, the word had a different, more poignant and wondrous quality to it. Her own prince of the fairy tales. Being hers in all ways, handsome and attentive. When he leaned over to glance over the side, she studied his profile in the magically lit darkness, the flutter of his hair over his brow and across his throat from the breeze.

As they ticked up another car, she saw an even more elevated view of the carnival, details lost and everything becoming a flirtation between shadows and light. Just like he'd said. The best of both worlds.

Her gaze drifted further, to the darkness beyond the carnival grounds. That darkness covered the inlet and the large spread of oaks that surrounded and buffered Tyler's property, and yet there was always an extra component to darkness, a weight to it that suggested it was a living thing, not just a curtain.

It reminded her of Marguerite's words, what would wait for her on the ground, what would continue to follow her. When Brendan had been holding her earlier, she'd been so close to letting it spill out of her soul. What if she could let some of it go up here? Would it float away and lose her, not be able to find her again? Would the rest lose some of its ability to cling to her so hard? Could she release a portion of it, just to see? Hell, it could be no worse than some of the other things she'd done tonight.

Trust and surrender. She bit her lip.

"Chloe." It was a soft murmur, and he laid his hand on her temple, letting her drop her head to his chest, tucking herself under his jaw. Her hands rested on his lap naturally, one finger worrying the inseam accessible from his casually splayed thighs. "You can trust me with anything, you know."

Maybe it was his timing. Or what had happened a little while ago. The knowledge in Marguerite's eyes that had hurt and yet not been wrong. Or maybe it was as simple as this Ferris wheel going up, one click at a time, like a clock face going toward the top of the hour, when all things started over, or began. Maybe it was the fact she wasn't looking into his face that made her finally decide to open her mouth.

"The thing with Marguerite's dad... More happened that day."

He remained silent, but he curved one finger over her unoccupied hand, lying limply along the same thigh.

"He... When he pulled Natalie away from me, and I was fighting him, trying to get her back, he shoved her and she fell down. She was too frightened to run, even though I screamed at her, told her to. Then he started hitting me..." She drew a deep breath. "When he broke my leg, had me on the ground, he...fell down on top of me. Pushed himself against me, from behind. Through my clothes. He grabbed my hair. It hurt so much, because he'd hit me in the face, but he whispered, 'I'm back. You thought I'd gone, but I'm never gone.'"

"Chloe."

"Please don't say anything. Not until I'm done." She stared out into that darkness. "He didn't do anything else. Just picked her up and left. I was... I mean, I know I couldn't have stopped him then, but I would have tried, would have tried to get up and go after them, but that single moment, it held me frozen. I know what he said was a message for Marguerite. He was delusional, imagining I was her for that second, when he did that horrible thing." She closed her eyes. *Oh Marguerite.*

She still didn't know all of it, but she didn't need to do so. She'd cared about Marguerite from the beginning. Even when the reticent tea shop owner had held her and Gen at such arms' distance, she'd still seemed to be yearning for a closeness she wouldn't allow herself to have. With that intuition Marguerite had praised so highly, Chloe had responded to it, trying to offer it to her in every way she could. She'd wanted M as a friend, as much as she wanted Marguerite to view her as a friend, as much or little as she could handle.

"Anyhow," she continued. "When he said that, he opened this door in my head that I've kept closed for a really, really long time. I've always known it's there, but I thought I'd figured out a permanent lock for it."

She stopped. "I don't know if I can do this. I really, really feel like I should, but I don't know..."

Both arms closed over her, and he drew her upper body further across his bare chest, as close to being in his lap as the restraining bar would allow. She could flatten herself against him as he held her head tucked under his with one of those long fingered, large hands that covered almost the entire side

189

of her face. He stroked her hair. The cars ticked up again. One from the top. They were so high up, above everything. His thigh pressed against hers, her hands gripping that anchor of solid flesh and bone. His heart beat under her ear. Then he said just the right thing.

"I'm here, Chloe. I won't let it have you."

The monster in the darkness. She closed her eyes, gave herself to a darkness that was all Brendan's scent and closeness, his heat in the middle of the night, a ward against all fear. And she said what she hadn't said since she was nine years old.

"When I was in grade school, I usually walked home from school with two other girls. But every Friday, I liked to take a different route. I'd go to the railroad tracks, and walk home along them, because of the wildflowers that grew along them, because of how quiet it was. I'd see rabbits and deer, raccoons. Angela and Tina didn't go with me, because it was a longer walk, and our parents had told us not to do that. They were worried about a train coming, hurting us. But I knew if I was old enough to cross the street, I didn't have to worry about being hit by a train." She couldn't summon a smile, didn't even try. "To be honest, I kind of liked going alone, because if I was really quiet too, the animals would come close to me."

Brendan had tensed, because of course it was obvious where this could go, but he kept petting her, kept being silent. Just there.

"I guess I got into a pattern of it, and someone was watching. He scared me at first, coming up out of the trees, but he said, 'I like watching the deer too. Did you know...there's a mother with twin fawns?' And I did know that. I'd seen her, always along that section of track. He sat down on the gravel bank, took out a sandwich, asked me if I wanted to share. He started talking about the deer and he was...it was like he understood about the quiet, and the animals, and how happy it made me sometimes, just to be there with them, by myself. So I sat down with him."

Her voice trembled then. "We were sitting there, and the mother deer came out with her fawns, a little ways down the track. He put his hand on mine, it was so big, and squeezed, showing me, and we were both so silent, watching her, and then she went away. Then he turned around and kissed me. Forced my mouth open and pushed me back against the gravel."

She shuddered at the memory, but it was not a rejection of Brendan. She was so grateful he realized that, keeping her close. Even though a soft oath came from his lips, and his arms tightened as if he could keep her from that long-ago harm, he didn't interrupt her, didn't keep her from saying what she needed to say. One more tick and they were at the top. Top of the world, everything above and below clear. Just the two of them.

"I struggled of course, tried to get away, and he dragged me into the trees. There was a little shack deep in the woods. He was so big, and he kept telling me it was okay, that it was going to be fine, that I was a good girl, and I understood about things. That he couldn't help himself, I was just so beautiful and perfect, and he knew I was going to be his heart, his treasure. He got me into the shack. There was a dirty cot there, but also all sorts of things, like what I collected in my room. Rocks, twigs with empty cocoon pods. Different shaped leaves.

"He begged me to calm down, said he'd show me the special rocks he'd found, and the tracks of a fox he had in a piece of dried clay. He helped me stop crying, made me shush and then he turned around to get the clay piece. I tried to bolt for the door. He grabbed me of course, and I fell. It unbalanced him, and I kicked him. I shouldn't have been able to hurt him, but I hit him right in the face with the sole of my shoe."

"So brave," Brendan murmured softly into her hair. "Such a brave girl." He'd started rocking her, just slightly, making the car rock too.

"I got away, and I ran. Further into the woods, because I was too frightened to remember which way to go, so I just kept

191

running. And somewhere along the way I saw the mother deer."

She pressed her lips together, throat dry. "You know, over the years, I thought maybe I made this part up, because I was a kid, and you know how kids sometimes do that to cope. But I guess it doesn't matter. I saw her. She was there, and I followed her, right into this glade she had for her and her twin babies. There was a tiny path into it that only she could see, that I never would have seen for myself. There was just enough room in that little glade for me to slip into it with her. She settled down with the babies curled against her. When I crawled in, pressed myself to one side, she didn't leave. She stared at me, in that way deer do, as if they're frozen, and the babies did the same. That's when I heard him crashing through the brush, coming closer.

"I guess I probably stared back at that mother the way she was staring at me, as if I couldn't move. She made this soft noise, and she and the babies became even more still. I realized that was how she protected them, teaching them to hide and not move. So I sat there, so still, when everything in me wanted to run, told me to run. But I knew that mother deer wanted to protect her babies more than anything, and so I did what she told them to do. I stayed there until it was full dark. When at last she got up and slid out with her babies, I followed her again, because I felt safer with her. But then I heard him again and knew he was looking for me."

So lost in the memory, she jumped when the Ferris wheel began to move. A slow turn that she knew would become a much faster spin, until they'd be flying through the night. She tightened her fingers on Brendan's leg, and he put his mouth on her ear, head bent over hers. "It's okay. I can hear you."

She nodded, actually liking how her voice was muted in her own head by the whir of the equipment, the building rush of the wind, as if it was carrying the memory away on the flow of words, as she wanted it to do.

"The deer disappeared, and it went on for hours. I would move through the woods, as quiet as I could, listening for everything, in the full dark. I ran into spider webs, was terrified of what might be crawling on me, but I was more scared of him. There were times I knew he was close. I saw a flashlight beam a few times, and pressed myself to the ground, then I would move again."

She took a deep breath, telling herself she was almost there, though she knew this was the worst part. "Just before dawn, I came to what I thought was a clearing, and it was a road. A road behind a neighborhood. I was so relieved, I started running down it, sobbing, looking at the houses, knowing I was going to be okay. Then he came out of the woods behind me.

"He wasn't making a sound, running faster than I was running, and I knew I wasn't going to make it, that nobody would be looking out their windows or be out in their yards, and he would just drag me into those woods again. I couldn't bear it. I started screaming for my mother, just screaming. I was so scared, I thought it was all in my head, that I wasn't forcing out any noise. But then this lady came out of the back of her house. She was letting her dog out before work, and she saw us through the trees. I crashed toward her, and she came running toward me, to help, shouting out for her husband. She said the man turned and ran back into the woods then."

The tremor she felt wasn't the Ferris wheel. But she told herself it was so long ago. It was okay. She was here. In the arms of a man who would never let something like that happen to her, would never let the monsters get her, no matter he'd only known her two days, no matter that she was likely to sabotage their relationship like a human grenade. She pressed her forehead into his chest, then turned her face outward to feel the breeze as they slowed, came up to the top again, giving her a light-jeweled and star filled view of the world.

"All those years..." She shook her head. "I know most kids deal with something like that differently, but I went

another direction. Like there was something in my head telling
me if I could make the world beautiful and full of sunshine, no
darkness would ever come to get me again. I remember sitting
with the therapist my parents had me see, and it was like, 'no,
I'm going to be fine.' I'd think about the deer and the rabbits,
and the flowers, and I'd know it was all right. I just didn't
think about those dark things. The therapist told my parents
that I had basically blocked it out, and might have to deal with
the fallout years later, but I knew it was okay. I was fine."

She lifted her head then, tilted her face so it was mere
inches from Brendan's. In his eyes, she saw all the things she
expected to see. Deep anger that anyone would try to harm her
this way, or harm any child. Compassion, kindness, strength.
And blissful, blissful quiet. She realized then that was what
she liked the absolute best about Brendan. There was such a
solid tranquility at the center of him, like the fulcrum of this
Ferris wheel. Allowing the world to turn, but solidly anchored.
She wondered if that had anything to do with him being a
sexual submissive, or if being a sexual submissive had created
it. Chicken or egg. Or if it was just him being Brendan, and all
the wonderful things that meant. She rubbed her forehead,
gave a little tired laugh.

"So, long story short, Marguerite's father said, 'I'm back,'
and it's like he brought his attack and that memory slamming
together. Now I can't get the boogeyman out of my closet. I
can't sleep…and sometimes my leg aches so much, like it's this
dull reminder all the time. It's stupid, because I *do* have a
wonderful life. I've had these two terrible moments in time,
and they really were just moments, you know? It makes me so
mad they can ruin my life despite being so short. It makes me
furious."

She was really shaking now, but then the Ferris wheel
revved up again, dropping them out of that top spot, taking
them down fast, building up for the final cycle. It whirled
faster and faster, the other occupants crying out in nervous

excitement and pleasure. It felt like too much, except she was at a still place in the universe, held against Brendan's chest.

"Yell."

She wasn't sure she'd heard him correctly, but he tilted up her chin, looked at her close up, his eyes vibrant as he spoke over the rushing wind. "Yell your lungs out. Here. Tell the universe how pissed off you are. Face outward, and let it out."

She remembered the exercises he told her he had his students do, teaching them to cry and rage, laugh and use every range of emotion they had, spilling it out into the world. She saw that resolve and encouragement in his bright gaze, coaxing her to keep this moment from breaking her in a way she wasn't ready to handle. Holding onto his hand, she straightened up as they ascended toward the heavens at maximum speed. Taking a deep breath, she put everything into it.

With the first note, she understood why, in some cultures, the women would shriek like banshees at grief, letting their pain be heard up to the heavens. Maybe they feared it wouldn't be heard otherwise, so much suffering in the world that God wouldn't notice a quieter plea.

The sound was torn away from her on the wind, so she did it again, and again, closing her eyes so she didn't have to see anyone's face on the ground as they sped past the lower level, again and again. She let her rage slash up through the sky, up toward the stars. Her eyes were tearing, but she shoved that reaction back and kept screaming until the wheel slowed and her breaths deepened, steadied. When the car came to a stop about halfway up, she realized they were starting to unload people and load the next group on.

She had to clear her throat, but his grip stayed tight on her, helping. She was proud she hadn't let a single tear through, had let the rage lead her cry of fury, even though she was shaking in a way that made her glad she wasn't trying to stand. "I'm so afraid, Brendan. It's like fifteen years of nightmares that I never had have been saving themselves for me, and every time I close my eyes I'm sure they're going to take me. Like I didn't experience what somebody wanted me to experience, something that I was supposed to handle differently. So I'm going to wake back up there in that shack, only this time it's going to be both of them. God, I can't stand it. I can't stand being this way, and I don't know what to do. I don't know what to do."

Damn it, her voice was breaking, and it wasn't like all those countless times before, those small leaks in the dam, or short, painful floods that she could battle back. Her head pounded so violently with the fear and pent-up emotion it was as if her skull might shatter from the force of it, her bones might rattle out of her skin. She couldn't breathe.

The bar was pulled back. He gathered her up in his arms, holding her close and curled up against him as if she was a child again in truth, and stepped back onto the ground. She didn't know if he spoke to anyone, reassured anyone about her. All she cared about was he took her back into that weighted darkness, walking away from the carnival, letting the lights dim behind them. He sat down on one of the many benches scattered over the back lawn for the convenience of guests. He held her as she battled her emotions, the boiling cauldron that threatened to overflow, erupt from her chest.

It took a long time. Though the fear and anguish didn't go away, she ran out of energy and got numb to it. On that horrible long ago night, in the deer glade, it had been like that a couple times. She'd gotten so exhausted, she'd nodded off, chased by uneasiness and dangerous numbness together.

He was rocking her gently in his arms, and she was clutching his flesh, kneading it, almost like nursing babies she'd seen, that reminder of the bond between them and the safe womb they'd had as a haven for far too short a time. She was too tired to be embarrassed, too tired to do anything.

"Chloe." It was the first time he'd spoken in a long while, and the soft, masculine timbre was a pure, soothing stroke of guitar strings to her raw heart.

"Yeah?" Her voice was sandpaper rough.

"Will you move in with me for awhile?"

His fingers drifted over her hair, her shoulders, making a circular, healing motion. Strong hand, long fingers. His voice was calm, matter of fact, as if his request had nothing to do with her outburst.

"I had a roommate for a while, so I'm not used to living alone. I'd prefer to have someone's company, you know. Hear something moving around, making noise, sharing a bathroom. Or a bath." Humor tinged his voice. "Saves water that way, you know."

"I...don't know. Can I..." She stopped, but he cupped her face, tilted it up to him as if he was cupping a lotus flower, teasing the petals of her lips and cheek, the curve of her ear.

"Ask me anything, Chloe. Anything."

"I don't know if I can do that. But I want...can we go there for at least tonight? I know you're supposed to be here, so if you have to say no—"

He rose, still holding her in his arms. "Do you have things in Marguerite and Tyler's house you need to get?"

She managed an ungraceful snuffle. "Yeah. Just one suitcase. I can walk, you know. Been doing it nearly all my life."

"And I can carry you. I haven't been doing it nearly long enough."

Chapter Thirteen

ஐ

He'd given her a serious glance with those Fae hazel eyes, and strode for the main house. She'd liked the noise and life of the carnival, but now, in the aftermath of her latest meltdown, she welcomed the quiet of the back gardens, the beauty of the Florida room that Brendan entered, shifting her in his arms. "Why don't I put you down here?" He nodded to a deep cushioned chair. "If you tell me what room you're in, I'll go up and get your things."

"It's the first bedroom on the left upstairs, but I haven't really packed it up."

"I'll know what's yours." He met her gaze. "If I overlook anything, Marguerite will bring it to the tea room. Just rest easy here, all right? Did you bring your car?"

"No. Marguerite brought me here."

"Okay, then." As he lowered her into the lounger, her hands tightened on his shoulders. She couldn't let him go, afraid of what might happen if she broke that connection. He pressed his forehead to hers. "I'll be right back, I promise."

A soft creak drew her attention to the doorway. Chloe saw Tyler's silhouette framed in it.

Brendan kept a loose hold of her hands as he straightened, letting her arms slide down in his grip. "Master Tyler, can you stay with her while I get her things? I'm going to take her to my place."

Tyler nodded, stepping into the room. Chloe wondered if the well of shame and humiliation ever ran dry, as she thought about her erratic behavior today. But when Brendan squeezed her hand, giving her a steady look that promised a quick return, she couldn't help clinging to his fingers. Fortunately, as if the men were in a Vulcan mind meld over her care, Tyler's hand closed over her wrist, so as Brendan's touch slid away, his took its place.

With his other hand, he drew an ottoman close to the lounger and sat down on it, reaching out with two fingers to smooth back a tendril of her hair. Then he reached into the pocket of his slacks and drew out a neatly folded and pressed handkerchief for her sweat-stained, makeup destroyed face.

"You know, guys don't carry those any more."

"There are many things that men don't do any more that they should. Particularly for women." Leaning forward, Tyler touched the fabric to her cheeks.

She fished about for something to say. "I'm sorry about leaving. And taking Brendan. I want to explain, but—"

Taking the cloth away, he put his hand on her face instead. It was a different feeling. Whereas Brendan gave her that feeling of absolute connection, with Tyler it was a reassuring command. "When and if you wish, you can."

"I don't know if he's exactly serious, but Brendan suggested I move in with him for a little while, since he's between roommates."

"Really?" Tyler lifted a brow.

"Yeah. That's the complicated part. I really want to, but most relationships don't start with 'Hey, why don't you move in with me?' I like him a lot, Tyler. I don't want to blow it for both of us, and if he turns out to be not the right guy, I don't want it to be over too fast. I want to savor the good before I find out he cross dresses or has bodies in his freezer."

"Some men look very good in women's clothes." But Tyler smiled.

"Does Brendan tell Marguerite a lot of things? Are they that kind of friends?"

An intriguing look passed over Tyler's face, here and gone. Chloe wasn't sure how to interpret it, but he inclined his head. "Brendan would trust Marguerite with anything."

"Okay. I told him something tonight. I'm pretty sure…it's something that Marguerite should know, but I don't think I can say it again. I haven't talked to anyone about it, Tyler, and I'm not sure I want anyone else to know. I know you and Marguerite don't have any secrets from one another either, but if he tells her, and then she tells you, you guys could pretend not to know, if I need you to do that. Right?"

A grim smile touched his firm lips. "Marguerite and I will do whatever you need to make you happy, little flower."

She gave a half chuckle. "I'm zapped, but not zapped enough to miss the fact that's a qualified answer. But it's okay." She realized she was leaning more of her head's weight against his hand, and pressing it to the lounger. "Tell Marguerite I do know it's wrong, but I'm going to let him take care of me for a little while, okay? I'm sure I'll say I'm sorry for it…" Her words were slurring, her head rolling against his broad palm. Vaguely she was aware of him easing her back on the lounger, down to a resting position, but she didn't have the energy to say anything further.

I just can't let him go, even if we're wrong for each other.

* * * * *

She was quiet on the ride to his place. The Jeep had an unfortunate center console, so Brendan couldn't keep her close to his side like he wanted, but he kept a hand on her as he held her hand, resting his palm on her knee. She leaned against the seat, turned on her hip toward him, as if she needed that closeness too.

He'd seen Chloe's face reflect myriad emotions now, and had made careful note of all of them. Part of it was the drama coach in him, scrutinizing how people expressed the countless emotions and multiple shades of gray in between. As a submissive as well as a drama teacher, he knew there were two physical languages. While a woman's face might reflect the universally recognized expression of happiness, there would be nuances to it, not only the unique signature to her brand of happiness, but subtle messages of what drove the happiness, how long it would last, how real the happiness truly was.

With her, his interest was more than his deep curiosity in the human condition. It was his sheer desire to understand her mind, anticipate her needs and wants, even before she herself might realize them. Because he'd watched her so closely, he'd understood from the beginning that there was more to what had happened that horrible day at Tea Leaves. Her surface expressions, no matter if they were was happiness or pleasure, had possessed a wariness, as if she knew that under layer, the story untold, was waiting in the wings, ready to turn everything she'd wanted to feel into a lie.

Something perilous had occurred tonight, perilous and cathartic at once. She was struggling with the idea she'd built her life on an illusion of happiness, foolishly, childishly pushing away the reality. However, in this too, he saw something entirely different, something she couldn't yet see.

The world was full of beauty and light, and reasons for joy. Rather than letting the adult world of darkness take that from her at the age of nine, she'd built her own tower, refusing to do anything less than embrace life fully, with her laughter and her joy. It made her remarkable, exceptional and courageous.

The fact that the incident with Marguerite's father had laid siege to that tower didn't alter her truth. It had only altered her belief in it, and he was determined to give her whatever she needed to help her see that, drive that dragon away.

Joy and happiness, darkness and rage had all visited her since he'd known her. They were all part of her, as they were part of everyone, but he knew which ones truly guided Chloe Davis.

As he pulled up to his townhouse, her tired eyes studied the door arrangement, a drama mask designed like a pumpkin's face, ensconced in a spray of autumn leaves. It was a reminder of the fall equinox that didn't match the warm Florida weather, but many residents, including him, insisted on observing the seasonal transition anyway. A little black rubber spider dangled from it, an incongruous touch of whimsy.

"Was the door arrangement a gift?"

"Yes and no." Because he wanted to do it, he lifted her hand to his mouth, nuzzled her fingers. She watched him, her lips parting. He knew such Old World gestures bemused her Bohemian personality, but the female animal beneath recognized and responded to them. When her fingers quivered, he increased his grasp on them. "When I was little, my mom was pretty busy, a decorator, and a really good one. Even though she didn't have a lot of time to transform our house for the holidays or passing of seasons, she made a production of decorating the door. She had me 'help' her."

He smiled at Chloe, rubbing his thumb over her fingers. "I'd say where I thought different things should go. In retrospect, I'm sure they were ideas that destroyed the artistry of her design. Like for Christmas, I'd want a gaudy lit-up Santa with a plastic face and rosy cheeks in the middle of the elegant wreath she'd arranged with white doves and silver and blue ribbons. But she helped me see where it would best fit. She'd talk me into putting Santa on the stoop, surround him with pine cones and sprigs of holly, perch a few doves there like the white of his beard. We'd spray frost snow flakes on the glass of our storm door, and they'd sparkle when she'd hang a single strand of white lights around them."

"She sounds nice."

"She was perfect. In the way a loving mother seen through the eyes of a five-year-old can be." He paused, glanced back at the door. "My parents were killed in a car wreck when I was young. As the years pass, you forget important details, no matter how long you try to hold onto them, but you remember small things. So I still decorate the door, with the odd gaudy touch."

"Like a rubber spider." Now it was her fingers that tightened on his. When he looked toward her, he saw compassion in her eyes, a softness to her mouth, but she didn't say any of the usual platitudes. He was glad for that.

Her brown eyes, when they were like this, reminded him of a cow. He didn't say that, unsure she'd understand the compliment, but when he looked at the liquid brown eyes of a cow, he always felt a tranquility, as if the placid animal, in her bovine simplicity, understood something no human ever would about making the most of each day, of every moment. He wanted to give that back to her.

Now though, he simply nodded. "Want to go in and see the rest of it?"

"The door arrangement is a way to keep it from overwhelming you, isn't it? Losing your parents."

"That's one way of looking at it. Here's another." Leaning over, he put his lips on hers, a gentle meeting of mouths, slow moving, a drift of feeling and physical stirring between them, quiet understanding. Yet when he started to draw back, she caught her fingers in his hair, holding him there so his eyes were inches from hers.

"I should take you home to my family this Christmas," she said. "My mother would adopt you in a heartbeat."

The warmth of his smile settled over Chloe, making her feel close to every part of who he was, and so glad to be here with him.

"Another way to keep things from overwhelming you is to realize that a house not only shelters you from the storm, it has windows to let in the light, hold it." He teased back a loose lock of her hair. "And I'd love to meet your parents. I don't think you realize how brave you are, Chloe."

"Brave enough to go into your house at the very least, right?" She managed to give him a faint smile. "Though I've heard horror stories about your laundry. And shoes like spiders. Maybe I'll sleep in the car."

"I keep the laundry safely locked away so it can't harm the innocent, and the spider shoes only appear for me." He made a face at her that almost made her laugh, but then he sobered. "Please come into my home, Chloe."

Dropping to a sensual murmur, he pressed his lips to her jaw, glided to the pulse in her throat so that she lifted her chin to give him better access. She moved her fingers from his hair to his shoulders, then down to clutch his shirt, holding tight as that brief touch threatened to send her floating away.

"Okay." She managed it on an indrawn breath. "You've bullied me into it."

"Don't move," he said, and then he was out the Jeep door and moving around to the other side. He was a little less put together at three a.m. than he'd been in his chain mail. But she liked the look of him in worn jeans and his faded Cirque du Soleil T-shirt with a fire breathing dragon. Unshaven, his hair tousled, he looked a little rough and unpredictable as he came around the vehicle. It wasn't a bad look for him, his Beaver Cleaver jokes notwithstanding.

He opened the door, helped her out, ready if she was still unsteady on her feet. She had an amazing feeling he'd be willing to carry her for the next decade if she needed it. At the same time, with his comment about her being brave, she didn't feel as if it stole any strength from her. Moreover, it suggested she still had some in her, somewhere. She'd give it the night off, hope it would have grown in size by morning.

Opening his front door, he guided her in, carrying her bag, which he set down in the entryway. "Feel free to look around anywhere," he said. "I'm just going to go check my messages."

She nodded as he moved toward the open kitchen. The living space was comfortable, a male abode with masculine furniture, but a style that underscored Brendan's background in theater art. There were earthy blends of color with splashes of warm reds in the sectional grouping in his sitting room. The entranceway had a series of black and white photographs, artistic renderings of two nudes, a male and female. Their positions were intimate. The male kneeling, head to his knees while the woman's long hair, a rich brown, draped over him like strands of a weeping willow, her body the slender trunk arched backward over him. In the next, the two models lay on blue velvet, the only color, as their black and white figures spooned together. The male was curved protectively around her, their legs and torso flush against one another.

The other two photos had a similar give and take theme, and then guided the eye to a much larger centerpiece for the same series, positioned alone on the wall over the sectional.

This one only showed the two from shoulder to hips. They were back to back, seated, the point of their buttocks on grass, marked with a scattering of tiny white wildflowers. Again the green was the only color, the humans in black and white. Their heads were averted from the camera and so emphasized the jaw lines, the arch of their necks turned from the viewer and each other. But their bodies were pressed so close their hips and shoulders touched, conveying connection and separation at once.

Several cushions and a woven blanket had been tossed across the sectional. On the side table was a pyramid of linked picture frames, forming a sculpture of photos.

Drawing closer, the first one she identified was Marguerite and Brendan, a shot taken of them after Marguerite's wedding. He was looking down at her, a light smile on his face. Marguerite's peace and happiness had been obvious that night, enough to make Chloe smile now in remembrance. The bride leaned into the curve of Brendan's body, as if the picture had been taken while they were dancing, the fairy lights and silhouettes of the large oaks in the background.

Another pair of pictures were soldered at the corners to link them diagonally. One showed a young couple with a boy of about four. The father squatted with the child between his knees while the woman was caught in a half laugh, her hand on her husband's shoulder, two of her fingers firmly clasped by the child as she leaned over them. The other photo was a department store type shot, a pleasant-looking older couple with an adolescent Brendan, their hands on his shoulders, a solidly middle class picture.

"My parents and my adopted parents," Brendan confirmed, returning from the kitchen to stand behind her. "I was very lucky to have them both. Ellen and Reid live in Dayton now, which is where Reid was from originally."

His tone was easy, no hidden meanings, and she was glad to know his adopted parents had appreciated his wonderful qualities as much as those who'd given him birth obviously had. If there was a heaven, she was sure it was a comfort to them to know he'd not lost that security, that vital need of a child to know he was specifically and specially loved by someone who felt it was their duty—and privilege—to be in charge of his safety and wellbeing.

In this rack of obviously significant choices, she was surprised to see a picture of herself.

It was also from the wedding. She'd still been recuperating from her injuries, enough that she'd looked a little thinner, the face bruises healed but the impression of them still somehow there. But in this shot, she was sitting at a table with Brendan, Gen and a couple of regular visitors to the tea room.

She'd been firmly instructed by everyone to keep her leg elevated. Brendan had it propped on his leg, his hand resting on her ankle as he leaned back, beer in hand. His lips were curved in a grin that suggested they'd all been laughing at something. She was laughing too, one of her hands clasped in Gen's, the other reaching out to grab Brendan's, as if they'd made her laugh so hard she was steadying herself with their touch.

Brendan and Gen were partially cut off in the picture, Chloe the center focus.

"Marguerite gave it to me." Brendan touched the photo, her face, without any obvious self-consciousness.

"Yet all those months, you didn't call me."

"I gave you my phone number. You didn't give me yours. Remember?" He said it without judgment in his tone, a simple fact. "I thought we hit it off that night, but there were things, the way you looked at times, that told me you needed time. Crazy as it sounds, I thought it might mean more to you, when you finally called, if I was ready to be with you, waiting for you, rather than forcing you to decide on me before you were ready."

He'd waited on her to call. For months. Wow. "Oh." Chloe absorbed that. "Either that's a really spectacular thing to say to overwhelm a girl, or the smoothest lie I've ever heard to cover being too chickenshit to risk rejection."

Brendan chuckled, not confirming or denying. Glancing at the several other photos, she saw a precocious-looking hound in one, and then some shots of what might be his students, clustered around him and dressed in costume for one of the community plays he'd probably helped produce.

She wanted to know the stories behind those as well, but not right now. She turned on her heel to take in the rest of the room. A flat-screen TV—the essential piece of male home décor. An assortment of books on art and theater, as well as some espionage novels. They were mixed with a fairly substantial movie collection, neatly arranged in handsome glass-faced cabinets.

"Did you know I was coming? Or are you always this scarily neat?"

"Which answer makes me seem less OCD?"

She gave a snort. She remembered how she'd thought it possible to mistake him for the gay stereotype, with his physical perfection, sense of style and interests. Having been the recipient of a direct blast of his unleashed sexuality, she knew he had a fully committed appreciation for the female form. Still, Brendan's program section at the auction hadn't noted a limitation to female bidders only.

"There's no picture of an old girlfriend, or boyfriend." She tested the waters, wondering why she was hesitating to ask him straight out if he was bi. "Or a current one, for that matter."

He gave her an easy smile. "Well, papering the wall with my conquests tends to put off the scores of dates I bring home."

"Yeah, right." She bumped him with her hip. "I can tell you're a real slut." Though she remembered his words. *I don't usually date outside the club...* It suggested he'd been telling the truth, when he said he'd been waiting for her call. She wasn't sure what to make of that. Truth be told, he was like nothing she'd ever met before.

When he slid an arm around her back, she automatically leaned into him, feeling her tiredness. "Am I prying?" she asked.

"No. Well, yeah, but I want you to be interested. Sometimes, depending on how a relationship ends, it's too painful to keep a picture, you know?"

"But do you keep them?"

"It depends. On whether that helps me move on or not. The last one, no."

She saw the shadow, registered the tension that tightened the biceps against her shoulder blades. "I'm sorry. How long ago?"

"Over a year. Before you think it, no, you are not a rebound." He gave her a little admonishing squeeze.

She believed him. But what about her? He was her first foray into a relationship, hell, even dating, since that terrible day. Her first attempt to open herself up in the way a good romance demanded, fully experiencing the tingling delight, wonder and adventure of falling in love again, wherever it ended up. Only she wasn't sure what she'd find in her heart, when and if she opened it fully again. She was afraid those spurts of unreasoning anger and desire to hurt, strike out, were evidence of the sharp slivers her heart had become.

She could see the ground level hallway off the sitting room led to a bathroom and home office. In his kitchen, where he'd been checking his messages, a small four-person table was visible through the pass through. Following her desire, she headed for the stairs to the second level. She had a sudden impulse to take him at his word, see, explore whatever she wanted, without asking permission. As she went up the carpeted stairs and reached the hallway, she noted there was a guest bedroom. It wasn't his, because it didn't have any personal articles. When he turned on the light, she could see two rooms off further down the hallway. More intriguing prints lined the walls. This time they were water scenes, shots that she assumed had called to the swimmer in him.

She glanced over her shoulder. He stood behind her, hand on the light switch, gazing down at her face in that intent way that made heat prickle on her skin and increased her awareness of where she was headed.

"I want to see where you were lying, that night I called you," she said, her voice husky. "I'd like to see your bedroom."

He nodded, gesturing her forward, letting her lead. He didn't say anything further as she stepped through the doorway. Her gaze fell on a king-sized shaker style bed of dark sleek wood. The throw was the dark, swirling blue color of the deep ocean. An oil painting positioned above the head board picked up the nautical theme. It depicted a storm-stirred sea against a lightning-illuminated bank of clouds, no other features except the turbulence of the waves and foam of the white caps.

She briefly noted his armoire and closet, a single dresser. One silk tie and jacket were folded over the arm of a straight chair. She imagined he'd been running late after work and had left them there before heading for Marguerite and Tyler's. Or maybe they were there for Monday. In her mind's eye, she saw him getting ready for work. Sitting down in the chair to pull on his shoes, standing in front of the dresser mirror to adjust the tie. Picking up his keys, sliding his wallet into his coat or pants. Through an open door, she saw a spacious master bath reflected in the mirror over the sink.

Her heart dared to give her another image. Her, living with him. Destroying all that neatness with her propensity for leaving her clothes everywhere. Turning on music in the morning to dance around him as he shaved at the mirror. He'd be smiling at her as she karaoke'd for him, garbled, because her toothbrush was in her mouth.

It hadn't even occurred to her heart's imaginings that she'd stay in the guestroom.

Brendan touched her lower back as he moved past her. He went to the nightstand and laid his cell phone in the charger there.

"Where do you —" She cut herself off, turned and went to the armoire. Opened it and let her gaze wander over the clothes hung to one side. Compartments on the right held a few sets of good shoes, an assortment of ties and slacks on racks. There were some built-in drawers and she opened the top one to find socks, underwear, the lower one revealing jeans.

Nodding to herself, she moved to the closet. She noted he shifted, as if he might stop her, or wanted to say something first, but when she glanced at him, he only gestured, confirming she was free to do as she pleased. He sat down on the bed, his eyes on her.

The door did have a keyed lock, so he could secure it if he wished. But it was open to her. While it turned under her hand, she didn't immediately pull it open.

She knew what had to be in here. The carnival had made clear being a sexual submissive wasn't a casual pastime in his life. It was innate to who he was. The person who wanted to be with him would need not only to accept that, but embrace it. She wished she could banish Mistress Lyda's words, but she couldn't, could she? Because she didn't know her feelings on any of it.

If she didn't open the closet, he might think she was rejecting that part of him. However, that wasn't why she was wavering. She didn't want the ugliness that had gripped her at the carnival to take over here. While she wasn't sure what had happened, she was pretty sure having the trappings and tools to put him entirely at her mercy had been a dangerous catalyst.

As she wavered between what she owed him and what she owed herself, the overhead light clicked off. It would have alarmed her, except there was still light thrown into the room from the hallway. And Brendan was here.

She didn't turn, but heard his feet cross the carpet. Then his hand closed over hers on the doorknob. He pressed close, the curve of her buttock against his thigh, his hip bone. Flattening his palm on her abdomen, he traced the navel through her dress, a teasing circle, then curved his fingers inward so his knuckles glided up her body, shifting to follow the line of her left breast.

He'd lingered at the navel, identifying that bump of scar tissue, but he hadn't commented on it. As his long fingers straightened so the pads grazed her nipple, before he closed over the curve fully, taking gentle possession, she whispered the truth of it.

"I used to have a piercing there."

"Yeah?" He disengaged her grip on the knob, and brought her hand back behind her, guiding her until she molded her hand over his right buttock. Her thumb tucked into his jeans' pocket, helping her keep her hand there. Her touch moved with cautious but unmistakable greedy pleasure over the well-toned muscle.

As he let that hand go, he slid his arm forward over her shoulder. She figured he'd cross over his other to clasp her other breast, but his destination was higher, his palm curving around her neck, one finger sliding over her cheek, thumb tracing her bottom lip. Slow caresses of her breast with the other hand made the nipple ache and flesh swell.

"What was your favorite piece of jewelry for it?" he murmured. "What did it look like?"

How could you speak when someone was stealing your breath? "It was a silver yin and yang symbol...with a diamond for the point of light in dark and vice versa."

"Who gave it to you?"

She shuddered as two fingers pinched the nipple. Her thighs quivered, her hips pushing back into that solid leg. "What if I said he was a sexy bad boy biker guy with six pack abs and a dragon tattoo on his biceps? Are you the jealous type?"

Nudging her head to the side, he put his lips on her accelerating pulse, right between his fingers. "What do you think?"

"I think you get underestimated in the dangerous bad boy department." She gave a half laugh, half gasp. "You don't have to get jealous. You make damn sure a girl has zero desire to be with anyone but you. It's a different form of possessiveness, more Mach...Machiavellian than Attila the Hun." She had to take a deep breath to get through a suddenly far too complex word, but that reaction increased the pressure of her breast against his hand, embellishing the squeezing, pleasurable sensation. Her nipple was stabbing his palm and she wanted to push it against him harder.

"Hmm. *Did* a man give it to you?"

"No. I bought it for myself. Rick—that was his name—took me to the bluegrass festival...where the vendor was. He spent all his money on his bike. He was...n-nineteen. You're really making it hard to...talk."

"Good." He'd continued down the side of her throat with that devastating hand on her cheek, his fingers tracing her nose, gliding over her lashes. It made her eyes close, then her teeth bit down on her lip as he nipped and suckled on her throat in a way that had her body moving restlessly. Heat and wetness grew between her legs, making her panties damp, making her want him to touch her there, feel it too.

She didn't have the navel piercing anymore because Marguerite's father had ripped the barbell loose. His face had been close, stark, horror-movie close, saliva spraying her as he screamed. *This is what a dirty whore wears. A slut. I've always been with you. I know what you became. What you are.*

Brendan's hands slid away, but only to turn her around, gently push her back against the closet door. Her fingers slipped out of his pocket regretfully, grazed his hip as he completed that turn. Closing his hands over hers, he held them out in the air to either side of them, letting them float erratically up and down, a drift of movement that helped steady what had suddenly become unsteady to her.

Keeping his gray-green eyes on hers, he eased down to one knee, flanking her with the other bent one as he let go of one of her hands, then the other, to place his hands on her hips. Leaning forward, he put his mouth on her navel through the thin fabric between them and drove that terrible memory away, the shame that went with it.

The moist heat of his breath dampened the area. That and the pressure of his mouth made her nerves respond, perhaps even more violently than if it had been flesh on flesh, no barrier between them. The deprivation somehow heightened her reaction.

"Can you..." Her voice was a cautious plea in the full dark, because she'd closed her eyes, one hand restlessly kneading his shoulder while the other found his hair, gripped.

"What, beloved?"

Beloved. Never would she have thought a guy could use such an old-fashioned word and make it sound like that, like it was supposed to sound. A vow of adoration in one, three-syllable utterance.

But then Brendan wasn't a "guy", was he? She'd dated guys, like Rick. A lot of them. Brendan was a man, everything that word should mean. Just like the word "beloved", it had a rich significance to it that was lost unless everything became really still, like this.

"If I need...want you to...can you..."

She shouldn't think about this so much, or she was going to mess herself up, but what if he couldn't do what she wanted? What she thought she understood about tonight, everything she'd seen, said it wasn't fair to ask this. But it wasn't anger or that dark ugliness motivating her now, and he'd said he'd give her anything. Anything.

As she waffled over it, he stood. As he got up, his body was so close it dragged along hers, his jeans, the shirt he wore, catching the thin fabric of her dress, pulling it up with the motion of his body so it was gathered between them, her hem rucked up and trapped between their thighs.

"Take me over." She flicked her attention doubtfully up to his face, wanting too much, too badly, to give herself a chance to be sensitive or debate the wisdom.

He gazed at her. Then, slowly, his lips curved to show his teeth. No question about it. It was a dangerous, bad-boy smile.

Chapter Fourteen

৪০

Closing his hands over both of hers, he brought her wrists up against the door, over her head, stealing her breath. Then he brought his head down so his lips hovered over hers, his eyes so close.

"Chloe." As her pulse slammed against those points in her wrist, held firmly beneath his hands, his breath caressed her face.

"Yeah." Her throat had gone dry, thick. His thigh slid forward, pressed against her mons, eliciting a quiet gasp, then lower, insinuating between her legs so she had to adjust her stance over him. The moment she did, he brought his knee up, an insistent, searing pressure against the thin panties she wore. The folds of her dress whispered over the denim-clad leg.

"Kiss me the way you want me to fuck you. Show me with your mouth and tongue, with your desire, how hard you want me to nail you against this wall."

Holy God. She let go of thought, guilt or consequences and surged up against his hold, hitting his mouth as if fueled by a firelake of pheromones. His grip tightened, a resistant counterpoint, and she growled into his mouth, scraping her teeth over his tongue, a tongue clever enough to be tangling with hers as she thrust savagely into his mouth, not thinking about finesse or seduction, just a desire to be straight out, Victorian romance-novel *ravished.* Taken over and taken hard. Pummeled, owned, so she'd know he was completely hers. A possession to seal the deal between them. She needed his response to her eager desire to know he'd give her anything of himself.

He had her arms, but her hips were free to move. She worked herself up on his thigh, pressing her hip bone into his cock, finding him blissfully hard. Her pussy contracted, already anticipating, needy for him.

Hiking her up under her arms, he let her climb up his body and wrap her legs around his waist, but instead of taking her against the closet as he'd intimated, he brought her over to his bed, to that ocean of blue.

He sat down on it, with her straddling him, hands lowering to grip her buttocks, work her against him. He used his strength to move her, though the friction and pressure had her adding her own insistence to it. She wanted him inside now.

Instead, he flipped her over onto the mattress, taking her down to her back, and held her wrists to her sides as he worked his way from her mouth down her throat again, to her breasts, but not the nipples, jutting with obvious insistence against the thin cloth.

"Brendan, suckle me," she gasped.

"I'm OCD, remember? I have to obey your first command, first." When she saw a devilish glint in his eyes, she got even wetter as her hands flexed under his and he only tightened his grip. "I'm going to take you over, make you hot, wet and panting. Make you mindless, just the way you want."

He worked his way down to the navel again, the skin so sensitive there she almost cried out as if he'd tongued her cunt. It convulsed as if he had. She bucked as his head cruised down, his lips over one hip bone, down to the top of her thigh, playing in that crease between thigh and sex, always that wet, hot mouth against a bare millimeter thickness of fabric.

If that wasn't enough torment, he spoke to her throughout, in that sexy, quiet rumble, as she gasped and pleaded incoherently.

His mouth dipped, just a touch of her pussy through her clothes and she bucked up like she'd been touched by electricity.

"Not quite wet enough," he said in a husky, seductive tone, and she cursed him. In answer, he flipped her onto her stomach, and began working his way over her ass, his tongue dipping into that seam between her buttocks, pushing silky cloth against the nerves with the firm pressure. He wasn't holding her arms now, but his hand remained on her lower back, stroking, exerting pressure to make it clear that was where he wanted her.

"Brendan." She shut her eyes tightly, thinking she would come just from rubbing herself against the cover, but she needed him. "Please. Fuck me."

His arm slid beneath her, pulled her to her knees. She was used to her boyfriends being larger than she was, and Brendan was no exception, outweighing her by probably eighty pounds and more than a foot taller than she was. She'd always loved that feeling of being sheltered by a man's strength, seeing the way they varied between gentle and rough in the way they touched her, depending on how worked up they were. This was unique, getting both at once. Brendan was never rough with her, but he was inexorable at the same time, a devastating seduction.

Air touched the back of her legs as he pulled the skirt up, folded it over her lower back. He slid the panties off, allowing him to thoroughly caress every inch of flesh from ankles to hips, except the area that wanted him the most.

But then he came back up and let his fingers glide down either side of her labia, carefully avoiding her clit. She realized she was shaking as if she had a fever, thinking of his lips on her navel, his hands on her wrists.

"I want your cock, Brendan. I want it now. I need it now."

He slid up her back, came down on either side of her with his long arms, the pressure of his chest canting her down, bringing her pussy and his cock into alignment. She made a soft, low cry at the feel of him brushing her thigh, the scratch of his opened jeans along her thighs.

"I'll take you wherever you need to go," he promised, breathing into her hair.

"Wherever I order you to go?"

"They're the same. Just one of them isn't always said with words. I hear it in your voice, what you want and need from me."

Had he done this with other Mistresses? A give and take, not only them commanding him to their will, but him knowing, watching a Mistress's actions and reactions, knowing what she most wanted from him? Was she now the beneficiary of such skills, though they both knew she was no Mistress?

Such disturbing thoughts fled. He'd cinched his arm around her waist, holding her fast, and now he began to enter her, his broad head starting to stretch her lips, make her tremble.

"No one's ever made me feel like you do." She turned her face into his arm, muffling the words against his skin. It was an impulsive, emotionally driven confession, but it didn't make it any less true.

She'd taken joy and pleasure in her relationships, however long or short they were, but she hadn't known it could ever feel like this. Vital. Coming home, when you didn't even realize you'd been away as long as you had. The beginning of a fire, a desire that was like an eternal flame, that only seemed to grow more fierce as he satisfied her, making her want him even more, again and again.

More than that, in this second, she felt clean. *I'm clean, I'm clean, I'm clean...this makes me clean.* She thought it was in her head, something she was chanting like a spell to change the past, transform her present and change her fear of the future, but then he spoke.

"You're pure love, Chloe. That's what you are."

He slid all the way in, filling and stretching her, and she cried out at the sensation, him seated to the hilt so his testicles pressed against her clit. All those internal muscles rippled along him like fingers, holding him tight. Brendan increased his grip on her waist as she pressed her face into the muscular arm he had braced on the bed.

"You're pure love," he repeated, his voice husky and thick. "And pure fire. God, you feel so sweet and tight. You're burning me up."

He drew out slowly, came back in, and all that arousal he'd built before he'd even entered her tumbled on the brink of eruption. He'd chosen to take her like this, in the most natural position in the animal world. Taken her, as she'd asked. Demanded. Needed.

He did it again, that slow, torturous withdrawal and glide back in. As she moaned, sinking her teeth into his forearm, his other hand descended, thumb sliding over the tiny area of scar tissue at the navel, down to her clit. Stretched as she was, he still managed to tease inside the labia, add stress to those outer lips, as if he might try to fill her even more, work his fingers in there on top of the already thick diameter of his cock. He didn't, just taunted her with the fantasy of it, his thumb rubbing a slow, perfect circle on the sensitive clit bud as she began to work herself back against him.

"Yeah, that's it, baby," he muttered. Her control flagged at the quiver she felt in his hard abs, his incredible restraint as he kept himself to the pace that would inflame both of them further, take her orgasm higher.

"Brendan, I want you to come with me. When I go, I want you with me."

"Want to feel my cock spurt in your sweet cunt?" His voice was a form of fucking all its own, thrusting into her psyche, dragging forth the emotional response that could make the physical one so much more intense. His breath caressed the sensitive shell of her ear. She pressed her forehead harder into the solid curve of biceps muscle, shifted her hand so it was over his, her fingers in the spaces, curling into the bed.

"Yes. Take me there. Get us there."

"We are. See it on the horizon. Feel my fingers working you, the feel of me against your beautiful ass. My balls hitting your clit, as I give...you...more."

He thrust with more power, and the sensation shot straight to her womb and into her throat. She cried out, now gripping his wrist, digging in, wanting more.

He gave her more, working her harder, holding her body against him, and it was the most incredible sensation, feeling as if she were being cradled like an egg, and ridden hard at the same time. Cherished and ravished both as he set his teeth to her shoulder, a long male growl in his chest. "Want to come inside you, Chloe. Want to fill you up."

"I'm...yes, come for me." She barely got the words out as his fingers, the movement of his cock inside her, the friction of his body on the outside, swept over like fire in truth, shoving her pumping body back into his. All those nearly there orgasms of the past few months came slamming together, like an army thundering out of the world of unfinished climaxes. They roared up on her, took her over.

She screamed, she was sure of it. It wasn't a short scream, but a long, drawn out cry. She had a brief second to wonder about neighbors, knowing there would be no doubt that what they heard was pleasure, not torment, though it could be the knife edge of both. Brendan knew that even better than she did.

His hot seed jetted into her, keeping her going. His cock was still slamming into her so she did feel the slap of testicles against her, an additional impact to her still spasming clit. The clutch of his powerful arm around her waist, hearing his guttural, primal sound of release, it was all beautiful. His climax kept her crying out through her own aftershocks, clinging to that supporting arm, gloriously aware it never slipped, capable of holding her up even through his own overwhelming response.

Capable of holding her through anything.

* * * * *

It seemed a long time before they came down. Her vision seemed fuzzy. Easing her to her side, he spooned behind her, like the photo downstairs, and she didn't mind thinking of them as black and white, tranquil shades of gray against the blue. The light from the parking lot thrown through the window illuminated the bedroom furnishings in soft relief.

Brendan left her briefly, with a kiss on her shoulder, to light two tapered candles he removed from a drawer and set up in a pair of pewter holders on the nightstand. As he went to turn off the hallway light, her gaze drifted over them. The bases were a pair of coiled dragons.

When he brought his warmth back behind her, she was gratified by how he fit his body to hers again, resting his arm over her waist. "You like dragons?" she asked.

"Dungeons and Dragons geek. Never quite shaken it." When she glanced up from the pillow, she saw he had his head propped on a fist as he studied her profile. Completely absorbed in her, in a way that made the kittens somersaulting in her lower belly purr. She turned away from him, toward the candles, and curled her toes when that clever mouth, the tip of the tongue, traced the valley of her spine. She was amazed to discover arousal was still simmering in her blood. He was so attentive, so attuned to her needs...

"I wish we could just stay like this." Reaching out, she passed her fingers through the flame, felt the brief kiss of heat. "That was...something. It made me feel humble. Content. And wanting to do it all again, as soon as I find the energy."

In answer, he closed his hand on her shoulder, eased her toward him again, down onto her back. First he took her fingers, the ones she'd passed through the flame, and studied them. She realized he was making sure she hadn't singed herself. Then he let her slide the hand free as he curved over her and put his mouth on the upper rise of her breast. His hair brushed her skin. His fingers gripped her waist as he shifted over to her nipple, closed his mouth there with a deep suckling pull, easy and quiet. Instead of kittens, now the desire in her belly was a lazy cat in a heated window sill, burrowing deeper in the joy of sunshine and complete, mindless lassitude. Everything in the universe was revolving where it should be.

She loved how he communicated so much without words, the way the most important things always were. "Oh. *Oh.*" She drew a trembling breath, the hand nearest him curving around his shoulder, finding his hair and threading into it.

It was astonishing how he could find what she wanted, and then give it to her. Not for a mere blink, not until his own desire kicked in, impatient to take them somewhere else, but as long as *she* wanted it. All his senses seemed tuned in to her breath, the tiniest movements of her body, every infinitesimal increase in her arousal. If he were watching a calm pond, he would be the first one to notice the tiny ripples from the movements of water bugs, or sense a fish coming close, but not quite breaking the water's surface.

Knowing that, it wasn't absurd at all to believe that suckling her nipples was the most important—the only thing—in Brendan's existence at this moment. Because it was what she wanted.

Trusting, she laid her other hand limply over her head, feeling like some kind of decadent princess again, lounging on her bed like a raft on an ocean, watching her servant pleasure her.

She'd thought of submission from the angle of whips, chains and contracts, vaguely disturbing internet sites and tonight's auction. But for the first time, she thought she was glimpsing the true essence of it, the elusive understanding of why he was like this. Why Marguerite had said it was hard to explain. It was better grasped when all things were stripped down to this, a sacred act of devotion.

As she shifted, her fingertips brushed one of the candleholders. Following it up past the guard, she caressed the candle's sleek column, liking the silken feel of hard wax. Following her train of thought, relaxing into the moment, she closed her hand over the base, lifted it.

It was amazing how steady her hand was as she brought it to hover over his shoulder, angled over her abdomen because he'd moved his attention to her other nipple now. His mouth intensified the coil of liquid lust spiraling through the curve of flesh, down through her lower belly and arrowing straight between her legs. She watched the movement of his head, his mouth, the way he cradled her breast, compressing it so the nerve endings all focused on his lips, teeth and tongue.

She tipped the taper, and hot wax pattered onto his shoulder. His skin shuddered like a horse's under the impact, but he didn't break his nursing rhythm.

At all.

It was one of the most erotic things she'd ever seen. He hadn't flinched, as if she could do anything she wished, anything that gave her pleasure.

She did it again, a different spot, and it was the same, though she felt a sympathetic burning sensation through the back of her shoulder, imaging how it must feel, how it stimulated the nerve endings there.

"Brendan," she whispered. "Kiss me."

He lifted his face, bathed in candlelit shadows, and put his mouth on hers. She was still holding the candle, and when she fumbled, trying to find her way back to the dresser with it without breaking that pleasurable contact, his hand closed over her wrist, helped her safely take it back to the table. Then she brought both hands back to his shoulders, wrapped her arms tight around him, giving herself to that kiss. Her fingers found the wax, already hardening, but still soft with lingering heat. He slid his arm underneath her, keeping her close to his chest, so their hearts beat together, and she realized both organs were moving at a faster pace, almost synchronized, like that first night.

"I want to be back inside you now." He looked at her through thick lashes, his gaze so intent. "Just to be inside you. May I do that?"

In answer, she curved her leg over his hip, welcoming him. Brendan shifted, bringing his weight onto her, watching every change in her face, the way she bit into her lip, the expression in her eyes as he brought his mostly erect cock back into her. As he eased in, she gave a small whimper at that brief giving sensation when he made it past the gateway, then she sighed over the slow, deep glide, all the way to the heart, that point of fullness, when things that were meant to come together did, a perfect fit in nature.

"You feel so good," she said in a hushed tone. "Like everything I've ever wanted. It scares me."

"Me too." The corner of his mouth turned up.

"Why does it scare you?"

"Because I know it's real."

It made her breath catch funny, somewhere between a sob and surprise. Since she wasn't sure what to say in reply, she fingered the wax on his shoulder, broke a piece of it away. It got away from her, tumbling down his back, lost in the ocean of covers.

He smoothed a palm down her side, all the way to her hip and then to the thigh muscle, crooked over his buttock. While he took his time with the gliding touch, she realized with some amazement he was also making sure her muscles weren't tense or tiring.

"You're not real," she whispered. "Brendan, don't you ever think of yourself?"

"I don't have to do that. I know what I am, what I want, Chloe. It's other people who need my focus. Like you."

"But do you want anything for yourself?"

"Your pleasure, your happiness. Your joy."

That brief ripple of fierce light in his eye should give her a burst of warmth, and it did. But still...

"A true slave can't want anything for himself." She punctuated the words with a sound of pure want in the back of her throat as he moved, a slow stroke, his gaze latched on her face. "Can't have desires. Beyond serving a Master, that is."

"Or Mistress." He bent, touched that clever mouth to the corner of hers, not impeding her ability to talk, but certainly taking away her desire to do so. His ass flexed under her legs, his shoulder muscles constricting as he shifted his body lower, his chest a solid wall, her breasts compressed beneath. As their abdomens touched, his cock made another slight but significant movement inside her, telling her he was hardening further.

"You've been reading," he added, the trace of amusement not lessening the burning desire in his face, the restraint that kept his jaw and chest muscles tense in a very appealing way.

"I read a lot during this week...getting ready. But it didn't tell me...everything. Tonight...those slaves and you... Do you know why you willingly..." *Submit? Need that? Want that? Crave it?* She knew she was coming back to that locked closet, and her questions would reflect more on what she wanted and her confusion about that, rather than his. But maybe one would lead to another. Since she wasn't sure how to word it, she asked the way she felt it. With great difficulty, because she was having to push past how he was distracting her.

"Do you know why you can't do without it? Can you do without it?"

His teeth closed on her carotid, making her body undulate, a slow roll attended by a keening note from her lips.

"Do you know why you prefer a man's cock inside you," he whispered, "instead of a woman's touch on your pussy?"

"No." Her whimper became a short cry as he executed a far more deliberate movement inside her. Her nipples, so aroused by him earlier, tingled with the response that glittered through her body like a shower of silver sparkles. "I just...I experimented, here and there, but I like...men. A lot."

His lips pulled into a smile against her throat. When he lifted his head, enough so their faces were close, his mouth was too inviting. She returned the favor, nibbling him back as he obligingly held still so she could taste and tease.

"Oh," she breathed. "I like that. Stay still, just like that."

She moved over his mouth, the lips slightly parted, and discovered a new erotic pleasure as she dipped into it with tongue and lips. He didn't move, not even a twitch. The only movement was his cock pulsing hard inside her, indicating how pleasurable and difficult at once it was for him to obey, stay motionless as her hands went down his back, traced the width of his shoulders, found the taper of his waist, and then dipped to grip his ass.

With an impish smile, she brought her hips up, taking him deeper, then let her hips sink back to the bed, a heated, moist stroke, all executed by her will. His thighs quivered, a shudder running through his shoulders.

"Brendan, why are you like this?" she repeated in a whisper. "What do you feel when a woman takes you over like this, pushes you to mindless obedience, makes her every wish your only desire, your only reason for living?"

She saw all that in his eyes and face, in the tension and compliance at once in his body.

"Because..." She was intrigued to see his gaze sweep down, his focus on her throat, the flush of desire across her sternum. His voice vibrated through her. "I feel...whole, like I'm doing what I'm supposed to do. I'm on the edge of being exactly what I'm meant to be, and there's no need for anything but to be...yours. When I get completely lost under a woman's touch, her power and control, swept away, I know this is what I want most. I'll do anything for her. For you."

It overwhelmed her, as so many things about him did. Despite the growing need in her thighs and pussy, the surging in that delicious part of her lower abdomen, reflecting the tiny spasms happening in her clit, she needed one more answer. Even so, her hips kept moving of their own volition to slide her increasing slickness up and down his cock.

"You've been with men."

"God, Chloe..." He bit back a groan as she clenched tight on him, so that the sucking sound of her now thoroughly wet cunt reached both their ears. "Yes, but never..."

He stopped, face constricting a brief minute, telling her she was testing his control, a quiet delight to her. "Never a Master," he said, his expression strained. "Except for training, or charity auction...which is different. Never a Master. Just...male lovers. Submissives. Like me."

"I don't think there's anyone like you, Brendan." She said it with fervent belief. Or maybe it was just that she'd never met anyone like him...for her. "Do you want to come for me?"

"Yes. Fuck, yes."

"But shouldn't I come first?"

She was teasing him, half serious, half sensual, and he caught both. He gave her a look of wry exasperation and something more tender before he gave a jerky, determined nod. Gripping him hard with those internal muscles, she slid back down like a slow, hot mouth.

"I don't think so," she said softly, watching him nearly choke on an oath. "I want you to come for me first, Brendan. Show me how much you want me."

Tensing her stomach muscles, she slid up his length again then down. Then up, a carousel ride, like when the horses were slowing. He was shaking his head, but now he stiffened in the grasp of her legs and arms, his eyes going deep green and rich earth brown. All the muscles in his handsome face tightened to the point he became a statue. "Oh God. Chloe."

"Now," she urged, working him just a little bit faster. "Look at me. I want you to look at me."

It was a sheer loss of control, of will, of everything but the need to release, to spill himself in her. His hips rose and plunged, the climax taking over, overriding even her command as involuntary movement took over. She encouraged it, whispering, and he let out a hoarse cry, his hips jerking beneath the clutch of her hands on his ass, his chest expanding against her breasts, trying to get the air it needed.

She'd thought to remain a fascinated audience, but as he pistoned inside her slick sex, the hot kernel of arousal she'd thought would take longer to build to eruption exploded. It took her unaware as his cock rubbed her deep inside, his friction on the outside galvanizing her swollen clit to convulse and reach climax again.

She couldn't hold her concentration then, arching her head back and crying out, a sound that echoed off the walls of his home, the space that held all the sights, sounds and essential being of this man.

Even if there were skeletons literally in that closet, she was pretty sure she was on her way to wanting to keep him indefinitely. Maybe forever, if she'd dare Fate by making such an absurd declaration. Though her mind might not have the courage, her heart whispered it all the same, echoing and mirroring his words.

Mine. *Mine.*

Yours.

Chapter Fifteen

ஐ

It felt so good to sleep. Really sleep, with no shadows or currents of uneasiness running through her dreams. She'd slept fitfully even at Marguerite's, but here, with Brendan's warmth curled around her, she'd woken only once, and that was to find his arms wrapped around her possessively. It was a side he didn't show as much when he was awake, but which dropped her pleasantly back into slumber.

After her outburst on the Ferris wheel, this felt like she'd lain down in the bottom of a wooden boat, sailing down a never ending, slow moving river. As she lay there and had no worries, she watched the clouds float above, the birds and forest insects making their usual noises of life in cacophonous song. The boat rocked her, a cradle in moving water, a river sister.

When she woke in the morning, she was surprised to realize she was alone. Well, not technically. The sheets and blankets that smelled like Brendan were tucked around her, an aroma security blanket, and he'd left her plush puppy in her arms.

Smiling a little, and realizing how long it had been since she'd woken with a smile on her face, she straightened, running fingers through her rumpled hair.

Her nose told her tea was being brewed, as well as coffee, a nice mingling of feminine and masculine scents. His Cirque du Soleil T-shirt was on the end of the bed, so she slid it on, liking the way it felt. Leaving the puppy in the blankets, she did a trip to the bathroom for the usual reasons—call of nature, and the important female need to make her morning wake up appearance as "naturally" appealing as possible when waking with a lover. Then she headed downstairs.

The kitchen was full of indirect sunlight from a pair of open French doors that led out to a little patio framed by potted flowering plants. Most were from the vine family, spilling out in lush handfuls, artfully arranged to look wild, making her think that Brendan had some of Tyler's green thumb.

Continuing proof of his fastidious nature, the counter was relatively clear, holding only a few silver computerized appliances. He was standing at the center island, cutting up strawberries. Wearing only a pair of cotton pajama bottoms that looked a bit stretched and faded, since they hung temptingly low on his muscular waist, he made an appealing picture. Particularly since he'd not yet shaved and his hair was tousled in a sexy way that would make her envious, if a wave of comfortable morning lust didn't wash it away.

"Good morning."

He looked up at her, capturing her appearance, from her bare toes to her unruly hair. Before she could have an instance of self consciousness, his gorgeous smile dispelled it. "Yes, it is. Particularly now."

"Charmer. Can I help?"

"I've pretty much got it. I was about to go see if you were ready for some breakfast."

She glanced at the clock, blanched. "It's ten o'clock."

"Yep. You needed the sleep." Leaning over the island, he snagged a piece of the T-shirt, reeled her in and around the marble countertop. Folding her into the shelter of his body, he brushed his cheek to hers, lips to her ear then her mouth, a caress that made her lay her palm on his chest, curl her other hand in the waistband of the trousers as she contoured easily into the curve of his body.

"You're so little," he mused, tapping his chin on the top of her head and giving her body a squeeze to underscore it.

"My father calls me Bug. Said it was because I was so short, yet always scuttling off to do something like I had six legs."

"Sounds fairly perceptive." Brendan chuckled. "Do you have any plans for the day?"

"I don't know. Do I?"

His smile broadened. Obviously, that had been the right answer.

"I thought we'd eat a light breakfast, then I'd take you to one of my favorite national parks to spend the day. There's a water view and hiking trails there. And an incredibly good deli on the way that could pack us a picnic."

"I'd like that." Despite a twinge of guilt. "You should have been at the carnival today, and last night. I'm sorry for that. I know it was a big deal, and I took you away from it." She'd have more apologies to make to M as well, she knew.

She gave a surprised squeak when two very capable hands lifted her onto the island, seating her bare bottom under the T-shirt on the cool surface. Brendan braced his arms on either side of her, his body pressed between her thighs as he gazed at her with that mixed tenderness and desire in his gaze. "I'm where I want to be, with the only person I want to be with. Besides which, I got lucky in the past few hours, a couple times, so you paid me back for any inconvenience."

She made a noise of mock annoyance, but then he caught her lips in a kiss, making it powerful, so reminiscent of the most intense moments of the early hours, she could only hold on as he pressed her back, his arm steady around her waist. He kissed her thoroughly before drawing back, leaving her out of breath.

"So, how does the picnic sound?"

"Well." She cleared her throat, giving him a narrow look to tell him that she wasn't completely bowled over, though of course she was. "I did have a couple other hot dates lined up, come to think of it."

"I'm your transportation," he pointed out. "So you've got zero chance of making those."

"Aren't you supposed to do what I say? My wish is your only desire? Or something like that."

She didn't know how comfortable he'd be with the teasing, but she needn't have worried. He gave her a pleasurably provocative look.

"Every sub has his limits."

"So a submissive is allowed to be possessive?" She thought of the way he'd slept, with that arm tight around her.

"You remember Mac and Violet, at the wedding? Mac's a sub."

"No way." She knew her eyes must have rounded and her mouth dropped despite herself. But who could blame her? She remembered the big cop, his protective demeanor toward his pregnant, feisty wife, who was also a state trooper. Violet was the only other adult at the wedding as short as Chloe. "He looks like he could take on a biker gang and win."

"He would. And he'd tolerate someone touching Violet, or sharing her, about as long as it would take him to throw the misguided bastard through a wall."

"Wow." She watched him reclaim the knife, begin to slice again as she sat on the table next to the cutting board. The marble felt intriguing on her bare ass, the slightly sore lips of her pussy. Her mind was turning. "This isn't really all that clear cut, is it?"

"People who are subs and Doms are as complex and diverse as any other person. You know what they say. A million people mean a million different religions." He offered her a strawberry. Thinking, Chloe took it from him with her mouth, but closed her hand on his wrist so she could lick the juice off his fingers. It was something to see him go still in that way she was beginning to anticipate. The way he watched her so closely, his muscles tightening like a dog on a chain. Hunger flashed through his expression as she suckled a finger, teased a palm with the tip of her tongue. She let her gaze drop as she did it, watched with feigned clinical interest as his cock thickened and stirred under the thin pants.

When she let him go at last, he started to lean forward. Testing, she put a restraining hand on his chest. "I want my breakfast," she murmured.

He straightened, a muscle twitching in his jaw, those hazel eyes holding her gaze for a moment before he quite deliberately lowered his attention back to his task.

Wow. She swallowed, not sure if she'd ruin her little experiment by jumping him now. Fortunately, he provided a distraction, so she didn't give away how lousy her willpower was.

He dipped his head toward his kitchen table. "I've been keeping some flowers for you, if you want to check them out."

Glancing that way, she saw a bouquet there. She realized the profuse number of blooms were paper flowers, made from what looked like magazine and news papers.

"Oh." As she slid off the counter, he offered a steadying hand, his palm managing to slide along her bare ass, revealed when the shirt hiked up. When he flashed an unrepentant grin at her, she swatted his solid abdomen, got a kiss on her abused knuckles for her trouble, but then extricated herself with a sniff to wander over to the table.

The flower shapes were held in careful wraps of green floral tape for the stems. There were a full two dozen, more than could have been done this morning, unless he'd been up awhile.

"I've been collecting them for you," he said. "You can pull each one off, open it to see what the picture or text is."

She touched one crinkled paper, slid it free of the tubular stem and unfolded it. The slick, heavy magazine paper showed a photo cut from a *National Geographic* article on an archaeological dig. Two sets of bones had been unearthed, skeletons who had apparently been buried in one another's embrace.

Brendan came to see, glancing over her shoulder. She smelled the scent of strawberries on him. "That was found at a Neolithic dig in Italy. The skeletons are somewhere between five and six thousand years old. I thought you'd probably consider that one for your happiness book. Then…there's this one."

Peering over her head, he slid his arm around her waist, pressing his body close to reach around her and pluck another picture. This one was probably from a perfume ad. Chloe saw a woman's slender back, bare down to the flare of her hips, her long hair held up in one hand to show the nape. A tattoo, shaped like a rope of autumn-colored maple leaves, twisted down her spine and then flared out into a free fall of the same leaves, as if they'd been scattered out toward the rolling landscape of her smooth buttocks. A butterfly rode on one spinning leaf, jewel blue wings catching the eye among all the earth tones.

"I'm sure that's airbrushed, not a real tattoo, but I thought you'd like it. You don't have to use any of them. Just throw away the ones that won't work. If—"

Picking up the hand on her waist, she brought it to her face, and inhaled strawberries. Pressed her face fully into his palm, her mouth against the callused heel.

She turned, standing so close to him they could be one person, her feet inside the span of his. She put her lips against the base of his throat by laying her hands on his arms and stretching onto her toes.

"I'm going to wake up and find you were the nicest, most incredible dream I've ever had," she mumbled against his flesh. "Damn it." Those sneaky tears were threatening again, and they weren't supposed to do that. Hadn't she let some of it out last night? Couldn't it be over, and she go back to being the Chloe she'd been? Why couldn't all the fairy tale enchantment of last night have lifted the curse of her rollercoaster emotions?

Before she could get upset about what felt like a giant step backward, he eased her down into a chair by the bouquet and dropped to one knee, framing her face as he kissed the corner of each eye, catching the tears before they happened.

Strawberries, heat and Brendan. As he moved his lips to hers, she let herself get swept away by him again, her hands naturally creeping up to hold onto his biceps. His body insinuated between her knees so they bumped against his hips, his upper thighs. When he lifted his head, she wasn't ready for what she saw in his face. She squeezed one unyielding arm muscle instead.

"Don't. Let's pretend I didn't get all weepy and weird. M says you're a swimmer. That you usually get up at some ungodly hour and go do a thousand laps."

She held her breath, waiting to see if he could respect her wishes, as well as blow off the top of her head with unrelenting lust.

"Today's a day off. I have something better to do."

As his gaze flickered, and he leaned in to take her mouth again, desperate humor fluttered in her chest, so she spoke right before his mouth closed the distance.

"Was that a double entendre?"

"I think it was a blatant suggestion, if you're willing. Instead of a thousand laps, I like the idea of bringing you to climax a thousand times." He kissed her mouth, her cheekbones, under each ear and then her collarbone, punctuating each word.

"I didn't open your closet." He'd been so generous, she felt obligated to mention it, though the expectations she might find there gave her gut a nervous twist.

"That's your choice, Chloe. It's not something I need or expect you to do."

Her brow furrowed. "Do you expect anything of me?" Putting her hands on his chest, she managed to hold him off, though the bulk of her mind was happy drifting in a fog of desire and tactile pleasure, no thought or accountability required.

When he didn't immediately answer, she made sure he met her gaze. "Brendan?"

"Yeah, I do." There was a trace of impatience in his eyes, but before she could determine whether she'd pushed into a vulnerable area, he brought it back to her. "I expect you to give yourself a break, and let me do whatever you want and need to make you happy this weekend." A brow quirked. "After all, you did pay for the privilege."

Maybe he meant it as a joke, but there was something beneath it, a dark quagmire that tripped off an alarm. Chloe tightened her grip on him, this time with a bite of nails. "Brendan, you're not a whore. If you think I believe that, just because I bought you at some auction..."

"Hey." He closed his hands on her wrists, his expression suddenly a lot more direct and forceful than she'd yet seen. "I didn't mean it that way, Chloe. I was teasing." At her look, he shrugged. "Yeah, it was a crappy joke. I was frustrated, because I don't want you to be worrying about things you don't need to worry about. Is there anything about last night that suggests I don't want to be with you, a hundred and twenty percent?"

Nothing except her own mind, telling her there was no way anybody could want to be with her. Not now, pitiful, weepy, dirty...

That word, the way it kept springing on her like a monster out of a closet, took her out of the chair and away from him, though she practically tripped over him. She moved quickly to the open window, drawing in deep breaths. *No. I'm done with this. Please stop.*

She focused on the pond that formed a center point for the townhouse development and tried to imagine herself in that boat again. When he laid his hands on her shoulders, she shuddered. "I'm sorry."

"You've nothing to be sorry about." Rather than making her face him, he put his chin on top of her head, folded his arms around her so she could hook her hands on his forearm, hold on as he swayed them back and forth, giving her a rhythm that helped calm her. "Chloe, other than last night, you haven't talked to anyone about all of this, have you? The things you're carrying around inside you, about Marguerite's father, and what happened to you when you were nine?" He kept his voice soft, so it didn't make the anxiety in her chest worse, though it didn't abate. "Have you cried about it, really let it out?"

She tightened her chin, shook her head. "I thought... You know, when it first happened, I thought I was all right. Getting better, at least physically, gave my mind something to do. Then afterward, when the nightmares started happening, I was so determined to do and be the way I was. But with every month my body got better, the nightmares were growing in my mind, taking away who I was, a piece at a time."

He murmured something incoherent, but he stroked her forearm. "You remember that first night, when I told you that you didn't have to handle this alone? Chloe, why are you trying so hard to do it that way?"

She'd let her head sink down on her chest, her arms folded against her under his grasp. Most of the time she didn't even realize she'd taken what she'd dubbed "the dead bird pose" until after it happened. She'd first noticed it as the way she woke from her nightmares, defending herself unconsciously. Recognizing it now brought forth that familiar desolation. "Because I feel like it's my fault," she whispered.

"What?"

Okay, she was wrong. *This* was the most forceful she'd ever seen him. He turned her in his arms, lifted her chin to make her look at his enraged and amazed features. It just widened the crack inside her further. "I know, don't say it. It's a stupid cliché, feeling that way. This isn't supposed to be me. I can control it, take care of it. I'm not a ...dirty whore, or slut, something not worth living. So disgusting, no one would want me. I have light inside me, and that light will drive out the shadows." Her fists clenched against his chest. "Only it's not, and the dark is winning, which must mean it's right…"

That did it. Her chest was tearing open again, so that she had to bend over it fully, hold herself as he followed her down to a hunched crouch on the floor, sheltering her.

"That's what he said to you, isn't it?"

"When he was chasing me in the woods, and he couldn't find me, that was what he was saying. And then Marguerite's dad, he said things like it too. Brendan, I know I shouldn't…they were horrible, terrible messed-up people, but they want me to be messed up too. How can I know they're wrong, and yet they still have this power over me?"

Sitting down cross-legged on the floor, he pulled her into that comfortable triangle formed by his lap. His hand burrowed under hers, her heart beating rapidly beneath his palm. He massaged, small circles, his other arm doing that rocking thing again. She had a fleeting thought that he would be the best father ever. If he had a girl baby, she'd be a daddy's girl all the way.

"It's all right. I'm here. You're not any of those things."

"I know. *I know.* I'm supposed to know it, right? So why does it feel like a lie? Why is it, when these things happen, that the first thing you feel is so alone? Like evil just closes around you, so nothing feels connected to you?"

At her lowest moments, she'd decided that was what hell was, total loneliness. She had to stop thinking about this. She knew better. She was going to lose it entirely in a moment, and Brendan would have to call for strait jackets and restraints. Come to think of it, he probably had some upstairs.

"Hey, shh…" He kept up that rubbing as she hiccupped and strangled her way through the minor panic attack, murmuring to her until she could take shallow breaths. "Easy, baby. Are you listening to me?"

When she nodded, he slid his fingers up her sternum to tease her cheek, bring her gaze to his worried face. "You know how, when kids are little, and an adult does something wrong to them, the adult will say, 'this will be our secret, don't tell anyone'?"

She nodded. Her eyes closed because it was easier, but she held on to his voice.

"It's no different when you're an adult. When someone hurts you, it's like they put those same kinds of shadows in your head. Those shadows tell you that you're all alone, that there's no one who can help, that you shouldn't burden anyone." He kept touching her face, but she still couldn't look at him. It was okay, though, because he also kept talking. "Chloe, the world is full of people who milk every little setback, become emotional hypochondriacs. You're not that kind of person. From that one night at the wedding I could tell you've made so many people happy. You've been so generous with your love. You can't see how much we want to help you, but I think that's because you've let those bastards close your eyes, make you believe for some idiotic reason that you don't deserve it."

He went from quiet and soothing to righteous fury, and every word cut through that chitinous layer, finding his way to her beneath, so when he feathered her lashes with a thumb, coaxing her eyes open, she couldn't look away from his fierce regard. "Where the hell is that coming from? Think about it. Why don't you deserve it? What one fucking thing did you do to deserve being attacked when you were a child, and then as an adult?

"I..." She didn't know, damn it, but that was how she felt. "I don't know. But why...if I didn't deserve it, *why* did it happen? Why?" Her voice came out a shrill, thin cry. Pain for her wounded his expression, made her crumble further, but he gave her an answer, in a low, determined voice that cut through every fear, told her she wasn't alone, that he wouldn't let her be alone, no matter how much those demons tried to make her feel that way.

"Nothing, Chloe. Not a damn thing. Well, I take it back. You *did* do something." At her look of surprise, he nodded. "Evil wants us to skulk in the shadows, be afraid of everything, of being happy and loving. So yeah, maybe your love of life and beauty attracted it. But you said to hell with it anyway—as a freaking child—and lived your life according to what you knew was right and true to your soul. As a result, when evil came for Natalie, you stepped into the line of fire and fought it. You didn't run. You fought as hard as you could, and because he was able to take some of his venom out on you, it took him that much longer to reach the eruption point with Natalie, giving Marguerite more time to get to them."

"You make me sound brave and amazing, and I'm not."

"You are," he said, and his expression told her he'd brook no argument. "You are brave, amazing, beautiful. If you were a muse, you'd be Joy. Pure joy. They didn't take that from you, Chloe. I've seen a hundred glimpses of it in the past couple days, and it shone like the stars the night of Marguerite's wedding. There was so much happiness in the air that night, evil didn't even have a chance of breathing there."

As she dropped her head to his chest again, hiccupping over another tiny sob, he let out a breath, went back to the soothing murmur. "You let your physical injuries be treated, and gave them time to heal. Now it's time to do the same for your mind and heart. Marguerite's close friend Komal was a counselor for abused children for years. I bet Marguerite would be more than happy to arrange a few sessions for you. Doesn't that sound like a good idea?"

She managed a sniffle, a dubious lift of her shoulder. After a pause, he caressed the curls gathered around her face. "Okay, think about it some. I won't hassle you about it further. For now. If you say it."

"W-what?" She sniffled ungracefully again, resenting the few tears that had squeezed out. Reaching up to the table, he found a napkin holder and brought a napkin back to her nose, massaging it to take the moisture away. It reminded her of Tyler with his handkerchief, as well as his words. *There are many things that men don't do any more that they should. Particularly for women.*

"Tell me what you did to deserve this, other than being insanely brave."

"I can't." It was just a word. She should be able to say it, even if she didn't feel it, just to fib her way past his demand, but that wall of darkness rose, like a dark sea, threatening to engulf her. "I can't." And that, more than anything else, told her he was right. She needed help. She knew she wasn't alone, yet her mind refused to let her believe anything else, as if her rational-irrational selves stood on either side of that wall, and her irrational self was the one holding her heart and soul hostage.

"Tell me, Chloe." He shifted her in one flexible movement, those lean swimmer muscles stretching her out on the linoleum beneath him, warm from the morning sun. Sunlight filled her eyes so her sense of him came through touch as he slid the T-shirt up her abdomen. The tips of his fingers brushed the lower curve of her breasts. But they were not his goal. When he leaned down and pressed his closed mouth directly against her clit, no teasing or warning, her breath shuddered out of her aching chest. "Oh."

"Tell me." A whisper in her ears, filtering through that dark wall. His tongue made a lazy circle, dipped lower, dipped deeper.

Her young body, with the imprint of his lovemaking so fresh on it from last night, was already moistening her, preparing her for him. He increased that wetness, taking his knuckles between her labia, pressing up. The hard emotions knotted up in her chest and yanked on something lower, making it impossible to focus on why she had to hold out, what she was fighting.

"Tell me. One word, Chloe. What did you do to deserve it?"

He shifted, his body between her legs, amazing her at how he took over this moment. *I know what you want and need...* He stretched out full length on her, holding her down. With no need to guide himself, he shifted his hips, found her and eased his cock into the opening of her pussy.

Steel velvet flesh gave enough to fit her shape as he pushed in through that wall, physical and emotional, and connected her to him, sinking deep, pulling her out of that dark well and bringing her to him. She opened her eyes because his hand was cupped over her brow, giving her a shield from the sun's bright beams, though she could still feel the heat coming through his palm. Once opened, she couldn't close her eyes against what she saw in his hazel eyes. He wasn't making a demand of her, standing detached from her. He was there with her, suffering with her pain, holding her hand, wanting her to say it so that he could take both of them to a better place. She held the key.

"Tell me, Chloe. Say it." He stroked, a deep, deep thrust that had her body rising to his, a withdrawal that made her tremble, all her nerve endings stretching toward him in pleasure. "Beloved. Brave girl. Beautiful angel. Sex goddess."

A small hiccup of laughter moved in her heart, and that bump in the road threw the darkness off. As if he knew, his eyes smiled, though it didn't lessen their intensity. "Fair maiden, a gift to us all. A child's soul and a woman's heart. You know it, Chloe. Don't let them take the gift from you, from all of us. What did you do to deserve it?"

Her response was a moan this time, because he was so damn good at this, so stubborn and seductive at once, his cock teasing everything to life, pushing through that dark wave, making her fear it would crash over her, topple her, but if it did, he was already there, in it with her. He wouldn't let her go. He had her now, was connected in a way no one ever had been.

"Chloe, tell me."

She realized then that she did want to look in that closet. Because whatever Brendan was—a woman's slave, her protector, the man willing to get on his knees to be what most men wouldn't contemplate—his heart made him what she wanted and needed. What she'd felt last night and right now. Someone who made her feel like her needs were his sole desire to fulfill, her pain something he'd do anything to heal.

"Nothing," she whispered as he came back in deep, and the word was lost in another whimper of pleasure. A climax was coming, but not like any she'd felt before. She was going to cut her raft loose or have it yanked free, but from the resolve in his set jaw, the flame of determination and desire in his face, she knew he was going to pull her through those dark waters. But what could she offer him in return?

"Nothing," she said, louder this time, hoping she was answering his question still and not her own. She grabbed his shoulders, lifting up to bury her face in his shoulder. "Nothing. I didn't do anything."

He banded his arms around her, and increased his pace just enough.

"Damn right," he muttered against her as she continued to say it, even as the climax took her. A few more stingy tears came too, wrenching her apart, but they were like the spray when a wave crashed, lost as the climax tumbled them over and over. Crying out, she rode salty foam and wet pleasure with him, muscles tensing and releasing, limbs tangling. They moved together in that tidal rhythm until they'd spent all their desire and were deposited, replete and still locked together, on a sun drenched, sandy shore.

Chapter Sixteen

ଈଠ

Afterward, they ate strawberries on his patio. Feeling drained and energized at once, she quickly decided sitting next to him in one of the green metal chairs that were roomy and rocked back on their squared bases wasn't adequate. So she'd straddled him, letting her legs dangle on either side of his hips, pleased by his hands curved around her bottom, holding the shirt and her modesty secure, and fed him strawberries with the cream he'd provided.

She quickly came to the conclusion that Cool Whip was the world's most perfect food when he sucked it off her fingers, taking his time as he seemed gifted at doing. Two could play that game. When she retrieved her fingers, she scooped more of the Cool Whip out with them and painted a curved line over his smooth pectoral, taking it off with three quick nips and swipes of her tongue, earning a skipped beat from his heart under her mouth.

"Do you shave your chest because you're..." She grimaced. "I don't know why I have trouble saying it. Or maybe I do, but I'm afraid I'll offend you."

For an answer, he shifted, propping his feet on his fire pit so she could lean back comfortably against the backrest his knees provided. Putting his hands beneath the T-shirt, he teased the crease beneath her breasts. "Tell me anyway."

She did, not merely because of his irresistible look, but because she needed to talk about something not related to what had just happened in the kitchen, the decisions she still couldn't bring herself to make. But she had to look down at his chest to say it. She put another dollop of whipped topping on it, her fingers dipping in and making tiny dots in the froth.

"It feels insulting to call a guy a submissive. Which, since you are one, suggests that's my hangup, not yours, right? I mean, I don't view you being that way as wrong...or...well, I guess I just didn't expect it to be sexy. I envisioned a male submissive as some wimpy person who'd hide behind me if I was ever mugged. Or who'd be afraid to tell the waitress the cook made me the wrong thing. Don't get me wrong, I'm not a 1950s kind of girl, I could tell her myself. There are just certain things..."

"A woman should expect from a man." His mouth tugged up. "I get that."

Yes, she knew he did. She was beginning to understand there was far more than one definition to this. "Well, anyway, I'm sure Submissive Males of America will do a PR campaign to improve their image—as soon as their Mistresses okay it."

"Like a public service commercial?" He narrowed his gaze at her in mock warning. She tried to suppress the humor quivering at the corners of her mouth as his thumbs swept down over her abdomen, tickling.

"Yep. It could start in a gym, with a bunch of sweaty guys pounding sandbags. Or better, in basic training, and then this female sergeant comes in, all tough in tight camouflage..."

She started giggling as he tickled her in earnest and squirmed in his lap. "Quit it. Okay, I'll stop, I'll stop. Hey, be still or you'll upset the whipped cream."

Leaning forward, she brought his retribution to a sliding halt when she put her mouth back on the Cool Whip, and the man beneath. His fingers gripped her hips as she licked and tasted. She gave him several more short nips, not entirely gentle, moving down to tease his nipple, registering the hardening beneath her ass and the increased demand in the grip of his hands. His mouth brushed the crown of her head, his breath rasping out on her muttered name.

"I just want to taste you," she said. "Nothing else."

She could want a lot more, she knew, but despite the dampness between her thighs and the tingle in her breasts from his caressing strokes just below them, she liked this, taking her pleasure of him, knowing she could keep it at just this level.

"Yes, that's why I remove it. And sometimes for swimming."

She lifted her head, licking the last of the cream off her lips. His eyes riveted on that motion, made muscles in her lower abdomen contract. "What?"

"That's why I remove my chest hair. For The Zone. And swim meets."

She cocked her head and straightened, seeing his gaze drop to her breasts, the aroused nipples evident through the cloth. The nipple she'd been tasting was a hard point as well, and she passed her fingers over it, at the same time she lifted the other hand and touched one of her own, feeling the arousal in both.

"Chloe. You're torturing me."

She nodded, but then gave him an impish smile. "Have you won any medals?"

"For swimming?" He gave her that sexy grin, teasing her right back. "Yeah. A couple."

Regarding him for a few minutes in silence, she listened to the sounds of the geese on the pond behind them. She bit into a strawberry herself, picking it up off the bowl next to them. "So what's in the closet?"

As he propped his head on the chair back, he gave her a lazy smile. "What would you imagine was in there?"

"Cuffs. Whips. Scalpels, electrodes. Maybe a portable cage."

"Exactly right. Now if you finish your strawberries, I can take you to the park."

She wrinkled her nose at him. "That was an evasion."

"Not entirely." Taking the bowl of Cool Whip from between them, he rose, holding her around the waist with such sure strength she was able to curl her legs around his hips, hold onto him as he walked them back inside. As he did, he brought his mouth to hers, spoke against her lips. "I'm concerned that if you don't get dressed, I'm not going to do anything more than fuck you, all day long. I've already had a hard-on longer than they recommend for Viagra."

"You say that like it's a bad thing." But she smiled and looped her arms around his shoulders. Pressing her face into the heat of his neck as he carried her back to the bedroom, she knew she didn't really care which he chose to do, as long as she could hold onto this feeling.

* * * * *

The park had lots of sequestered places to spread a picnic blanket and enjoy privacy, as well as the water view the park offered. Despite her earlier energy, when they reached the park she'd lain down on the picnic blanket, her head on his thigh as he talked about the waterfowl, the campers they saw, a quiet run of words that sent her off to dreamland.

Waking some time later, she was amazed to find he hadn't moved, making sure her rest was undisturbed, her cheek pillowed on him. He'd slid down so she could rest her neck more comfortably, with her head on his abdomen. It was a particularly aggressive growl from that stomach that she thought had woken her, but the waking view was a pleasure. Denim covered thighs, ankles crossed to cradle the groin area in that nice curved way that jeans did. His feet were still in his hiking boots. Just past them, she saw the water, rippling with wind and the air traffic of herons and seagulls and the occasional boat passage.

When she turned her head, the upward view wasn't bad either. He had an arm propped under his head, and was gazing up into the trees. There was a worn paperback next to him. The stage play *Camelot*.

"I don't think I've met anyone as comfortable with himself in my whole life," she observed in a groggy voice, not wanting to disturb the peaceful hush over their world.

He slanted a glance down at her, his hazel eyes showing pleasure at her being awake, though no impression that he'd been impatient with her sleep. "I have. It was this really hot girl I met at a wedding last year. Lucky me, she finally took pity on me and decided to give me a call."

She smiled, curling her hand in his shirt over his stomach. "You sound hungry. You should have eaten, or woken me."

"You needed the sleep to keep up with my voracious sexual appetite. Are you hungry?"

She snorted, but nodded. He sat up, putting his arm around her back to hold her close, help her as she rose as well, running a hand through her short curls to loosen them from the compression of her nap. She hoped she hadn't drooled on his shirt, but thankfully a discreet glance showed no evidence of that.

As he unpacked the sandwiches they'd picked up, along with the assorted tidbits of chocolate and crackers, chunks of fruit and cheese he'd thrown in from his house, she studied his profile, thought about that night at the carnival. A question was still hovering in her mind, but she found she wasn't yet ready to ask it. Instead, she pointed to the paperback. "There's a playbill for that up at Tea Leaves, on the community board. I think Marguerite plans to take a group of the neighborhood kids. Are you in it?"

"No. I'm the coach and helping with the production for the students who are."

"Did you ever act yourself?"

"All the time, growing up. I enjoy it, but I'm better at teaching people with a real talent for it, bringing that talent out. I also do a couple night classes for people who don't want to perform in public, but like to tap into that part of themselves. It gives you skills a lot like Toastmasters, self-confidence, public speaking, etc." His eyes sparkled. "Of course, I eventually talk a lot of them into auditioning for the community plays."

"You'd be a great Lancelot."

He lifted a brow. "I was always partial to Percival. His interest was serving the king and the ideals of Camelot, not achieving greatness. Lancelot seemed torn. He wasn't ambitious, but he had a great need to be the best. He saw that as service to the king, and it was, but it diluted his focus on his primary duty."

"And hence, his love for Guinevere, as much as he didn't want it to happen." Chloe smiled. "Course, I think they should have become a threesome. I mean, Arthur loved Lancelot as much as Guinevere, just in a different way. It would have been hard for Mordred to claim they'd betrayed the king if they were all sharing a bed together. If they'd been a little more sexually enlightened, Camelot might have persevered."

"I think the idea would have given T.H. White and Lerner and Loewe a heart attack. Sandwich or chocolate first?"

"Both. Well, Loewe was gay."

"Gay doesn't mean a predisposition to a threesome." Brendan laughed.

"How about you? How do you feel about sharing?"

His eyes sharpened on her, considering. "That depends on the lover. I've had some that prefer sharing, some that don't. I do what gives them pleasure."

"What about me? What if I wanted to share you? Or have another guy, both of you...with me?"

For so long she'd been so focused on herself, she'd forgotten how good she was at reading faces. That skill came in handy now, because the look she saw was so quick, she would have missed it if she hadn't been looking for it. As he began to open his mouth, she put her fingers on it.

"No, don't say anything. You wouldn't like it, but you were going to say you'd do what makes me happy. You know, you're not exempt. You're one of those 'lovers' whose desires should be taken into consideration as well. If I fell in love with you… If, my present dysfunctional behavior aside, I *am* in love with you…" A tremor, not unpleasant but definitely scary, went through her stomach at the look in his eyes, but she pressed on. "What you want would be as important to my happiness as what I want is to yours."

"What you want is always going to be more important to me, Chloe."

"Maybe. Because you're wonderful and unreal. But even superheroes should have a line." Despite her humor, her brow creased, noticing how he broke the link between their gazes to arrange the food on the blanket. She reached out, put a hand on his wrist, stilling him. "Look at me."

A tiny muscle in his jaw twitched, but then his gaze flicked up, showing her those hazel eyes had become far more guarded. She'd seen traces of it since they'd met, but if there was a fortress inside Brendan, protecting his deepest needs, she was pretty sure this subject kept bringing her right to the locked drawbridge.

"I don't know a lot," she said quietly, "but I do know that being a submissive doesn't mean you have to be okay with everything your lover wants to do. If that was the case, all those program designations wouldn't have been necessary. And you'd have let me go down on you without a seatbelt. Maybe you've had some really inconsiderate assholes in your life that made you feel like you've failed if you don't give them everything they want. But I think I'm different for you, Brendan. I think you want specific things with me. Things that would be limits, conditions. Like wanting me only for yourself."

"Chloe—"

"I think I said not to talk," she said mildly.

Whoa. She'd surprised herself on that one, as much as him. But she tried not to let it show in her face as she took her fingers up to his lips, caressed them. His attention was riveted on her, the increased focus she'd noted he demonstrated when a woman took the reins, so irresistible in its flood of power. She pushed that back, though, keeping her concentration where it would do more good for both of them. She hoped. "Have you ever thought that your possessiveness toward me, your desire for exclusivity, might be something I want from you? That it makes me feel special?"

He closed his hand around her wrist as if she were made of glass. However, as her pulse ratcheted up, she had a feeling if she tried to withdraw her arm just then, he might have resisted. Just for a moment, giving her the thrill of confirming her theory.

He seemed to be struggling with his own thoughts, so she decided to let him off the hook. For now. "Someone promised me lunch," she said.

He nodded, kissed her palm, and then let her go. She stayed in that quiet space for a few minutes, enjoying the view as he reached over her legs to open the wine cooler. It shifted him to his knees, and she put her hand on his side, thinking of a horse, the living, fluid heat of muscle under the powerful beast's flesh, just like this one. She moved her hands down, one over the other, as if she was brushing him, until one palm rested on his hip. He glanced at her over his broad shoulder, his hair falling like a silky mane in truth.

"Those Mistresses. Have they ever spanked you?"

His brows lifted, a slight tug at the corner of his mouth as she cupped his buttock, followed the curve of it. His eyes darkened as her fingertips found the center seam and descended, her thumb caressing the curve of his testicles beneath denim.

"Yes, but not so much the 'Mommy, I need a spanking because I've been a bad boy' psychology. " He lifted a shoulder. "That area has a lot of nerve endings, connected directly to the cock, and Mistresses like getting those worked up, connected directly to the cock. They like giving pain as well, and the ass is a good place for that, harder to do permanent injury but still possessing the necessary psychological impact, the connection of punishment with authority and safety. Love and dominance both."

"Wow. That sounded so...teacher-like." She imagined it, imagined them getting that response out of him. Their hands on his trembling body, taking him places that she couldn't. That she never would. Her fingers dug in. "When they spanked you, did they put you over their laps and paddle you like you were six? Is all of what you just said bullshit, and when it comes down to it, to the moment itself, you actually *are* looking for Mommy to punish you?"

"Would it bother you if I was?" When he gave her an even look, withdrawing the wine and sitting back on his heels, her hand slipped away, both dropping back into her lap.

"I'm not sure why I asked it that way," she said slowly. "Why I felt so angry, all of a sudden."

"At me, or yourself?" He kept his face carefully blank as he poured.

"Both. And the whole world, for a second. I don't know what's the matter with me. I mean, I don't judge people like that. It wouldn't matter to me if Gen liked to sleep in a cradle and suck her thumb, or Tyler liked to dress in women's clothes, as long as they were okay with it, and it didn't hurt anyone else."

"You aren't contemplating making Gen yours," he pointed out. "Judging is all right when it's for yourself, Chloe. Deciding what you want and best need for your own happiness. No shame in that."

"But there is shame in making someone else feel bad about who and what they are, just because it might not mesh with who and what I am." She closed her eyes at his look. "I'm not saying you and I don't mesh...I just... Oh God, just shut me up."

He touched her nose, a whimsical gesture that brought her eyes back open. "I would be very disturbed to know Tyler dressed in women's clothes."

She caught the sadness at the back of his expression, though. Her heart hurt at his attempt to make her feel better. She wondered if he already knew it, that in the end they wouldn't suit. Had he come to that conclusion, decided he was willing to be her Mr. Right Now, even if he couldn't be Mr. Right? That made her angry in a different way.

She reached out abruptly, gripped his hand. "You'll do what I...command you to do?"

He cocked his head. "Mostly, yes. If it's not a command that harms you."

She shook her head. "Don't let me hurt you, Brendan. Don't let me take weird, fucked-up potshots at you for reasons I can't understand, and just take it. Okay? Please, I'm begging you. Don't let me do that to you."

Touching her full bottom lip, he ran his thumb over the indentation of her chin. "You'll never have to beg me for anything, Chloe."

Turning away, he began to set up their lunch. Unsure what to say, she watched him open the deli wrappers, lay out her sandwich on a napkin, then unwrap the homemade brownie and pour her a glass of wine. Did he do it unconsciously, serving her like this, rather than handing her a sandwich to unwrap herself or fixing his own food at the same time?

Clearing her throat, she took up her sandwich. As she did, a pair of mated geese and their goslings moved along the water's edge, looking like a postcard.

"So back to this closet. I really want to know. Do you keep things there you take to the club?"

"Sometimes. My last relationship, we were roommates, and we used some of those things at home. A lot of what's in that closet is club wear, though, because Mistresses tend to like presentation." He gave her a nudge, a half smile that she was sure was intended to make her feel a little better, rather than lower than a slug inching along the gravel. "You know how women are."

"I expect a drama professor would be very comfortable dressing the part." Despite her guilt, her mind quickly shifted to imagining a few things and wondering about her own private fashion show. But his comment gave her a distracting little pang. "So you said that relationship broke up a little over a year ago?"

"Yes. Shortly before Marguerite got married."

"So I guess you were telling me the truth." She slanted him a glance. "I'm not a rebound."

"You wouldn't have been that, even if you called right after the wedding. That relationship was over."

"Did you love her?"

His expression shifted. "Him. I loved him at one time, but was never in love with him."

"How do you know?" She was always interested in how people defined being in love. Though the path to it differed for everyone, she'd noted that long term relationships seemed to have certain things in common, things she'd always longed to experience. That commonality suggested there was a universal truth to love, an idea that seemed very reassuring, like proof of Divinity.

"Because this feels entirely different." He gave her a briefly intense look that rocked her back on her heels, metaphorically speaking. She cleared her throat.

"I'm not quite sure what to do with that yet, so I guess I'll steer us into safer waters." She brightened abruptly. "Do they have boats here? Like canoes?"

He nodded, looking bemused and amused at once. "After we eat, can we go out on one?" she continued. "It's like this dream I have. I want to lie on the boards and look up at the sky while you paddle."

"All right." Reaching out, he cupped the side of her neck, ran his thumb over her throat, the sensitive windpipe. The genuine smile forgave anything, gave her permission to release the memory of her ugly behavior as if it had never been. To do and be something entirely different.

Thinking about that, she decided she wasn't as hungry as she'd thought. Not for food. Setting the rest of her sandwich down on the cooler, she shifted, aware of his attention as she eased herself down to her back. Dropping one arm over her head, she reached out to him with the other. "Come here, Beaver," she said in a throaty voice.

"God, you are so good at being adorable and desirable at once," he murmured.

Wanting to let the latter take precedence, she closed her hand over his shirt front and tugged, bringing him from his leaning position down toward her.

Responding to her desires, he moved his body over hers. Her small hands slid down his back, then lower, lower, until she rested on the rise of his ass, the line of his hip, and curled her fingers into his belt loops. He sucked in a breath as one bare foot slid up his calf, her thighs rising to cradle him.

"When you said I was confident, that night at the wedding," she whispered, "why did you think that?"

"Because you were very independent, but not obnoxious about it."

"Do feminist women annoy you?"

"No." He gave a despairing half chuckle as she brought his pelvis closer to the juncture of her thighs, her softness against his hardness, even with the layers of denim and skirt between them. "I'm grading papers in my head."

She rubbed herself against him, a slow circle. "Tell me what you think is obnoxious."

"I get irritated with women who say they don't need a man to be happy."

She raised a brow. "Why is that?"

"Because it's bollocks. If you're a hetero woman, you need a man. If you're a hetero man, you need a woman. A homo man needs a man, and so forth. Everyone needs someone to love them, to stand at their back, be in their corner, inside their soul. Someone who isn't required by blood ties or even the parameters of friendship. Someone who looks at you, the good and the bad, and flat out can't help wanting to be with you. Very few people come into this world as whole pieces, or reach adulthood without some pieces broken off. We all need the other pieces of the puzzle to find happiness."

This was like her dream too. Having him over her was like the sky passing above, the scenery changing like his emotions, but always constant, always there. She tightened her legs on him, ran her hand up his back. He'd caught up with her change of mood, one hand sliding beneath her, thumb sliding along the line of her bare spine beneath her shirt, the other braced by her head. He held the pressure of his hardened cock against her in obedience to her will, but also to destroy it, she was sure.

"If you had a happiness book, Brendan, what would be in it? And no fair saying pictures of me to distract me."

"It wouldn't be to distract you," he said. She played her fingers through his hair, threading, stroking slowly, while his fingers curled in need, digging into her brown locks.

"It would be whatever reminded me of feelings like these. The shadow of a woman's smile..." His thumb followed her cheek. "It reminds me of that song from Camelot."

He hummed it briefly, a hint of the melody in his voice as he spoke. "There was this brief, amazing moment, where everything was perfect. And they called it Camelot." Then, switching to Shakespeare, he quoted, "'The more I give to thee, the more I have, for both are infinite.'"

"Romeo and Juliet," she said softly. He was irresistible. She drew him down, touching his mouth with her own, that first sweet moment flavored with the chocolate she'd eaten for lunch, and then it was all Brendan. A deep, abiding kiss. She'd never thought what a sweet, wonderful word that was, *abiding.* So many meanings, all good.

She spoke against his lips after a long time, her body feeling heavy, like it was in water, tipped out of the canoe, turned by currents and tides, her will given up to nature's course.

"Turn over. I want you inside me, and I'll put my skirt over us, so that we won't scandalize anyone." *Much.*

She'd never really thought seeing two people make love should be considered something shameful or dirty, or something that would traumatize young eyes. Indian parents used to do it in the same teepees, for heaven's sake. However, she didn't want to be interrupted by a forest ranger, so she was willing to be as discreet as possible, even given their location, screened by trees.

Moving his knee outside of her leg, he rolled them, with the sinuous grace and male strength she expected to see when she watched him swim.

"Do you swim with a league?" she asked, her voice low and throaty. "No, I want to do it all. Just keep your arms loose, out to the sides like that. To avoid suspicion from the prudishly repressed." Her amused gaze lifted, became more serious. "And so I can control how I want this to go."

"It's sort of like a league, yes. You can come..." His voice hitched as she spread the gypsy skirt over his chest and upper thighs, shifting over his groin. She hadn't worn panties, wanting the feel of air on herself after the constant pleasuring of the past twenty-four hours.

"I can come?" she prompted, with a wicked grin. "I thought that was up to me."

"You can come swimming with me, if you want." He drew in another unsteady breath as she reached beneath all that fabric and slipped the button of his jeans, taking the zipper down slow and careful. The front of his boxers were already damp from arousal.

"You can use your hands. Just to work them down."

He did, managing it with her balanced on him, and then groaned when she shifted, rubbing her slickness along his now free cock, pressing it to his belly as she made it slick as well with slow, subtle movements. There was only forest behind them, so she opened her shirt, let him see the firm and bare curves of her breasts, since she'd also left the bra behind today. The wind fluttered the shirt, giving him a brief glimpse of the full left curve, the jutting nipple.

"Chloe," he murmured. "God, you're so beautiful."

The look in his eyes, the way his hands tightened, not quite closing, as if he was imagining her breasts in their grasp, made such simple, non-poetic words ignite with a fire that increased her own desire. She continued that slow rub, and then, reaching beneath her, tipped his heavy weight up enough to fit herself onto him. Holding his gaze, she moved forward and then back, sliding down his length like hot fudge down the side of a sundae, too good to resist a bite and wanting more.

The birds continued chirping, calling back and forth. The afternoon sun diamond paned through the trees, jagged bits of gold reaching through to touch his face, bathe all those wonderful muscles, the lines of his body. He was like a living happiness book laid out before her, every page seen and unseen. She wanted to read every word, see every image. Touch every page of that book, front and back.

"I love your cock," she breathed. "I love the way it feels inside me, how when I rise and fall on it, the ridge of your head stretches me, makes me feel hotter from the friction." The fire in his gaze grew, but she wasn't finished.

"I love to watch your face when I do this." Cupping her breasts, she grazed her nipples with her fingers, her heart rate increasing at the way his eyes latched onto the movement, his regard heating her fingers.

"The way you're looking at them, makes it feel like these are your fingers touching me. The way you press your lips together, it's as if you're already tasting them. You'd taste the strawberry lingering on them from this morning, because your mouth was on them then too."

"Do you like knowing I have to wait until you tell me I can do that, suckle your nipples?" His voice ran shivers up her spine.

"Yeah. I do."

His hands closed on the grass, muscles bunching, power rippling over his shoulders as she purred her next words. "I love the way you work so hard to stay still when I'm working your cock inside me this way, squeezing, pulling. Stroking." She let her body move in those tiny increments, doing just that. "I'm imagining how your balls are drawing up, wanting to come inside me. How long you'll keep waiting for that one single word from me. Waiting for yes."

"I want to see you come," he said, in a growl that tingled up her spine, because of the need in it, despite the fact he kept his hands where she'd ordered.

The rising desire twined the physical and emotional together. Lust was gaining an intensity that made her want to give him honesty. She didn't want him to merely forgive her earlier ugliness. She wanted to ask for it, make amends. The honesty was as much a part of what she needed in this moment as the release, one necessary for the purity of the other.

"What you are, what you've done, it's like going to a circus, Brendan." She went completely still, holding him within her, fingers digging into his chest to bring his attention to her face, despite her breathless tone. "It fascinates and saddens me both, because it's not my world. I feel like an actor on a stage, pretending to be Guinevere, not really her, because I don't feel it the way you do."

His fingers flexed against the grass again. She knew she'd want them on her soon, but she had to get this out, give him the truth, so he could have it to protect him from her next horrible spurt of anger. "That's what I should have said," she whispered, "rather than making that horrible remark. But I want you, Brendan. So much. I want to know that none of it matters, that you want me too. I know I'm different from those other Mistresses. I need to know that's okay, but I'm afraid it's not."

He lifted his hands then, shifted his upper body so that he could cup her face, let her feel the strength that was reflected in his expression. "I won't come until you believe it, Chloe. No matter what you do to me." His eyes, all three colors, were vibrant. "Not now, not later, not while I'm by myself. Not until you believe it enough to say the two words you'll say to me then, and mean them with everything you are."

Keeping his gaze on hers, he lay back down, deliberately dropped his arms back to the sides as she'd commanded.

The steel of his cock moved in her, aching for her to milk it to completion. She could override him, she thought, squeeze and taunt until biology defeated will, but looking at the resolve in his eyes, she wasn't sure she would in fact succeed. She might not know what made up those fortress walls she'd run up against earlier, but now she had a sense of what lay behind the drawbridge. Whatever hung in the balance between them was essential to who and what he was, and she'd uncovered it, touched it with her words and body.

More than a little overwhelmed, she curled her fingers into his shirt, his muscles flexing beneath her palms. "Would you, could you, in a park? Can you, will you, in the dark?"

Slowly, that intent resolve was replaced transformed by of humor as he picked up on her bastardized Dr. Seuss reference. "Only at your word, Sam. That's what I want. Who I am."

When she would have lifted off him, he disobeyed orders, settling his hands on her hips, holding her in place. "It doesn't mean you can't come. You want to, I can tell." Even now, he'd worked under the skirt, and before she could think to protest, she'd arched up with a hiss as his thumb found her clit, pressed and began those highly skilled, intuitive circles.

"Brendan," she gasped, her hand on his chest becoming a tighter clutch as she rocked involuntarily on him. "This...isn't...fair...to you."

"It's not about fair. It's about giving you pleasure, letting you take it. This cock is yours, Chloe. Use it. It's yours."

The demand nearly melted her brain. Heedless of who might be watching now, she was lifting, plunging, feeling him thrust harder, matching the spiral of response churning up from where his fingers were. His gaze followed her breasts, the way each downward impact made them quiver, the flutter of the open shirt showing him the dark flush color of her nipples. She saw that press of lips, how he wanted to suckle them, and part of her wanted that too. But the other part was fascinated enough to go down a little harder on him, make the quiver become a definite wobble, a provocative jiggle where the nipples were making his mouth water to taste them. All male animal beneath her, between her thighs, all under her control. Yet holding the reins felt like such a delicate business, as if any moment he'd break forth from the leash, even knowing he wouldn't.

"Brendan—" Realizing she was about to come hard, and there were people who were in hearing distance, she still couldn't make herself stop.

In a swift move, he drew her down against his chest, palm flattening under her shirt against her bare back. He held her close, her movements rubbing her clit against firm muscle and bone, his cock moving inside her still. He was iron all over, so she felt the powerful fight, the strain to hold onto his control as she went over, turning her mouth into his neck so her cries were muffled, her body twitching on his, the skirt ruffling over her ankles and his knees.

She wanted him to come. She really, really did, wanted to feel it, but she couldn't say that word. She wanted to test him, just as he'd predicted. As she spiraled away on the tide of her own release, she wondered how someone she hadn't let all the way into her soul already seemed to understand and know every room, light and dark.

Her knight had gotten over her drawbridge and much further into her fortress than she'd gotten into his.

She just hoped the dragon inside hers wouldn't end up tearing him to pieces.

Chapter Seventeen
ശ

How could a woman not fall for a male willing to bind himself to self-denial for her own pleasure? Or was that self-abstinence? She wasn't sure what term applied to a man willing to deny his own release, while she used him to fuck her brains out whenever she wished.

It was possible he got off on it, some equivalent type of psychological orgasm. Maybe. However, she suspected the truth was far more complex and more than she wanted to explore right now.

They'd spent a few more hours in the park, going on that canoe ride, walking the hiking paths in the hushed pine forests. At one point, they'd helped a young girl corral her escaped pair of Jack Russell terriers. The dogs considered being chased a game, up until Brendan, thinking fast, stripped down to his boxers and plunged into the water with the leashes. They'd followed him, yipping excitedly, and he'd gotten hold of the collars and snapped the leashes back on. He'd emerged with laughter and triumph in his face, as well as thin cotton plastered to his privates and backside in a way that had stirred her anew, as well as any other woman in the park with a pulse.

But while he might have masochistic tendencies, she tried to quell her unexpectedly sadistic ones. It was difficult, particularly when he didn't spare himself, being as physically affectionate as he'd been all along, stopping to give her long, drugging kisses on those paths as her hands ran up his back and down over his ass. When she leaned into him, she registered the tremor in those muscles, the turgid state of his cock, her barest touch hardening him further, his cock jumping eagerly. However, it was his mind—and her word—that were

263

the leashes that kept him in check. She had to admit, it was heady, powerful stuff.

It was also very convincing. Despite what he was, she thought back to the auction, all the beautiful women. Except for a respectful nod to Marguerite at Tyler's table, his attention had all been for her. Earlier, on the picnic blanket, it had been indescribable. When he gazed up at her from the ground, his cock hard and demanding inside her, everything in him focused on what she wanted and needed, denying the ache and primal need of his own body through her orgasm...it had been mind blowing.

Perversely, such commitment made it hard for her to resist the compulsion to give him his release, give him those words that would do it. For some reason, it made her recall her readings, the term "topping from the bottom", where a submissive controlled the direction. It had been discussed as a negative, where the submissive wasn't truly being pushed to where they needed to be, a true release of control. Which brought her back to Mistress Lyda's uncomfortably knowledgeable eyes.

Oh how the hell could she really know whether or not Brendan was doing something like that, and whether or not it was good or bad, for either one of them? She wasn't a Mistress, and Brendan had said she didn't need to worry about those kinds of things, anyway.

She'd dated everything from a rough and semi-violent biker to a computer analyst who had an addiction to X-Men comics. Her natural curiosity and acceptance, BVA—Before Violent Attack—had let her get beneath the surface, find the polish of the roughest, uncut gems. She'd always been satisfied with her journeys, sad but accepting when she knew it was over.

Brendan had fit none of that pattern so far. They'd met a year before the first real date happened, and here they were, just a few days later, in deeper and faster than any relationship she'd ever had. She couldn't imagine—and desperately didn't want—for it to end, but this was unmarked wilderness. Still, so far he hadn't let go of her hand once, never making her feel lost or alone in there. He was like meeting a mysterious and yet reassuring guide in a forest, one she wasn't sure she valued solely for being a guide, or being who he was.

"Steam is starting to come from your ears," Brendan mentioned. They'd left the park, agreeing to stop at his favorite coffee place to pick up a hot beverage, because the inlet temperature hadn't been as comfortable as the fall Florida weather. He put the vehicle in park and stretched his arm over her seat, teasing her hair with his fingers.

"I can't go swimming with you," she said, reaching for earlier, safer topics. "You know, when you said I could go with you?"

He lifted a brow. "I didn't mean we were going today. The dip wasn't planned."

She chuckled, but shook her head. "I mean I can't swim."

"Not at all?"

"No. My parents don't swim, and I was involved in a lot of things growing up. Art, nature classes, music, so that somehow got overlooked. We didn't live near any water, no friends with pools, so it never became an issue. We went to the mountains for hiking, but if there were streams we didn't go in unless it was for wading."

"Do you own a swimsuit?" His attention wandered over her knit button down shirt. It showed decent cleavage, particularly highlighted with the wooden Tree-of-Life pendant she wore nestled there. "Preferably a bikini. It's much easier to learn to swim in a bikini."

She pressed her lips together in a smile. "I'm sure. You're going to teach me?"

"Everyone should know how to swim. And you'd love it. At that park we went to today, there's a hike to a creek area that not a lot of people know about because it takes a while to get there. There's a cave, and you can swim into it, listen to the

drip of the water off the rocks. You'd love it," he repeated. His fingers shifted, tracing the soft skin beneath her eyes. "But that's not why steam was coming from your ears."

"No. But I need to keep thinking on it. Okay?"

"Okay." She could tell it took him some effort not to push, suggesting that, whatever being a submissive meant, it didn't mean he would blithely accept everything she dictated to him. Coming around the Jeep, he opened her door for her, handed her out. As he did, she mercilessly let her body bump against his groin, a passing stroke of her hip. "I'm glad those boxers were too wet to wear under your jeans."

"I'm glad you were willing to keep watch while I stripped them off in the bushes and put my jeans back on." He gave her a wry look, not just about that, but also telling her he was well aware she was enjoying her power over him. "That group of teenage girls was making me pretty nervous."

"A big, strong guy like you, afraid of a pack of naturally curious fourteen-year-olds?"

"'Pack' being the key word there," he said, making her laugh again. "Do you want some coffee?"

"Hot chocolate for me, with whipped cream and marshmallows."

"Does it come any other way?" When he slid his arm around her shoulders, she looped hers low on his waist, hooking her fingers in his waistband and feeling the movement of bare skin and hip bone under her touch.

"You know, Brendan, I'm not going to hold you to what you said, in the park." She grimaced over the surge of guilt. "You don't need to—"

"Yeah, I do." He brushed a kiss over her brow. "Not until you say it, Chloe."

"What if I order you to abandon that idea? Climax a hundred times?"

"I'd say I'll need hydration, fast."

She scowled at him and his evasion, but nature intervened before she could pursue it further. Their timing for departing the park had been propitious, because the sky had been darkening during their drive. Now a roll of thunder greeted them as they got out of the Jeep, sending them into the coffee shop, which was too crowded for the personal conversation to continue.

The late afternoon rain shower arrived as he was paying for their purchases, the lights flickering at a particularly sharp and brilliant shard of lightning. She loved storms, so she'd moved to a table for two at the window to watch while he waited for their order. She'd offered to pay, but he'd given her a look of mild horror and waved her off to get them napkins.

Old-fashioned, weird, submissive, gorgeous, mysterious guy-thing. She held onto the smile that thought brought, and eyed the thrumming flood of rain, the gray sheets of it coming down, broken into panes by the wind. The way the trees moved in the background, behind the shopping center across the street. Florida thunderstorms often blew up fast and scary, but she was pretty sure it would already be dying off before they left.

Brendan joined her then, sliding her cup to her. "Can we admit to Marguerite we stopped in at a coffee shop?"

"I got hot chocolate, so I'm safe. But she'll sniff out your treason." Chloe grinned. "Of course, Tyler prefers coffee over tea. She finally put a small pot on the counter for him, and she stocks his favorite brand."

"Does she give him a hard time about it?"

Chloe lifted her nose and gave him an imperious look, doing her best Marguerite impression. "'If you insist on drinking cowboy swill instead of a civilized beverage, you can't share in any of my substantial profits.'"

Brendan laughed. "Yep. That's exactly how she'd say it."

"I've never liked the taste, but I love the smell of coffee," Chloe confided. "It smells so reassuring, you know? It definitely has a very male aroma. My dad drinks it before work, so maybe that's why I've always thought about it that way." She folded her arms on the table and leaned in now, her eyes sparkling as if sharing an important secret. "Truth, I think M has started to like it for the same reason. It reminds her of how Tyler smells in the morning, all coffee and unique Tyler-aroma."

"What about you?" He stretched out one leg so it was on the outside of her hip, smiling a little as she slid her foot out of her ratty canvas sneaker and placed it on his foot, pressing down so he could feel the pressure of her toes through his Nikes. "Do you like the aroma of Tyler in the morning?"

"If he offered me ten minutes to take complete and total advantage of his body, are you asking if I'd leap on it like a starving wolf on raw meat?" Her eyes danced at his expression, but she laid a hand on his. "If you've had both men and women, you know there's no denying the man is a feast for the senses. He's just powerful, and..."

When she sought the explanation, he had it ready. "Commanding. Completely in charge of himself and everyone around him. A hundred percent Dominant. Hard for any woman to resist."

His tone remained neutral, but she couldn't argue with any of it, or deny what was left unsaid. *Unless the woman was a Mistress.* Marguerite's situation was an unusual one Chloe knew that, even with her minimal exposure to that world. Two Dominants didn't often come together the way Marguerite and Tyler had.

"Yeah, I guess you could say that," she admitted. "But joking aside, he loves Marguerite with every cell of his being. It's so obvious, that's what adds to how wonderful I think he is. It makes him something different to me. He's so good to her and...even before what happened to me, Gen and I knew there were terrible things in her past that made her how she is. Was. You still see it in her, but he's healing a lot of that. The open wounds are becoming scars." She gave him a steady look. "I guess you know some of this. How long have you two known one another?"

His fingers tightened on hers. "Marguerite and I were in an orphanage together. When she was fourteen and I was six. I was there about six months before I was adopted."

"Wow. I knew she said you were childhood friends, but I didn't realize." She digested that. "You kept in touch all these years."

"No. I didn't know where she was until a few years back, when I saw her at The Zone. Even then, she didn't recognize me, but I knew her. I eventually let her know, and we renewed the friendship."

"That's not fate, that's divine intervention." She shook her head, amazed. "I mean, what are the odds? Is that why you walked her down the aisle, because she was a link to your past? Or her past, rather?"

Brendan lifted a shoulder, drew her hands closer to him, pulling her attention back to his face. "In a way. Chloe, I think it's time—"

"Brendan."

Chloe's gaze rose at the address, but not so quickly that she didn't notice Brendan stiffen before he raised his attention to the man who'd approached their table. He was tall, lean and athletic like Brendan, making her wonder if he was a fellow swim team member. Handsome face and stylishly fashioned brown sandy hair showed off a movie star jaw line and prominent cheekbones. He had a model's face, with a pair of sea green eyes to match. His mouth was held in a way that gave Chloe a moment's unease though, his eyes a little too probing as they shifted between them.

"Haven't seen you for awhile. You don't usually stop by here this time of day. Still swimming at the Y in the mornings?"

"Yeah." Brendan rose, offered a hand, the handshake of men who were acquainted but who hadn't seen one another in awhile, though Chloe noted the touch lingered a little longer than would have been expected. She couldn't tell who'd prolonged the contact, though. "This is my friend Chloe. Chloe, this is an old friend of mine. Tim."

Before her lips could form a pleasant greeting or she could offer her hand, Tim's gaze had returned to Brendan, dismissing her so curtly it left her blinking. "Looks like you're playing on the other side of the fence now."

Brendan gave him an even look. "I was always bi, Tim. You knew that."

Tim chuckled, a harsh sound. "You aren't bi. You just want one Mistress, and the rest of us are sloppy seconds. You could care less if we have cunts or dicks."

The words, spoken so low and deceptively pleasant, took a moment to sink in, a razor blade hiding inside the façade of a sugar-coated tea cake. Chloe sucked in a startled breath, but it was then she registered what was burning in Tim's gaze, what had given her that moment of unease. She hadn't been dismissed as much as he simply wouldn't look at her, refusing to acknowledge Brendan was with someone else.

"You didn't have to stop and talk to us," Brendan said, just as low, but the gray in his eyes had darkened to match the storm clouds outside, the glitters of green like the flashes of lightning. "If the only reason you did is to be an asshole, you can just keep going."

"Does she know she'll never measure up to your precious Mistress? Of course, looking at her, I doubt she's man enough to take you up the ass, anyway."

That caught the attention of some of the nearer tables, and Chloe felt a flush burn across her cheeks. Brendan's expression changed. The current of rage that jettisoned through him was strong as the vibrating thunder. When he surged forward, she reacted instinctively. She slid between the two of them, pressing her back firmly to Brendan's chest, putting a quelling hand on Tim's.

In hindsight, it told her something pretty significant about how she felt with Brendan. She'd become far more timid about inserting herself into a potentially volatile situation, but this time she hadn't hesitated. Of course, once there, surrounded by combustible violence, her mind was jerked back to the memory of a face thrust into hers, saliva spraying her as his screamed accusations hurt her ears.

She struggled past that. Though she was standing between two men simmering with past ill feeling, her head barely coming up to their chins, Brendan would never hurt her, even if it meant backing down from a fight. Nor would he let anyone hurt her. She knew it. Because she knew that, she stayed where she was, hoping it would defuse before the young female manager, even now glancing over at them warily, called the cops.

"You son of a bitch," Brendan said, trying to keep his voice down. "I've done nothing to deserve that from you. And she sure as hell hasn't. Apologize to her, or I'm going to ruin that bleach job you've had done on your teeth."

"She's protective," Tim ignored him to give Chloe a mocking look. "Like a cute Pomeranian."

Chloe gritted her teeth. "Seems to me you weren't enough for him, either, because he's not with you."

"No one's enough for him, sweetheart," Tim scoffed. "Except his Mistress Marguerite. She's the only one he's ever begged to brand him like her personal slave."

Brendan went rigid behind her, his hands closing on her biceps, whether to steady her or thrust her out of the way, she didn't know. But she couldn't move anyhow. She blinked. "W-what?"

Brendan said something else to Tim, but she didn't hear it. Instead, she was spinning back to the very first night Brendan had stayed with her. When she'd first seen the brand. She remembered how she'd come out of the bathroom, looked at it while he'd been lying on his stomach. The way she'd pressed her mouth to it, with the odd idea she was overriding someone else's claim on him.

She thought about the *fleur de lis*, the way his eyes changed when she passed her fingers over it. *I won't refuse to answer any question you ask, but I'm requesting that you hold off on that one… I don't want to scare you off. I like being with you too much.*

Studying her face, Tim nodded with satisfaction, stepped back. "I'll see you around, Brendan. Payback's a bitch, isn't it?"

"You're a coward," Brendan said with venom. "You're too scared to strike out at your real target. Which is a good thing, because if she didn't finish the job she started, her husband sure as hell would. You're still running scared, Tim. Being an abusive bully and running scared."

"Excuse me," Chloe mumbled. She pushed away from them both, not really caring if they pounded one another to crumb cake. Heedless of the rain, which was still falling but fortunately had gone to a more gentle drizzle, she got out the door, hardly aware of the people coming in that she bulled her way through.

Her mind was swirling with it. Marguerite. Mistress Marguerite. The brand. The way Brendan acted toward Marguerite, and her toward him. Then her mind dragged her to how protective M was. *Take care of yourself or we will do it for you…*

What better way than to send her someone who would watch over her, show an almost inhuman propensity for putting her needs before his? No lover acted like that, male or female.

No, it made no sense. Marguerite wasn't duplicitous. But she was very secretive, and Chloe didn't completely understand this odd world of Domination and submission. Particularly what a Mistress could or couldn't command a slave to do.

She closed her mind. It was easier to think of nothing, because behind the pain of betrayal was the return of nightmares, the feel of brutal hands, the insidious whispers through the night.

Slut, whore, liar. None of what you think is real…

"Chloe."

His shout made her feet move more quickly. She couldn't stand the idea of him touching her, being near her. She was a billion years old, and the touch of another organism, anything living, was capable of disintegrating her, just like those bones under glass she'd seen at a museum once when she was young. Before she was nine, before she realized that everyone was like those bones, and they all lived in fragile containment environments, so easily shattered.

She yelped as she was forcibly jerked backward, a moment before she'd have stepped off the curb into the four-lane Tampa traffic. Horns and squealing wheels blasted open the door of her emotional fog like a SWAT team entering, ratcheting up her heart rate and adrenaline so abruptly pain grabbed her chest. She struggled against the arms holding her like iron bands, fighting to be free. Oddly, she realized she still had hot chocolate taste on her tongue, the remembered pleasure of a few minutes before.

"You really need to *not* do that when you're upset," Brendan muttered in her ear. "Chloe, calm down. Breathe. Just breathe. You're okay." He got her to one of the coffeehouse benches set under the spreading canopy of a couple live oaks, providing some coverage from the rain.

He eased her head down to her knees but she pushed against him, letting him know her chest hurt and she needed to sit up. While he backed off, he remained cloyingly close, his hand seeking her fingers. She pulled them out of reach, crossed her arms over her chest.

As she oriented herself, she realized Tim was a few feet away, his face white, short of breath. Apparently he wasn't a totally unredeemable asshole, because he'd run out here with

Brendan when they both realized she wasn't aware of her surroundings.

"She okay?" He spoke tersely.

"Go away, Tim." Brendan's voice was flat, dangerous. "You don't want to be here."

The face of Brendan's former lover became wooden, but he nodded, turned away. In a matter of steps he was out of her field of vision, probably headed to the parking area. Vaguely she wondered what flavor latte he'd gotten from the shop before he chose to ruin her day.

Brendan's awkward silence cut her, but his words were little better. He cleared his throat. "Would you like me to go get your hot chocolate?"

The half snort, half hysterical chuckle spat from her lips like a curse, full of scorn and self-deprecation. "Sure. Why not? I mean, you don't want to let five bucks go to waste, just because I feel... Hell, how *am* I supposed to feel about this?"

"However you want."

"Of course. Of-fucking-course." Chloe surged up and rounded on him. "It's always about what I want, what I feel. So what, did she order you to do whatever I needed if I called you?"

The shock and hurt on his face was so instantaneous, she had some small comfort in knowing she was off base on that, at least. "Chloe, everything I've said to you, felt about you, is real. I told you that I didn't want to lie to you, and I told you why."

"Because you were afraid it would scare me off." She rubbed her forehead. "I remember. I just...I never imagined this. God, that's why she's so protective of you. You're hers."

"As much as you are. That's the way Marguerite is about everyone she..." He stopped, but she finished it, bitterly.

"She loves."

"But it's not like that between us."

"Of course not. But it's not some Sir Percival routine, lady from afar. She branded you, Brendan. She's been at the club *with* you, not just with you." The flicker in his gaze told her she was right, and the knife drove in a little more. "So she's probably done all sorts of weird, perverted—"

"It's not perverted," he snapped, real anger sweeping his expression.

It wasn't a word she normally would have chosen, either, but Tim seemed to have rubbed off on her, and those words that had been trundling through her head with every stressful moment came forth now. *Dirty. Filthy. Perverted.*

However, it was his anger that froze her in her tracks, not the abrupt flashback possessions of her mind that were no longer a big surprise to her. "When you got pissed off at Tim a few moments ago, it was the first time I'd seen you get ticked off about something. And it was because of what he said about her."

"It was because of what he said to you, in front of you."

"And now," she continued, as if he hadn't spoken, "this is the first time you've ever raised your voice to me. Again, because of her. The first time you have a fucking real opinion on anything, and it's about her."

"It's not like that. Chloe, I've told you—"

"I should have seen it. Even that night at the auction, you looked at her first. I was so overwhelmed, because you latched onto me like some guy dying of thirst in the desert, but you looked at her *first.*"

"Chloe, you don't—"

"Understand?" She shrugged, though the hated tears were threatening. Why had she ever gone down this road? Like she needed a relationship barely begun to fall apart, on top of all the other shit she'd been handling in her head, her heart? "No, I don't. It's not my world, is it? It won't ever be, because it's not who I am. So how can any of this be anything more than an Alice-trip-to-fucking-Wonderland? You wear her brand, Brendan. I know what that means, if I don't know anything else. I want to go. I'm going."

She turned on her heel, wouldn't look at his face, not wanting to register any of his emotions, because she was having a hard enough time holding onto her own. For that nice, short time in the park, she'd felt like she was getting a grip of things. She should have known it was a farce.

"I'll take you."

"No. I have friends near here. I'll walk, crash there. Get one to pick me up—"

"Chloe." His hand closed on her arm. Surprisingly, when she tried to shrug him off, he didn't budge. It brought her gaze unwillingly back to his face. His expression was tense, his mouth a straight line, eyes unhappy but determined.

"You're upset, and I about pulled you out from beneath a truck. Even if you were completely calm, I'm not going to leave you on a city block to go find yourself a place to stay, miles from home. Come back to my place." Before she could object, he held up his other hand. "I'll find someplace else to stay. You're more comfortable there right now. There's no reason you shouldn't take advantage of it."

"Correction. *Was* more comfortable there." She felt meanly vindicated when he flinched, but what did he expect? She was supposed to lie in his bed, smell his scent, think of what they'd done there, and then think of Marguerite…

"Fine, you can drive me. But not to your place. We can pick up my stuff there, but I want to go home. We all know I'm safe there, I'm just being paranoid."

"Chloe."

"I'm tired of talking right now," she snapped. "Either take me home, or get out of my way so I can call a cab."

* * * * *

If there was a Guinness Book of World Records for the Most Awkward, Miserable Car Ride in History, Chloe knew this would be right there at the top of the list. Brendan tried to talk to her a couple times, but she simply looked out the window, her arms crossed over her chest, knees drawn up. She'd refused to put on her seatbelt. With a sigh, Brendan had reached across her. He probably hadn't noticed how she closed her eyes, tightening into a smaller ball to steel herself against the brush of his body as he pulled the seatbelt over her, guiding it with firm patience to the right position before he snapped it in place.

After that, there was the brief stop at his place. She went in to retrieve her bag. He stood at the door, waiting on her. Because she didn't want him to come into the bedroom, she hurried, stuffing her few items in, and then sped back past him, across the threshold.

"Chloe—"

She shook her head, beat him to the car by several moments while he locked his door, came after her. The drive out to her place wasn't short, and she kept her attention turned to her open window, her face in the rushing wind. He may have said something a couple times, but she didn't listen. One part of her wanted him to shout at her, grab her arm, shake her, do something to show it mattered to him, but the other part of her clung to the cocoon of silence, sure that any attempt to strip it away would be more than she could take.

She didn't think about the darkness that would soon cloak her home, or the remoteness of her place. Hell, if necessary, she'd sit on the back porch all night, hidden in a small corner where no ax murderer would think to look for her. He could look for her in all the usual places. Bed, kitchen, even bathroom. But she'd be outside, part of the night itself. Empty, not feeling, not thinking, completely transparent. Evil could look right through her, because there was nothing left to take, at least for tonight.

She wasn't a drama queen. She knew this would pass, because all pain did. But this was one too many right now. If Brendan started to make her feel alive again, like it could be okay, she'd grab onto that illusion until she lost herself forever.

When the Jeep crunched down her driveway, she saw St. Frances sitting on the porch, his eyes glowing in the deepening twilight. She'd had a neighbor checking in on him, giving him food and water, so he looked well fed, only mildly interested in her return. Which she knew would change as soon as he had a person to curl up against in the bed, to give him extra tidbits. Companionship.

Brendan put the Jeep in park. "I'm going to come in and check the house for you. Then I'll go."

"I'll wait out here," she said tonelessly. She felt him looking at her for a minute, then he got out, came around. He faked her out, halting his forward progress abruptly and turning back to the open window. Before she could draw back, he'd put his hand out, curled it around her neck, tilted her chin up with his thumb.

"Chloe, don't do this. Please talk to me. I'll tell you anything you want to know."

"I don't want to know anything." She pulled away, shook her head. "I can't handle knowing, Brendan."

"So tell me what you're thinking, then. Give me something I can work with, Chloe. Let me help make it better. I can't leave you, knowing you're feeling like this." He leaned against the window, so close that if the door hadn't been in the way, their bodies would have brushed. She was cold. She missed his warmth, remembering how they'd arrived at the coffee shop earlier, his arm over her shoulders, hers around his lean waist. Her finger hooked on his belt, hips bumping with that casual intimacy of two people who might already be sleeping together, or just indicating the inevitability of their doing so.

She stared at his hand, gripping the frame. If she didn't give him something, she knew she couldn't end this, couldn't escape. And fortunately or unfortunately, something was bubbling up inside her at his words. "I did it in a church once, when I was sixteen," she said at last. "Had sex in a park after sundown. Stripped off all my clothes to go skinny dipping. I thought those things made me adventurous. Tolerant. So when Marguerite told me more about her lifestyle..."

She curled a lip. "God, I hate that word. It's like a choice between Cape Cod or Victorian architecture, living on a six-figure income versus a five-figure one. It's a stupid word."

"Yes, it is," he said cautiously. She glanced at him. He was a good listener. He was. And he hadn't lied to her. Though it didn't make it hurt less, it was something. He was worried how she felt. It mattered to him. She mattered to him. Which made it all so confusing, and painful.

"I guess I'm realizing that there's a difference between being willingly adventurous and trying to figure out things beyond your normal understanding of the way the world is. No point of reference, right?" She suppressed a frustrated sigh. "Then there's realizing I'm not above jealousy. It feels...it's a terrible feeling. I don't like it."

He closed a hand over hers, hard. "I didn't want to hurt you, Chloe. And I don't know how to tell you not to be jealous, but it's different with Mistr—Marguerite."

She swallowed a jagged lump. "That's what you prefer to call her, isn't it? Mistress."

He nodded, uncomfortably. "I know you don't want to hear it, but I need to tell you. I could say I've never had sex with Marguerite. That the only thing she's ever allowed me to give her directly is a kiss. But the things we did at The Zone were sexual, so I guess that doesn't mean much. I did intend to tell you, if we reached this point together. It's just..." He sighed. "You're right. You may never fully understand the way this works, Chloe, but as far as I can tell, most people never fully understand those they care about. What's more important is that they love each other, and want to love each other to the very best of their ability."

She stared down, past her painted toenails. She'd left her shoes off and the canvas sneakers were in the floorboards, her feet braced on the edge of the seat as her legs remained bent against her, a modified fetal ball, instinctive shielding. But he was playing with her fingers, tiny strokes of the knuckles. She couldn't seem to pull her hand back.

"I can tell you that there's a difference between what I've shared with Marguerite and what I hope to share with you, but I know that would sound like a boatload of crap, like a million other guys have said to justify past relationships. So I will say this." She heard him draw a breath. "Marguerite is my Mistress. I love her, I've served her in the past, and I'll always honor her. I'll never deny how important she is to me."

As numb as she'd thought she'd gotten, each word cut, but then he came to the end of it. "I'm not in love with her, though. I never have been. And I expect it's obvious that she's not in love with me."

Chloe raised her chin to look at him. Those eyes, so many shifting shades of gray, green and brown, were holding hers, though his face was strained with the effort, and she registered the tension in his shoulders. He wanted to soothe, to comfort, to physically demonstrate his devotion to her. She couldn't deny her body trembled with a desire for that, but it also had a vengeful need to slice into him.

Instead, she fought for some sense of stability inside, while the afternoon birds chirped and St. Frances came down to lie on the gravel and begin a thorough bath. "You always call Tyler 'sir'. That's part of it too, isn't it?"

Brendan nodded. "She belongs to him. It's a reminder that I respect that bond and will never dishonor it."

She pressed her lips together. Reaching back to get her tote, she pulled it forward. "I need to get out now."

He opened the door for her, and she slid out. He stood in that opening, but she held the pack defensively between them. "Brendan...I think you're a really good person. And maybe...I don't know if I can do this or not. I just need to think about it, work it out. Okay? So you need to go now."

"I'll call—"

"No." She shook her head, spoke before she lost her nerve. "Don't call me and don't come back. I'll work this out. If I think...I can handle it, I'll call you. Okay?"

The look that came into his eyes made her wonder if her heart had cracked, because pain shot through her chest, so sharp she had to stay very still a moment. She saw resignation. He wouldn't fight her, would accept what she wanted. He'd said that from the beginning, hadn't he? That he was all about doing whatever she wanted. Maybe that was why women went for those pushy, more dominant guys. Because women could be so confused about what they wanted, sometimes it was nice to have a guy who forced the issue and made the decision for her.

But honestly, she wasn't sure if that approach was what she wanted right now either. Dominant, submissive or none of the above, several hours ago she'd had no doubt she wanted this man more than anything. That hadn't changed. She just didn't know if she could handle the past—or hell, the present—that came with him.

"All right." Before he let her by, though, he leaned in. She stiffened, thinking and perhaps hoping he was going to kiss her mouth, but he relieved and disappointed her by kissing her forehead, cupping the back of her skull as he did it. When his hand tightened there, digging into her curls, it brought tears to her eyes. She could feel how hard he was holding back his emotions. Why was he doing so? Why wouldn't he snarl and snap? Demand and rage?

Because that wasn't who or what he was, was it?

When he spoke, his tone was rough, his lips moving over her skin. "Whatever you decide, Chloe, my life is better because of the short time we've had together. And I fucking want you with all my heart. So if you change your mind, or even just want to talk some more about this, let me know. I'm a phone call away."

Chapter Eighteen

₰

She hadn't been scheduled to work until after the carnival, so she had two days to stew at home. She thought about quitting. Brendan would have called Marguerite, told her that Chloe knew. Of course he would. That thought alone spiked the ugly ball of anger in her stomach. But what *was* Brendan and Marguerite's relationship now? She and Tyler were obviously bonded, and no matter how willing Tyler was to pleasure two women at once, Chloe didn't need any special intuition to know he wasn't the type to share Marguerite. Period. She pitied the guy who thought otherwise.

So where did that leave things? She knew she had no point of reference for the kind of relationship that Brendan and Marguerite might have. Maybe if she'd given Brendan more of a chance to explain... But she didn't want it explained. She wasn't ready to be soothed or coaxed into accepting a rationalization from a guy who thought making her happy was more important than making it clear they had no future.

Yeah, she knew how that sounded, but she knew what she meant, damn it.

She didn't want to see Marguerite, but she wanted to go to work, double damn it. She'd slept poorly and ended up sitting on the back porch as predicted both nights, huddled in a blanket and fitfully dozing, listening to the nighttime insects, St. Frances purring on her lap. The house was scarier than the outdoors. Walls blocked a view of what was coming after you.

So she got dressed. She even put on jewelry and makeup, taking time with her hair in a way she hadn't in a while. When she came out on her front porch, she had a momentary hope, a despicable one, that Brendan would be there, miraculously showing up like he had after that first night. Of course he wasn't. He was respecting her wishes, the jerk. Getting into her car, she slammed the old Toyota's squeaky door and caught a glimpse of herself in the mirror.

The reflection looked about as inviting as a washed-out corpse dolled up by a mortician, curls fluffed around sunken eyes, a painted mouth that looked garish. Yeah, she'd taken care with her appearance today, but it hadn't been because she'd been feeling better. It was because she was viewing Marguerite as a competitor, wanting to show her she could be as attractive to Brendan, in one of those insanely irrational moves at which women excelled.

Yanking a wet towelette out of the glove compartment, she wiped it all off. Scraped her hands through her hair like a dog with fleas. Then she put the car in drive.

She didn't remember much of the trip into town, didn't turn on the radio. She could work on autopilot if she needed to do so. She'd perfected that these past few months, hadn't she? She'd get through, even though Tea Leaves had been her last sanctuary.

When she came into the tea room, it was still about a half hour before opening. Gen and Tyler were at the center island in the kitchen. Tyler was finishing up his coffee, wearing slacks and shirt, coat hung over the chair, suggesting he'd brought Marguerite in to work and planned to do some business in Tampa today. They glanced up as she entered, and Gen's brow rose at her appearance, but she didn't say anything. Eggshells. She wondered if they were as tired of walking around on them as she was.

"Yeah, I look like shit," she said. "You can say it. I'm not going to fucking break, you know."

"I think you're already broken, sweetling," Gen said quietly. "You want some tea this morning? There's a good chamomile blend that Marguerite—"

"Has been making me choke down regularly. Yeah. It's done a hell of a lot of good."

"That's enough."

Chloe snapped her attention to the end of the counter, where Tyler had leveled a look on her with those amber eyes. That look mashed the words flat on her tongue, an act of self-preservation. She'd never been a child who feared her father, but her dad, like many loving fathers, had that point past which his child knew he would not be crossed. Tyler had that look now, and she had a crazy feeling he wasn't above taking her behind the woodshed for a good strapping with his belt if he felt she needed it. In some ways, she wished she was back in that time of her life, because usually her dad had done it when she'd been out of sorts about something. Somehow the punishment had defused it, refocused her. Helped the tears come.

Was that part of it for Brendan? The release of pain? Demons he couldn't exorcise? Oh hell, she didn't want to go down that road.

When Tyler rose from his stool and stepped over to her, she wanted to draw back, but she couldn't. The gentleness of his touch on her face, at odds with the sternness of his voice, almost unhinged her. She had to quit her job. She'd known it when she woke up this morning, recognized it more than once over the past couple days. She needed to leave it all behind. Maybe she'd drive to the opposite coast, like she'd done in college a couple times. Go hang out on the beaches, braid people's hair. Be homeless, live in a pretty box decorated with rainbow colors and scraps of beads and ribbons that advertised her trade. Be a part of nothing.

"Tell Marguerite—"

"You need to go talk to her," Tyler said. "She's in her private garden, having tea."

Marguerite did that on rare occasions, following her own unique mixture of Japanese and English tea etiquettes that were as important to her as her yoga. It happened on occasions that usually coincided with Marguerite having a bad day herself. Great. So Brendan *had* told her. Though she expected it, it still hurt. *We're all sloppy seconds to his Mistress...*

"I don't want to see her. You can just tell—"

"Did I give you the impression this was a choice?"

Gen became still as a mouse behind the counter, and Chloe wondered if her own eyes had become wide as saucers, like her co-worker's. That shift in tone was as subtle as a tiger going from lazy interest to keen fascination with a grumpy badger right outside the tiger's camouflage of marsh grass. Tyler's hand on her face remained just as gentle, though, which was the disturbing part.

"She doesn't want to see me."

"You're wrong about that. You've been on her mind for quite a while now. It's time to resolve it. Go tell her what's on *your* mind. Get it over with. Stop hiding behind your anger and your fear. It's not fooling anyone, not even yourself."

"What about you?" She stared at his silk tie, knowing she couldn't meet that gaze for long. "Are you fooling yourself, about her and Brendan?"

Gen's indrawn breath told her that being fired might be the least of her problems, but when there was nothing but silence, she looked up. Tyler was studying her with a lifted brow. "So he told you."

"I found out. Then he told me."

"Mmm. Chloe, the relationship Marguerite and I have isn't really your business, but I will tell you this. I'm not concerned about Brendan and Marguerite's relationship. I know her heart. And you used to know it as well, better than you ever realized. She is protective of him, and of you."

"Why does she need to be protective of him? He's a big strong guy."

"Brendan was involved with someone who abused his submissive...generosity, for lack of a better word. I agree with you, that he's a grown man and can protect himself, but she doesn't want to see him hurt like that again."

Tim's bitter face swam up in her mind. She didn't want to feel anger on Brendan's behalf at the thought of someone abusing him, but it came anyway, curling her hands. "Why would Brendan let that happen? I mean, again—big strong guy."

"Chloe, it's possible to strip someone to the bone without ever laying a finger on them. You just need to know what kind of weapon to use."

There were many layers of meaning under that, all of them there in Tyler's gaze, too painful for her to face. She looked away. Brendan had said he broke up with his last relationship a few months before their wedding. Which meant, if he had a Zone membership, and a...friendship, with Marguerite, then he and M were never an exclusive item. Of course, did knowing that make things better or worse?

"I'm mad at her. It's not a good time to go talk to her."

"Actually, I think that's the perfect time. Go." He nodded to the side door. "And, if you're entertaining ideas of heading toward your car, instead of toward her garden, I'd rethink that. I'm a great deal faster than you are."

She sighed, rubbed her face, resenting him, resenting all of it, not wanting to look at Gen and resent the look on her face, either. "I just can't deal with it."

"Yes, you can." He shepherded her toward the side door, held her arm an extra moment. "Face your fear, Chloe. You'll feel better when you do."

"You're a bully, you know that?" But her tone was resigned, not accusing. A reluctant frisson of reassurance coursed through her at the faint amusement in those amber eyes.

"So I've been told. Repeatedly. It doesn't help her get away with anything, any more than it's going to help you."

* * * * *

Marguerite poured her a cup of tea, setting the pot back down on the cozy, and leaned back. She didn't speak right away, inhaling the aroma from her own cup. Chloe curved her hands around the smooth ceramic, needing and wanting the warmth, despite the protest in her stomach against putting anything in it. She was finding it hard to even look at Marguerite, the overwhelming beauty, the shadows and secrets in the pale blue eyes. Maybe because it would make her despise herself more, and face the fact she was as much hurt by Marguerite's silence as Brendan's sin of omission, no matter that he'd told her up front that there were things he would tell her in time.

I love you. Why did you push me toward him, knowing...

"Chloe." Marguerite spoke, but Chloe didn't lift her head. The woman sighed, put down her cup. Slim fingers and long silver white nails came into Chloe's field of vision, settling on the table cloth. "Do you have any idea how difficult it is for me to see you like this every day?"

"Sorry," Chloe responded tersely. "But if you wanted him for yourself, I guess you should have kept him. Worked out some permanent threesome with you and Tyler, though I'm sure that wouldn't have gone over too well."

At the pregnant silence, she had to lift her head. As she'd always known, it was difficult to surprise Marguerite. But there was no mistaking that she'd done it now. The shock on Marguerite's face was entirely genuine. The brief spurt of vindictive satisfaction was swept away by mortification.

"He hasn't told you anything, has he?"

"Who, Tyler? Have you been confiding in Tyler?"

"No." Chloe pushed away from the table, but couldn't get up. "I thought Brendan had..."

"Whatever Brendan feels for me, Chloe," Marguerite said carefully, "I can guarantee he would never break a confidence with you, unless he felt you were in danger. Would you like to tell me what has upset you so much?"

Chloe gazed at her hands miserably. The warmth from the tea cup was slipping out of them. "First, tell me what you meant, about it being hard to see me every day. Have I become such a lousy employee lately that you're thinking about firing me?"

"It has been hard for me to see you, knowing that it's my past that has hurt you this way." Marguerite shifted. "Now I'm suspecting I personally have hurt you as well. That makes seeing your misery all the more unbearable, though it gives me hope I might be able to fix my part of it."

Marguerite's visibly strained expression took Chloe back, to the day Marguerite had bent over her broken body, knelt in blood and shattered glass to touch her, tell her help was on the way. "Chloe, you could become the most horrible employee Tea Leaves ever hired, and I wouldn't let you go, or let you give up on yourself. I would never stop being your friend, caring about what happens to you. Loving you."

The tautly strung barbed wire anger fell into a tangle inside Chloe. "M..." She reached out then, clumsily, almost toppling her tea cup, but she managed to grasp Marguerite's hand. Unless she initiated it, Marguerite often stiffened at sudden contact, but this time, she not only let Chloe curl her fingers over hers, she brought her other hand down on top of them, holding her in a strong, sure grip.

"M, about your dad... You have to know, I don't blame you for a minute of that. Not a single second. From what I know...what I learned, of what he was to you, I think you are one of the strongest, most incredible people I know. Which is maybe why I hate myself so much now. Because I'm so jealous and angry at what you and Brendan have. And confused, about what that brand means, how that affects what he and I have. I don't know what to say or do toward you. I feel like slapping you or scratching your eyes out, because you're so bloody perfect, how could any man not love you? I don't usually let things like that bother me, because I know people are meant for each other or not, and I used to feel beautiful and desirable, but I've felt so ugly and miserable lately…

"Then, on top of that, there's this whole part of his life that I can't feel, you know? I can learn it, I can learn the language, but there's no way I can *feel* it, you understand? So where does that leave us? And you and me?" She could barely talk now. "You and Gen, the tea room, you all were helping me hang onto what shred of sanity I have, and when I found out about the brand…"

"That was taken away as well. Oh Chloe." Marguerite grasped her other hand, holding them both on the table between them, so tightly. "My family was broken apart, you understand? But I found one, made one, and I did that with your help. Yours and Gen's, Tyler's. Even Brendan. You are my family. I love you so very much, Chloe, and I don't think you realize how much I need to love you. Whatever else there is, we will work it out, I promise, but you must believe in that one thing, have hope in it. I need you back, Chloe. Your laughter and your joy."

Her grip tightened further. "There have been times, watching you, that I've gone into my office and done everything possible not to scream my rage. It has made me so unspeakably furious that something else I valued was taken because of this pestilence that was my childhood. It has hurt me more than I can express, not knowing how to fix it, how to give you back what my father took from you."

Marguerite broke off. Not only was it the longest emotional outpouring Chloe had ever heard from her boss, she was amazed to hear Marguerite's voice tremble at the end, her right eye glistening with the hint of an actual tear.

Before the attack, Chloe had never feared her own emotions. It was as she'd told Brendan, her strategy had been to embrace every ounce of life, living without fear. Marguerite had known such fear in her childhood that it was Chloe's night on the train tracks, multiplied by a factor of ten. As a result, the austere owner of Tea Leaves had always been so regimented with her feelings. Each emotion was carefully vetted before it was sent out to represent her.

Therefore, seeing her close to a breaking point shocked Chloe to her toes, making her realize the true vulnerability of the invincible. Their need for reassurance could be completely overlooked.

"I've been so fucking self-absorbed," she murmured. "Here I was, caught up in Brendan, and it never occurred to me..."

"No, hush. It shouldn't have. That's not why I'm telling you this." Marguerite pressed her lips together, gave her hand a squeeze and sat back, closing her eyes and picking up the tea.

Though she said nothing further, Chloe understood she needed a minute. To tell the truth, so did she. She gazed down at the caramel-color of the blend Marguerite had given her, one of the green teas, probably one of her concoctions specifically geared toward dissipating tension. However, as they sat there quietly, she heard a foot on the cobblestones. Despite the intensity of the moment, she felt a rush of warmth. There was one who never overlooked Marguerite's needs.

Tyler stepped into the garden, his paper under his arm, obviously about to head out, but checking in with her before he left. Marguerite kept her eyes closed, and when he bent to touch her cheek, she stayed that way. Her head tilted into the press of his mouth, though, as his other hand cupped her skull, held her that way.

After a moment's pause, he turned his gaze to Chloe. With a bemused expression, he leaned forward and kissed her forehead as well, stroking her hair. Chloe found herself leaning into that same reassurance. She mumbled her "I'm sorry," into his shirtfront.

When he leaned back, his eyes were as kind and compassionate as they were stern and uncompromising earlier. "Forgiven, little flower."

"You're really scary, you know. I guess you've convinced terrorists to give up their plots and everything, so you have practice."

"The women in my life require a different approach." Humor rippled across his handsome face. "The terrorists are far less work."

* * * * *

After he left them, they were silent a few more moments, but an easier feeling was between them, surrounded by the aroma of tea, morning sunlight, and late blooming flowers. The buzz of insects. "The night at the carnival," Chloe asked at last. "You disapproved of me being there. Why?"

Marguerite adjusted the tea pot on the cozy, smoothing the lace edge with slim fingers. "It was the wrong setting. A submissive's needs can be confusing and overwhelming for someone who's not a Dominant. A submissive tends to have a lot of conflicting emotions, a push-pull, so to speak. It's also difficult for a submissive like Brendan to instruct a Mistress, because he is wired to please. Plus, for someone like you, who isn't part of the D/s world, a setting like that can overwhelm you with the physical side of what it means. D/s is, at its heart, psychological. It's a power exchange, where a Dom takes the surrender of a submissive and makes the most of that for both of them."

"So he needs a Mistress, somebody to tie him up and do things to him, things like I saw at the carnival." Chloe sighed. "I mean, freaking Level Ten pain threshold? I'm not like that, Marguerite. It's not that I couldn't learn, it just doesn't feel like me."

Marguerite shook her head. "Done the right way, Brendan will respond the same way to a command to give his

Mistress a foot massage as he would to being whipped." At that astounding statement, she leaned forward. "Some subs need the restraints and caning to be fulfilled. But not him. How much D/s can or can't adversely affect a relationship has a great deal to do with the two people involved. Brendan loves you, Chloe. I can see it in his face, and that love will continue to grow.

"He is unique, in that the most elemental level of his submission has to do with a woman's willingness to let him care for her, to do what it is she wishes and see her pleasure in that. What Brendan needs, more than a Mistress, is someone who understands what his submissiveness is truly about. And that's the challenge and test of acceptance you face, not whether or not you are a natural Domme."

Chloe drew a breath. "Is it wrong for me to feel a little pissed off at you? A little possessive of Brendan, kind of like I don't want you around him, or touching him again?"

"No." The wry humor in the other woman's face did a lot to loosen Chloe's gut. "In fact, I find it very reassuring. You want him. Perhaps could even love him in time."

If I don't already. Chloe knew that thought was there on the table, as obvious as the gleam of sun on the teapot. "The way he calls Tyler sir. Brendan said that he initiated that."

"Yes, Brendan did that himself. He understood, based on what we have been to one another, that it was necessary to be clear how he views himself in relation to Tyler's claim over me."

Okay. Chloe thought it through. "But you were mad at me for more than that. Tyler said you're protective of him, and you thought…I felt like you thought I'd abused his trust."

"Didn't you?"

"I didn't know what I was doing. I…" Chloe came to a stop before that level pale blue gaze. Goddess, it was eerie how both of them could do that look. "Yeah, I did."

"You needed to exorcise some demons. Another reason the setting was not a good one."

"But isn't pain part of submission?" She remembered wanting to hurt him, a couple times, that desire to strike.

Marguerite cocked her head. "When you wanted to hurt him, up on the platform, it felt wrong inside you, ugly, violent. Right?"

At Chloe's nod, shadows came into Marguerite's eyes. "You know the small scar Tyler bears under his eye?"

"He said he had a gardening accident."

"No. I did that to him. Because I wanted to hurt him." Marguerite met her gaze. "There is a difference between giving pain to your submissive for your mutual needs and pleasure, and using him as a whipping post for your own wounds, your fear and pain. You intuitively knew the difference, which is why it felt wrong."

Chloe pressed her lips together. "I don't think I'd ever feel okay giving pain to anyone, no matter the reason. I understand some people, like Brendan, may take pleasure in that, but it's not me."

"If your love for one another goes the direction I expect, knowing what I know of both of you, you won't have to worry about that." Marguerite arched a brow. "What is it you like about touching Brendan?"

Though unexpected, the change of direction wasn't unwelcome. "Well...besides the fact it's like eating really good cake, I like the way he acts when I touch him."

"Yes, you do." That ghostlike smile on her lips, Marguerite nodded. "The more we fall in love, Chloe, the more deeply we bond with another. Our preferences change, grow, because we are so wrapped up in pleasing one another, nothing else matters."

Chloe considered that. "He said something, when we were out on a picnic. That he gets irritated with people who claim not to need anyone, who confuse being defensive and obnoxious with independence. It was an unusual thing to hear a guy say."

"It's not unusual for Brendan. He lost his mother young, and understands that loss of stability, how it feels when there is no safety net of love or connection to another in your life. Someone could certainly misinterpret that as weakness in a male."

Marguerite's level look spoke volumes. Chloe remembered her reluctance to call Brendan a submissive for that very reason. Yet he'd made her feel protected and cosseted every minute they'd been together. Every minute her fucked up mind had let him, and sometimes when it hadn't.

"I don't," Chloe said, with enough conviction that Marguerite's jaw eased. "He made a joke about it, though. He said if a terrorist had showed up at your wedding, everyone would crowd behind Mac and Tyler, because they have that out front, alpha-hero thing going, to take charge and lead everyone out of danger. But it doesn't make Brendan…" She sought the right words, but Marguerite already had them.

"He'd make sure every woman and child there was tucked behind Mac and Tyler, and then risk his life drawing the line of fire until they got them out of harm's way." Marguerite nodded in perfect understanding. "A soldier is just as brave as the colonel leading the troops, because he has to have the courage to follow, to believe that winning the battle is the most important thing. That's what Brendan is."

Percival. She remembered Brendan's words about the knight.

"As I said, Brendan is a more intuitive submissive, Chloe. He doesn't always need you to clearly state what you want. He seeks it out, as part of his nature, and strives to meet it, perhaps to excess. But no, he's not a doormat. Not in the least. He won't let you abuse him, though he might undervalue his worth, accept less than what you could truly give him, if you don't find the courage to do so."

Okay, there was a warning there, that streak of protectiveness showing in Marguerite's eyes that Tyler had mentioned. Chloe felt less threatened by it now, knowing Marguerite had a similar feeling toward her, but it did turn her toward that uneasiness she'd felt a couple times during her conversations with Brendan. An uneasiness because of his unwillingness to tell her what *he* wanted.

"The night at the carnival, how would you have done it...when he was tied up?"

"I'd have told you first and foremost it wasn't about sticking six inches of molded rubber up his backside, any more than religious faith is about two sticks tied together in a certain way. That's a tool for expressing your faith, not the sole focus of it."

Rising abruptly, Marguerite drew Chloe out of her seat. She moved them a few steps into an open area of the garden, where they stood on a platform of slate tiles next to a gurgling fountain formed by smooth stones. The winter bushes here had a light, sweet smell.

Turning Chloe away from her, Marguerite took her palm down Chloe's back, a slow trail of sensation. "Imagine you're him, Chloe. He wants to give himself to you utterly. You gag him because he needs to be helpless to your love, however you want to express it. He's given up his voice, his freedom, to give you pleasure in this precious moment. To take you both on a journey together. He's hard for you, his mind, soul and heart riveted upon you. You have commanded all his attention."

Her hands settled on Chloe's hips, her body pressing close, giving Chloe an unexpected charge of sexual energy, with an emotional twist. "Now imagine you're wearing that strap-on. You put the tip in his anus, exert pressure and slide forward, easing in, so slowly, registering every single response of that body, heart, soul and mind to you."

Chloe thought of Brendan's body accepting her, those beautiful muscles straining, head fully back on his shoulders, ass tightening in delicious display, flexing against her. If she'd moved forward, she would have felt it, that push followed by a sudden slick giving, a dildo accepted in a man's ass the way a woman's cunt would accept his cock.

Marguerite brushed her lips against her hair. "Different as day and night, isn't it?"

"Yeah." Chloe swallowed as Marguerite let her go enough to guide her back to the chair, easing her down on weak knees before taking a seat herself. Though she had no obvious feathers out of place, Marguerite's gaze remained compassionate, gentle. It made something crack inside Chloe's chest, remembering arousal and pain sawing together against her breast bone. But she'd be brave enough to take it a step further.

"M...I haven't asked, because I'm not even sure I could understand. But what is he to you?" More importantly, what was she to him? Brendan had answered the question, for certain. *I'm not in love with her, and she's not in love with me.* But she wanted Marguerite's answer to it.

"I was his Mistress, Chloe." Marguerite pressed her lips together. "I *am* his Mistress. You're right, you may not be at a place you can fully understand how that doesn't impede or detract from where the two of you are going, but it doesn't. There is no active sexual or romantic relationship between us, and there never will be again, unless that is something the four of us find agreeable. Brendan and I are bonded, because of who and what we are to one another, but what the two of you have will exceed it, if your hearts desire it."

"I do," Chloe said slowly. Reassurance and apprehension both came with hearing the truth of it spoken. "But M, I think...I need to understand better. I don't know enough to know what I need to ask here, but...can you help me?"

Marguerite studied her in that peculiar way she had, as if she was sifting through a variety of things about Chloe that Chloe couldn't even see in herself.

"You need to understand the core of what he is. I think you're already mostly there, but you need to have an experience with it, untainted by your own fear and pain. You'll go where you need to go then, find out who you are, who he is. It's a thing of raw, perfect beauty."

Chloe turned her gaze back to her tea cup. "What if I'm not undamaged enough to set aside fear and pain? It's like chicken and egg, M. I want him, but I may be too messed up right now. Do you think it's best to let him go until I get it figured out?"

"Like the chicken and egg, I think he may be the key to helping you figure it out. He has chosen you, and will be whatever you need him to be."

"I just want him to be him."

Marguerite met her gaze. "I'm glad to hear it. You may be able to help him with that."

So Marguerite knew. What had she said? *What Brendan needs, more than a Mistress, is someone who understands what his submissiveness is truly about. And that's the challenge and test of acceptance you face.* Before she could pursue that further, Marguerite shifted. "If you are willing to do this, I can set it up. It may require me to have some brief exposure to Brendan in my capacity as his Mistress. But only to give you both a gift, I hope."

Chloe digested that, thought about seeing Marguerite act as "Mistress" toward the man she felt, in an inexplicable way, was hers. "Can I think about it a little while?"

"Of course." Marguerite's lovely hair, pulled back in a comb, fell alongside her shoulder as she leaned forward again, touched Chloe's face, the lightest of contacts over sensitive nerves. "The option is entirely up to you. What I most want, Chloe, is for you to find your happiness again. Not for my sake, or Brendan's, but for your own."

Chloe got lost in that blue gaze, how close Marguerite was. Her reassurance, warmth, love, it all wrapped around her. She could get up now, go back to work. In fact, she even started to do so, giving Marguerite a tired smile. Her boss squeezed her knee, leaned back. Chloe knew she'd pick up her tea cup and go back to her meditation. Session done, lots of progress made. After all this, which had been emotionally draining, it would be okay to let it go for awhile, right?

However, for the first time in forty-eight hours, it didn't hurt so much to think about Brendan. Which meant she couldn't help but think of what he'd told her in his small kitchen, how he'd held her beneath him, helped her from shattering. And now Marguerite, saying that she could help Chloe understand Brendan's soul...if her own fear and anger didn't get in the way.

She did want him. After nearly a year of vacillating on nearly every decision, that want galvanized her to think about what healing really meant. It meant taking the scariest step imaginable, defying those dark voices that told her not to reach out to anyone, that she could handle this herself, that it would eventually go away...

"M, I think..." She turned around, faced Marguerite again. She couldn't figure out why the words were sticking in her throat, or why it got worse when Marguerite put down her teacup and rose, her brow creasing at whatever she saw in Chloe's face.

It was too hard. The tears she'd held back for so long surged up into her throat, as if this very second was the key moment, when they knew the dam would break and the flood would begin. She couldn't do it.

She couldn't not do it.

"I wanted to be strong, like you, not let them win. Brendan told me they only win if they cut me off, you know. If I don't trust anyone or let myself be vulnerable." The words poured out at once, jumbled and insensible, so painful she couldn't breathe. She choked the words out anyway. "I can't do this on my own. I'm afraid, and scared all the time, and angry, and ashamed... I need help. Goddess, I need help."

When Marguerite closed the distance between them in barely a second, her arms immediately there, no doubt, no hesitation, Chloe grabbed hold of the taller woman like a panicked drowning swimmer. "I can't fix it. I don't know how...and they hurt me, and made me afraid to live... I'm afraid to cry. I can't..."

She didn't know how Marguerite called her, or maybe Gen had been watching all along, but suddenly Gen was there too, so they held her between them, forming a solid protection all around her. She had to trust them. Brendan had told her she could. She knew she could.

The dark memories rose, bringing violent hands and faces, anger and hatred, such that the evil and helplessness of it all drowned her. She went down in it and let go.

It was like being in a nightmare, only she wasn't. She could scream out her rage and hurt, cry as if she'd never stop, so hard she choked on the sobs, and yet they were holding her, keeping her between them as she struggled against the horror of it all, of everything that had been taken from her, that had come back to haunt her.

"Help..." She kept repeating that one word, and they held her tighter, pressing kisses on her face, stroking her hair, refusing to let her trembling body break apart. They all sat, folded on the pea gravel together, the fountain a hushed reassurance all its own. Evil had come here, the place she'd always assumed was safe, but it hadn't destroyed it. It hadn't destroyed her. They wouldn't let it. She wouldn't let it.

"Thank God," Gen said softly, after a long time, when her sobs were becoming shuddering gulps of air. "Oh precious, you should have done this a long time ago. We've always been here for you."

"Always," Marguerite repeated. "You're going to be fine."

Chloe realized that Marguerite's face was streaked with tears too, a remarkable validation of its own. In that moment, she knew it didn't mean a damn, what her boss was to Brendan or Brendan was to her, because those tears destroyed her, made Chloe forgive everything. Marguerite had known exactly what she'd felt, what she'd needed all along, and yet had suffered the heartbreak of knowing nothing could help her until Chloe reached out herself.

It made her sorry and painfully reassured all at once. Family. This was what family did. Shelter in the storm, and even more than that. Remembering what Brendan had said, she knew that when the storm passed, they were the ones that would give her the strength to open those windows again, let the sunlight in, not fear its touch on her cold soul.

"Easy, dear, dear girl," Marguerite said. "It's all right. We're going to help you."

* * * * *

Tyler hadn't left. He knew his wife's moods, and the tea ceremony she'd done for herself had been a sign of the stress. She would need him when this conversation was over, no matter how much—or how snappishly—she'd insisted she was fine, before Chloe arrived this morning. So he'd simply gone into the alleyway, taken a seat on the wrought iron bench, tucked in between a Buddha statue and a small, spilling mountain of impatiens. He'd checked the stock reports, eyed a stray tom who considered spraying the leg of that bench before Tyler's anytime-you-feel-lucky look had him sauntering off.

As he occupied himself, Tyler kept tuned in to the conversation. Fortunately, he was close enough to follow it fairly well. When the flood finally came, he felt the same relief Gen expressed, even as his gut ached at the girl's outpouring. He knew how strong his wife was, just as Chloe had said. So strong, she could break into a million pieces inside at the pain of someone she loved as much as she loved Chloe, and still not show a single crack on the outside. Which was why she had him.

When the weeping wound down at last, he slid back into the garden. Chloe had sunk back into the chair, with Gen standing behind her, stroking her hair. The girl's forehead was against Marguerite's shoulder as she gave the occasional snuffle, her body shaking in that flu-like aftermath that came to victims of trauma when they finally let it go.

When Marguerite glanced up, her mouth softened in rueful acknowledgment that said she wasn't surprised to see him. "Chloe," she murmured, covering Gen's hand on the girl's skull. "We're going to take you upstairs to the bedroom. We'll close the shop today, and you, Gen and I are going to curl up in the quilts with ice cream and tea cakes, overdose on chocolate and watch a marathon of your favorite movies. I'm going to call Komal, and later in the afternoon, I'm going to drive you to her house. You're going to talk to her. And you're going to keep visiting her, until you and she agree that you don't need to see her anymore. All right?"

"I'm so tired."

"Well, you're going to sleep for a little while, while Gen and I handle close up. Tyler will take you upstairs."

Chloe shifted her head then, registering his presence next to Marguerite. His hand was on his wife's shoulder. "Gonna carry me, just like Clark Gable?"

Gen smiled, bending to kiss the top of her head. "Without the implied ravishing."

"Well, that sucks." But that was just for form's sake, he knew. Chloe was so exhausted from ten minutes of crying, Tyler could tell she only wanted the oblivion of dreams. And apparently one other thing. "Gen…"

"Yeah, sweetling?"

"Can you get… there's a stuffed dog in my bag. Can you get me that?"

"I sure can."

Chloe accepted Tyler's ever present handkerchief with a tremulous half-chuckle. "I keep messing up all your handkerchiefs."

"Don't worry. I have plenty more. And a devoted little wife who washes and irons them for me."

Marguerite gave him a lifted brow, the slight look of disdain he adored. "You must be keeping her locked in the basement, because I haven't seen her. Polygamist."

Since Tyler's extremely capable housekeeper Sarah took care of their every domestic need, Chloe knew the humor was for her benefit. Still, it was appreciated. She focused back on Marguerite.

Gen returned then, the plush Rottweiler in hand. "It's a shame the guy that gave it to you isn't in that bag," she observed as she handed it over. Chloe shook her head.

"Next time he sees me, I want to do it right. Like you said, M."

"We'll worry about that soon."

"Pretty soon," Chloe said. "I miss him a lot."

"Pretty soon, then. But today, we deal with you."

"I haven't been really fair to him. To any of you. You've been good friends, and I don't deserve you."

"That's not at all true." Tyler squatted so they were at eye level, put his hand on Marguerite's knee and his hand on Chloe's shoulder. "You've been here whenever Marguerite or Gen needed you. I want to hear you say you deserve every bit of their friendship. No ice cream until you do."

When he held her gaze, telling her he was serious, she looked toward Marguerite. "He is relentless," she informed her, with a glint that might have been amused commiseration. "And he's also absolutely correct."

"All right." Chloe remembered Brendan had done almost the exact thing with her, with a gentler but no less determined approach. It gave her a new thought, seeing the two loving men, opposite sides of the same coin. Dominant and submissive.

"I deserve you guys. I deserve…to feel good again, and to be happy. And I'm going to."

"Good. Put your arms around my neck, little flower."

She gave Marguerite's hands a hard squeeze, somehow reluctant to let go. Given that she was being offered the chance to put her hands on Tyler, that was saying something. But if she was afraid her emotions would sweep her away without that lifeline, she needn't have worried. Tyler put his arms under her in the chair and lifted her, bringing her close to his solid body as Marguerite and Gen's hands slid from her, one more caress, telling her they were all three there, and it was going to be okay.

She almost believed it.

* * * * *

After settling Chloe upstairs in the canopy bed, stuffed Rottweiler in her arms, Tyler sat with her, waiting for her to drop off to sleep. She mumbled soft things to the dog, to the absent Brendan and to herself before she gave in to slumber. It only took a few moments. Knowing the signs of mental and physical exhaustion, he returned to the lower level when he was sure she was well under.

The women had finished the closing, but Marguerite was on the front porch, explaining to some early arrivals they had a family emergency but would be open in the morning, complete with a complimentary first cup. True to her regular clientele, she got warm wishes that everything would be all right, and a promise to return the following day.

When she came back in, Gen was in the kitchen, but he was sitting in his favorite seat in her tea room, a chair that gave him a direct line of sight to both the front door and the kitchen, as well as the large mirror that was the two-way window in her office where she could watch the floor. It was where he'd sat down the first night he'd come calling on her, an amusingly old-fashioned sentiment, but one he applied to that situation.

Now she moved to sit down across from him, but he took her wrist, guided her onto his lap. Since the door was locked and Gen was occupied, she capitulated, letting out a sigh when he folded his arms around her, guided her head to his shoulder.

When she spoke, he wasn't surprised where her thoughts were. She was so fragile, in so many ways, but she could also rival Boadicea for unflinching courage to do what needed to be done. "When you offered to have him killed in prison, I should have said yes. If I could turn back time, I would. I'd do it. With every tear she shed, I wanted to do it more, until I felt consumed by it."

"It's not who you are, angel. You'd do it now, with the knowledge you have, because you'll fight anything to the death in defense of those you love or consider yours. But you didn't know then, and you're not a cold-blooded killer. You also don't believe you're God, able to predict people's actions."

She was quiet for a bit, her fingers curved into his back muscles. "I need to find you a job. Always meddling. You're not busy enough."

"I'm plenty busy enough. But nothing is more important to me than you. I know this has been hard."

"She's just young. She and Brendan, they're both so young. Trying so hard to please, afraid of hurting one another, rather than understanding you have to be who you are with one another, the dark as well as the light. You helped me with that."

"You think they're meant to be together."

Marguerite's lips curved in one of her serious smiles as she tipped her head back, let him see the shadows in her eyes receding. "Absolutely. But sometimes people can involve their heads too much in their decisions, and the right ships will sail right past each other."

"It's a good thing we didn't."

"It might have something to do with the fact you intercepted my ship, blasted a shot across the bow, and then tried to ram me when I was going to sail away."

"Well, whatever works." Tyler drew her close, unrepentant. "It will be okay, angel. She has us, and Gen."

"And Brendan." Her lips pressed into the hollow of his throat. "He's only begun to love her as much as he will, if she lets him. I know it."

Chapter Nineteen

ဆာ

Dear Brendan,

I was wrong, you know. About a lot of things. I told Marguerite it was okay to tell you what was happening with me right now, my visits with Komal, but Komal and I agreed this letter is a really good idea. I'm not reading it to her, though. I want it to be between you and me.

Here it is. I hope you haven't given up on me, on us, because I don't want to give up on you. Whatever we're going to be deserves a real chance, and that's part of why I'm seeing Komal. You helped steer me the right way, helped me find the courage to finally admit I needed help. I want to be the person you met at the wedding, not just for you, but for me. Every time you kiss me, or touch my body, or say something that makes butterflies tumble around in my stomach, I want to feel the joy of that, of all those tiny steps toward falling completely, irrevocably in love with you.

I can't see you right now. I know I don't have to be perfect to be with you, but I don't want what happened at the carnival to happen again. You feel like taking care of me is part of the whole love and relationship thing. Well, I feel the same thing about you. There's something you and I need to get straight between us, and I want my head screwed on right when I have that discussion with you.

So I hope you'll be okay with seeing me soon, and know that I'm thinking about you every day. Oh, and Prince sleeps with me every night. That's the name of the dog you gave me. And before you accuse me of being unoriginal, not naming him something quirky and precocious, like Basil, Rupert or Bill, did you know that your name comes from Brendanus, a Latin form of the Irish name Bréanainn? That's Welsh, and it means – you guessed it – Prince.

* * * * *

For a few days, she stayed at Marguerite and Tyler's home in Tampa and worked with Komal almost daily. The day after she sent the letter, she received a basket of chocolates, the bite-sized Dove Promises. That and a set of red roses, twined around the wicker. Once she started working at Tea Leaves again, each morning a new paper rose was left inside the screen door. New things to add to her happiness book. A poem, a quote, a picture of something that delighted her, whether it was an elderly man with a kitten on his shoulder, or a field of lavender in a Midwest town.

Gen teased her, said her admirer had walked right out of the pages of a sappy romance novel, but Chloe knew her cynical co-worker was as touched by it as any woman would be. Marguerite gave the paper rose a pursed lip look, told her if Brendan was harassing her to let her know. She'd put out a restraining order. It made Chloe chuckle, as she was sure their austere boss intended, though Marguerite gave nothing away except possibly a quick twinkle through her pale blue eyes.

It made her happy, but also anxious to be with him. So it was, after three weeks, she'd had enough and knew it was time. When she hesitated, Komal had given her a smile and pressed her hand.

"Chloe, you don't have to finish therapy and be completely healed for you to embrace love again. All you had to do was be willing to be helped, and feel like you have taken control of your life again. You have." The comfortably sixty-something Indian woman had shifted on her oversized sofa and offered Chloe another lemon drop. "So when you want to see Brendan is entirely up to you."

Yesterday wouldn't be soon enough. But she wanted to do it right, so she spent time talking about it with Marguerite, discussing her approach, what she wanted to do, just as they'd talked about that fateful day in the garden. Therefore she asked Marguerite to draft the next letter she would send to Brendan.

When the woman was done with it, she brought it to Chloe. They were in the Tea Leaves kitchen, Chloe preparing a lemon cake for the afternoon visitors. When Marguerite laid the heavy stationery on the butcher block, Chloe looked down, then raised a brow. "It's pretty brief. That's all you need to do?"

Marguerite nodded. "Yes. Only one more thing is needed."

Chloe looked back down at the note.

Brendan. West wing. Holograph room. Friday 9 p.m. Staff member will give you further instruction. Wait upon my pleasure.

"So what's missing? Other than full sentences, a greeting of some kind…"

Marguerite handed her the calligraphy pen. "Your signature."

Chloe nodded. Took it in hand. She signed with a flourish, then included a smiley face and a couple Xs and Os, for hugs and kisses. When she glanced up at Marguerite, mischief dancing in her eyes, Marguerite leaned in, kissed her forehead.

"There's my girl," she said, satisfaction in her voice.

* * * * *

The Zone was the Florida area's most exclusive fetish club, and it showed. Chloe had been to an opera house when she was young, and been overwhelmed by the jewel toned carpets, huge chandeliers and winding staircases. This place had the same odd mixture of macabre and beauty as a Phantom of the Opera set. Marguerite circumvented the dance floor areas and public play area, however, which Chloe knew might have made her far more nervous than she was. Instead, Marguerite took her to a lower level where the changing areas and rented private rooms were.

She felt okay about being here. It was like being at a masquerade, because everyone was wearing different things. She saw people in Goth wear, full bondage, even a couple people completely nude except for collars and leashes, which was like the carnival. She also saw masks of all shapes and descriptions, from full head masks to Mardi Gras masks with sparkles and feathers. She herself blended in well, and felt as mysterious and dangerous as her outfit suggested.

It had been all her idea, the setting, the costume. In truth, it was a private fantasy of hers she'd never had the resources to try...or a lover she trusted enough to try it out. At first she hadn't been sure she should tell Marguerite about it, thinking Brendan might decide it meant more than it did, but Marguerite had been reassuring on that score.

Chloe, a lot of women have Domination or submission fantasies. It doesn't mean that they are in fact Dominants or submissives. We are very sexually imaginative creatures, and we like a variety of situations to explore that. Brendan has a fairly good grasp of who you are. Trust in that.

Some of the playrooms had windows, and Marguerite explained they could allow two way, one way or no viewing, depending on the Master or Mistress's preference. As they walked past the ones that allowed viewing, at least from their side, Chloe digested the various scenarios. Pony play, sensory deprivation and pain, pure psychological Domination. She stopped at the Victorian drawing room, where apparently a male butler was being severely chastised by a Master for spilling his brandy. The "butler" had been pushed over the arm of a wingbacked chair and forced to suck his Master's cock while his trousers were dropped and he was enthusiastically caned by another Master.

Chloe blinked, somewhat mesmerized by the action, as all three men were handsome males, and the butler had a superior ass, but then Marguerite was tugging at her elbow, drawing her onward. Chloe's brow creased, though, as she passed a window with a mother and child scenario. The male was cradled in a woman's arms, suckling her breast as if he were a nursing infant, though he was wearing a cock harness. She was swatting his organ with what looked like a wooden spoon, making him flinch. His toes curled at every strike, however, and he was leaking from the tip of his very erect cock.

"It's kind of strange, but as different as all these are, there's something similar about a lot of it. Isn't there?"

"Yes. You're picking up the undercurrent. It's all about letting go. Surrender and trust. It's as different for each person as any personal need is." Chloe looked toward her. Marguerite wasn't here to be part of a scene or the upstairs nightclub atmosphere, but she wore a snug skirt and soft blouse thin enough to outline a feminine camisole beneath. Her hair was pulled back, showing the pearl and silver necklace she often wore, that Tyler had given her at their wedding. A gift Chloe had finally realized was Marguerite's collar.

Thinking how that had dumbfounded her, she had that momentary sense of despair again, that she would never understand any of this, but she reminded herself that she didn't have to. This was about Brendan and her.

"Did Brendan find those things with you? Surrender and trust?" Chloe dared the question. She no longer felt angry about them, but she had to admit there was a tingle of jealousy she was trying to accept and defuse.

"He found a Mistress in me. But he didn't find his heart. Chloe, there are people who come to the club and go home to wives or husbands, children, none of whom know a thing about this part of their lives, and never will, because they come here to satisfy their craving."

"But this is part of Brendan," Chloe responded. "It's part of how he acts, how he makes love, how he speaks and thinks."

"Yes, it is. Which means, as I told you, if he's chosen you to serve, whether or not you're a Mistress doesn't matter. "

"I don't want him to serve me. I want him to love me."

"In Brendan's mind, they are the same thing." Marguerite grasped Chloe's hand. "I will always have his respect, his devotion. But you are well on the way to having his heart. He has to trust you enough to admit that, to acknowledge he wants something for himself. A Mistress breaks a submissive down to his deepest needs. As unusual as it sounds, if you can be his Mistress this one time, compel him to admit what he wants for himself, then ever after it will be far less important that you are not a natural Domme. The reason I think you have run into troubles, from his side of things, is that he is avoiding that admission and therefore falling back on serving you as a Mistress in ways that you are not comfortable accepting."

"So I have to get him to admit he wants me more than the moon, the stars and the universe combined." Chloe cleared her throat. "Piece of cake."

Marguerite adjusted her glance to the next viewing pane, and the amusement in her eyes curved her lips. "Do you remember him?"

Chloe glanced to the right and recognized Marius, her waiter. She winced, noting that he was stretched out on a cross naked while a Mistress worked on him with a paddle, leaving large rectangular blocks of reddened skin on his ass with her liberal swats. His fine set of shoulder and ass muscles were tight, his fists clenched. She noticed his cock was in some form of electronic sleeve that appeared to be rippling like... Her eyes widened as Marguerite nodded.

"It simulates the feel of a woman clenched around him. Mistress Allison has probably told him he's not allowed to come until she finishes her punishment. And if you know what to look for, you can tell Marius is loving it. He's a pure slut. He loves to play, to be bad, to be punished. But it's never casual, even if the submissive himself tries to pass it off as a playful bit of kink. He wouldn't keep coming back if it was. There is far more to Marius, something that needs a regular Mistress, rather than his constant trolling."

As they strolled onward, Chloe asked, "What does Brendan need?"

"I expect you will be the first, and perhaps the last, to fully answer that question."

The answer gave Chloe a flutter of butterflies, a mix of anxiety and anticipation. "But if I had to guess, based on what I know of him, I'd say it's the need to assure the woman in his life he is there for her in all ways. He's constantly testing himself, making himself worthy the way all knights do, feeling that they can't lay their heads in the lap of their chosen lady until they've absolutely proven their devotion."

Chloe bit down on her lip. "Brendan doesn't take anything for himself. I want him to do that, Marguerite. God, at times I was vicious to him, and he wouldn't strike back."

"No, he wouldn't. He felt like he had to rescue you from the clutches of the memories that were holding you captive. Every time you struck at him, he didn't interpret it as you striking at him, but the enemy beyond your reach. Only you can convince him the battle is won." Marguerite gave her a shrewd look. "Or convince him that's not the battle you need him to fight, that what you need from him is far different.

"It is as essential for him to understand that, as it is for you to accept you deserve his unconditional love." Marguerite's expression turned upon her, hawk fierce now. "None of us are perfect, none of us do everything we should in this world. But that doesn't mean we aren't worthy of love, and accepting every bit of it offered to us."

Chloe nodded. "I'm learning to believe that, M. I promise."

Marguerite gave her another tight smile. "Then I have no doubt you will get Brendan to admit he wants you more than the moon, the stars, and the universe combined. Do you want him, Chloe?"

"Yes," she said softly. "But I want him to be happy more."

"That's what he wants for you. When two people want each other to be happy so much they're willing to break their own heart to let the other go, it's kismet. Two idiots canceling one another out."

It startled a chuckle from her. "Great vote of confidence there, M."

"You are two idiots I love." She cocked an ironic brow at Chloe. "'Nothing is so strong as gentleness, nothing so gentle as real strength', right? There are women who don't understand that, but I think you do."

When Chloe nodded, Marguerite gave her a satisfied look. "Brendan would fight dragons for you, but he doesn't think fighting for you to be his exclusively is noble, unless he's convinced that's what you want for yourself. If you are," M's eyes sparkled, "then prove it to him. Use your intuition. If you are successful, you'll have a very difficult time *ever* getting rid of him."

She took Chloe by the shoulders, turned her to see that they'd reached their destination, the holographic room. Marguerite's voice was a murmur in her ear. "You may not be a Mistress, Chloe, but you are a very strong-willed young woman who knows what you want. Go take it."

* * * * *

When Marguerite had described the capabilities of the holographic room, Chloe had been entranced. Enough to contemplate joining The Zone solely to have access to that room. Then she'd heard about the membership fee and changed her mind. Instead, she'd coax Tyler to sneak her in to play during daylight hours in exchange for her cookies and cakes. Marguerite claimed those were the only thing that could make him beg.

Yeah, right.

She'd asked for the Gothic vampire program, and so she stepped into what looked like a London street a couple

314

hundred years ago, the pavers wet with a recent rain, the dim glow of street lamps thrown against an alley wall. A secluded place, no disturbance possible at this late hour. One lantern had been removed, the hook now holding something entirely different.

Her heart was in her throat, seeing him for the first time in weeks. She'd gotten flushed several times on the way here, just thinking about being close to him, but right now her libido jumped and jittered as if a cattle prod had been jammed up its conceptual ass. He was in black trousers and boots, a manservant caught unawares when out on an errand. The white shirt with ruffles had been torn open down the front and raked off his shoulders. It was still partially tucked in so it hadn't fallen to the floor. The work of a very creative staff member, she was sure.

The pants were probably a bit tighter than they wore them in the day, but she wasn't complaining, looking at the visible evidence of his arousal. Chloe leaned back against the door, folding her hands beneath her backside to contain them. While she steadied her breath, she recalled another vital piece of advice Marguerite had given her. It had been a few days before this night, when her questions had been coming thick and fast. As opposed to now, where everything inside her was starting to get very still and…right.

* * * * *

"It's not first and foremost about the power, Chloe." Marguerite took a tray of her cookies out of the oven as Chloe stirred the dough for another batch. They were expecting an afternoon tea party for twenty women celebrating a birthday, and Gen was frosting tea cakes as they worked on the cookies. Her tall boss glanced at her, and then, with a bemused smile, wiped a smudge of flour off Chloe's nose. "That's part of it, but the way that vanilla or butter is part of your recipes. The cake is his gift of trust to you. During a session, he offers you everything he is in return for one-hundred percent of who you are in that moment. It's a place where you lay both your souls bare without saying a word, and you make time stop."

"What if I don't know how?"

"There are many things about BDSM that require practice and training, but this isn't one of them, specifically because that's not your goal." Marguerite gestured with a spatula. "You have a gift of knowing purely with your heart. You can give love as easily as God gives breath, laughter as easily as the flowers bloom after rain."

The woman paused, met Chloe's gaze. "My father didn't take that from you. You locked it away as the precious gift it was, afraid you'd lose it, that it would shatter if you didn't hide it away. But with Brendan, you can take it out again, offer it. This is the type of man who, when you think you've been wounded beyond repair, will make sure you have all the time, room and love you need to heal."

"The mother of all handymen," Gen teased, though her voice was gentle as she swiped a finger through Chloe's batter.

"That violated several health code requirements," Marguerite reproved, then did the same, licking the batter off her index finger thoughtfully. "He's sanctuary. The port in the storm, not to hide, but to go out in the storm, stretch your hands up to the raindrops, feel the wind and not be afraid. He's the ship you can trust."

Gen slipped out to go get more flour. While Chloe didn't feel the need to hide anything from her, she was glad for the moment to get a little more one-on-one. "But what we're talking about doing, at The Zone. He'll be bound. As if he needs to be released, as if *I'm* the one to rescue him."

"No." Marguerite took up the spatula again, began to free cookies from the tray. "He's bound because he is at his strongest, gives you the most of himself, when he surrenders to you. While Brendan is the type of submissive who can do that without the chains, this takes you both back to the symbolic, reminds you both of what he can be to you. And you to him."

* * * * *

Chloe stood in the shadows. He was blindfolded with the cravat that would have gone with the outfit, but they'd left his sensual mouth free to speak, and now he did.

"Is someone there?" he asked quietly, knowing there was, because she'd opened the door. She wouldn't be surprised if he knew it was her, but he would let her lead this, let her set the parameters, not try to set it on the course he wanted. Topping from the bottom. Something a submissive like Brendan would never do, not once he was in scene.

She'd wondered if she would dare step into that circle of light with him, but now she did, her boot heel making a scrape on the floor which was a temporary stone overlay mat, a cobblestone to match the holographic background. The only actual physical things were a few crates, the wall and lamp post, but it all looked so real. There was a fog drifting through the air, the wet smell of the earlier rain. That, and her outfit, helped her become completely what she wanted to be in this moment.

She came out of the shadows and fog, enjoying the scrape of her heels on the stone, the way he cocked his head listening, how his hands tightened around the chains holding his hands above his head. When she reached him, the first thing she did was palm his cock, that hard, impressive curve beneath the stretched fabric. He sucked a breath through his teeth.

"Did you keep your promise, Brendan?" she asked softly. "You sent me all those chocolates. Was that to tell me you saved all of this for me?"

"Every drop. I haven't touched myself since you last did it. Please, let me see you. I need to see you."

Instead she rose on her toes, put her lips to his throat, curved them back and let him feel the prick of fangs. He stiffened at the pressure, and she put her hand on his side, curving inward with the long sharp nails she'd also donned. For good measure, she rubbed her mound over his taut thigh and almost groaned herself at the pleasure of it. "It's dangerous to be out on the streets this late at night. No telling what trouble a groomsman will find."

A long pause, then he cleared his throat. "Yes, my lady."

She smiled, delighted that he'd injected a bit of what sounded like Cockney dialect into his voice. "Didn't you know there are creatures of the night that seek blood? A man's seed. They'll drain him dry of both."

"And which will you be seeking, my lady?"

"I want it all," she whispered, and lifted up onto her toes, clinging to his shoulders to take his mouth.

For the first second, she was just hanging on, because at that contact, he became a ravenous animal, telling her how much he had in fact missed her. He clamped down over her lips, his body straining toward her, his tongue sweeping in to tangle with hers. Exploring the enamel of her pricey but very authentic-looking fangs, he tasted her mouth, tasted her as she tasted him.

As the kiss dragged on blissfully, she pressed herself against him, let him feel the rest of her ensemble. It was a black sleek corset over a skirt made of strips of black silk that looked like they could have been spun from a spider's web. The strips went all the way up to the waist and parted to show her bare skin, nothing beneath it. The corset was strapless, so her breasts rose high, cradling the ruby and pewter pendant between them. The pewter looked like fangs, the rubies like drops of blood dangling from them.

Reaching up, she tugged the cravat free of his eyes. She didn't drop it, though, preferring to tie it around his bare throat, so he felt the restriction as she knotted it. Hooking her fingers in it, she suckled his bottom lip and then eased back enough he could sweep his gaze over her, taking in her black-lined eyes, the red crimson of her lips, the way Gen had done her hair so it was a froth of exotic curls around her face.

"Holy God," he said fervently, deep pleasure in his eyes, but deep need as well.

"Not exactly the way to entreat a soulless creature of the night," she observed, a touch of a smile on her lips. "What do you want, Brendan?" She backed up a step. "This pussy? These breasts?"

"Yes," he said low, gaze burning as her hands ran over them, caressing, stimulating.

"How about this heart, this soul?" She asked that quietly, and watched his expression change, as she knew it would.

"I want to give my lady pleasure. I want to give you pleasure."

She retreated another step. "Do you remember the game Red Light, Green Light, Brendan?"

He studied her, his hazel eyes so vivid and intelligent. A hundred thoughts were tangling with the lust he was obviously feeling, such that the heat of it emanated against her, made her want to get closer, not further away. But she knew what she wanted, and she was going to have it.

"I remember it."

"Good. Here's your question. What do you want? With each wrong answer, I back a step toward the door. If I reach it, step through it, we weren't meant to be."

"Chloe."

"No." She shook her head. "I need the right answer, Brendan. For both our sakes. What do you want, Brendan? For yourself?"

"Your happiness."

She took a step back as his brow furrowed. "But I do want your happiness."

"For yourself, Brendan. What do you want?"

"A hi-def sound system."

That might have thrown her off balance, but something entirely different happened. All those things Marguerite had told her, warned her about, kicked in. His shields were closing against her. She didn't need to have her Mistress merit badge to know how to respond.

"Really, a joke? Defensive." She took another step back. "I'm not repeating the question. I have better things to do. Keep answering." Lifting her hands, those long nails, she trailed a fingertip down her throat, to the upper curve of her breast. He watched her, with the hunger of a vampire in truth in his gaze.

"I want to fuck you."

"Easy enough to see. Still a distraction." She took another step. Two steps more, and she'd be at the door. She'd never felt like this before. All the power was hers, as well as total resolve. The calm inside her might dissipate into a chaotic storm if she had to step outside that door, but she'd do it if she had to. For this moment, however, she felt what she suspected Marguerite might feel toward a bound male, at her mercy, forcing him to confront something in himself he didn't want to confront.

Yes, she felt the power of it, the sense of control. But this was someone she cared about, she wanted. He'd helped her, and she could help him now, for both of them. Such a different feeling from the carnival.

She'd always been so closely in touch with what she wanted, a child of impulse and laughter, love and happiness. Marguerite had been right. It wasn't gone. It would take time to coax that Chloe back into existence, but in some ways, this was the shadow side of that person, who knew that embracing what she truly wanted was what mattered.

Life was too short to give any less of herself, or demand any less, from the male she was almost sure she'd be willing to spend the rest of her life with, if he'd just say what she knew he wanted to say. The shadow and light would come together at last, and she'd be an even better person than she'd ever been before.

"You know, when I saw you the night of the auction, I compared you to a young Druid priest, someone so dedicated to his art and craft, a treasure. But something's lacking, Brendan. There's a difference between those you serve and the one you love above and beyond it all." She spoke the last words softly. "So last time. What do you want for yourself?"

The look on his face was a true struggle. He was fighting something far down inside himself, so painful she could almost see internal organs begin to bleed from the strain. He'd seemed so strong, so balanced, and yet she'd known, felt the shadow. So had Marguerite. Intuition.

"Chloe, I can't... I'm not like that."

"Not built that way." She nodded, though it was an effort. She put her hand on the latch. "I'm glad I met you, Brendan. And I'm sorry it didn't work out for us. I wish you only the best. But I want the man, not the priest."

She stepped out.

Chapter Twenty

"No." Brendan stared at the door, feeling the chains on his arms as if they were looped lower, tightening around his chest. What the fuck did she want from him? How could she ask from him what wasn't his to give?

Why couldn't he give himself that? Was he going to let her walk away?

What do you want? Whatdoyouwantwhatdoyouwant…

The raw, uncertain feeling was an old wound, but one he hadn't experienced at this level in some time. It wasn't welcome, and he immediately wanted to banish it. He gave Mistresses what they wanted, damn it, so there was no uncertainty. No surges of volatile emotions like this, but Marguerite had hit it on the head that day in the auditorium, hadn't she? The answer was in the center of that tumultuous sea, as treacherous a place as the spooky London street depicted around him. He didn't want a choice. Didn't want to take that risk.

That day in the auditorium, he'd looked toward the stage when Marguerite was bringing that shameful knowledge forth. He'd looked toward the unattainable grail.

In his mind's eye, a grail always sat on a dais, brilliantly lit among darkness. He'd told Chloe he liked the idea of being Percival. A knight seeking that grail because it served his king. In reality, he hadn't ever thought of being the one who found it, grasped it, accepted the consequences and challenges of being worthy of it.

He'd told himself that was because the focus couldn't be on recognition, winning the prize. The focus had to be on the dedication and unswerving loyalty to the quest. He'd made the journey the art form, not the completion of the task, because she was right. Marguerite was right. He was fucking terrified of what that light would show inside himself. A small boy, crouched in a corner, learning that his mother was never coming back, that fate had taken her away from him, because he wasn't worthy of her. She was the grail. Now Chloe was on that same dais.

Jesus. And he meant it as a prayer. Closing his eyes tight, he faced the inevitable, that he could accept this about himself, always be the perfect submissive, the one who every Mistress wanted for a night, or he could put spurs to his horse, so to speak, and see if he couldn't actually grasp that grail, dedicating himself to everything it required and meant.

"I want you," he whispered. Even spoken low, the words were rough, thick, as if by never having been said before, his mouth had difficulty forming the words. The desolation of the night reflected his inside, his loneliness now, knowing what was walking away from him. It lanced him with such pain, he thought a vampire's fangs actually tearing into him might feel good. "Chloe."

He pulled against the wrought iron of the lamp post that had been welded into a temporary plate in the floor. It didn't have any give. "Come let me go," he called out, an urgent demand to whatever staff was watching him. Someone had to be, because no one was ever left unattended in a room. But maybe Chloe hadn't realized that. He had to go after her. "Chloe!"

He yanked again, using his full strength. Not caring that he might destroy the prop, he put his feet against it and shoved, hoping to loosen the bolts. "Chloe, I want you. Come back!"

Just when he thought he was going to have to start bellowing, the door opened. He'd twisted around, gotten the chains wrapped over the cuffs and couldn't see, but that didn't matter. "Get me down. I have to go after her." He'd never spoken to anyone at The Zone like that. He'd always performed as a submissive in all ways, toward staff as well as Doms, but damn it, this was too important. Logically, he could always call her, text her, send her a fucking letter, but even the dumbest hero knew timing was everything. He couldn't lose the chance.

"I'm right here." His queen of the night was holding him steady, soothing him with long scarlet nails and worried brown eyes as he tried to catch his breath, feeling the cut of the chains in his wrists. It had been less than a couple minutes, he realized, but it felt much longer, the journey in his mind a jump of twenty some years.

"Oh Goddess, your fingers are turning blue." Finding the key hanging on the wall, she came back, dragging a crate over that had been used as an alley prop. She stepped up on it to unlock the cuffs on his wrists so he could slide free of the snarled chain slack. The position put her enticingly shaped cleavage right at his face. When he got free, he banded his arms around her hips and back, taking his lips to that moist crease, then biting the fullness around it. Dropping the key, she wrapped her arms around his shoulders.

"I'm right here," she gasped. "I didn't leave. I didn't even take my hand off the latch on the other side."

His knees felt weak, but he managed to get off the cobblestone and lay her down on a pallet draped in velvet in the shadows, a convenience if she'd decided to take their scene to the semblance of a vampiress's boudoir.

As he laid her down, he followed her, propping on his elbow, his body braced between her legs. When she curved a leg over him, he felt the bare brush of her pussy against the front of the tight dark trousers. He wanted to rut on her like an animal, but she had more in store for him. Closing her hand on his shoulder, she pushed at him, hard. He let himself be knocked over on his back as she straddled him with that shapely, mouthwatering hook of her thigh.

"I'm sorry, I didn't catch that last thing when I left the room." Her expression was serious, despite the slight teasing note to her voice. She was right back in scene, completely in control. Her fingers hooked in that cravat around his neck, tightening the slack in a way that made his cock pulse hard beneath the clamp of her pelvis. She moved against it, rubbing him.

"I want you. Only you." It was harder with her looking at him. "Is that okay?"

"More than you know." Testing him, she arched a brow. "And if it wasn't?"

He understood, because his hands tightened on her, slipping down to mold over her backside, letting her feel his arousal for her, the need in his body. "Well, I guess I'd just have to say the hell with what's okay or not and convince you that I'm right, that I'm the only one you need."

Her eyes warmed on his face. "More, slave."

A smile pulled at his mouth. "I want you. *You.* For myself. All for myself. Mine."

"No matter if I think you're a completely worthless drama dweeb beneath my notice?"

"Even then. I still want you. Heart, body, soul, everything from your deepest thought to your most casual gesture. I want to see all of it, be a part of all of it."

"If I try to shake you off, you'll stalk me like a predator?"

"Until you have to get a restraining order, and even that won't stop me. Even if you call on Tyler and Mac for reinforcements." It felt so damn good to say it, mean it, see how it lit her face up with everything he wanted to see in her eyes. He'd been such an idiot for withholding it from her, and found himself ashamed that he'd put her through the stress of wresting it out of him.

She took a deep breath, let it out with a shudder. Gave him a beatific smile at odds with the dark vampire-of-the-night fangs and expression. "Good. Now why the heck was that so hard?"

He chuckled, he couldn't help it. Though she was sitting quite solidly on him, he felt as if a weight lifted right off his chest. "I don't know. Chloe, I've been dying for you, three weeks now."

"I'm yours," she reminded him with a smile full of seductive promise and open- hearted need. "Take what you need."

But it was Chloe who took, reaching between them before he could do it and opening the trousers, taking him firmly in hand. Her noise of pleasure almost put him over the edge. When he reached up toward her, she shook her head, that feline smile still on her face as he obediently dropped his arms back over his head, though his fingers clenched with the desire to touch, grip. She was indulging that desire fully, working him in her grasp, even as she began to rub her mound along the base of his cock and testicles, letting him feel how wet she was.

"Chloe," he said, urgent need filling his voice. "Damn it. Please."

He didn't ever make demands, but he did now, letting her feel that every part of him was rigid with desire for her, not just what she was working in his hand.

"I don't want you to ever forget to give me what I want, when I want it," she said, those dark-rimmed eyes fixed on his face.

"Never." His gaze coursed greedily over her breasts, the flirty roll of those rubies back and forth over the high curves. "Let me suck on your nipples."

"Unlace the front."

Easier said than done, with hands that were almost shaking with the power of his need. "Rip it," she suggested, and almost before the words were out of her mouth, he'd put his hands on it and yanked. It didn't rip, but it loosened enough that her breasts spilled free and his hands closed over them, at the same moment she shoved him back down again.

She slid up his body with her eyes fixed on him in hot demand.

"First, you eat my pussy. I want to come on your face. You won't come until I say it's okay. I want to feel that hard cock inside me."

Was it the clothes? He didn't care what made her act like this wanton vamp now, as long as it was genuine, and he could tell it was, a role she was delighted to play. Something in her face told him she was on the right path again. Not necessarily the girl she'd been before her attack, but some new compilation of her own sculpting.

As for him, he didn't care if one night she was Chloe, the vampire of his dreams, or tender, giggling Chloe, retying the bow on Prince's plush neck. Or pensive Chloe, gluing pictures in her happiness book. Mischievous Chloe, winking as she slipped him and Tyler pieces of free cake at Tea Leaves when she thought the eagle-eyed Marguerite didn't see. He wanted to discover every face. He wanted to make her happy and enjoy every damn day of knowing she was his.

He told her that, in rough, broken language as she covered his face, straddling him but staying just out of reach of his mouth as he spoke, his breath caressing her labia, already moist with her honey.

"Good," she whispered, and came down on him, letting him bury his mouth and nose into that bliss. His hands came up, cupped her bare bottom through the strips of the barely there skirt. The slick surface of her boots pressed against his sides, the hard heels turned in toward his rib cage, digging in as if he were her personal mount.

He was good at oral sex, and he used all his skill now, sucking on her clit, taking slow, dragging licks of the outer labia and then penetrating her like his cock, swirling inside and closing his mouth over the whole vulva to put light pressure on it as his tongue came out, darted here and there, went back in, making her work herself against his face. Her breath came faster, a dew of perspiration and the moisture of the fog on her flesh. He made noises of his hunger against her, and she tortured him further. Leaning back, she wrapped her small hand around his cock, tugging hard on it as she rocked against his mouth.

Ah, God... He couldn't come. He wouldn't, as much as he wanted her, because she'd told him not to, because... oh hell.

He had so much control, but he'd missed her too much, and having her cunt in his face, her bottom rubbing against his chest, her knowledgeable fingers on his cock, was just too much for any man. He prided himself on obeying a Mistress's most outrageous demand, but all he managed was a strangled protest against her. She didn't take the hint, didn't let up. In fact, she deliberately tightened her grip and rolled it up the length of his shaft, flicking the vein beneath with her thumb, letting him feel the bite of the long nail in his tightening testicles.

She flipped in a quick, lithe movement he hadn't expected, straddling his head from the other direction, and put her mouth over him just as he released. She took him into the back of her throat as her ass moved rhythmically in front of his face, her pussy brushing his chin so he angled his head and made damn sure the vibrations of his guttural roars were felt all the way up through her womb as his hips bucked up, driving his cock into her mouth.

It was the pleasure of nearly a month of self-denial, all for her, everything he wanted. It made him wonder why it really had been so hard for him to say, but he knew. And he owed it to her to explain why.

However, first things first. As the orgasm slowly died away, even in the grip of the agonizing aftershocks, he applied himself to her cunt again, nibbling, thrusting, and giving her the occasional tease on her anal rim with his nose, the press of his lips.

She enjoyed the hell out of it, gasping and moving on him, but just as he sensed her about to approach that peak, she turned, taking it away from him. She sat back down on his loins like a queen on her throne, chin up and skin flushed, breath coming fast, nipples taunting him over the loosened corset.

"If you want me to come, you'll have to get hard for me again," she said in a throaty voice. "But first you'll have to be punished, won't you? Because you broke your promise to me. The promise you made in the park."

"Yes." Whatever she wanted to do was fine with him. Hell, she could shove a poker up his ass and he would take it from her.

"Then get up and face that wall over there."

* * * * *

Chloe could tell there were things he wanted to say to her. Marguerite had said things would boil up once the wound was lanced, but she wanted to make it even easier for him, break him open so it would all come out at once. When he rose, his height shadowed her such that she trembled with the desire to move into that shelter, hold him to her. She could do that if she wanted to. She could be and do anything here with him, because he wanted her. Everything she was.

In some ways, he'd been telling her the truth all along, though it hadn't hit the target dead on, as she'd sensed. He did want to please her, make her happy, do as she desired, because that was what you did when you wanted, needed and loved someone with all your heart. It amazed her that it had been so difficult for both of them to say and acknowledge such a gift, embrace it with everything they were from the very first moment. However, the one thing she'd always known about humans — they weren't always very sensible.

Or predictable. Because, though she wanted the comfort of his embrace, she wanted something more right now. She wanted to test something in herself, see if she could navigate that roller coaster of angry, lustful emotions she'd felt at the carnival.

He moved past her, his eyes on her face, but had to break the contact to go to the wall. She enjoyed the view, the graceful power of his male body. She'd had him refasten the snug trousers and dwelled on the way his ass shifted, the flex of muscle in his back and broad shoulders. All hers, every fine inch of him. When he reached the wall, she spoke again.

"Put your hands on the wall, just above your head, out to either side."

He did, and she glanced to the corner. In another cluster of artfully placed shadows, a variety of tools appropriate to the environment had been hung on a brick façade. She moved to it, conscious that his head had turned, tracking her movements, and probably indulging in an eyeful of her walk in those heeled boots, the sway of her hips. She could feel the dampness of her thighs from his mouth and the arousal that had trickled down, tickled by the strips of the skirt. Her shoulders were bare and pale in the dim light. Her curls were pinned up, exposing her neck and the silk cord of the pendant.

Conscious of his regard, she knew he would be anticipating her turn back toward him in the corset, pulled open to show her breasts fully, but still supported so they thrust out provocatively. She could torment him by making him close his eyes, but she wanted to feel the heat of that gaze on her. Revel in the clean, healthy desire of it.

She passed her fingers over a riding crop, a flail and what appeared to be an electric cattle prod. A coiled whip, paddles, switches. She'd read enough to know which ones to leave alone, knowing they required skills she didn't have to use safely. Perhaps leaving them here anyway had been a test of Marguerite's, or proof to boost her self confidence, showing how much she'd progressed in just these three weeks from her unreasoning anger.

She paused over an item she didn't know. A teardrop-shaped hoop, slightly larger than her hand, attached to a handle. The hoop appeared to be made of some kind of semifirm rubber. She picked it up, liking the weight and that it wasn't much longer than her arm from elbow to fingertip.

She came back to him. The minute she turned, he'd returned his attention to the wall as if he hadn't been staring at her, though she could tell he was watching her out of the corner of his eye. Suppressing a smile, she came up behind him and used the top edge of the thing to trace the line of his spine, from nape to the waistband of his trousers.

"What is this?"

He cleared his throat. "It's a branding hoop. It leaves temporary marks."

"Mmm." Reaching forward with her free hand, she tugged the shirt that was mostly off anyway out of the pants, dropped it to the side. "Undo the top buttons of the trousers again. I want them low enough that I can see all of your back."

So she could see that brand, now that she knew who'd done it, why it was there. She needed to see it, see how it made her feel.

He'd hesitated at that, but then he lowered his left arm, moved the hand in front of him and obeyed. The fabric tightened over his buttocks briefly, even more than it was already, then he tugged and the trousers dropped several inches, sliding away from the *fleur de lis*, and coming to rest just past the rise of his ass.

When she traced the brand with her fingertips, he trembled. "How does this make you feel?" she murmured.

"Good." He rested his forehead against the wall, both sets of fingers back above him, curling inward in response to the sensation. "It feels…like you're taking ownership of it."

Almost exactly an echo of what she'd felt the first day she'd seen it, not knowing then even what it was.

"I am," she said. His fingers tightened further, his body rippling with a wave of emotion she could feel. It was overpowering to know they were both feeling something so strongly, even barely touching. He awaited her pleasure, and she could take as long as she wanted to absorb the emotion, savor it. She didn't need to give him anything else until she was ready.

"All right," she said at last. "You should have told me about the brand from the beginning, shouldn't you have?"

"Yes."

"Yes," she echoed, affirming it. "You should have told me that you wanted me."

"Yes."

"You shouldn't have come, because you promised me you wouldn't, not until I said those two words."

"No." As he pressed his forehead to the wall, she saw the fierce desire gripping his expression, making her even more needy for him.

She took a step back, gauging where she'd need to be. "Does this hurt a lot?"

"It can, depending on how much strength you use."

Level Ten pain threshold. She remembered that from his program entry, the night of the auction. But still... "Is there any way I can hurt you incorrectly with it?"

"It's a good idea, with any tool, to stay above the kidneys." Reaching back, he showed her where with a fingertip pressed above that area on his back. Then he returned his palm to the wall. "Best also to stop before you draw blood, though this will only do that if you keep hitting the welts it creates, over and over. The Zone doesn't allow bloodletting without special permission."

"All right, then. Three strikes. Unless I like it and decide to do more."

He pressed his forehead to the wall again, nodding, and she saw that delicious tremor run through his body. She didn't have to understand why he craved it to be aroused by his response, and that too, was a new and exciting revelation. He'd told her that by giving her pleasure, it would give him pleasure. She hadn't considered how much the reverse could hold true.

Moving away from him, she did a couple practice swings against the lamp, watching how much the rubber gave. The lamp vibrated with the impact when she put a little more strength against it. Nodding to herself, she came back to him.

"I'm not sure the lamp post did anything to deserve that, the way I have."

She suppressed a smile, and trailed the hoop down his back again, teasing it over the brand. "Keep it up, and I'll make it much worse."

"Keeping it up isn't a problem. Not watching you walk with your breasts out like that, and glimpses of your pussy through the strips of the skirt. I want to put my mouth on the boots, bite through it to your ankle. Work my way up to the top, and slide my tongue around the edge, behind your knees. Kiss your beautiful, perfect ass. God, please do it, Chloe. You're making me crazy."

The plea and demand made her put aside rational thought and go for intuition. She swung. The rubber hit with a sharp slap noise in the middle of his back. She'd put some strength behind it, and a curved crescent appeared on his flesh, pain and pleasure both shuddering through him. She did it again, harder, just below it, earning a muffled grunt, his shoulders bunching. Once more made a triangular trinity of intersected crescent marks, radiating heat and pain. She did it twice more, high and low, then once more, in the center, over the original three. The power of his stillness, of his submitting to her torment, of his hunger to serve her, washed over her like a drug. Goddess, she'd had a taste of this the night of the carnival, but this was so, so different.

Because this was about their pleasure, not just her dark cravings. She was soaking wet, and it was as much from his response as her own. He stayed against the wall, his hands flat, but the sense of restrained power there was pure lust, waiting to be unleashed at her command.

Even so, as she watched the welts rise on his skin, she felt sympathetic pangs in her own flesh. Setting the hoop aside, she moved in, and placed her palms over them. Heat, as she'd sensed, and he drew in a breath at the abrasion of that mere light touch. Reaching around to slide her fingertips down his abdomen, she arrowed into the open trousers to find his cock hardening again. It jumped spasmodically against her touch.

Leaning in, she pressed her lips to the first welt. Then the second. Kissed every one of them, again and again, as his trembling increased beneath the kneading, slow rhythm of her touch on his cock, her caresses to his back with her moist lips.

"I'm sorry, Brendan."

"For what?" he rasped.

"For not liking to hurt you."

"I'm going to turn around now. I want to hold you. Is that okay?"

"It's way more than okay."

He turned then, a blink of time, and had his arms around her, holding her close. They leaned against the wall, her palms folded over his back, keeping the rough texture of the wall from scraping those welts. "Please say those two words," he murmured against her hair. "I'm going to go crazy if you don't."

She closed her eyes, drew a breath and tipped her head back, because she wanted those forest-like eyes so close, his mouth so touchable she had to trace it with her fingertips.

"You're mine, Brendan," she said. "Fully, in every way. Whatever you need or want, it's here. We'll figure it out. I believe that, down to my Passionate Pink painted toenails."

His smile blinded her, or maybe it was the easy tears that spilled from her eyes at his reaction, so heartfelt and giving. He kissed every one. When she put her fingers on his mouth, they passed the next few moments in a silent game of him nipping and nuzzling at her fingers, catching and holding one then letting it go, until they were both smiling.

"You're gentle, Chloe," he said at last. "I love that about you. I love everything about you." Taking a breath, telling her that he was working at what she'd started, he spoke. "I've been with Mistresses who shared me, and I had no claim or demand on who they had in their life, but that was part of who we were to one another. If I thought you were the type of person...maybe I could give you that, but I don't think you are. I know you aren't," he added hastily, at the warning glint in her eye.

With the raw emotion she heard enter his voice, he captured her heart even more. "I've never wanted something as much as I want you, Chloe. I've never had someone I wasn't prepared to let go. Someone I wanted to keep, more than anything else. I was fine with that, until I met you that night at the wedding. I wanted to call you a hundred times, but I didn't, because I told myself it had to be about what you wanted, not what I wanted."

"Idiot," she decided. "We could have been fucking like minks months ago."

He choked on a laugh. "I'm sorry for that, but also because, by doing that, I made you go through it alone all those months. I could have helped."

She shook her head. "I think things happen at certain times, for certain reasons. You know what I mean?"

"Yeah, but it doesn't make me wish any less that I could have been there for you."

"Except for a couple times at the carnival, and even then it felt...sort of wrong, you haven't called me Mistress."

"Nor have you demanded it." He cocked his head, seeming to consider what he was going to say next, how she would take it. She tightened her grip on him, drawing his attention.

"Tell me anything, Brendan. Don't hold back."

He nodded. "Marguerite...she's my Mistress. Clear cut. What you and I are is less definable to me. Meeting you...it opened a room I'd kept closed, for a very long time. In fact, I'm not sure I've ever opened it. What I want isn't exactly different, but the form is. You're who and what I want, in all ways. If I'm being fair, I'd have to say you're both to thank for that."

Moving her hands down to the brand, she touched it, watched his eyes darken, felt the combined weight of two women's hold on him, and didn't feel threatened by it anymore. "I agree," she said softly.

He tilted her chin up, and now his mouth was so close it made her dizzy. "The night I called you Beloved, that seemed to come closest to it, you know?"

She nodded, too full of happiness to speak. Just as he'd opened himself up to her to embrace the possible treasure of love between them, this past month she'd been doing the same, rediscovering the treasure of herself, something she would never take for granted again. Brendan was the best possible reward for it.

She cupped her hand around his neck, guided him in backward steps toward that pallet again, and when she leaned back against his arms, he understood, taking them down until he was laying full on top of her, and the tears and joy and desire were all there. She pushed at the skirt, and he helped, closing his hands gently on hers to take them out of his way, telling her he would take care of her.

His cock slid in, long and deep, coming to rest in a well of her soul that embraced him with every emotion spinning there. She closed her legs over his back, her heels on his buttocks, feeling the loosened trousers beneath them.

"I want to do this again later tonight," she whispered. "At home, with no clothes on either of us, just bare skin to bare skin. I want to fall asleep with you inside me, Brendan."

He held her gaze, setting fire to her body with slow movements. Her clit tightened against the rub of his body, telling her that she would be climaxing in his arms in a matter of minutes. "We can do that. I'd like that." His voice fell to that sexy murmur that made her even hotter. "Taking care of the woman I love, who belongs to me as much as I belong to her, is what matters most to me."

"Good to know," she managed. "And as much as I like having my own personal groomsman in a London alleyway to ravish, after this...I want to go home." She bit down on a groan, a near whimper, and exulted in the fire that flared in his gaze. His cock was as hard as if he hadn't just come, and she knew she'd bring him to climax inside her again. She wouldn't go over alone. "You asked me to move in with you, Brendan. I don't want that."

Before he could wonder, she added, on a gasp, "What I want is for you to move in with me. I want you to move...your bed there..." Oh Goddess. "I want to always remember the first night. When you laid on that ocean-like spread of yours and put your hands on yourself, bringing yourself to climax for me."

"Bring yourself to climax for me now." His voice was rough, urgent, and his hips started moving faster, his hands gripping her body. "Let me come inside you."

"Now," she agreed, her breath catching in her throat. "Let me feel you."

It was fire, sweeping from that joining point, melting their bodies together, making them twist and arch, struggle and move in a dance of inches, that took them far out into a part of the universe carved just for them. He swallowed her scream in his mouth, kissed her with all the need and ownership that she gave right back to him, telling him that whatever else happened here, whatever journey they traveled, she knew she wanted this to be forever. She believed in forever. Thanks to Brendan.

When their carousel at last eased to a stop, their bodies trembling, slick, his arms were banded tight around her. As her fingers curled into his chest, he pressed his forehead to hers.

"I'll move in with you. I'll bring my bed. I'll do and be whatever you want, Chloe. Always."

She pressed her hands to his temples, letting more tears come, ease them both. "Anything that makes us both happy," she said. "That's all I could ever want."

* * * * *

They did resolve to go to his home that night, since the hour was late. They slept on his bed there, with plans to move it the next day. He made love to her as she'd requested, his body stretched out on hers, breast to chest, hip to hip, legs and feet tangling. As his body moved inside her, slow and easy, as if they were on the ocean in truth, they came to a crest together. His hands framed her face as they both reached the pinnacle, and then they held each other close, content to say nothing, be nothing in the darkness but everything to one another. It was then she remembered something else Marguerite had told her.

"What if I have days I want him to just hold me, make love to me without permission and the D/s thing?"

Marguerite had run a reassuring touch down her arm. *"Chloe, we all have our needs, but there are no rules when it comes to love. I have no doubt that whatever you each need, you'll be that for each other. Because whatever God or Goddess is, love is Their greatest gift. Nothing gives Them more joy than to see it embraced, with every ounce of our souls."*

Holding him close, Chloe didn't doubt it in the slightest. No darkness could take it away from them.

Epilogue

&

Chloe considered the swimming pool, her gaze wandering from the largest part, where there were lap lanes marked off for team swimmers and people using their Y membership to do their daily exercise regimen, over to the square shaped "deep end", featuring two diving boards. One was about three feet above the pool. The other appeared much, much higher.

She'd just discarded her cover-up. It was a warmish late fall day, but it wasn't warm enough to completely convince her of the wisdom of jumping into an outdoor pool. A very warm male hand touched her bare back then, sliding around her waist to her hip and curving with relaxed intimacy there. His fingertips teased the side bow of the skimpy gold bikini, giving a discreet little tug.

"Hey." She shot a narrow look up at him. "Don't even think about it."

Brendan gave her an easy smile. "Just making sure it was secure before you jumped in."

"Yeah, right. You're always thinking of me." She gave him a once over, though, arching a brow. He wore pasted-like-skin shorts that he said cut down on his draft, helped him move faster through the water. She had no objection, since it outlined his ass in a way that reminded her vividly of how she'd dug her fingers into the hard muscle of it only a few hours before. They'd lain in their bed and he'd been sunk inside her to the hilt, thrusting hard enough to rock the headboard against her wall, until she came to a screaming, over-the-top climax.

But it never seemed to be enough. She was looking forward to taking full advantage of her first swimming lesson to curl her arms and legs around him, rub herself against the nest of cock and testicles held so snugly under the suit. She'd get him hard enough he'd be embarrassed to step out of the pool.

His finger dipped to her throat, followed her neck to the joining point of her collar bone, down to the ample cleavage formed by the hug of the bikini top. He lingered there, a light caress of the upper curve. "You know, when you were looking at me, your nipples got tighter," he murmured. "You were thinking about what we were doing a little while ago, weren't you?"

"You know I was." She indulged her desire to lean into him, thread her fingers through his loose hair, though he had a swimmer's cap in hand he apparently intended to put on if he did laps. She preferred the idea of his hair wet and slicked back against his skull, the ends brushing his shoulders, and thought about making him leave it off. His hands had settled on her hips, thumbs over hip bones, long, clever fingers tracing the elastic band of her swimsuit bottoms in the back, making those sensitive nerves ripple in response. She took a breath before she lost her focus and just jumped him.

"I'm going to go off the high dive."

He blinked. "We haven't even gotten into the water yet."

"I know that."

"I was going to teach you to swim."

She nodded, moved away from him, headed for the board. "That's the plan."

"Chloe, you're going to jump off the board into twelve feet of water. You're shorter than that. Much."

"I know. I was reading this article last night that said people tend to drown themselves and others when they panic. If they believe they're completely safe, they're far more likely to survive. Probably because they're working with their rescuer, instead of trying to drown him."

"I'm not going to ask why you were reading articles about drowning the night before your first swimming lesson."

"Best not." She'd reached the ladder, but when she put her hand on it, his clamped over hers, holding her to the concrete decking. Looking up into his face, her heart wrenched at the concern and amused frustration in his features. She needed to work on his sense of humor, but other than that, she thought he was as close to perfect as any girl could want. Any woman. Any wife.

Wow. She'd never had that thought before. She wondered what he would think about it, but from his frown, she realized it might be too much of a segue. His brain might explode, and she liked it inside his head.

"I don't think this is a good idea," he said.

"There's no danger, as long as someone's around to help me get to the side, right? So, unless you're going to disappear in the next two minutes, I assume I'll have your help."

"What about that pecan pancake breakfast someone made me? I might get a debilitating cramp and be helpless to assist."

"My cooking never gives anyone cramps," she said loftily. Latching onto his neck, she gave a little hop, wrapping her legs around his waist as he caught her in reflex, bracing her between him and the ladder. His hands felt good on her bare flesh, and his breath had the sweet, lingering scent of her pancakes, as well as something else. She leaned in, teasing his mouth with hers, her tongue dipping in to slide along his. "You taste like me and pecan pancakes," she whispered.

"I know. It makes me want to eat you both all over again." His hands tightened. "Chloe, I won't let you get hurt."

"I know that. That's why I'm going to try a back somersault with a half twist." At his expression, she burst out laughing. "I'm kidding. I'm just going to jump off, feet first. I'll be fine. You'll be there. Right?"

He cupped her skull in both hands, gave her a look of tender exasperation. "You know that men with black hair have a tendency to prematurely gray, particularly when they're under stress?

"I think you'd look really sexy with silver in your hair. In fact, we could try it out, dye one lock. You'd look like one of those superheroes. Like Ioan Griffud in the *Fantastic Four*." Giving him a cheeky grin, she twisted her upper body to take hold of the ladder rung just above her. Agile as a monkey, she loosened the hold of her legs to put her feet on a rung below it. His hands guided her, but held on one extra second.

"Remember to jump out as far as you can," he said. "You want to clear the board. And nothing fancy. Just a straight out, feet-first jump. Don't bounce on the board first."

"Got it, sir." Knowing how he reacted to the undercurrents in such an address, she was amused to see it startle him. "Who knows? Maybe I'll hit the water so fast this tiny bikini will be ripped right off."

"You think I'd set aside your wellbeing in favor of seeing a little extra skin?"

"Well, you're male. It's biological. I wouldn't hold it against you."

She started up, but was brought up short by a healthy, stinging slap on her left ass cheek that made nerve endings ricochet response right through her pussy and arrow up through her belly. She snapped her head around. "*Hey*, I didn't think you knew how to do that kind of thing."

"I know how to do it pretty well," he remarked, leaning on the ladder and giving her a heated once up and down. "When the moment calls for it. When you call for it."

"I think I might be insulted, or really turned-on. I'll let you know." Now she hesitated, her bravery faltering over one key point. "This pool *is* heated, right?"

"Eighty-three degrees." He slid his knuckles along her calf. "Chloe. I love you."

She drew in a breath, her fingers fluttering out to touch his face. He caught her wrist, turned his mouth into her palm. "Brendan."

Before she could say anything else in response, he put her hand back on the ladder's side, closed it there firmly. "Two hands at all times," he said. "And be careful, the rungs can be slippery. I'll be here to catch you."

"I know you will." He stayed beneath her as she ascended. When she made it to the top, he moved to the side, where he could see her. He glanced up at her with a half smile, arms crossed over his bare chest. He was beautiful, there was no denying that, but she realized he'd stolen her heart because of what was inside him. He could look like the most average man alive, even unattractive, and that heart would have called to her. She was sure of it.

"I love you too," she murmured. "Enough to marry and keep you forever. Goddess, I don't believe it."

When she perused her surroundings, she discovered that, as high as it looked off to the side, it was higher when one was actually on it. Maybe she was a bit crazy.

But when she walked to the end, she saw him still there. Standing on the edge, ready to dive in, come down to the bottom and help guide her up. To fortify herself for the jump, she imagined herself as a brave heroine who was throwing herself off the side of a pirate ship to save herself from being debauched. She didn't have to worry, because from the depths of the sea, strong arms would come around her, and a pair of hazel eyes, the green like trace colors of an ocean indeed, would meet hers. A merman, there to take her to safety, to give her breath from his body so she could see all the magic of his world, and never fear being alone and afraid again. Never doubt that magic would always exist in the world, particularly if one knew how to open the window, let the light in, and have the courage to look for it.

Looking down at her toes gripping the end of the board, any trepidation she had about heights vanished. Taking a breath, she jumped outward.

She had a brief impression of his face, that flash of a smile as he dove, already marking where she would land. As she plummeted, bubbles streamed above her and she saw him coming toward her, smooth kicks and twists of his body like a merman in truth.

She wasn't afraid. Not the slightest, even knowing she didn't know how to swim. She put her arms out to her sides, experiencing the buoyancy of her body, and knew it was natural, being in the water like this. Something she didn't have to fear. This feeling was a glimmer of herself, the self she'd been before, only stronger now. She'd been getting those glimmers a lot more now, as if diamonds were starting to sparkle through the cracks that bad experiences had formed, creating a new kind of beauty in her outlook.

She knew who she could trust, who her friends and family were. Most importantly, she trusted herself again. Trusted herself to love Brendan, to learn how to love him in the way they both most wanted. As he came up beside her and she looped her arms around his neck, she pressed her mouth to his underwater, something she'd always wanted to do. She laughed into his mouth at the way his arms curled around her, how she could tangle her legs over the backs of his thighs, and float and spin, and listen to that silence underwater that was somehow so...full.

As he took her toward the surface, their bodies still intertwined, she realized it was so simple. While the way they felt, what they needed, might be complex and unique, love was the common denominator between them. Whatever he needed, that was what she wanted to be for him. She wanted to take care of him as much as he wanted to care for her.

She looked forward to the adventure. The joyous pleasure of it, of a life together. Of life itself.

Also by Joey W. Hill

&

eBooks:

Board Resolution
Branded Sanctuary
Chance of a Lifetime
If Wishes Were Horses
Make Her Dreams Come True
Nature of Desire 1: Holding the Cards
Nature of Desire 2: Natural Law
Nature of Desire 3: Ice Queen
Nature of Desire 4: Mirror of My Soul
Nature of Desire 5: Mistress of Redemption
Nature of Desire 6: Rough Canvas
Snow Angel
Threads of Faith
Virtual Reality

Print Books:

Behind the Mask (*anthology*)
Enchained (*anthology*)
Faith and Dreams
Hot Chances *with Rhyannon Byrd*
If Wishes Were Horses
Nature of Desire 1: Holding the Cards
Nature of Desire 2: Natural Law

About the Author

ഔ

I've always had an aversion to reading, watching or hearing interviews of favorite actors, authors, musicians, etc. because so often the real person doesn't measure up to the beauty of the art they produce. Their politics or religion are distasteful, or they're shallow and self-absorbed, a vacuous mophead without a lick of sense. From then on, though I may appreciate their craft or art, it has somehow been tarnished. Therefore, whenever I'm asked to provide personal information about myself for readers, a ball of anxiety forms in my stomach as I think: "Okay, the next couple of paragraphs can change forever the way someone views my stories." Why on earth does a reader want to know about me? It's the story that's important.

So here it is. I've been given more blessings in my life than any one person has a right to have. Despite that, I'm a Type A, borderline obsessive-compulsive paranoiac who worries I will never live up to expectations. I've got more phobias than anyone (including myself) has patience to read about. I can't stand talking on the phone, I dread social commitments, and the idea of living in monastic solitude with my husband and animals, books and writing is as close an idea to paradise as I can imagine. I love chocolate, but with that deeply ingrained, irrational female belief that weight equals worth, I manage to keep it down to a minor addiction. I adore good movies. I'm told I work too much. Every day is spent trying to get through the never ending "to do" list to snatch a few minutes to write.

This is because, despite all these mediocre and typical qualities, for some miraculous reason, these wonderful characters well up out of my soul with stories to tell. When I manage to find enough time to write, sufficient enough that the precious "stillness" required rises up and calms all the competing voices in my head, I can step into their lives, hear what they are saying, what they're feeling, and put it down on paper. It's a magic beyond description, akin to truly believing my husband loves me, winning the trust of an animal who has known only fear or apathy, making a true connection with someone, or knowing for certain I've given a reader a moment of magic through those written words. It's a magic that reassures me there is Someone, far wiser than myself, who knows the permanent path to that garden of stillness, where there is only love, acceptance and a pen waiting for hours and hours of uninterrupted, blissful use.

If only I could finish that darned "to do" list.

I welcome feedback from readers - actually, I thrive on it like a vampire, whether it's good or bad. So feel free to visit me through my website www.storywitch.com anytime.

Joey welcomes comments from readers. You can find her website and email address on her author bio page at www.ellorascave.com.

Tell Us What You Think

We appreciate hearing reader opinions about our books. You can email us at Comments@EllorasCave.com.

Why an electronic book?

We live in the Information Age—an exciting time in the history of human civilization, in which technology rules supreme and continues to progress in leaps and bounds every minute of every day. For a multitude of reasons, more and more avid literary fans are opting to purchase e-books instead of paper books. The question from those not yet initiated into the world of electronic reading is simply: *Why?*

1. *Price.* An electronic title at Ellora's Cave Publishing and Cerridwen Press runs anywhere from 40% to 75% less than the cover price of the exact same title in paperback format. Why? Basic mathematics and cost. It is less expensive to publish an e-book (no paper and printing, no warehousing and shipping) than it is to publish a paperback, so the savings are passed along to the consumer.

2. *Space.* Running out of room in your house for your books? That is one worry you will never have with electronic books. For a low one-time cost, you can purchase a handheld device specifically designed for e-reading. Many e-readers have large, convenient screens for viewing. Better yet, hundreds of titles can be stored within your new library—on a single microchip. There are a variety of e-readers from different manufacturers. You can also read e-books on your PC or laptop computer. (Please note that Ellora's Cave does not endorse any specific brands.

You can check our websites at www.ellorascave.com or www.cerridwenpress.com for information we make available to new consumers.)

3. *Mobility.* Because your new e-library consists of only a microchip within a small, easily transportable e-reader, your entire cache of books can be taken with you wherever you go.

4. *Personal Viewing Preferences.* Are the words you are currently reading too small? Too large? Too... ANNOYING? Paperback books cannot be modified according to personal preferences, but e-books can.

5. *Instant Gratification.* Is it the middle of the night and all the bookstores near you are closed? Are you tired of waiting days, sometimes weeks, for bookstores to ship the novels you bought? Ellora's Cave Publishing sells instantaneous downloads twenty-four hours a day, seven days a week, every day of the year. Our webstore is never closed. Our e-book delivery system is 100% automated, meaning your order is filled as soon as you pay for it.

Those are a few of the top reasons why electronic books are replacing paperbacks for many avid readers.

As always, Ellora's Cave and Cerridwen Press welcome your questions and comments. We invite you to email us at Comments@ellorascave.com or write to us directly at Ellora's Cave Publishing Inc., 1056 Home Avenue, Akron, OH 44310-3502.

COMING TO A BOOKSTORE NEAR YOU!

ELLORA'S CAVE

Bestselling Authors Tour